CRUSH THE KING

Also by Jennifer Estep

THE CROWN OF SHARDS SERIES

Kill the Queen

Protect the Prince

Crush the King

THE ELEMENTAL ASSASSIN SERIES

Spider's Bite

Web of Lies

Venom

Tangled Threads

Spider's Revenge

By a Thread

Widow's Web

Deadly Sting

Heart of Venom

The Spider

Poison Promise

Black Widow

Spider's Trap

Bitter Bite

Unraveled

Snared

Venom in the Veins

Sharpest Sting

THE MYTHOS ACADEMY SERIES

Touch of Frost

Kiss of Frost

Dark Frost

Crimson Frost

Midnight Frost

Killer Frost

CRUSH THE KING

A CROWN OF SHARDS NOVEL

JENNIFER ESTEP

HARPER Voyager

An Imprint of HarperCollins*Publishers*

HarperCollins books may be purchased for educational, business, or sales promotional use. For information, please email the Special Markets Department at SPsales@harpercollins.com.

Harper Voyager and design are trademarks of HarperCollins Publishers LLC.

FIRST EDITION

Designed by Paula Russell Szafranski
Maps designed by Virginia Norey
Title page and chapter opener art © mashakotcur/Shutterstock, Inc.

Library of Congress Cataloging-in-Publication Data has been applied for.

ISBN 978-0-06-279769-8

20 21 22 23 24 LSC 10 9 8 7 6 5 4 3 2 1

To my mom and my grandma—for your love, your patience,
and everything else that you've given to me over the years.

To Gayle and Karen—for being my book buddies and
such good friends.

And to my teenage self, who devoured every single epic fantasy
book that she could get her hands on—for finally writing your
very own epic fantasy books.

Bellonans are very good at playing the long game.

—TRADITIONAL BELLONAN MOTTO

ACKNOWLEDGMENTS

My heartfelt thanks go out to all the folks who help turn my words into a book.

Thanks go to my agent, Annelise Robey, and my editor, Erika Tsang, for all their helpful advice, support, and encouragement. Thanks also to Nicole Fischer, Pamela Jaffee, Angela Craft, and everyone else at Harper Voyager and HarperCollins.

And finally, a big thanks to all the readers. Knowing that folks read and enjoy my books is truly humbling, and I hope that you all enjoy reading about Evie and her adventures.

I appreciate you all more than you will ever know.

Happy reading! ☺

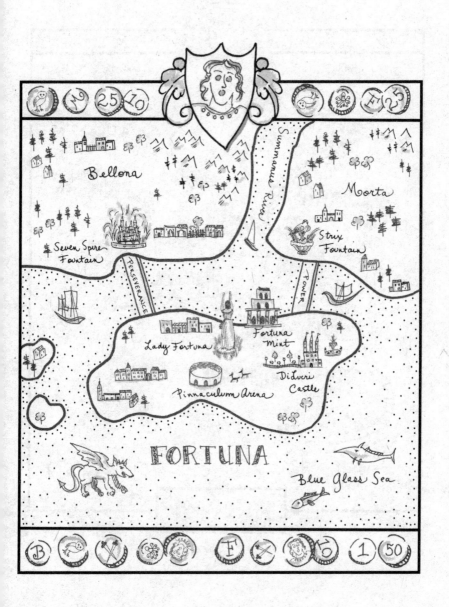

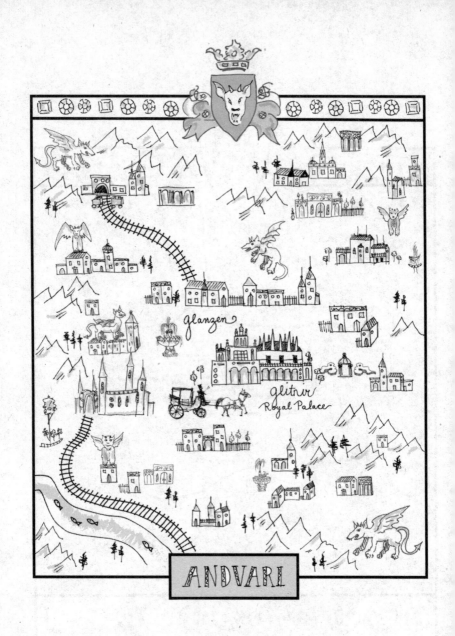

ANDVARI

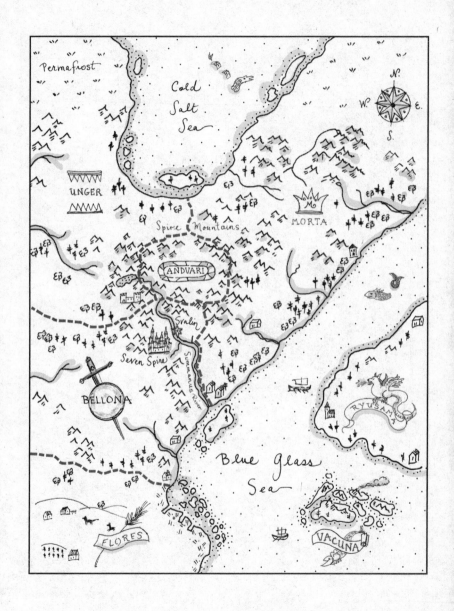

PART ONE

LET THE GAMES BEGIN

chapter one

The day the Regalia Games truly began for me started out like any other.

With me dancing, dancing, dancing as fast as I could.

"Move! Move!" a stern voice barked out. "You're falling behind the music!"

I grimaced, but I quickened my pace, my bare feet slapping against the wooden floor, my arms sweeping up, down, and back again, my fingers flexing, twisting, and pointing. Loud, lively music trilled through the air, and I did my best to match my movements to the rapid beat.

"Arms up!" that stern voice barked again. "Fingers wide! Toes pointed! Now, hop! Hop! Hop! Hop!"

All the bloody hopping made me feel like a bunny stumbling around a field, but I did as commanded. The music cranked up, singing out even louder and faster, and I continued to flail my arms and legs, desperately trying to keep up with the relentless rhythm.

I had been dancing on and off for more than an hour, and exhaustion slowed my feet and dragged down my arms. I turned my head to ask my torturer if we could finally stop the session, but she barked out another command.

"Don't look at me! Look at yourself! See your mistakes!"

If she saw my sour expression, she didn't care, so I focused on my own reflection again.

I was dancing in front of the floor-to-ceiling mirrors that lined one wall of the dance hall. My shoulder-length black hair was pulled back into a low ponytail, and my normally pale cheeks were now tomato-red from my prolonged exertion. I was wearing my usual royal-blue tunic, along with black leggings, although I'd removed my black boots and socks. This dance was traditionally performed barefoot, and the parquet floor felt as cool and smooth as glass under my hot, sweaty toes.

Even though I was supposed to be watching my form, I couldn't help but glance around at everything else in the mirror. The large, cavernous hall was made of gleaming golden wood. White crown molding shot through with silver leaf ringed the ceiling, which boasted three round crystal chandeliers that resembled glittering oversize snowballs. The fluorestones embedded in the chandeliers blazed with white light, all the better to show off my many mistakes—and all the ogres around the room.

Fierce, snarling ogre faces were carved into the wooden walls and much of the crown molding, while silver ogre figurines dangled from the bottoms of the chandeliers like wind chimes, although there was no breeze to make them merrily *tinkle-tinkle* together. Still more snarling ogre faces were painted in deep forest-greens and bright scarlets on the floor squares, as though the entire room were one enormous game board. I was dancing on top of several faces, and I kept expecting the creatures' gleaming white teeth to erupt out of the wood and bite my heels every time my feet hit the floor.

I was dancing alone, although several musicians were sitting in the corner, playing, playing, playing their flutes and violins as fast as possible. My torturer was lounging in a plush green velvet chair a few feet away.

Out of the corner of my eye I spotted a flash of silver zooming toward me. I grimaced again, knowing what was coming next, but I didn't move out of the way.

Thump.

The blunt end of a silver cane stabbed into my right thigh. The poke wasn't quite hard enough to bruise, but it was definitely forceful enough to get my full attention. I staggered to the side, but I didn't stop dancing. That would only make her poke me again, even harder.

"Don't let your mind wander! Or your gaze!" she snapped. "You must focus on the dance and the dance alone!"

I opened my mouth to snipe that it was hard to focus when she kept stabbing me with her bloody cane, but she cut me off.

"And don't even *think* about talking back to me."

"Yes . . . my lady . . . Your wish . . . is my command . . . And your happiness . . . is my utmost concern . . . and only true joy . . ." I wheezed, then lifted my hand and snapped off a mocking salute to her.

Over in the corner, one of the musicians guffawed, the sound even louder than the quick melody.

My torturer turned her stern gaze in that direction. The musician started, surprised by her sudden, unexpected attention, and his bow slipped off his violin strings, causing a sharp, earsplitting *screech*.

"Enough!" she snapped. "That's enough! Stop playing!"

The music abruptly cut off, and silence dropped over the dance hall, the sudden quiet seeming even more deafening than the boisterous notes. I stopped dancing, dropped my head, and put my hands on my hips, trying to get my breath back.

The woman sitting in the velvet chair stabbed her cane against the floor and climbed to her feet. She was dressed in a dark green tunic, along with black leggings and low black heels that made her almost six feet tall. Her wavy coppery hair brushed the tops of her shoulders, and her golden amber gaze was sharp and critical. Wrinkles grooved into her bronze skin, but her sixty-something-year-old body was strong and muscled, and she didn't really need her cane. Other than to poke me, of course.

The woman eyed me a moment, then focused on the musicians again. The ogre face on her neck kept staring at me, though, almost as if it could sense my unkind thoughts about its mistress.

All morphs had some sort of tattoo-like mark on their bodies that indicated what creature they could shift into. My torturer's mark was a snarling ogre face with the same coppery hair and amber eyes that the woman herself had. The ogre's eyes narrowed, and its lips drew back, revealing its many pointed teeth. The creature wasn't happy with me either.

Despite the disapproving glower, I winked at the ogre. I was rather incorrigible that way. Morph marks often mirrored the expressions and emotions of their human counterparts, and the ogre rolled its eyes, just like its mistress had more than once during my training session.

Lady Xenia, my torturer-slash-dance-instructor, stabbed her cane at the musicians. "Leave us! Now!"

She didn't have to tell them twice. The musicians clutched their instruments, grabbed their sheet music off the metal stands, and scurried out of the dance hall. The violinist who'd laughed at my cheeky salute gave me a sympathetic look, and I winked at him too. He grinned back, then fled with the others.

Xenia turned and stabbed her cane at me. The ogre head on top of the silver stick matched the morph mark on her neck.

"You shouldn't encourage the musicians. They're here to work, not laugh at your pitiful attempts at humor."

I sidestepped her cane, limped over to a bench, picked up a towel, and wiped the sweat off my face and neck. "Since when is dancing so much bloody work? Dancing should be *fun*."

She shook her head. "No. The Tanzen Falter is not *fun*. Not for you, Evie. Not if you want to gain that alliance with Queen Zariza."

"She's your cousin. Can't you convince her to align with me some other way? We both know that Unger joining forces with Bellona and Andvari is in the best interests of all three kingdoms."

"Zariza might be my cousin, but she is still the queen of Unger, and she answers to no one, not even me," Xenia said in a matter-of-fact tone. "Just like you are the queen of Bellona and answer to no one."

I snorted. "Tell that to Fullman, Diante, and the other nobles. Because they are all quite convinced I answer to them and them alone."

Xenia shrugged, neither agreeing nor disagreeing. "Regardless, Zariza *will* challenge you to dance during the Regalia, and you must be ready. Beating her at the Tanzen Falter will show your strength. Plus, it's the only way she's going to align with you."

I shook my head. "I will never understand why you Ungers turn everything into a dance competition."

"Because we are a *civilized* people. Unlike you Bellonans with your gladiator traditions. To you barbarians, everything always ends in a bloodbath in an arena." She sniffed her disapproval.

I wanted to point out that many Ungerian dances ended with the loser being executed, but I held my tongue. About that, at least. "Well, you do realize you're not supposed to poke the queen of Bellona with your cane, right?"

Xenia sniffed again. "This is *my* dance hall, and I will poke whomever I like, whether it's you, Zariza, or some other queen who dares to step through those doors."

"Then I'm glad that I'm not a queen," a voice drawled, "and that I don't have to learn how to dance."

A woman ambled into the room. She was around my age, twenty-seven or so, and tall and muscled, with braided blond hair, golden amber eyes, and lovely bronze skin. She was wearing a dark green tunic, along with black leggings and boots. A dark green cloak was draped over her shoulders, but the long, flowing fabric did little to hide the enormous spiked silver mace dangling from her black leather belt. As if the weapon wasn't intimidating enough, a morph mark was also visible on the woman's neck—a fearsome ogre face, also with braided blond hair and amber eyes.

Paloma, my best friend and a former gladiator, studied Xenia and me. "If you two are finished with your twirling lessons, perhaps we can get on with the more important business of the evening."

Xenia sniffed for a third time. "No business is more important than dancing. You should pay more attention to it. After all, it's part of your heritage."

Paloma frowned. "What do you mean?"

She gestured at the morph mark on Paloma's neck. "You're an ogre, which means you have some Ungerian blood in your family. Didn't your parents ever tell you that? Or teach you any Ungerian dances?"

Paloma shifted on her feet, clearly uncomfortable. "No. My father was from Flores, and I don't remember my mother ever saying that she was from Unger."

Paloma's mother had disappeared when she was a child, and Paloma had no idea what had happened to her. Perhaps even worse, her father had kicked her out when she was sixteen because he thought her morph mark made her a monster. So Paloma's inner ogre and apparently Ungerian heritage was something of a sore spot.

Xenia stepped closer, peering at the ogre face on Paloma's neck. "I've never paid much attention to it before, but your mark is quite striking. It reminds me of . . ." Her voice trailed off.

"What?" Paloma asked in a low, guarded voice.

Xenia shook her head. "Nothing. Just an old silly hope."

She smiled, but her expression was more gritted teeth than easy happiness. Even more telling, the scent of her ashy heartbreak swirled through the air, burning my nose with its sharp intensity. My mutt magic let me smell people's emotions, everything from soft, rosy love to hot, peppery anger to Xenia's sudden grief. She must be thinking about her child, the one she had lost through her own supposed foolishness.

I wondered if Xenia saw something of her lost child in Paloma. I had often thought my two friends were a lot alike, especially when it came to their morph marks with their bright amber eyes and distinctive locks of hair. I'd never voiced that thought to either of them, though, and now didn't seem like the time.

I cleared my throat, breaking the awkward silence. "Paloma's right. We need to get on with things. Are the others in position?"

"Yes. Serilda, Cho, and Lucas are in the plaza," Paloma replied. "They'll be ready to move if something goes wrong and this mysterious person isn't really a Blair."

This time, the scent of my own ashy heartbreak filled my nose. Earlier this year, my cousin Crown Princess Vasilia had killed her mother, Queen Cordelia, and the rest of the Blair royal family—*my* family. The Seven Spire massacre had been part of an elaborate Mortan plot to put Vasilia on the Bellonan throne and plunge our kingdom into war with Andvari.

Through a series of unexpected events, I had survived the massacre, become a gladiator, killed Vasilia, and taken the throne.

Now I was widely considered to be the last Blair, something that saddened me more than I'd ever thought possible. Most of my cousins might have been as vicious as coral vipers, but they hadn't deserved to be slaughtered just because the Mortan king wanted to wipe out the Blairs with their Summer and Winter bloodlines and powerful magics.

But a few weeks ago, Xenia had started hearing whispers about someone using magic in Svalin. Someone with gray-blue eyes, tearstone eyes, Blair eyes, just like mine.

The news, the rumors, the mere *hope* had stunned me.

After the massacre, Serilda and Cho had searched for months for another survivor, another Blair, with no luck. Once I was on the throne, I had ordered Auster, the captain of the palace guards, to expand the search into the countryside, in hopes that some of my cousins had managed to avoid Vasilia's turncoat guards, fled from their homes, and were in hiding. We hadn't heard the softest whisper that anyone else, any other Blair, had survived the slaughter.

But Xenia had.

In addition to running her dance hall and finishing school, Xenia was also a spy, one of the best in all the kingdoms. Over the past few weeks, she and her sources had heard more and more rumors that a Blair was hiding somewhere in Svalin, the capital city of Bellona.

Tonight I was finally going to see if the rumors were true.

And if they were, if this woman really *was* a Blair, then I hoped we could work together to protect Bellona, not only from the Mortan king, but from everyone who wished to hurt us and our people. I'd only been queen for about six months, but I was already tired of shouldering the heavy burden alone. I needed *help.* I needed another Blair, someone I could depend on, and especially someone I could leave my throne to if the worst happened and the Mortans finally managed to kill me.

Something that was a distinct possibility with the Regalia coming up.

My heart lifted, and the scent of my own warm, sweet honey hope filled my nose at the thought of finding another Blair, but I forced the emotion down, down, down. All the other rumors had turned out to be just that, and this one would probably be more of the same.

I wiped the last bit of sweat off my face, then tossed my towel onto the bench, grabbed my black leather belt, and buckled it around my waist. A sword and a matching dagger hung from the belt, both a dull silver color with the same crest embedded in their hilts—seven midnight-blue shards fitted together to form a crown.

The weapons looked heavy, but they were actually quite light, since they were made of tearstone. Not only could tearstone absorb, store, and reflect magic like other jewels, but it also had the unique property of offering protection from magic, deflecting it like a shield would knock aside an arrow in a gladiator bout. The dark blue shards in the hilts would divert quite a bit of magier power, as would the weapons' silvery razor-sharp blades.

The sword and the dagger had saved me from being assassinated more than once, and I never went anywhere without them. I also had a matching shield, but it drew far too much attention, so I had left it in my chambers at the palace.

Once the weapons belt was fastened around my waist, I focused on the two identical bracelets—gauntlets—that gleamed on my wrists. Both were made of silver that had been shaped into sharp thorns, all of which wrapped around and protected the design in the center—another midnight-blue crown of shards.

My personal crest as Everleigh Saffira Winter Blair, the queen of Bellona.

A crown-of-shards crest was also stitched in silver thread on my blue tunic, right over my heart, and I had several actual crowns that boasted the same design, although I hadn't worn any of them this evening, since I was trying to be incognito. Plus, I always worried about a crown falling off my head, especially when I was doing something as vigorous as Xenia's dance training.

I had rolled up my sleeves to better track my arm movements during the lesson, and I slid them down, hiding the bracelets. I also grabbed a midnight-blue cloak and settled it around my shoulders, making sure the fabric covered the crown-of-shards crest on my tunic.

"Wish us luck," I said to Xenia.

"No."

"No? What do you mean *no*?"

Xenia shrugged. "Luck is a pointless expression and a silly sentiment. You work hard, and you train, and you prepare. Luck has nothing to do with your success or failure."

Paloma nodded her agreement. Traitor. I glared at my friend, but she shrugged at me much the same way Xenia had. "She's right. Luck is for fools and children."

"You're no fun either."

Paloma shrugged again. "I'm not here to be fun," she said in a matter-of-fact tone that I both admired and hated. "I'm here to keep you alive."

I sighed, knowing I couldn't win with either one of them. "Well, then, let's get on with it."

I started to head toward the open doors, but Xenia raised her hand, stopping me.

"I hope you find what you're looking for, Evie," she said in a kinder voice. "And that some part of your family has survived."

A sad, wistful expression flickered across her face. Once again, the scent of Xenia's ashy heartbreak filled my nose, and she leaned on her cane a little more heavily than before, as if she really did need its support.

"Thank you," I said in a soft voice.

She shrugged, then snapped up her cane and stabbed me in the arm with it. "But no matter what happens tonight, I expect you back here at the same time tomorrow for your next lesson."

Paloma snickered, and Xenia whipped around and poked the younger woman with her cane just like she had me.

"And you too," she ordered. "Even if you don't know anything about your heritage, you can still learn the dances."

Paloma opened her mouth to argue, but Xenia stared her down, and my friend sighed. "Yes, my lady."

Xenia nodded in satisfaction and strolled away, *tap-tap-tap*ping her cane on the floor.

I slung my arm around Paloma's shoulders. "Looks like I have a new dancing partner. Just think. This time tomorrow, Xenia will be stabbing *you* with her bloody cane."

My friend gave me a sour look. I laughed, and together we followed Xenia out of the dance hall.

CHAPTER TWO

Xenia had some other business to take care of, so Paloma and I left her finishing school.

It was almost six o'clock, and the sun was slowly sinking behind the Spire Mountains that ringed the city. The December air was already quite chilly, and it would turn even colder once the last golden rays vanished behind the high, rugged peaks and took their meager warmth along with them. My nose twitched. A faint metallic scent hung in the air, indicating that it would snow later tonight.

Only a few people were walking on the side streets that flanked Xenia's finishing school. Most had their heads down and their arms crossed over their chests, trying to stay as warm as possible in their hats, scarves, coats, and gloves, and no one gave Paloma and me a second look as we made our way over to one of the many enormous square plazas that could be found throughout Svalin.

We stood in the shadows in a narrow alley that ran between two bakeries and looked out over the plaza. Brightly painted wooden carts manned by bakers, butchers, farmers, tailors, and other merchants lined all four sides of the area, while a large gray stone fountain of two girls holding hands bubbled merrily in the center.

People of all shapes, sizes, stations, and ages moved across the gray cobblestones, going from one cart and merchant to the next and shopping for bread, meat, cheeses, and vegetables. Still more people cut through the plaza, bypassing the colorful carts and loud, squawking merchants, skirting around the gurgling fountain, and steadfastly trudging home after a long, hard day at work. Miners, mostly, wearing thick dark blue coveralls, boots, and hard, ridged helmets, all of which were coated with light gray fluorestone dust.

I opened my mouth and drew in breath after breath, letting the air roll in over my tongue and using my mutt magic to taste all the scents swirling through the plaza. Fresh warm bread and almond-sugar cookies from the bakeries next to the alley. The coppery stench of blood from the meat on the butchers' carts. The sharp, tangy cheeses. The bits of dirt on the farmers' sweet potatoes and other produce. The fine layers of crushed, chalky stone clinging to the miners.

I sensed all that and more, but the one thing I didn't smell was magic.

Normally, I would have welcomed its absence. More often than not I sensed the hot, caustic stench of magic only when someone was trying to kill me. But this evening, I found the lack of power disappointing.

"I don't like this," Paloma muttered. "What if this rumor about another Blair is just a trick to get you out of the palace and into the city, where you're more vulnerable? And leaving Xenia's finishing school without any guards is just asking for trouble."

In addition to being my best friend, Paloma was also my personal guard, a job she took very seriously.

"Coming here without any guards is part of the plan. We're

trying to blend in, remember?" I arched an eyebrow at her. "Besides, didn't you once tell me that a gladiator and an ogre morph like yourself is worth twenty regular soldiers?"

"That was Halvar." Paloma's chin lifted with pride. "But he was right. I *am* worth twenty soldiers."

Halvar was Xenia's nephew and a powerful ogre morph. He and Paloma were good friends, along with Bjarni, another ogre morph. Halvar and Bjarni had also helped me more than once, and the two men were currently staying at Seven Spire palace and working with Captain Auster.

I rolled my eyes. "Well, you might get a chance to prove how many soldiers you are worth. Xenia is just as skeptical about this rumor as you are. If the two of you are right, then we're probably going to run into trouble."

Paloma's eyes gleamed with anticipation, and the ogre on her neck grinned, showing off its jagged teeth. "I haven't been in a real fight in a while." She plucked her mace off her belt and gave it an experimental swing, making the spikes whistle through the air. "It'll be good to get in some practice before the Regalia and knock the dust off Peony."

It took me a moment to realize who—or rather what—she was referring to. "You named your mace *Peony*?"

She gave me an incredulous look, as if my question were utter gibberish. "Of course. Years ago. Haven't you named your sword yet?"

"No."

"Well, you should. And your dagger and shield too."

My hand dropped to the sword belted to my waist, and my fingers traced over the crown-of-shards crest in the hilt. The sharp points of the shards digging into my skin always comforted me. The sensation reminded me of all the other Bellonan queens—especially the Winter queens—who had come before me.

Hmm. Maybe I should take Paloma's advice and name my sword . . . *Winter*. Nah, that was too obvious, too on the nose, too cliché. I'd have to think of something more original.

Paloma kept swinging her mace, as if she were warming up for a gladiator bout.

"Why *Peony*?" I asked.

She froze mid-swing and lowered the weapon to her side. "My mother always wore peony perfume," she said in a low, raspy voice.

The smell of salty grief gusted off Paloma, overpowering her own natural scent—soft peony perfume mixed with a hint of wet fur. Sympathy filled me, and I reached over and squeezed her shoulder. My friend gave me a small, sad smile, then turned her attention back to the plaza.

"I still don't like this," she repeated. "You're far too exposed and vulnerable, and that cloak is barely a disguise. At least put your hood up so people can't see your face so clearly."

I opened my mouth to point out that half the people in the plaza were wearing cloaks and that her swinging that giant mace made her far more noticeable than me, but Paloma and her inner ogre both gave me a fierce glare. So I bit back my words and pulled up my hood, hiding my black hair and casting my face in shadow.

"I don't know why you're so worried," I said. "It's not like we came here alone."

I waved my hand at the fountain in the center of the plaza. A forty-something woman with slicked-back blond hair, tan skin, and a scar at the corner of one of her dark blue eyes was tossing pennies into the fountain, as though she were making wishes. She was wearing a black cloak, although her white tunic with its distinctive black-swan crest peeked out from beneath the flowing fabric. She also had a tearstone sword and dagger belted to her waist, just like I did.

Serilda Swanson, the leader of the Black Swan gladiator troupe and one of my advisors, discreetly waved at me, then pointed her finger to her right.

I looked in that direction and focused on a forty-something man with glossy black hair, black eyes, golden skin, and a lean, muscled body on the far side of the plaza. He too was wearing a black cloak over a red jacket and a ruffled white shirt. A sword and a dagger hung off his belt as well, and a morph mark was visible on his neck—a dragon face with ruby-red scales and gleaming black eyes.

Cho Yamato, the Black Swan ringmaster, was leaning against a bakery cart, nibbling on an apricot cookie. Cho had a serious sweet tooth, as did his inner dragon. He noticed my gaze and winked at me, then gestured up at the roof of a building across the plaza.

A man was standing next to a silver spire that decorated one corner of the roof. He was tall and handsome, with dark brown hair, bright blue eyes, tan skin, and a bit of stubble that clung to his strong jaw. A midnight-blue cloak was draped over his shoulders, and his black tunic was perfectly tailored to his muscled chest. He too was wearing a sword and a dagger, although he kept flexing his fingers, ready to unleash his lightning magic at the first sign of trouble.

I drew in a deep breath. Even among all the floral perfumes and musky colognes swirling through the plaza, I could still pick out his unique scent—clean, cold vanilla with just a hint of warm spice.

Thanks to my mutt magic, scents and memories were often tangled together in my mind, and his rich, heady aroma made my heart quicken, my stomach clench, and hot, liquid desire scorch through my veins. All sorts of images and sensations washed over me. My lips on his, our tongues dueling back and forth, my fingers sliding through his thick, silky hair, my palms skimming down his bare muscled chest, then going lower and lower, even as his hands slid across my skin . . .

Lucas Sullivan, the magier enforcer of the Black Swan troupe and my unofficial consort, grinned, as if he knew exactly what I was thinking about and couldn't wait to return to the palace to make it a reality.

I grinned back at him. That made two of us.

"Oh, quit mooning at Lucas," Paloma grumbled. "That will get you killed quicker than anything else."

I gestured at the plaza again. "See? The others are in position, and I am perfectly safe. Now we just have to wait and see if anyone shows up."

In addition to hearing whispers that another Blair might still be alive, Xenia and her many sources had started spreading their own rumor in return—that *any* Blair who came to this plaza tonight would be taken in and guaranteed safety at Seven Spire palace.

Xenia and her network of spies had been spreading the rumor for about two weeks, and my friends and I had come to see if anyone would take the bait.

Paloma eyed the people moving through the plaza. "Even if this woman, this supposed Blair, does show up, how are we going to find her? There are hundreds of people here. We might not even see her."

"I don't have to see her." I tapped my nose. "My magic will let me sense hers."

"But you don't even know what she is," Paloma pointed out. "She could be a magier or a master or a morph. Or she might just be a mutt like you are. It might not even be a woman. Maybe it's a man."

I shrugged. "Magic is magic. I can always smell it, no matter what kind it is or who it belongs to. Besides, if there's even the smallest bit of truth to the rumor . . ."

My voice trailed off, and a hard knot of emotion clogged my throat. That treacherous hope was rising up in me again, but I pushed it back down.

"You still need to be careful," Paloma continued. "It wouldn't surprise me if Maeven started this rumor to lure you here so she and the rest of the Bastard Brigade can try to kill you again."

Maeven was the bastard sister of the Mortan king and the one who had orchestrated the Seven Spire massacre. She was also the leader of the Bastard Brigade, a group of bastard relatives of the king and the other legitimate Mortan royals. Over the past several months, Maeven and her Bastard Brigade had tried to murder me numerous times, although I had managed to thwart most of their schemes and stay alive—so far.

"You might be right," I admitted. "Maeven is certainly clever and devious enough to float a rumor about another Blair to get me here, but I have to learn for myself whether it's true. And if it is a plot, then we'll kill her assassins, just like we have before."

"And if it's not another Mortan plot?" Paloma asked.

"Then we'll find out exactly who this person is, where they've been hiding, and how they've managed to stay alive. And especially why they didn't come to Seven Spire after I took the throne and decreed that Blair survivors should return to the palace."

Part of me was happy that one of my cousins had potentially survived the slaughter, but part of me was also dreading the family reunion. I was only queen because all the other Blairs were dead. What if this mysterious cousin was higher in line for the throne? What if they had a better claim on the crown? What if they had more magic?

And if any of that were true, then came the biggest question of all: Should I step aside?

That was what protocol and tradition would dictate I do.

But what was best for Bellona? Because I couldn't imagine anyone else—Blair or otherwise—who wanted to protect my kingdom and her people more than I did.

I hadn't wanted to be queen, but now that I had finally secured my position, I didn't want to give it up just because someone else had had the good fortune to survive the massacre. If I was being brutally honest, I also didn't want to give up all the power and privileges that came with being queen. It was heady and thrilling to be respected and even feared, especially since I had spent years being the royal stand-in, the royal puppet, at Seven Spire. Perhaps that made me petty and selfish, just like Vasilia had been.

But most of all, I didn't want to give up the throne because of how it would impact my chances of finally taking my revenge on Maeven and the Mortan king. I wanted to make them suffer for what they'd done to the Blairs, to my family, to *me*, and I had a far better chance of getting that revenge as queen, rather than going back to just being Lady Everleigh.

"Well, I hope this person shows up soon," Paloma grumbled, breaking into my turbulent thoughts. "I don't want to stand around in the cold all night."

She stamped her feet and pulled her green cloak a little tighter around her body. Autumn had already come and gone, and winter was quickly taking hold in the Spire Mountains. In addition to the impending snow tonight, the wind had a bitter chill that promised even colder, harsher weather was on its way.

"Don't worry. Xenia and her spies said to meet at this fountain at six o'clock, and it's that time now. Someone should show up soon."

Paloma sighed and stamped her feet again, but the two of us held our position in the alley, and Serilda, Cho, and Sullivan remained in their spots around and above the plaza.

As the sun set, fluorestones flared to life inside the surrounding buildings, as well as in the streetlamps that lined the plaza. The soft golden lights must have made the goods look even more attractive, because the merchants were still doing a brisk business, and it was hard to pick out anyone suspicious, much less a familiar face.

Ever since Xenia had told me that one of my cousins might still be alive, I had been racking my mind trying to figure out who it could be, but I hadn't come up with any possibilities. So I stared out into the plaza, peering at everyone who walked by.

I was so busy studying the faces of the adults that I almost missed the girl.

She was young, fourteen or so, and dressed in several layers of thin, grubby rags. Her clothes might have been dark blue at one time but were now almost black with grime. Her face wasn't much better. Dirt streaked across her pale cheeks, and her nose was red from the cold. A gray winter hat covered her head, although her dark brown hair stuck up at odd angles through the gaping holes in the knit fabric.

The girl stopped about twenty feet away from us, next to a bakery cart. Her head snapped back and forth, as if she were looking for someone, although she soon focused on the area around the fountain. She tapped her hand on her thigh in a nervous rhythm and shifted on her feet, like she was ready to run away at any moment. A few red-hot sparks flashed on her fingertips, flickering in time to her uneasy motions, but she quickly curled her hand into a fist, snuffing out the telltale signs of magic.

I drew in a breath, letting the air roll over my tongue and tasting all the scents in it again. The warm bread, the sweet cookies, the bloody cuts of meat, the chalky fluorestone dust. I pushed aside all those aromas and concentrated on the girl. My nose twitched, and I finally got a whiff of her scent—the hot, caustic stench of magic mixed with a sweet, rosy note.

"There," I whispered, pointing out the girl to Paloma. "I think it might be her."

Paloma peered in that direction. "Who is she? Do you recognize her?"

"No. I've never seen her before, but I can smell her magic. She's definitely a fire magier." I hesitated, trying to push down my treacherous hope yet again. "She could be a Summer queen. Lots of them had fire magic."

"Then what is she waiting for?" Paloma asked. "Serilda is still throwing pennies into the fountain. That's the signal."

It had been Xenia's idea to say that any Blair seeking refuge should approach the blond woman tossing pennies into the fountain. The girl had come to the right plaza at the right time, so she must have heard the information, but she still didn't approach the fountain.

Instead, she stared at Serilda a second longer, then turned around and ran away.

For a moment, I stood there, stunned. My friends and I had been plotting this for *days*, and everything had been going according to plan. But now, instead of talking to Serilda like she was supposed to, the girl was heading deeper into the crowd and getting farther away with each passing second.

Desperation propelled me forward, and I charged out of the alley.

"Evie!" Paloma hissed. "Evie, wait for me!"

But I couldn't wait, not without losing sight of the girl, so I chased after her.

The girl must have had some practice picking her way through crowds, because she slipped through the throngs of people as easily as one of the Black Swan acrobats could tumble across the arena floor.

Several times I lost sight of her, only to push past someone and see her gray hat bobbing along in the distance. I felt like a fisherman trying to reel in a particularly difficult catch. Every time I almost got close enough to latch on to her shoulder, the girl sped up and put three more people between us. She never looked back, but I wasn't exactly being subtle with all my pushing and shoving, and she must have realized that someone was following her, given the annoyed shouts that sprang up in my wake.

"Evie!" Paloma hissed again from somewhere behind me. "Slow down! You're going to get your fool self killed!"

She was probably right, but I couldn't slow down. Not until I knew whether this girl was a Blair. The burning need to know—and the rising hope that I wasn't the only one left—drove me onward.

The girl broke free of the plaza and darted onto one of the side streets. I glanced back over my shoulder. Paloma was still pushing through the crowd behind me, but Serilda, Cho, and Sullivan were nowhere in sight. Not surprising, given how much farther across the plaza they'd been. Well, my friends would just have to catch up.

I quickly followed the girl, racing around the people ambling along and window-shopping. My boots clattered on the cobblestones, my hood slipped off my head, and my cloak streamed out behind me like a dark blue ribbon, but I hurried on.

I reached the end of the street. Just when I thought I'd lost her completely, I spotted the girl's gray hat disappearing into an alley. I hurried to the entrance and stopped, peering into the dark corridor.

The alley ran for about fifty feet before opening into another, much smaller plaza, but no carts and merchants were set up here, and no pretty stone fountain bubbled in the center. Instead, cracked wooden boards, broken bottles, busted bricks, and other trash littered this area.

Buildings flanked the plaza, with another alley leading out the far side, and debris was piled in heaps along the walls, as though the people living and working in the rooms above opened their windows and tossed their garbage outside, not caring where it landed below. The stench of sour milk, rotten meat, and other spoiled food almost knocked me down, and I had to pinch the bridge of my nose to hold back a sneeze.

In just a few streets, I had gone from one of the most affluent parts of Svalin to the beginning of the slums. Sadness filled me, the way it always did at the thought that people—*my* people—lived like this, but I shoved the emotion aside.

I held my position at the alley entrance, looking and listening, but I didn't see the girl running out the far side, which was clogged with trash, and I didn't hear any footsteps. She must still be in the plaza somewhere. Maybe she thought I was a threat. Maybe she was hiding until I left. Or maybe this was her home.

I peered at the piles of debris lining the walls, but there was no pattern to them, and I didn't see any makeshift shacks made of scraps of wood, metal, or stone. Still, as nimbly as the girl had slipped through the crowd, she could easily slither behind a stack of boards or hunker down behind one of the overflowing trash bins.

I glanced back over my shoulder, but I didn't see Paloma. Despite her dire warning that I was going to get myself killed, I wasn't a complete reckless idiot, and I realized that this would be the perfect place for assassins to ambush me. But I also couldn't afford to lose the girl, so I drew my sword and cautiously crept down the alley, peering into the shadows. I also tasted the air again, trying to pick up the scent of the girl's magic, although all the rotting garbage made it difficult—

Something rustled behind a trash bin. I froze.

A large, fat black rat sauntered out from behind the bin. It paused in the middle of the alley, staring at me with its bright black eyes before scurrying away and disappearing into a pile of trash on the opposite side.

I let out a tense breath and crept forward again. I stopped in the open space in the center of the plaza and slowly turned around in a circle, studying the piles of debris.

The sun had finally set, and the murky gray twilight was quickly being swallowed by the oncoming night. A few lights burned in the surrounding buildings, but they did little to drive back the encroaching darkness. If the girl was hiding here, I couldn't see her, so I drew in breath after breath, tasting all the scents in the air again. It took me a few seconds to push past the garbage, but I finally got a whiff of hot, caustic magic.

For a moment, I thought it was the girl's magic, and my heart lifted with fresh hope. Then the scent washed over me again. This magic had much more of an electric sizzle than the girl's fire power—and it was far too strong to belong to just one person.

As soon as the realization filled my mind, the shadows around me started moving, shifting, and rising, as people slithered out of the piles of trash and climbed to their feet.

One second, I was alone. The next, I was surrounded by ten magiers. Paloma had been right.

It was a trap.

CHAPTER THREE

I tightened my grip on my sword, held my position, and waited for my enemies to advance.

The magiers crept a little closer, then spread out, forming a loose semicircle around me. They were a mix of men and women, old and young, and all shapes and sizes. No crests or symbols adorned their black cloaks and tunics, so I couldn't immediately tell who had sent them. Some of the magiers were clutching swords, but they all reeked of magic, their power burning like colorful torches in their eyes.

One of the magiers stepped forward. His dark brown hair was slicked back from his tan forehead, and a trim goatee clung to his chin, while his eyes were a light, bright topaz. He was my height, although his muscles bulged and strained against his tunic with every breath, making him seem as puffed up as a child's balloon full of hot air. I wondered if he would let out an audible *pop!* if I stuck him with my sword. I rubbed my thumb over the hilt of my weapon. I wanted to find out.

Since the man didn't immediately attack, I focused on the girl standing next to him, the one I'd been chasing. Now that I was closer, I could see that she didn't look like any of my cousins, and her eyes were dark brown, instead of gray-blue like mine. Even though I'd known that she wasn't a Blair the second the magiers had sprung their trap, disappointment still flooded my stomach. The cold, sick sensation quickly drowned all my warm, sweet honey hope, and the scent of my own ashy heartbreak punched me in the nose.

I forced myself to ignore the feeling and study the rest of the magiers. None of them had blond hair and purplish eyes like Maeven and so many of her relatives did, but the magiers could still be members of the Bastard Brigade. No one wanted me dead as badly as they did.

"Well, well, well," the man drawled, breaking the silence. "I was hoping to capture a few guards, maybe even a royal advisor. I didn't expect to hook Queen Everleigh herself. It truly is an honor, Your Majesty."

He gave me a low, formal bow, and several of the other magiers snickered at his blatant mockery.

The girl huffed. "Oh, quit preening, Ricardo. I was the one who lured her here. All you had to do was wait for me to show up—"

Ricardo stepped forward and backhanded the girl, cutting off her complaint. The solid, heavy *thwack* of his hand cracking against her face boomed like thunder through the plaza. I grimaced at the sound.

Ricardo must have had a bit of mutt strength, because the girl plummeted to the ground like a brick dropped from a window. For a moment, she lay still and stunned, but then she slowly pushed herself back up to sitting. She blinked a few times, shaking off the hard blow, then gingerly touched her hand to her cheek, now a screaming scarlet underneath the dirt on her skin.

Ricardo loomed over her and flexed his fingers, as though he wanted to hit her again. "Don't *ever* take that tone with me, Lena, especially in front of our guest."

Guest? What was he talking about?

The other magiers shifted on their feet, but none of them spoke, and none of them came to the girl's defense.

Lena bristled and dropped her hand from her cheek. A few red-hot sparks flashed on her fingertips, as though she were thinking about blasting Ricardo with her fire power, but he crossed his arms over his muscled chest and stared her down. Lena wilted under his glare, and the sparks vanished.

"Sorry," she muttered. "I just wanted some credit for doing my part."

"And you'll get it," Ricardo said. "And gold and more—*after* we deliver her."

Deliver me? More confusion filled me, although it was quickly replaced by growing dread. The magiers *were* going to kill me . . . weren't they?

Lena frowned, as if she shared my confusion. "But I thought we were going to torture whomever we captured for information about the Regalia, then leave their body in one of the plazas as a message. That's what he told us—"

Ricardo smashed his boot into Lena's ribs, making her yelp with pain and topple over onto her side. He towered over the girl, anger pinching his face. "You take your orders from *me*," he snarled. "And I don't answer to *him*. None of us do. Don't make me remind you of that again."

Lena blanched and ducked her head, like she was a tortoise trying to hide in the shell of her grubby clothes, and the coppery stench of her fear gusted through the plaza, even stronger than the smell of the magiers' collective power.

I wondered who they were planning to turn me over to. Maeven? The Mortan king? Someone else? All sorts of horrible images and scenarios flashed through my mind, most of which involved Maeven slowly torturing me to death with her lightning.

My heart dropped, my stomach clenched, and my breath froze in my throat, but I shoved my fear and dread away and studied the magiers again, trying to figure out who was the most vulnerable. All I had to do was kill one or two to break through the line of them. Then I could run out of the alley before the others caught up with me.

A ball of fire flared to life in Ricardo's hand, and he gave me a flat stare, as if he had guessed my plan to cut my way through the other magiers. Beside him, Lena scrambled back up onto her feet. Her cheek was still red from his slap, but she reached for her magic, and a ball of fire filled her palm as well. A few more of the magiers summoned up their fire and lightning, while the rest raised their swords.

"You're coming with us, Your Majesty," Ricardo purred. "Whether you do it with your face intact is entirely up to you."

He waggled his fingers, and the fire in his palm burned a little brighter, as though it were a hungry monster that was eager to melt the skin from my bones. The hot, crackling stench of it filled the air, even more pungent than the rotten filth that polluted the plaza. Ricardo was clearly the strongest magier, although Lena was a close second, and the fire in her palm sparked almost as much as his did.

I was still holding my sword in my right hand, and I curled my left hand into a fist, then coated it with the invisible force of my own cold, hard power. Ricardo might be strong in his magic—but he wasn't stronger than *me*.

"I'm not going anywhere with you," I snarled.

He laughed, and Lena and the other magiers joined in with his chuckles. "If you want to get burned, Your Majesty, that's fine with me," he purred again. "It's always so much more fun when our guests resist."

He summoned up even more fire, but I didn't flinch at the searing flames, so he sneered at me. "Do you really think your tearstone sword is going to stop me from scalding you? I'd heard you were arrogant, but I didn't realize you were delusional as well."

Like most people, Ricardo assumed that my sword was the source of my power, that the silvery tearstone blade and the blue shards in the hilt were what protected me. He was wrong.

"I don't need my sword to destroy your magic. I can do it all by myself." I twirled the weapon around in my hand, then lowered it to my side.

"You might be a queen, but you're a fool," Ricardo hissed. "Perhaps you'll be a bit more humble after I've burned off the first few layers of your flesh."

He reared back his hand and tossed his magic at me. Not enough to kill me outright, but more than enough to severely burn me. The fire streaked through the air, the flames growing hotter and stronger as they chewed up the distance between us.

At the last moment, right before his magic would have slammed into my chest, I snapped up my left hand and flexed my fingers as though I were flicking water off them. In a way, that's exactly what I was doing. Only instead of water, I was throwing my magic at his.

The cold, hard, invisible force of my immunity slammed into his fire, shattering it like glass. The red-orange flames exploded in a roar of black smoke that boiled up and quickly wisped away in the winter breeze.

I casually brushed a stray ember off my right shoulder, snuffing it out just like I had the rest of the fire.

Ricardo's topaz eyes widened, and he jerked back in surprise. "How did you do that? I thought you were just a mutt who could smell things."

To most people, even my own Bellonans, I *was* just a mutt, a common, if condescending, term for folks with simple, straightforward powers like extra strength or speed. Even among mutts, my enhanced sense of smell was considered a weak, laughable ability, and most people thought I had only a faint spark of magic, and no real, significant power.

Those people were right—and wrong. I was a mutt, in every sense of the word, but I was also a master, someone who could control and wield a specific object or element.

And my element was *magic*.

I had always known that I was immune to magic and that I could destroy other people's fire, lightning, and ice just by pitting my power, my strength, my *will*, against theirs. But I'd recently discovered that I could do other things with my immunity, like control where other people's magic went or how much of it was used. I was still learning new tricks, and one day I hoped to be able to wield my immunity as easily as I did the sword in my hand.

I could have told Ricardo all that, but he didn't deserve any explanation. No, all he deserved was to die screaming. Him and everyone else who'd been stupid enough to threaten me, trick me, and especially make me feel all that damn *hope*. Icy rage surged through me, freezing out everything else. Forget running away to safety. I was going to end Ricardo here and now.

So I crooked my index finger at him. "Why don't you come over here and find out how I did that? If you're not too much of a coward. Using a girl to trap someone is easy enough, but actually battling a Bellonan queen yourself is a bit more challenging."

Anger filled Ricardo's eyes, a muscle ticked in his clenched jaw, and more fire erupted on his fingertips, even stronger than what he'd just thrown at me. But I didn't flinch, and I didn't back down.

"You think your little trick is going to save you from *me*? From all of *us*?" He gestured at Lena and the other magiers. "You shouldn't have come here alone, Winter queen. You're going to suffer for your arrogance."

I smiled, baring my teeth at him. "Who said I came here alone?"

Lena and the other magiers were so busy watching Ricardo threaten me that they weren't paying any attention to what was happening around them—like the shadow that was creeping along one of the alley walls and heading in this direction.

Paloma let out a loud roar, charged into the plaza, and swung her mace at the closest magier. The other woman never even saw her coming. The magier's head caved in like a soufflé taken out of the oven too early, and she dropped to the ground without making a sound.

Paloma roared again and charged at the next-closest magier, who whipped around to face her, along with several others.

Ricardo snarled with anger, reared back, and threw another fistful of fire at me. This time, I used my immunity, along with the blade of my tearstone sword, to swat away his magic like it was an annoying fly.

The fireball exploded against one of the building walls, igniting the rotten wood, spoiled food, and other filth piled there. Smoke, sparks, and red-hot embers boiled up into the air, hanging over the plaza like a thick, foul fog, but I sprinted through the stench toward Ricardo.

He snarled again, yanked two long knives out of his black cloak, and stepped up to meet me. He brought both knives down at once, attempting to cut through my defenses, but I whipped up my sword and blocked his attack.

Clang!

The loud crash of our blades banging together rang through the plaza, momentarily drowning out all the other grunts, yells, and screams. That one single note of sound turned a key deep inside me, and phantom music started playing in my mind. Xenia might be teaching me the Tanzen Falter, but Serilda was the one who'd trained me to treat each battle like it was a dance to the death. I let the quick, pulsing beat of that phantom music sweep me away, and my body moved to the rhythm, even as I pushed Ricardo back and twisted to the side.

He growled and slashed out with his knives over and over again, trying to drive the blades into my heart. He wasn't trying to capture me anymore. Now he wanted to kill me as badly as I did him.

I danced away from his blows and launched my own brutal counterstrikes in return.

We kept hacking and slashing at each other, even as we waded through the broken glass, chipped bits of stone, and other debris that littered the ground. The *crunch-crunch-crunch-crunch* of our boots added another layer of sound to that phantom music playing in my mind, and I hummed along to the beat, even though no one could hear it but me.

On the other side of the plaza, Paloma swung her mace at every magier she could reach, punching the spikes into first one body, then another. My friend was easily holding her own, so I turned my attention back to my enemy.

Ricardo feinted and lashed out with one of his knives, trying to catch me off guard, but I whirled to the side and knocked that blade out of his hand. The knife tumbled end over end along the cobblestones, shooting off a few weak silver sparks before it landed in a pile of dirty rags.

Ricardo snarled again and swiped out with his other knife, but I knocked that one away as well, and it spun to a stop near Lena's feet. The girl was hugging the closest wall, trying to stay out of the wild, deadly melee.

Lena backed away, but Ricardo darted forward, grabbed her shoulder, spun her around, and hooked an arm around her neck. Fire exploded on his fingertips again, and he held the burning ball close to Lena's face. She shrieked and tried to pull away, but she couldn't break his tight hold.

"Stop!" he barked. "Everyone stop right now!"

His voice boomed through the plaza, and everyone actually listened to him.

Paloma had already killed four of the magiers, and she had her mace raised to take out a fifth one, but she slowly lowered the weapon to her side. The remaining magiers lowered their swords as well and backed away from her.

Ricardo glanced at Paloma and the other magiers, making sure they weren't going to move, then looked at me again. He grinned and took a step back, dragging Lena along with him. Then another step, then another.

The bastard was using the girl as a human shield. The fight hadn't gone his way, and now he was going to run, just like that fat rat I'd seen scurrying through the garbage earlier.

I snapped up my sword and moved forward. He wasn't getting away.

Ricardo stopped and brandished his fire at Lena again. "What the fuck are you doing? Stop! Or the girl dies!"

I shrugged. "Go ahead. Kill her. I don't care."

Lena's eyes bulged, and the scent of her sour, nervous sweat filled my nose.

"What do you mean, you don't care?" Ricardo asked. "I saw your face after I hit her. You didn't like my disciplining her."

"That wasn't discipline—that was cruelty, plain and simple. And no, I didn't like seeing it." I stared him down. "But just because I don't like something doesn't mean that I won't do it in order to protect myself and my kingdom."

His eyes narrowed. "You're really going to let me kill the girl?"

I shrugged again. "That girl led me into a trap and was more than willing to trade my life for whatever gold you'd promised her. So go ahead. Melt her face off if you like. If she has to die so that I can get to you, then so be it."

Lena gasped at my harsh tone, and fear filled her face.

"You're bluffing," Ricardo hissed. "We've all heard of Queen Everleigh and her great heroics to save Bellona from the evil Mortan empire. We all know that you're far too noble to let me murder this girl right in front of you."

I laughed, the sound even harsher than my words had been. "I'm not that noble—or stupid. Even if I was, you're forgetting something important."

"What?" he growled.

I gave him a razor-thin smile. "I told you before. I don't need my sword to destroy your magic."

Before he could react, I snapped up my left hand and threw my immunity at him.

Admittedly, my power wasn't very impressive in a visual sense, since it was more like a blast of cold wind than the hot, tangible flames still burning in Ricardo's palm. But it slammed into him like a tidal wave, snuffing out his fire and knocking both him and Lena down.

Paloma roared again, hefted her mace high, and attacked the remaining magiers, while I focused on Ricardo and Lena, who were rolling around on the ground.

"You bastard!" Lena shrieked, scrambling up onto her knees and drawing her fist back to punch him. "You were going to kill me to save yourself—"

Ricardo drew another knife out of the folds of his cloak, whipped it up, and slashed it across her throat. Lena let out a choked scream and toppled over onto her side. She clamped her hands around her neck, but blood gushed out from between her fingers.

So much blood—too much blood.

Lena stretched up one of her hands, silently begging me to help her, but there was nothing I could do. A few seconds later, her outstretched hand dropped to the ground, while her other hand slipped off her neck and landed in the blood that was rapidly pooling underneath her body. She didn't move after that.

Ricardo scrambled to his feet and darted toward the alley, trying to escape, but I surged forward and sliced my sword across the back of his thigh, opening up a deep cut. He screamed and stumbled sideways. His boots slipped on some broken glass, and he hit one of the metal trash bins, bounced off, and landed on a pile of boards. The rotten wood snapped like matchsticks under his weight, and he ended up on his ass in the middle of the splintered debris.

I glanced over my shoulder. Paloma had killed the last of the magiers, and she came over to stand beside me.

I focused on Ricardo again. "You treacherous bastard. You didn't have to kill that girl. She was working for you."

Ricardo let out a harsh, mocking laugh. "Please. Lena would have stabbed me in the back the second she got the chance. She wanted all the gold we were going to get for this job. So did everyone else. It was just a matter of time before she and the others started plotting against me." He shrugged, as though the magiers' collective greed mattered as little to him as the girl's life had. "So, yes, I did have to kill her before she tried to kill me."

Maybe Xenia was right. Maybe my Bellonan gladiator heritage had made me more barbarian than queen, because his twisted logic actually made perfect sense to me. So many people had tried to murder me over the past year that I could easily understand—and even appreciate—the idea of killing someone before they tried to kill you.

"Well, you won't be hurting anyone else." I stabbed my sword at him. "Get on your feet. Now. You're going to tell me who you're working for and what they want with me."

Ricardo looked at Paloma, who casually propped her mace on her shoulder, even though drops of blood and bits of gore were still dripping off the sharp spikes and splattering onto the ground. The magier blanched and turned his attention back to me.

For a moment, I thought he was going to do the smart thing and surrender. Then his eyes narrowed, another sneer twisted his face, and the caustic stench of his magic filled the air again. Ricardo feinted and swiped out with his knife, as though he were going to cut me, even as he lifted his other hand to blast me in the face with his fire.

I was expecting the sneak attack, and I slapped his knife away with my sword. Then I dropped to one knee, surged forward, and slammed my left hand down onto his chest.

The second my palm touched his body, I sent my immunity shooting outward, as though it were a giant, invisible fist that I was hammering straight into him. The red-hot flames crackling on his hand immediately snuffed out, but I was angry, so I hit him with my immunity again, this time focusing on the fire, the magic, burning deep inside his body. Ricardo screamed with pain and lashed out with his inner fire, trying to scorch through my cold, hard power and char it to ash, along with the rest of me.

He was strong in his magic—but he wasn't stronger than *me*.

I hammered him with my immunity again. And again, and again, until the fire burning in his veins, in the very center of his black heart, started to crack and splinter. Ricardo screamed again and started beating at me with his fists, desperate to escape. He managed to hit me in the chest a few times, but the hard, heavy blows just fueled my own anger. I reached for even more of my power, even more of that icy rage deep inside me, and slammed another burst of magic into him, stronger than all the others.

CRACK!

That one note boomed in my ears like a thunderclap, making me flinch, although Ricardo and Paloma didn't seem to hear it. In that instant, I felt something inside the magier just . . . *shatter,* like his body was made of delicate glass that I'd just punched to pieces.

I glanced down, half expecting to see blood come gushing out of his chest, but my hand was still pressing down on his heart, and there was no blood or visible injury.

Ricardo looked up at me, gasping for breath. "What . . . have you . . . done?"

I let go of my immunity and yanked my hand off his chest, but it was too late. He pitched backward onto the ground, as though all his strength had suddenly deserted him, and his arms and legs started convulsing. The violent tremors lasted for about ten seconds before they abruptly stopped.

Ricardo's head lolled to the side, his topaz eyes frozen open in pain and fear, and a thin trickle of blood oozed out of his nose.

The magier was dead.

chapter four

I let out a tense breath, dropped my hand to my side, and sat back on my heels, still stunned by what I'd just done.

Ricardo's chest was whole and unbroken, with no visible injury, although blood kept dribbling out of his nose. But I could see one thing very clearly—the outline of my hand in the fabric of his black tunic, right over his heart.

I hadn't meant to kill the magier. At least, not before I'd gotten some answers about who he was working for. No, I had only wanted to douse Ricardo's fire to keep him from burning me, but I'd gone too far, and I'd killed him. And not with my sword.

With my magic.

I glanced down at my hand. Even now the invisible strength of my immunity crackled along my fingertips, as though it were a living weapon that was ready—*eager*—to be used again. I let out another breath and curled my hand into a tight fist. That was the only way I could pretend it wasn't trembling, along with the rest of me.

Paloma crouched down and studied Ricardo's body. "What did you do to him?"

I clenched my fingers into an even tighter fist, still trying to stop that damn trembling. "I think that I . . . crushed his magic . . . with my immunity."

Paloma heard the tremor in my voice, and she gave me a curious look. "I thought your immunity only let you dampen someone's magic for a few seconds, not completely destroy their power. And I didn't know destroying someone's magic would actually kill their physical body too."

"Me neither," I whispered, my fingers still trembling. "Me neither."

Paloma grinned and clapped me on the shoulder, almost knocking me over. "Well, good for you for figuring out a new way to kill people. I'm impressed, Evie. And a little jealous."

The ogre face on her neck also grinned at me, heartily approving of this new, lethal skill that I seemed to have.

Paloma stared at the dead bodies sprawled across the plaza. "No blond hair, no purple eyes. None of these magiers look like Maeven. Do you think they were related to her? More members of the Bastard Brigade?"

"I don't know. Let's see if we can find anything that tells us who they were."

Paloma moved over to the other side of the plaza and started rifling through one of the dead magiers' pockets. I scooted forward and did the same thing to Ricardo, since he was the closest one to me.

Ricardo had certainly been fond of knives. In addition to the three blades he'd pulled on me, I found two more tucked into a belt, at the small of his back. All the knives were perfectly balanced, with razor-sharp edges, but no crests or symbols adorned them, and no metal-master marks were stamped into the blades. Still, I laid them aside to take with me. Perhaps Serilda or Cho would see some clue in the weapons.

Next, I searched through the pockets stitched inside Ricardo's black cloak, as well as the ones in his leggings, but I only found a few gold crowns and other coins. I set those aside too. Money was money, after all.

I glanced at Paloma. "Find anything?"

She shook her head. "Just weapons and money. I'll keep looking."

Paloma and I moved from one dead body to the next, but we only found more weapons and money. None of the magiers was carrying anything personal that would identify them. Then again, assassins rarely left behind obvious clues.

Disgusted, I tossed a few more coins onto the pile I'd made, then looked out over the plaza again. There was one person we hadn't searched yet—Lena.

Paloma was busy with another body, so I went over and crouched down next to the dead girl.

Lena's eyes were still open, her dark brown gaze fixed and glassy in death, and the deep cut on her neck looked like a crooked, scarlet smile carved into her skin. The coppery stench of her blood, along with the growing rot of her death, overpowered the garbage in the plaza, and I had to choke down the bile that rose in my throat.

I didn't mourn her passing—after all, Lena had led me into this trap—but sorrow still filled me as I stared at her young, pretty features. She had given me hope that another Blair was still alive—hope that was now as dead as she was.

My sorrow faded, washed away by waves of anger, shame, and embarrassment. I should have known better. I should have known the rumor was too good to be true. I should have realized that it was a bloody trap right from the start. But instead, I'd foolishly let myself *hope,* and now I had nothing but a sick, roiling stomach and an empty, aching space in my heart.

"Evie?" Paloma asked. "Are you okay?"

"I'm fine," I growled.

I pushed my feelings aside, leaned forward, and rifled

through Lena's pockets the same way I had Ricardo's. She also had several knives, but they were nothing special, so I tossed them onto the weapons pile. I moved on to the pockets in her leggings and other layers of clothing, but I didn't find anything inside them, not even a few coins.

Frustration filled me, and I sat back on my heels. I was about to give up when I noticed a small lump on Lena's chest, one that was somehow sticking up through her grubby clothes.

Curious, I leaned forward again and probed the lump with my fingers. At first I thought it was a button, but it seemed too large for that, so I kept pressing on and around the lump. Lena was wearing something underneath her clothes.

Even though her neck was a cut, bloody mess, I hooked my fingers into the tops of her tunics and yanked them all down. A thin gold chain glimmered around her throat. I fished it out of the thick, sticky blood that covered her skin, drew it up over her head, and held it out where I could see it.

A gold pendant dangled from the end of the chain.

At first glance, the pendant seemed to be a simple round coin, but a closer look revealed that it was stamped on both sides. One side featured two crisscrossed knives that resembled Ricardo's and Lena's weapons. The symbol seemed vaguely familiar, although I couldn't remember when or where I had seen it before, so I flipped over the pendant.

A woman's face was stamped on the other side. A common enough symbol, except for one thing—the woman's eyes and mouth were all shaped like tiny coins.

I was so shocked that I almost dropped the pendant. I definitely recognized this symbol, although I wished I didn't. A woman with two coins for her eyes and a single coin for her mouth was the crest of the Fortuna Mint.

"Oh, bloody . . ." My voice trailed off, and I couldn't even finish the curse hanging on my lips.

Most people viewed the Fortuna Mint as a bank, since the Mint printed and accepted coins and currencies from various kingdoms, while other folks stored precious jewelry, artwork, and heirlooms in its supposedly impenetrable vaults. The Mint also dealt in rarities and hosted lavish auctions where everything from hard-to-find antiquities to exotic spices to unusual creatures was sold to the highest bidder.

The Fortuna Mint was run by the DiLucri family, as it had been ever since its founding centuries ago. In many ways, the DiLucris were an unofficial royal family who wielded their collective wealth and power to its fullest extent, influencing everyone from common merchants to lords and ladies to kings and queens.

I looked at the pendant again, then down at Lena, then over at Ricardo and the rest of the bodies. They weren't members of the Bastard Brigade. No, the dead magiers had worked for the DiLucris.

Intimidation, kidnapping, extortion, assassination. The Di-Lucris would quietly help you with all that and more, but they were most famous—or rather infamous—for their bounty hunters. The DiLucris trained and employed a legion of bounty hunters to collect on outstanding debts owed to their Mint, as well as procure rarities and carry out special missions. You could run, but you couldn't hide for long from the bounty hunters—or geldjagers, as they were also known.

I'd had the misfortune to encounter some geldjagers before, so I knew exactly how skilled and vicious they were and that many of them wore small gold-coin pendants to prove their identities.

Lena had said that her group had been sent to Svalin to torture whomever fell into their trap for information, but once Ricardo had realized who I was, he'd wanted to kidnap me instead. The thought of being casually sold from one horrible person to another like a purloined painting or a stolen necklace filled me with disgust, but I shouldn't have been surprised.

After all, it had almost happened to me before.

Oh, yes, the geldjagers had definitely been working for the DiLucris, and I couldn't help but think they were working for the Mortan king as well. I could imagine the king ordering me to be brought in alive just so he could have the pleasure—and certainty—of finally murdering me himself.

The DiLucris charged a high price for their geldjagers, but the Mortan king could easily afford their exorbitant fees. Or perhaps he'd promised the DiLucris something else. Contracts with Mortan merchants, fertile farmlands, or maybe even some noble title and a place in his palace. Or perhaps the DiLucris were breaking with their tradition of supposed neutrality and aligning themselves with the Mortans outright.

But all that really mattered was who Ricardo had wanted to deliver me to. The DiLucris, so they could fulfill their contract with the Mortans? Or perhaps Ricardo had been thinking about cutting the DiLucris out of the deal and taking me directly to the Mortan king. Either way, the DiLucris working for or with the Mortans was a disturbing development.

Paloma finished searching the last of the magiers and straightened up. "Did you find anything?"

I got to my feet to tell her about the pendant, but a voice cut me off.

"Highness!" someone yelled. "Highness!"

"Over here!" I called out.

Footsteps slapped against the cobblestones, and Sullivan sprinted into the alley, along with Serilda and Cho. All three of them were clutching swords, although they lowered their weapons when they realized the danger was dead.

Sullivan hurried over to me, reached out, and cupped my

face in his hand. His blue eyes searched mine, and he gently stroked his thumb over my cheek. "Highness?" he asked, all sorts of worried questions squeezed into that one word.

I reached up and grabbed his hand. "I'm fine, and so is Paloma. It was a trap, but we turned the tables on them. I'm sorry I ran off. I didn't mean to worry you."

He nodded, accepting my explanation, then dropped his hand and stared at the dead magiers. "Who were they? More members of the Bastard Brigade?"

Serilda bent down and picked up one of Ricardo's knives from the weapons pile. She twirled the blade around, then held it out where Cho could see it. Worry creased his face.

Serilda tossed the knife down onto the pile with the others. "No. These are geldjager blades."

"I think you're right." I showed my friends the coined-woman pendant that Lena had been wearing.

"The DiLucris sent geldjagers to Svalin?" Sullivan shook his head. "That's bold, even for them. Usually they only dispatch their pet vipers when there is serious money to be made."

"But who hired the geldjagers to come to Svalin and start that rumor about another Blair being alive?" I asked. "Was it Maeven? The Mortan king? Or did the DiLucris do this on their own? Who was Ricardo hoping to deliver me to? And for what purpose?"

"Ransom?" Cho suggested. "Maybe the DiLucris were going to sell you to the highest bidder, whether it was Bellona or Morta or someone else. That would be a good way to create even more tension between the two kingdoms, as well as make the DiLucris a hefty profit. The Mint trades in money, power, and favors, and auctioning off a queen would have netted them all three."

"Or this whole thing could be about payback," Serilda said. "Maybe Vasilia or Cordelia made some deal with the Mint. Maybe the DiLucris want to get their money back one way or another, now that the other Blair queens are dead."

"Maybe," I murmured. "It could be any one of those things or something else we haven't even thought of yet."

I studied the gold pendant again. Perhaps it was my imagination, but the three tiny coins in the woman's face winked at me like evil eyes, as if they were warning me that this was only the beginning of this latest plot against me—and that things were only going to get worse.

Every sly glimmer of gold made another match of anger flare to life in my chest. I was used to the Mortans trying to kill me, but the DiLucris had sent their operatives to *my* city, *my* capital, to torture and kill whomever had been unlucky enough to fall into the geldjagers' trap.

No one threatened my people like that—not without suffering the harshest of consequences.

I thought you were just a mutt who could smell things. Ricardo's sneering voice filled my mind. He'd thought I was weak, and no doubt so did his employers, which was why they'd launched such a sly, vicious scheme.

Well, I could be sly and vicious too. Paloma and I had already killed the geldjagers, but their masters needed to be reminded that they fucked with Bellona—and underestimated me—at their own peril.

"Well, whoever they were working for, geldjagers roaming the streets of Svalin is troublesome, Evie," Cho said. "Very troublesome."

"You're right," I snarled. "This does mean trouble—for my enemies."

"What are you thinking, highness?" Sullivan asked.

I stabbed my finger at Lena's body. "The girl said the geldjagers had been ordered to send me a message. Well, I'm going to use the geldjagers to send a message of my own right back to the DiLucris and the Mortan king."

An hour later, I once again found myself in a plaza surrounded by dead bodies. But instead of the rotten, trash-strewn city slums, I was now standing in a fresh, clean, open space along the Summanus River. Seven bridges led from the city of Svalin across the river and over to Seven Spire palace. Each bridge had a name, and I was standing at the end of the one called Retribution.

Very appropriate for what I had in mind.

Unlike many of the city plazas, the one at the end of the Retribution Bridge didn't feature a bubbling fountain, pretty statue, or grassy park. No, this plaza boasted a large stone platform with several trapdoors set into the bottom and sturdy scaffolding rising up and running along the back of it.

This was where people were executed.

Criminals, mostly, who had committed atrocious acts that demanded severe, permanent punishment. Once judgment was handed down, the condemned were brought from the palace dungeon to this platform, where they were hanged until dead for all the people of Svalin to see.

Tonight, I'd decided to use the platform for a slightly different purpose—to display the dead geldjagers.

Several palace guards wearing short-sleeve blue tunics topped with silver breastplates were standing on the platform, wrestling with the bodies and stringing them up with ropes. Even though the geldjagers were already dead, their remains would hang here until I said otherwise.

"Snap to it, men!" a loud voice barked out. "Queen's orders!"

The shouts came from a fifty-something man standing on one side of the platform. He was a tall, stern, imposing figure with short gray hair, brown eyes, dark bronze skin, and a lumpy nose that had obviously been broken multiple times. He was wearing a short-sleeve blue tunic, just like the other guards, but the feathered texture of his silver breastplate marked his importance, as did my crown-of-shards crest emblazoned in the metal over his heart.

Auster, the captain of the palace guards, hopped off the platform, walked over, and bowed low to me in the traditional Bellonan style. I had repeatedly told Auster that he didn't have to bow every single time he saw me, but the captain was a stickler for tradition, at least in front of his men.

"My queen," he said, straightening up. "Is everything proceeding according to your satisfaction?"

I stared at the platform. The guards had slipped the ropes around the geldjagers and were slowly hoisting the bodies into the air. "Yes. Thank you for seeing to it on such short notice."

"Well, perhaps if you had told me that you were planning to leave Xenia's finishing school without any guards and kill a bunch of assassins, I would have been better prepared." Auster didn't bother to keep the dry sarcasm or chiding tone out of his voice. He hadn't been happy that I hadn't informed him of my plans.

"I didn't want you to worry, and I didn't want a bunch of guards marching through the plaza and potentially scaring off whoever came to the meeting." I sighed. "But most of all, I hoped that the rumor was true, and that another Blair was still alive."

Auster's face softened. "I would have hoped it too. I still do."

His voice came out as a low rasp, and the scent of his salty grief washed over me. Like me, Auster had also witnessed the Seven Spire massacre. Even worse, he'd failed in his duty to protect Queen Cordelia, something that would always haunt him, just like it haunted me.

Thinking about the dead queen made me turn and stare up at Seven Spire palace on the other side of the river. The palace was the crown jewel of Svalin and the kingdom of Bellona, and the structure spiraled up, out, and into the side of Seven Spire Mountain before ending in seven tearstone spires that seemed to reach all the way up to the moon and stars. Balconies, terraces, and metal lifts adorned the outside of the palace like strings of fluorestones, honey cranberries, and cornucopia balls on a yule tree, but my gaze locked onto the massive columns that supported the structure.

In tribute to Bellona's history, gladiators were carved into the columns, along with swords, shields, daggers, and spears, as though the warriors and weapons were all frozen in some epic battle that stretched across the entire face of the palace and was threatening to spill over onto the surrounding mountains.

Gargoyles with curved horns and long tails tipped with arrowlike stones were also carved into the columns, along with strixes, hawklike birds with wide wings that looked just as sharp as the gladiators' swords. A few caladriuses were also scattered across the columns, as though they were hiding amid the chaos of the perpetual battle. The tiny, owlish birds might be much smaller, but they were just as powerful as the other creatures.

The artistry of the carvings was exquisite, but what made the columns truly eye-catching was the fact that they were made of tearstone. In addition to both absorbing and deflecting magic, tearstone also had another dual nature—it could change color, going from bright starry gray to deep midnight-blue and back again.

Given the evening hour and the soft light streaming out of the palace windows, the columns were such a dark blue that they almost looked black, although the gladiators and creatures still seemed to move back and forth, lifting and lowering their weapons and wings, and fighting for supremacy.

Despite the beautiful scene, my heart started to ache. The shifting colors represented the Summer and Winter lines of the Blair family—a family that seemed to be extinct, except for me.

I turned away from the palace. "You still think another Blair is alive?"

Auster shrugged. "I don't know, but I plan to keep searching. I might not hear as many whispers as Xenia, but I have my own spies, and I'm going to investigate every single Blair rumor that they bring to me. Besides, it doesn't hurt to hope, does it?"

But that was the problem—it *did* hurt to hope, more than I'd ever imagined.

Auster gestured at the scaffolding. "Are you sure about this, Evie?"

"Yes. The DiLucris and the Mortans need to be reminded what happens to people who are foolish enough to cause trouble in Bellona. And not just them, but all the other kings and queens and anyone else who thinks that Bellona is weak—that *I* am weak."

The words left a bitter taste on my tongue. Oh, I knew that I wasn't weak, not after everything I had been through over the past year, but others didn't feel the same. Most people in Bellona and beyond still believed that I had only lucked into the throne by accident, and my perceived weakness when it came to both my reign and my magic was the source of many of my problems. Displaying the geldjagers' bodies was the first step to fixing that. I had other steps in mind, especially when it came to the upcoming Regalia, although I wasn't quite sure how to accomplish them yet.

"*Weak* is a word that I would never use to describe you, my queen," Auster said.

I huffed. "You're my captain. You have to say that."

He shook his head. "I wouldn't say it if it wasn't true."

The strong scent of his lime truthfulness washed over me, and I inhaled the aroma deeply, even though it burned my nose. Auster's quiet, steady belief meant far more to me than he knew. Now it was time for me to earn that belief—and the respect of everyone in Bellona and beyond.

"I want more guards patrolling the plazas, just in case we didn't kill all the geldjagers. Coordinate with Xenia, pool your spies, and see what news your collective sources have about the geldjagers, the DiLucris, and the Mortans. Also, have Halvar and Bjarni step up their work with the palace guards. I want them firmly in command and ready to defend Seven Spire when we leave for the Regalia."

I paused. "I also have some . . . ideas for the Regalia, some things I want to accomplish while we're there, but we can talk more about those in the morning."

"Yes, my queen." Auster jerked his head to the side. "Before I go, is there anything you would like me to do about your current audience?"

It was after eight now, and most of the nobles, senators, guilders, and other wealthy, important citizens who roamed the Seven Spire halls had either retired to their chambers inside the palace or returned to their homes and apartments in the city for the night.

Most, but unfortunately not all.

A short man with thinning blond hair, blue eyes, pale skin, and a bulging belly was standing off to one side of the plaza. His arms were crossed over his chest, and he was studying the geldjagers' bodies with a critical gaze. Lord Fullman was one of the wealthiest—and most demanding—nobles at Seven Spire. He'd scurried out here less than fifteen minutes after a wagon had delivered the bodies, and he'd been watching the proceedings ever since.

And he wasn't the only one.

A woman in her seventies with short, curly iron-gray hair, golden eyes, and ebony skin was standing a few feet away from Fullman. Lady Diante was another wealthy, powerful noble, although she was far more skillful and patient when it came to playing courtly games than Fullman was. Diante had waited a full half hour before coming to the plaza, and her expression was more thoughtful than critical.

Auster eyed the two nobles. "I could always hoist up Full-man with the rest of the bodies." A smile creased the captain's face. "It would be fun to watch him kick and squirm."

"As entertaining as that would be, his screams would wake the entire palace and probably the rest of the city." I shook my head. "I would never subject my people to such a horror as that."

Auster let out a low, amused chuckle, then bowed to me again and headed back over to the platform. The captain walked right past Fullman like he didn't even see him stand-ing there. Fullman glared at Auster's back before scurrying over to me. Diante followed him, albeit at a much slower, more measured pace.

"Queen Everleigh," Fullman cooed, plastering a smile on his face. "I didn't realize you had such excitement planned."

"I would hardly call stringing up a bunch of dead bodies *excitement*," I drawled.

Diante chuckled at my rebuke. She and Fullman were bit-ter rivals, and each always took great pleasure in anything that harmed the other, even something as simple as words.

Fullman shot her a withering glare and turned back to me. "Yes, well, do you think this is wise? From what I've heard, these people were geldjagers who worked for the DiLucris."

"Yes, these geldjagers did work for the DiLucris. I don't know who they were after or what bounty they were sent to col-lect, but they were using their magic and weapons to harass the plaza merchants, along with innocent shoppers, so Serilda and Cho put an end to them."

That was the story my friends and I had concocted, and Paloma, Sullivan, Serilda, and Cho were already inside Seven Spire, telling it to anyone who would listen. By morning, it should be all over the palace. Auster would make sure that it spread throughout the ranks of the guards and the servants, while Xenia and her spies would whisper about it to the rest of the city.

Fullman's eyes narrowed, as though he didn't believe my lies, but he drew in a breath, ready to try another tactic. "Yes, but displaying their bodies in such a fashion could send the wrong message. That we are hostile to DiLucri interests, and to the Mint itself. Or have you forgotten that the Regalia will soon begin on Fortuna Island?"

No, I hadn't forgotten that the Regalia was taking place on the DiLucris' home island. As much as I hated to admit it, Fullman was right. I was thumbing my nose at the DiLucris days before I was scheduled to travel to their territory.

Not the smartest thing I'd ever done as queen, but in this case, being seen as strong and vicious was more important than being smart and tactful. Displaying the geldjagers' bodies might make the DiLucris think twice about attacking my people again. And if it didn't, well, I would keep giving the DiLucris visual reminders of how Bellona dealt with her enemies until my message finally sank in.

But I wasn't going to share my thoughts with the pompous lord, so I lifted my chin and peered down my nose at him. "I think it sends just the right message—that no one, geldjager or otherwise, comes to *my* kingdom, *my* capital, and terrorizes *my* people."

I stared at him a moment longer, then glanced over at the platform. The guards had hoisted the last body into the air, and Auster waved at me. I waved back and started walking toward the bridge.

I had thought—hoped—that my harsh response would be the end of things, but Fullman was nothing if not persistent, and he trotted along beside me, his short legs churning to keep up with my longer, smoother strides. Diante followed us at a much more stately pace, content to watch the other noble's frantic machinations.

"Actually, there is another urgent matter I must discuss with you," Fullman said.

I sighed, but I stopped and faced him. Otherwise, he would chatter at me all the way across the bridge. "What?"

"I'm wondering why you haven't chosen Tolliver to compete in any of the Regalia events, especially the Tournament of Champions."

Each kingdom sent a contingent of its best warriors, magiers, masters, and athletes to the Regalia. There were dozens and dozens of contests, everything from who was the strongest mutt to which magier could juggle the most balls of fire at one time to which cook master could bake the best cranberry-apple pie. Medals and money were awarded, but for many winners, the real prize was bragging rights for themselves and their respective kingdoms.

As queen, I had the final say on which Bellonans got to participate in the Regalia, including the Tournament of Champions, the most prestigious event, with a hefty prize of ten thousand gold crowns. Everything at Seven Spire was *always* a competition, but few items were as hotly contested as the Regalia slots, and the nobles had been showering me with flattery and fancy gifts for weeks, in hopes of swaying my opinion about who should enter what events. Fullman had been among the most persistent and annoying, especially when it came to trying to get his son Tolliver into the tournament.

"I'm sure Tolliver has far better things to do than fight in the tournament," I said, trying to tell Fullman no without snapping and losing my temper as I so often did with him.

But of course Fullman didn't take the hint. He never did. "But Tolliver has been training for months. Besides, someone from our family has been in the tournament for the last five generations. It's a time-honored tradition for a Fullman to compete, and Tolliver should lead the Bellonan warriors, just as I did when I was his age." His chin lifted, and his chest and belly both puffed up with bloated pride.

"I certainly admire Tolliver's . . . dedication," I said, once again trying to be diplomatic. "But Paloma is the highest-ranked gladiator in Svalin and one of the top-ranked gladiators on the continent. She's earned the right to lead the other warriors and represent Bellona."

A disgusted sneer twisted Fullman's face, and he threw up his hands in frustration. "But she's not even from Bellona! She's some Floresian ogre morph of questionable lineage!"

Red-hot anger roared through me at the way he so casually dismissed my friend and her skills and mocked her heritage. Paloma was right. She was worth twenty of this pompous, arrogant bastard. No, not twenty. Two hundred. Two thousand. Two million.

Fullman must have realized his grave mistake, because he quickly lowered his hands and schooled his face into a more neutral expression. "Not that there's anything wrong with Floresians. Or ogre morphs," he added, although we could both hear the lie in his high, nervous tone.

"Let me be clear," I said, my own voice growing colder and more menacing with each and every word. "Tolliver is a piss-poor fighter. He doesn't even like to get his tunic dirty. He never did, not even when we were children. He will get eliminated in the first minute in the first round of the tournament. Paloma, on the other hand, will easily advance, probably all the way to the finals. So *Paloma* will be representing Bellona in the tournament, along with whomever else I choose. Not Tolliver."

"But . . . but it's my family's *tradition*," Fullman sputtered.

"I care about family traditions, but I care even more about

winning. And we both know that Bellona won't win anything—not one *thing*—if Tolliver competes."

I glared at Fullman, daring him to contradict me, but for once he did the smart thing and shut his mouth, although hot, peppery anger blasted off him, along with a strong note of smoky deception. I'd pissed him off, and he was planning to retaliate. Well, this wouldn't be the first time some noble had started scheming against me, although Fullman had enough land, men, and money to do more damage than most.

"You're going to regret this," he hissed.

"That's the beauty of being queen—I never have to regret anything."

I kept glaring at him, letting him see that I wasn't the least bit intimidated. An angry red flush stained Fullman's cheeks, and he spun around and stormed across the bridge, heading back toward the palace.

The sharp *slap-slap-slap-slap* of his boots quickly faded away, but it was almost immediately replaced by another, softer set of footsteps. Lady Diante glided forward and stopped beside me. I'd been so focused on Fullman that I'd forgotten she was still lurking around.

"I hope you enjoyed the show."

"Seeing you put Fullman in his place? Absolutely," she murmured in a soft, silky voice. "Little things like that always brighten my day."

I snorted out a laugh.

She smiled, and a bit of genuine warmth crinkled her face. Diante could be as ruthless as any noble, but there were times like these when I thought she almost respected me—at least until she tried to undercut me with some new proposal that would benefit her family. But I couldn't fault her for that. Seven Spire was its own sort of arena, and everyone was always ready, willing, and eager to stab their rivals in the back to further advance their own position and standing.

"What can I do for you, Diante?" I asked, getting down to business.

"I also wanted to inquire about the Tournament of Champions."

I sighed. "Let me guess. You want one of your grandsons to compete."

She shrugged. "We both know that you've chosen Paloma with good reason, and you're right in that she could potentially win the tournament." She paused. "But I would like you to consider Nico for one of the slots."

Nico was one of the best warriors at Seven Spire and especially skilled at archery. I'd already been considering him for the Tournament of Champions, along with the separate archery competition. I had expected Diante to suggest some relative with no skill at all, someone she wanted to placate or appease, like Fullman had with Tolliver, but she was offering me a perfectly reasonable choice, one that all the other nobles could agree on. It made me even more suspicious about what she was really up to.

"The two of us have had our issues," Diante continued. "But Nico is a fine warrior, and he deserves to be in the tournament. All I'm asking is that you judge my grandson on his own merits, and not on mine."

I kept eyeing her, but once again, she seemed sincere, and she smelled strongly of lime truthfulness. More important, she was right. I *should* judge Nico on his own skills, and not on the problems I had with his grandmother.

"Very well. Nico will be an excellent addition to the tournament, as well as the archery competition. You can inform him of my decision, and tell him to report to the royal lawn in the morning to train with Paloma and the others."

Diante dropped into a respectful curtsy. "Thank you, my queen."

She straightened, but instead of leaving now that she'd gotten what she wanted, she stared at the platform in the distance. Her golden gaze flicked from one dead body to the next, and a thoughtful expression creased her face. "You're doing the right thing displaying the geldjagers like this."

Her approval surprised me. "Why would you say that?"

She turned toward me. "Because the DiLucris are one of the biggest threats to Bellona. They covet our land and tearstone mines just like the Mortans do. My family has had several run-ins with the DiLucris over the years, and their geldjagers have killed many of my people. Men, women, children."

The scent of hot, peppery anger blasted off her, searing my nose with its sudden, sharp intensity. Diante owned fruit orchards in the southern districts, many of which bordered the Summanus River close to Fortuna Island where the DiLucris made their home.

"In some ways, the DiLucris are even worse than the Mortans," Diante continued, her voice dripping with disgust. "They don't care about tradition or honor or playing the long game with their enemies. They just butcher and pillage whenever the mood strikes them. Two years ago, a group of geldjagers burned one of my pear orchards to the ground. Not because my people had done anything to them, but just because it amused them. Just because they wanted to watch the trees burn."

She fell silent, but memories darkened her eyes, and more peppery anger surged off her, along with a strong note of salty grief. This was by far the most open, honest, and vulnerable Diante had ever been in my presence, although the cynical part of me couldn't help but think that it was a carefully scripted act in order to manipulate me into doing whatever it was that she wanted.

"I've never heard you speak about anyone like this before, especially not a family as powerful as the DiLucris," I said, trying to determine her motives.

She shrugged again. "That's because I never had anyone willing to listen before."

"What do you mean?"

"When I told Cordelia about the geldjagers, she said that the DiLucris were too rich, too far away from Svalin, and too well guarded on their island to attack. She did *nothing*." Diante spat out the last word, then drew in a breath, visibly trying to rein in her temper. "But tonight, you actually did *something*."

"I didn't do it for you."

She shrugged yet again. "I know, but I appreciate it all the same."

I drew in a breath, tasting her scent, but she still reeked of lime truthfulness. She really was glad that the geldjagers were dead and on display. They must have killed someone she deeply loved, for her to despise them this much.

However, I still wondered why she was being so candid. Was she trying to warn me to be careful during the Regalia, since the Games were being held on the DiLucris' island? Was she hinting that the DiLucris were in league with the Mortans? Was she trying to push me into going after the DiLucris? Or did she have some other plan in mind?

"May I offer you some advice, my queen?" Diante asked, although she didn't wait for my agreement before speaking again. "Since you have picked this path, you need to continue on it, especially during the Regalia. Be bold, daring, brutal, and above all merciless. It's the only way anyone is going to take you seriously."

"I don't need a reminder of just how little people think of me, both here in Bellona and abroad." My voice came out louder and harsher than I had intended, and my cheeks burned with embarassment, despite the cool night air.

Diante dipped her head in apology. "I meant no disrespect. Truly. I have come to think quite a lot of you over the past few months, Everleigh. So have the other nobles. It's the fools like Fullman who continue to underestimate you."

She gestured up at the palace columns in the distance. "You rather remind me of a caladrius. Such a normal, innocent, quiet facade, but so much raw power lurking underneath. I admire how you hid your true strength from everyone at court. Smart of you to play that long game, especially when Vasilia was alive."

"But?" I asked, still wondering where she was going with this.

"But the time for hiding has passed. Something I think you already know, given your order to display the geldjagers' bodies. It is time to show your true strength, Everleigh, when it comes to both your reign and your magic. And it is especially time for you to play your own long game."

Her words mirrored my own thoughts, although I would never tell her so.

"Why, I think you could be one of the finest queens Bellona has ever known, if . . ." She deliberately let her voice trail off.

I sighed and asked the inevitable question. "If what?"

"If you quit worrying so much about what your actions might cost others." Diante gave me a speculative look. "You have people who will fight, kill, and die on your command, and yet you still prefer to handle such things yourself. It's no secret that you would much rather put yourself in danger rather than your people. An admirable, if foolish quality in a queen."

She paused. "Isn't that why *you* faced down the geldjagers this evening?"

I didn't respond, although I was cursing on the inside. It

seemed as though my story about Serilda and Cho killing the geldjagers hadn't been as convincing as I'd hoped.

At my continued silence, Diante's golden eyes narrowed, and a pleased smile crinkled her face. "Not a flicker of emotion at my accusation. Excellent. That skill will serve you well during the Regalia."

I arched an eyebrow. "I wasn't aware I needed your approval."

She let out a low, amused chuckle. "That's because you don't. *You* are the queen of Bellona. You have convinced me of it, Everleigh, and I am not an easy person to sway. Now it's time for you to convince everyone else—for all our sakes."

Once again, I didn't respond.

"Now, if you'll excuse me, my queen, I'm going to tell Nico the good news about the tournament." Diante's expression turned smug. "Along with Fullman, of course."

I snorted out another laugh. "Of course."

Diante curtsied again, then glided across the bridge, heading back toward the palace.

I watched her go, turning her words over in my mind. Diante was right. By displaying the geldjagers' bodies, I had chosen a new path, a bolder path, one where I would finally show my true power. Now I had to figure out how to stay on this path and achieve my ultimate goal, the thing I had secretly been dreaming about doing ever since the Seven Spire massacre.

Diante was also right about something else—I was already worrying about what my actions would cost my friends and how I could complete my mission without getting us all killed.

But I was too tired to puzzle it out tonight. Ensuring my kingdom's survival, along with my own, was a problem for tomorrow.

Unfortunately for me, I *always* had plenty of problems for tomorrow.

CHAPTER FIVE

I left the geldjagers' bodies behind in the plaza, crossed the bridge, and headed into the palace.

Given the late hour, the wide hallways and spacious common areas were deserted, and I didn't run into any other nobles. Guards were stationed here and there, and they all snapped to attention when they spotted me. I nodded at them and went to my chambers on the third floor.

The double doors were standing open, and I walked inside to find Sullivan surrounded by women.

One of them was about my age, with dark honey-blond hair, blue eyes, and rosy skin. She was quite pretty, as were the other two women, who were both younger but had similar features. All three were gathered around Sullivan, who was standing on a round dais with his arms held out to his sides and a pained expression on his face. Thick bolts of fabric, fat spools of thread, and plump pincushions glittering with needles littered several nearby tables.

I leaned against one of the doors and crossed my arms over my chest. "I stay behind to oversee Auster and his men and come back to find you besieged by beautiful women. The life of a consort truly is a grand one."

Calandre, my thread master, and Camille and Cerana, her two younger sisters, looked up at the sound of my drawling voice. The two teenage girls tittered and sidled away from Sullivan, as though they'd been caught doing something they shouldn't have, but Calandre raised her measuring tape and went back to work. The three women had been in my chambers every night this week, designing, sewing, and perfecting my and Sullivan's Regalia wardrobes.

"I feel like a bloody puppet," Sullivan muttered, still holding his arms out to his sides. "If I'd known that being your consort meant this sort of cruel, prolonged torture, then I would have reconsidered declaring my love for you."

Camille and Cerana gasped at his grumbled words, but I grinned.

"Ah, the trials we suffer for love," I said in mock sympathy.

Sullivan's eyes narrowed, but a smile curved the corner of his lips.

"A royal ball will be held every single night of the Regalia," Calandre said in a patient voice, as though she'd explained this more than once. "You need new jackets and tunics for all of them, not to mention the other events you're scheduled to attend. And not just any old clothes, but proper garments that are as fine as what the other royals will be wearing. Things that will make you look strong and imposing."

"Oh, I think that Evie is strong and imposing enough for the both of us," Sullivan joked.

"Absolutely," Calandre agreed. "And you have to look as polished as she does. Otherwise, you will completely clash with the gowns and other garments I've designed for her. I won't have you ruining all my hard work just because you have the patience of a petulant child."

Sullivan looked at me for help, but I held my hands up in surrender.

"You should listen to Calandre," I said. "She knows her fashions better than anyone."

Sullivan grumbled something under his breath, but he lifted his arms a little higher. Calandre winked at me and kept right on working.

Fifteen minutes later, the thread master announced she had finished recording Sullivan's measurements, and she and her sisters packed up their supplies and left the chambers. I thanked them for their time, then closed and locked the double doors behind them.

A long, tired sigh escaped my lips, and I leaned back against the stone.

"Problems with the nobles?" Sullivan asked, stepping off the dais. "I saw Fullman and Diante heading out of the palace earlier."

I sighed again. "Fullman questioned my every decision regarding the DiLucris and the geldjagers before threatening me for not including Tolliver in the Tournament of Champions."

Sympathy filled his face. "And Diante?"

"She asked me to include Nico in the tournament, which I agreed to do." I paused. "And then she said that I'd made the right decision displaying the geldjagers' bodies. She was actually quite supportive."

I told him everything Diante had said, including how the geldjagers had burned her orchard and killed her people. The only thing I omitted was her advice about continuing down my bold, brutal new path. I wanted some more time to think about that before I told Sullivan my true plans for the Regalia.

"Maybe she's finally warming up to you," Sullivan suggested. "Or at least hates the DiLucris enough to align with you on this."

I shrugged. "If I had to bet, I would say it was her hatred of the DiLucris that made her so approving. Diante might be inscrutable, but she wasn't faking her rage, grief, and heartache. I could smell how angry she was."

Sullivan studied me. "She sided with you, but you still seem upset. Why? Did she say something else?"

"No. But Diante's story and facing down the geldjagers earlier reminded me of . . ." My voice trailed off, and I couldn't finish my thought.

"Of what?"

"Of some things that happened after my parents were murdered." I shook my head, but I couldn't stop the awful memories from flooding my mind.

"You've never told me much about your parents," Sullivan said. "Or what happened to you right after they died."

I shook my head again. "It's not something I like to dwell on. And I have far too many problems right now to start digging up painful memories of the past."

Sullivan studied me a moment longer. Then he shrugged out of the dark blue cloak that Calandre had draped over his shoulders, tossed it aside, and prowled over to where I was still leaning against the doors.

I watched him come, admiring his strong, confident stride and tall, muscled body. Even now, after all our weeks together, I still couldn't believe that he was here, that he was mine, and that he loved me just as fiercely as I did him.

Sullivan stopped in front of me, his body a few scant inches away. He tilted his head to the side, and his blue, blue gaze locked with mine. A slow, devastating smile spread across his lips. "Well, if you don't want to focus on your bad memories, then you should let me help you make some new ones."

My heart stuttered, my breath caught in my throat, and hot, liquid desire started simmering in my veins. "What kind of memories?"

He gave me another wicked smile. "The kind this consort specializes in."

He leaned forward and braced his hands on the door on either side of my shoulders. My lips parted, and my body tensed with anticipation. Sullivan loomed in front of me, his handsome features blotting out everything else. My eyes began to flutter shut, and he drew closer to me . . . and closer . . . and closer still . . .

Sullivan kissed the tip of my nose.

My eyes snapped open. He leaned back and grinned, smugly pleased with his teasing.

"A kiss on the nose?" I muttered. "Really?"

"What were you expecting?" Sullivan kept teasing me. "Some grand romantic gesture? I already did that on the Pureheart Bridge, remember? Or perhaps you wanted me to sweep you off your feet and spin you around the room."

I rolled my eyes. "Sweeping me off my feet is a bit much. Especially since I am perfectly capable of standing on my own two feet. Besides, I'd probably get dizzy if you actually spun me around."

"But?"

"But I wouldn't have minded something a bit more passionate," I grumbled. "We've only been together for a couple of months. That's far too early for you to be kissing me on the nose and tucking me into bed like we're an old married couple."

Sullivan's smile widened, and his eyes burned like blue stars. "Oh, highness," he murmured in a low, husky voice that sent a shiver racing down my spine. "I would be quite happy to tuck you into bed. All you had to do was ask."

I arched an eyebrow, silently daring him to give me another chaste kiss on the nose. For a moment, I thought that was exactly what he was going to do, but Sullivan dipped his head, surged forward, and crushed his lips to mine.

Every single part of him filled up my senses. The firm feel

of his lips against my own. The quick, sure thrust of his tongue into my mouth. The warmth of his body heating the air between us. His vanilla scent tickling my nose with its faint, intoxicating hint of spice.

The kiss ended as quickly as it began, and Sullivan drew back, his hands still braced on the door on either side of my body, still not touching me. Not yet.

"Now, that's more like it," I whispered in a breathless voice.

He grinned again. "Oh, highness. I'm just getting started."

He leaned forward as though he were going to kiss me again, but this time he aimed lower, and his lips landed on my neck. I tilted my head to the side to give him better access, even as his hands crept up and started working at the silver crown-of-shards clasp on the front of my cloak. The garment drifted down to the floor, pooling at our feet.

Sullivan drew back, then leaned forward and kissed the other side of my neck. This time, his fingers worked on the laces on the front of my tunic, quickly loosening them. I lifted my arms so that he could draw the garment up and over my head, along with the soft, thin camisole underneath. He tossed them both aside, then snaked his arm around my waist, turning me around so that his chest was pressed against my back. Even through his tunic, the delicious heat of his body sank into my own bare skin.

Sullivan kissed my neck again, while his hands slid up my stomach and cupped my breasts. He gently squeezed them, then rolled the nipples between his fingers. That heat in my stomach spread through the rest of my body, and I sighed and arched back against him.

"If you like that, highness, then you're going to love this next bit," he rasped.

"I know I will," I murmured, lifting my hand to stroke the side of his face.

His hands left my breasts and slid lower. This time, he worked on the laces on the front of my leggings, undoing them as quickly and skillfully as he had the ones on my tunic.

His hand slid inside my leggings and then down below my silken undergarments. I turned my head to the side so that I could look up at him. Sullivan stared back at me, another wicked grin on his face. Then he leaned forward and kissed me again, flicking his tongue against mine, even as he cupped my warm, wet heat.

I hissed at how good it felt.

Sullivan rubbed his fingers back and forth, caressing that most intimate part of me. That warm desire in my veins burned brighter and hotter, turning into sharp, throbbing need.

"Sully," I rasped, urging him on. "Sully."

He kissed my neck again, his tongue skipping over the frantic, pounding pulse in my throat. I drew in a breath, but all I could see, feel, taste, smell was him. With every slide and glide of his fingers, Sullivan teased me a little higher until finally that sharp, throbbing need exploded into a tidal wave of pleasure. I cried out and sagged back against his body. He wrapped his arm around my waist again and pressed a kiss to the top of my shoulder.

"Like I said, highness," he whispered against my skin. "All you had to do was ask."

I shivered, then turned around so that we were face-to-face. I smiled and leaned forward, as though I were going to kiss him, but at the last moment, I gave him a peck on the nose instead.

Sullivan raised his eyebrows. "Using my own trick against me? That's not fair."

"Who said anything about fair?" I grinned. "Especially when we both know that it's more fun *not* to play fair."

I leaned forward again, kissing his neck, just like he had done mine. This time, my fingers went to work on the laces of his clothes. Sullivan lifted his arms, and I drew his tunic up and over his head, tossing it aside. I stopped to admire his bare muscled chest, then skimmed my fingers over the faint scars that cut across his skin, slowly working my way lower and lower. I undid the laces on his leggings, then we both stepped out of our boots, peeled off our socks, and shimmied out of our remaining garments.

When there were no more barriers between us, I stepped close to him again. Sullivan's hands fisted by his sides, but he didn't reach for me. Not yet. We stood there, staring into each other's eyes, both of us breathing hard, anticipating what was coming next.

I had thought to play a slow, teasing game just as he'd done with me, but I wanted him too badly to wait any longer, so I tangled my hand in his hair and drew his lips down to mine. Sullivan growled and started to pull me closer, but I put my other hand on his shoulder and stepped forward. I walked Sullivan all the way over to the bed in the back of the room. His legs hit the edge of the mattress, and he fell back onto the soft blankets.

Sullivan propped himself up on his elbows, while I looked him over from head to toe. His rumpled brown hair. The stubble on his chin. His bare muscled chest. The hard length of him just waiting to be claimed.

"I pictured you like this so many times," I confessed in a low, husky voice. "Here. In my bed. With me."

He held out his hand. "Then come and have me, highness."

I threaded my fingers through his, and he pulled me down onto the bed with him. I took all the proper herbs and precautions, as did he, so there was no worry between us, only desire.

We kissed, our lips and tongues crashing together time and time again, even as our hands slid over each other's body, kneading, caressing, and bringing as much pleasure to the other as possible.

I rolled Sullivan onto his back, then straddled him. My

hand closed over his long, hard cock, and I stroked him the same way he had me. Sullivan arched back, his hands fisting in the blankets. But he was just as impatient as I was, and he reached for me again. I leaned forward, and he pulled me down on top of him, thrusting into me at the same time.

We both moaned. I kissed him again, driving my tongue into his mouth, while his hands roamed up and down my back. Then I rose and started rocking my hips, taking him a little deeper inside with every quick slide.

Sullivan anchored his hands on my hips, urging me on, and I rocked harder, faster, moving in exquisite pleasure with him until we both finally cried out and reached our release together.

Afterward, Sullivan kept his promise. He tucked me under the blankets, then spooned against my back and drifted off to sleep. I slept as well, but some time later the soothing blackness receded, replaced by memories I would have rather forgotten . . .

I had never been so hungry.

My hunger was like a gargoyle in my belly, constantly growling, grumbling, and demanding to be fed. But there was nothing in the snowy woods to eat, unless I wanted to gnaw on some pine cones.

I eyed one of the spiky brown cones that littered the ground. Would eating a pine cone kill me? I didn't know, but it certainly wouldn't be good for me. Then again, neither was wandering around the woods in circles.

Three days ago, I had stumbled away from the ruined remains of Winterwind, my family estate. My father, Jarl Sancus, had been poisoned with wormroot by Ansel, my traitorous tutor, while my mother, Lady Leighton Larimar

Winter Blair, had been murdered by a Mortan weather magier while we'd been fleeing from our home. I'd gotten lucky and had managed to kill the weather magier, and I'd been wandering through the woods ever since.

I thought I'd been walking south, heading toward the nearest town, but I must have gotten turned around in the trees because I hadn't come across any signs of civilization. No hunters stalking deer, no one chopping wood, not even a traveler on the way to Unger or Andvari. My only company was the bluefrost doves softly cooing in the treetops, and for all I knew, I was the last person alive on the entire continent. But staring hungrily at pine cones certainly wasn't doing me any good, so I wrapped my arms around my still-growling stomach and trudged on.

The only good thing about walking through the woods was that there was plenty of water. I stopped in a clearing, scooped up a handful of snow from the ground, and shoved it into my mouth. The cold crystals froze my tongue before they slowly, reluctantly melted.

I was still crouching down, shoveling snow into my mouth and trying to pretend that it was something more substantial and filling, when a faint crack rang out.

I froze. Another crack rang out, and then another one, falling into a steady rhythm that I recognized as footsteps.

Someone was coming this way.

I stayed frozen in place a moment longer, then my mind sluggishly kicked into gear, whispering a warning. As much as I longed to find someone to help me—or at least give me something to bloody eat—Mortan assassins could be roaming around, searching for survivors of the Winterwind attack. I surged to my feet, but before I could hide behind a tree, two people strode into the clearing.

They stopped and stared, as surprised to see me as I was them.

One was a man, more than six feet tall, with dark brown hair, eyes, and skin, and a long, bushy brown beard. He was bundled up in a black cloak trimmed with shaggy brown fur that made him look like a grizzly. He was carrying a knapsack on either shoulder, with another, larger one strapped to his back. Several small bags were also fastened to his black leather belt, along with a piece of rope with a box dangling from the end. Black cloth covered the container, hiding the contents.

The other person was a woman with long blond hair, blue eyes, and milky skin, who was as petite and slender as the man was tall and stocky. Her black cloak was trimmed with sleek purple feathers, making her resemble a small, elegant strix.

The two of them must have been traipsing through the woods for quite some time, given the snow that crusted their black boots, but they looked warm and cozy in their thick cloaks, as though the chilly air wasn't bothering them. I had to clench my hands into fists to keep from shivering in my thin blue dress.

"Hello, there, little lady," the woman crooned in a soft voice. "What are you doing out here?"

"I'm . . . lost."

It was more or less the truth, and it seemed to be the safest, most plausible explanation. I couldn't tell these people, these strangers, who I was or what had happened at Winterwind. Not until I knew for certain that they weren't Mortan assassins.

Part of me still wanted to bolt into the woods, but that hadn't done me any good the last three days, so I forced myself to walk forward, as though I weren't afraid of them.

"Can you help me find my parents? We were heading toward Andvari and stopped to make camp a few hours ago. My mother sent me to get some firewood, but I couldn't find any, and I got turned around. All these stupid trees look the same." I let out a weak laugh, hoping they wouldn't realize how ridiculous my story was.

My mother and father had proudly told me how good we Bellonans were at playing the long game, at waiting, lying, plotting, and otherwise manipulating people in order to get them to do what we wanted. My mother had told me countless bedtime stories about Bryn Bellona Winter Blair and how my gladiator ancestor had used her wits, skills, strength, and magic to found our kingdom. I wasn't trying to do something that grand and important, but I had a sneaking suspicion that my survival depended on my playing the long game now, even though I had never attempted it before.

The woman glanced at the man, who shrugged. She looked at me again, another, wider smile creasing her face.

"Of course we can help. What happened?" She gestured at my dress.

I looked down. My dress was torn and ripped from the Winterwind attack, and blood also stained the tattered fabric, turning it more brown than blue. My blood—along with my mother's blood.

Thinking about how the Mortan weather magier had killed my mother made bile rise in my throat, but I swallowed it down and focused on the strangers again.

"Oh, I . . . tripped and fell. Don't worry. It's not as bad as it looks. Just a few cuts and bruises."

The woman nodded, seeming to accept my feeble explanation. "We were just about to stop and make camp." She gestured at the clearing around us. "This looks like a fine spot. Why don't you stay with us? We can talk about the best way to find your parents over a hot meal."

She was still smiling and saying all the right things, but the smoky lie of her words curled through the air, along with her sour, sweaty eagerness and the man's sharp, orange interest. I didn't know what these people wanted, but they certainly weren't planning on finding my nonexistent parents. Even worse, they both reeked of magic. The woman had the charred aroma of a fire magier, while the man was probably a mutt with enhanced strength, given how many knapsacks and bags he was so easily carrying.

Once again, I was tempted to run into the trees and try to lose them in the growing darkness, but another, stronger shiver swept over me, and my stomach grumbled again. I couldn't trust these people, but maybe I could stay with them long enough to at least eat some food. At this point, I'd take whatever crumbs I could get, no matter how dangerous the situation might be.

So I forced myself to smile back at the woman as if I didn't know that she was plotting something horrible. "Thank you so much! I'm so happy I ran into you!"

The woman glanced over at her partner, her expression turning much sharper and far more predatory. He shrugged again, agreeing with whatever she was silently asking.

The woman looked at me again. "My name is Rocinda, and this is Caxton. What's your name?"

"Ev . . . ie. My name is Evie . . . Sancus."

I had been about to say Everleigh Blair, but I couldn't use my real name. Not with these strangers.

Rocinda smiled again. She really needed to work on faking a happy, pleasant expression. She was showing so many teeth that she looked like a witch in some old fairy tale who was eager to gobble me up. "Hello, Evie. You can tell us where you think your parents might be while we set up camp."

I gave her a sunny smile in return, as if I had no clue that she was literally lying through her teeth. "That would be wonderful!"

Rocinda and Caxton slung their knapsacks down onto a patch of ground that was clear of the snow that dappled much of the clearing. Caxton also unhooked the rope from his belt and tied it around a nearby tree branch. The box on the end of the rope swung side to side like a clock pendulum ticking off the seconds. He didn't remove the black cloth from the box, so I still couldn't see what was under it.

Rocinda dug into her knapsack and pulled out several items wrapped in thick brown paper and tied off with string. She produced a knife from the folds of her feathered cloak, sliced through the strings, and unwrapped the papers, revealing long strips of beef jerky, thick wedges of cheese, and dried bloodcrisp apples and honey cranberries. The scents of the salty meat, buttery cheeses, and sweet, tart fruit made my stomach grumble again.

"Want something to eat?" Rocinda offered me a wedge of cheese.

"Yes, please. Thank you."

I drew in a breath, but the cheese was just cheese, and not poisoned or tainted, so I sank my teeth into it. The sharp, tangy flavor exploded on my tongue, and I almost moaned with happiness. The cheese was nothing special, just a common cheddar, but it was still one of the best things I had ever tasted.

I quickly polished off that wedge of cheese and two more, while Caxton dug a small pit, arranged stones around it, and filled it with pine cones, along with some branches that he broke off the nearby trees. Rocinda used her magic to light a fire, then put some jerky strips into a small cast-iron pot, along with water, a few potatoes, and a couple of chopped carrots. Thirty minutes later, she passed me a steaming mug of rich, hearty stew.

While I was waiting for it to cool down enough to eat, I studied the magier again, and I spotted a small round pendant hanging off the thin gold chain around her neck. I glanced over at Caxton. He too was wearing a pendant and chain.

"That's a pretty necklace," I said. "Where did you get it?"

Rocinda seemed startled by my question, but she grabbed

the chain, leaned forward, and held out the pendant, which was a gold coin stamped with a woman's face. She watched me closely, like she was expecting me to recognize the symbol, although I didn't.

She leaned back and let go of the pendant. "I got it on Fortuna. The island has a very famous statue of a gold woman."

That was all she said, although I got the impression there was far more meaning to her words. Rocinda gestured at the mug in my hands. "You'd better eat your stew before it gets cold."

The three of us sat there and sipped our meal. Rocinda peppered me with seemingly innocent, friendly questions, like who my parents were and what they did. I told her that my father was a miner, while my mother was a bookkeeper. Not rich by any means, but well enough off to make her think they might offer a reward for my safe return.

Caxton remained silent through the interrogation, slurping down several mugs of stew, although he kept glancing over at the box. Whatever was hidden underneath the black cloth must be quite important, given how often he checked to make sure the container was still secured to the tree.

Lies and plots aside, the meal passed by pleasantly enough, and the stew drowned out the grumbling gargoyle in my stomach. By the time we finished, the sun had set and the moon and stars had appeared in the night sky.

While the stew had been cooking, Rocinda had given me a black cloak from her knapsack, and I pulled it a little tighter around my body. The weather had been surprisingly mild over the past few days, but the temperature was steadily dropping, indicating that it was going to snow. Despite the danger, it was a good thing I had run into Rocinda and Caxton. Without their food, cloak, and fire, I probably would have frozen to death tonight.

Rocinda packed up the leftover food, while Caxton pulled

out a knife and started trimming his fingernails with the sharp
blade. Neither one of them was wearing a sword, but they both
seemed to have plenty of long knives tucked away in their cloaks.

I subtly patted the side of my dress, feeling a hard lump
beneath the fabric. They weren't the only ones with a blade
hidden in their pocket.

Rocinda finished her work, then gave me another fake,
toothy smile. "I think it's time that we got some sleep."

"But what about my parents?" I asked, as though they
really did exist. "Shouldn't we start looking for them? They must
be so worried."

Rocinda and Caxton exchanged another inscrutable look.

"I'm sorry," she said. "But it's far too dark. We'll look for
them first thing in the morning, though. I promise."

Once again, I could smell the smoky lie of her words, but
I crumpled my face, as though I were deeply upset at being
separated from my parents. She reached over and squeezed my
hand, trying to soothe me.

I felt her fire magic the second her skin touched mine.

Rocinda had used her magic to light the campfire earlier,
but she was far stronger than I'd realized. I would have to be
very careful how I played my long game. Otherwise, I wouldn't
survive the night, much less escape from her and Caxton.

"It's okay," I said in a small, sad voice. "I understand. You
don't want to get lost in the woods too."

"Exactly!" she replied. "Now, why don't you go to sleep?
Everything will seem much better in the morning."

I lay down by the fire and let her cover me with a blanket,
although the stench of her magic clung to it—along with more
than a little coppery blood. Somehow, I held back a shudder of
revulsion and wished Rocinda and Caxton a cheery good night.
Then I rolled over, so that my back was to them and the fire.

I shifted around for a few moments, as though I were trying

to get comfortable on the hard ground. After an appropriate amount of time, I settled down, then slowly let my breathing become deep, steady, and even, as though I were sliding toward sleep, although I kept my eyes cracked open. The first chance I got, I was going to slip into the trees and get as far away from my supposed new friends as possible.

Twenty minutes passed, maybe thirty, before Rocinda and Caxton began speaking in low voices. They must have thought I really was asleep.

"I can't believe our luck," Caxton murmured. "I thought we'd be out here for another two weeks searching for Winterwind survivors. But to have one of them just fall into our lap? It's the best luck we've had in a long, long time."

"Not just a survivor," Rocinda said. "That girl is a Blair. Didn't you notice her eyes? They're gray-blue, just like all the other Blairs I've seen. The DiLucris won't believe it when we drag her in front of them. We'll get top dollar for her from the Mint."

"Fuck the Mint," Caxton said. "We should sell her ourselves. I bet the king would give us a sack of gold crowns for a live Blair to use in his experiments . . ."

King? Which king? And what kind of experiments?

Instead of answering my silent questions, the two of them kept murmuring about all the awful people they wanted to sell me to, like I was a fat wheel of cheese they were hauling to a marketplace.

At first I was stunned, then sick, then afraid. But the longer they talked, the more my turbulent emotions crystallized into rage—this cold, cold rage that iced over my heart and hardened my resolve. These people weren't kidnapping and selling me. Not as long as I still had breath to fight them.

While Rocinda and Caxton continued their talk of riches, I kept my breathing steady and even, pretending that I was still asleep. Slowly, very, very slowly, I slid my hand into my right *dress pocket. I still had the dagger my mother had given to me at Winterwind, the one I had used to kill the Mortan weather magier.*

With my weapon in hand, all I had to do now was wait for the right moment to escape . . .

Something heavy fell across my chest, startling me awake.

For a moment, I thought I was back in the woods that horrible night, and Rocinda and Caxton had discovered that I was awake and were coming to hurt me. Then a soft murmur sounded, the scent of vanilla mixed with spice filled my nose, and a warm, strong body shifted on the bed next to me.

I exhaled. Sullivan was sleeping beside me, and we were both safe in my chambers at Seven Spire.

I lay there for several minutes until my heart quit racing, my breathing evened out, and the sweat cooled on my body. But try as I might, I couldn't quite shove my memories away, close my eyes, and go back to sleep. Eventually, I rolled over and glanced at a clock on the nightstand. Almost midnight.

If I hurried, I could still make my rendezvous.

Despite my awful nightmare, I was warm and comfortable next to Sullivan, and I debated whether to leave him. But I wasn't drifting off to dreamland again anytime soon, so I slipped out of bed, threw on some clothes, and grabbed my sword and dagger.

Even in the middle of the night, a queen's work was never done.

CHAPTER SIX

Normally, when I left my chambers for my midnight rendezvous, I used the secret passageway hidden behind the bookcase along the wall. But tonight I unlocked one of the main doors and walked through the palace.

Perhaps it was my bad dream or the geldjager attack, but I wanted to make sure that no more enemies were creeping around Seven Spire. Everything was quiet, and almost everyone was tucked away in their own chambers.

A few guards were roaming around, but I easily avoided them and climbed the stairs to the fifth floor. No one was moving on this level, not even a guard, so I opened a door at the end of a hallway, slipped through to the other side, and locked it behind me.

At my entrance, the fluorestones embedded in the ceiling clicked on, bathing the area in soft white light. This room was average in almost every way. It was neither small nor large and was filled with ordinary, serviceable furniture—chairs, a vanity table, a bed, an armoire, a writing desk. The adjoining bathroom was also unremarkable, as were the collective contents. Dresses, tunics, and leggings hanging in the armoire. Lotions, perfumes, and berry balms sitting on the bathroom counter. A jewelry box perched on the vanity table.

The only thing that made this area special was that it used to be Maeven's room, back when she had been masquerading as the kitchen steward and plotting to kill Queen Cordelia.

My friends and I had searched this room for clues many times, but we'd largely come up empty. Knowing what kind of honeysuckle perfume Maeven liked or ogling her stunning jewelry collection didn't help in my war against her and the rest of the Bastard Brigade.

Still, I found myself coming here more nights than not. I wasn't quite sure why. Perhaps I simply enjoyed the peace and quiet. No one, not even Paloma or Sullivan, ever thought to look for me here. Or perhaps I was just obsessed with Maeven the same way she seemed to be with me, with both of us desperately trying to uncover the other's weaknesses so that one of us could finally kill the other. Either way, I intended to use the room as my own private escape for as long as possible.

I sat down at the writing desk. Two items were gleaming on the wooden surface—a bronze pocket watch and a silver signet ring that both featured a fancy cursive *M*. The letter was engraved on the watch's cover and embossed in silver on a flat piece of jet in the center of the ring, which also featured tiny amethysts, along with feathers etched into its band.

The pocket watch had belonged to Ansel, my treacherous tutor, who had died in the woods outside Winterwind when Marisse, his own cousin and another member of the Bastard Brigade, had murdered him. The signet ring belonged to Maeven, and it was the only noteworthy thing she had left behind when she and Nox, another Mortan royal, had fled from Seven Spire the night I'd killed Vasilia and taken the throne.

I reached into my pocket, drew out the gold chain and pendant that Lena had been wearing, and set them on the desk. The three coins that made up the woman's eyes and mouth glimmered like gold stars. The Fortuna Mint pendant was another piece to add to my macabre collection of jewelry that my enemies had worn. Enemies who were all dead now, except for Maeven.

The desire to tear her to pieces for what she'd done to my family rose up inside me, and I gave in to my rage, leaned back in the chair, and let myself imagine choking the life out of Maeven with my bare hands. Then I slowly, reluctantly pushed the fantasy aside. I had something else in mind for Maeven, something far worse than a quick and easy death, but only time would tell whether I'd triumph in my long game with her and she'd get what she so richly deserved.

Still thinking about my plans for Maeven, I glanced over at the freestanding mirror in the corner. The long oval glass housed in a plain ebony frame looked like another ordinary piece of furniture, but it was actually a Cardea mirror that let people see and speak to each other over great distances.

I had discovered the mirror a couple of months ago, after Maeven had sent an assassin to Seven Spire to try to kill me, and I had spoken to her through the glass several times since then. Perhaps it was strange, but I actually found myself looking forward to our talks. Maybe because this was the only way I had to keep track of Maeven and figure out what new plots she was hatching. Or maybe it was because the two of us understood each other better than anyone else ever could, as weird and wrong as that was. Either way, I waited, wondering if Maeven would appear tonight.

About five minutes later, the scent of magic filled the chambers, and the mirror started glowing with a bright, silvery light. I stood up and walked over to the mirror, which was now rippling as though it were made of water instead of solid glass. The silver glare quickly faded away, and the surface of the mirror smoothed out, revealing Maeven's chambers, which were much like the ones I was standing in here at Seven Spire. But to my surprise, she didn't appear on the other side of the glass.

A boy did.

He was thirteen, maybe fourteen, with black hair, pale skin, and a body that was all long, thin, spindly arms and legs, although I could see subtle hints of the strong, solid man he would grow into. His head was turned to the side, and his profile and the shape of his nose, lips, and chin were eerily similar to Maeven's.

This had to be Maeven's son. Dahlia, Sullivan's mother and another member of the Bastard Brigade, had said that Maeven had children, and I was finally getting a look at one of them. I wondered if he was already as cruel as his mother was.

The boy didn't seem to realize that I was watching him. Instead, he kept looking at something on his side of the glass, something out of my line of sight.

"You have to go through the mirror," he said in a low, desperate voice. "It's the only way."

At first I thought he was talking to Maeven and telling her what to do, as strange as that would have been. Then talons scraped on the floor, and a creature hopped into view.

A strix.

The strix was a hawklike bird with bright purple eyes, a sharp, pointed black beak, and curved black talons. Its feathers were a deep, vibrant amethyst, and every single one on its broad, strong wings and long, wide tail was tipped with a glossy black marking, making the creature look like it had onyx arrows attached to its body.

Mortan soldiers often rode strixes into battle, and the creatures were one of the reasons why Morta was such a threat to Bellona. Not only did the creatures grow to be larger and stronger than Floresian horses, but they were also taught to attack with their wings, and those hard onyx points on their feathers were sharp enough to slice a man to shreds.

This strix was about the size of a large dog. It wasn't a baby, but it wasn't fully grown yet either, just like the boy wasn't a child and hadn't yet morphed into a man. Still, even now the creature was dangerous, and my hand dropped to my sword.

"*Please*," the boy begged, a louder, more desperate note in his voice. "Just hop through the mirror. That's all you have to do. Then you can break through a window and fly away. You can finally be *free*, even if I can't."

The strix shook its head and ruffled its wings in a clear, re-sounding *no*. It didn't want to go through the mirror. But the more important question was why the boy wanted to send it *here*.

Was this Maeven's latest scheme? The other members of the Bastard Brigade hadn't succeeded in killing me yet, so maybe she was going to start sending strixes after me. Although if that was the case, why not send one that was fully grown? And what did the boy—her son—have to do with this?

I decided to find out.

"I'm sorry to disappoint you, but this mirror only lets peo-ple see and talk to each other," I called out, rapping my knuckles on the ebony frame. "It doesn't let you send things through to the other side."

The boy jerked and stumbled back, almost tripping over the strix, who squawked in surprise and hopped out of the way. The boy's head snapped around, and he finally looked at me. He also had Maeven's eyes, those dark amethyst eyes that were so beau-tiful and yet the bane of my existence at the same time.

"What—what are *you* doing here?" the boy asked.

"This mirror is in *my* palace, so *I* have every right to be here."

His gaze swept over me, lingering on the tearstone sword and dagger belted to my waist. His face paled, and he shifted on his feet and wet his lips. "You're—you're the Bellonan queen," he finally whispered.

"Yes, I am. Now, who are you and what are you doing in Maeven's chambers?"

He grimaced, but he kept quiet.

"You might as well tell me. Or would you prefer that I ask *your mother* the next time I speak to her?"

He jerked again in obvious surprise. Unlike his mother, the boy was terrible at hiding his emotions. "How—how do you know that I'm Maeven's son?"

"Because you look just like her. I've seen enough members of the Bastard Brigade to recognize Maeven's spawn."

The boy grimaced again, and hurt flickered in his eyes. I wondered if he was a bastard like his mother was. Probably, given his reaction.

Even though he was a Mortan and the son of my most hated enemy, a surprising amount of sympathy filled me. Over the past several months, I had watched Sullivan deal with being a bastard prince, along with Dahlia's betrayal. Even if she loved the boy, it couldn't be easy having Maeven for a mother. I could also hear Diante's voice whispering in my mind, asking me to judge her grandson Nico on his own merits, instead of my complicated feelings for the lady herself.

"What's your name?" I asked in a gentler tone.

The boy stared at me with suspicion.

"I'm going to find it out sooner or later. You can tell me now, or I can ask your mother. Since it doesn't look like she's around, I imagine that she'll be very upset about you using the Cardea mirror without her permission."

The boy grimaced for a third time. Oh, no. He definitely

didn't want Maeven learning about this, which made me even more curious as to what exactly *this* was.

"If I tell you my name, will you promise *not* to tell my mother that you saw me here?" he asked, that desperate note in his voice again. "Or that Lyra was with me?"

It took me a moment to realize that Lyra was the strix. Interesting. I didn't think the Mortans were sentimental enough to actually name the creatures.

"I promise. Now, who are you?"

The boy eyed me with suspicion again, but his shoulders slowly slumped in defeat. "Leonidas."

"Hello, Leonidas. My name is Everleigh. Now, why don't you tell me why you want to send Lyra through the mirror and into my palace?"

He shook his head. "I don't want to send her into your palace. Not really. I don't care where she goes, as long as it's far away from here."

I didn't have to ask him where *here* was. From my conversations with Maeven, I knew that the Cardea mirror was in her chambers inside the main Mortan palace. "Why do you want to send Lyra away? She seems very fond of you."

The strix had turned the onyx points on her wings down and was nestled up against the boy's leg like she was a puppy who wanted to cuddle with him, despite the fact that her head came up past his waist. Leonidas curled his arm around Lyra's back and hugged her closer to his side, and I could smell their rosy love for each other through the mirror.

The two of them reminded me of Gemma, the crown princess of Andvari, and Grimley, her gargoyle. Leonidas seemed to have the same sort of deep, close relationship with the strix as Gemma did with her gargoyle.

"Stay with you, Leo," Lyra chirped in a high, singsong voice.

I blinked. And Lyra could talk, just like Grimley could.

Tears gleamed in Leonidas's eyes as he stared down at the strix. "I want to stay with you too," he said in a low voice. "But we both know what will happen if you don't go."

Lyra shivered, and the onyx tips on her feathers pointed straight up, as if she were a porcupine getting ready to defend herself against some horrible threat. After a moment, she settled back down and pressed her body against Leonidas's side again.

"Stay with you," she chirped in a louder, firmer voice.

"Even if you could pry her away from your side, you would still have another problem." I rapped my knuckles on the glass, making it ripple. "Like I said before, you can't send anything through this Cardea mirror."

A stubborn look filled Leonidas's face, and he pushed up the sleeves of his light purple tunic. "*I* can send something through to the other side. All I have to do is use my magic."

Power sparked in his eyes, and the scent of his magic drifted through the mirror—hard stone mixed with sweet honeysuckle. The aroma was sharp, old, soft, and fresh, all at the same time, as though his magic hadn't matured any more than his body had. But I had sensed a similar scent before, so I knew how strong he was going to be someday—and exactly what kind of magic he had.

My eyes narrowed. "You're a mind magier."

Leonidas's hands clenched into fists. He didn't say anything, but his lips pinched together, and a muscle ticked in his jaw. Maeven really needed to teach her son how to lie. His emotions were written all over his face for everyone to see and use against him, and her too.

Including me—*especially* me.

"So let me get this straight. You want to use your magic to send Lyra through the mirror and into my palace." I gestured at the chambers around me. "Most people in Bellona don't like strixes very much. Queens don't like them very much either, especially when they're coming from Mortan assassins."

Leonidas shook his head. "I'm not an assassin, and I'm not sending her there to hurt you. I'm sending her there to escape, so she can finally be *free*, even if I can't."

He'd said the same thing to Lyra before he'd realized that I was watching, and the raw, naked worry and clear desperation in his voice made me bite back my retort. I opened my mouth to ask what he wanted to protect the strix from, but a sharp *bang* sounded in the distance, like a door had been slammed shut—or thrown open into the wall behind it.

Leonidas whirled to his right. I couldn't see what he was looking at, but his eyes widened, and the twin scents of his coppery fear and ashy heartbreak gusted through the mirror. "It's too late," he whispered.

"Too late for what?"

He gave me an anguished look. "To save Lyra."

I opened my mouth to ask him another question, but he waved his hand, and that bright silver light flared in the glass. When it vanished, the boy was gone, along with his strix, and the mirror was just a mirror again.

I frowned at my own reflection. Who was going to hurt Lyra? Maeven? Someone else? And why would they harm a strix, one of their own creatures?

I crossed my arms over my chest, thinking about everything he'd said, but I had no way of finding out the answers to my questions. Still, I had learned something important about Maeven's son.

He was very, very afraid of something—or rather, *someone*.

And that someone had to be the Mortan king. The boy hadn't flinched when I'd said Maeven's name, other than the normal way all children did when they were worried about getting into trouble with their mothers, but he hadn't been able to bring himself to say the king's name.

More of that surprising sympathy filled me. I might despise Leonidas's mother and the rest of his family, but he couldn't control who his parents were or the situation he'd been born into.

I stood by the mirror for five minutes, wondering if the boy might return or if Maeven might appear, but the glass remained smooth and still. I turned away from the mirror to leave, when my gaze fell on the jewelry still sitting on the writing desk.

I walked over and stared down at the bronze pocket watch, the silver signet ring, and the gold-coin pendant. All the tokens of my enemies. I started to leave them here, but something made me scoop them up off the desk.

They felt as cold and heavy as anvils in my hand, and the mix of metal and jewels dug into my skin. But in a strange way, I welcomed the chilly weight and the pricking sensations. They reminded me that I had survived these enemies—and gave me hope that I could survive all my others.

I tightened my grip on the jewelry, then left Maeven's chambers and locked the door behind me.

I should have returned to my own chambers, climbed into bed next to Sullivan, and tried to get some sleep, but I wound up on the royal lawn instead.

It was completely deserted, and not even the guards were patrolling out here, given the cold, blustery wind and the snow fluttering down from the midnight sky. The hard, tiny flakes had already gathered on the flower beds, iron benches, and towering trees, and I felt as though I were standing in a giant globe, watching the snow swirl all around me.

The snow-dusted grass crunched like bones under my boots as I walked over to the low stone wall that cordoned off the lawn from the cliffs and the two-hundred-foot drop to the Summanus River below. I drew in a breath, pulling the chilly air deep down into my lungs, then looked out over Svalin.

I had always enjoyed the view of the city from the royal lawn, but the contrast of the black night and the white flakes made it even lovelier than usual. Lights still burned in many homes and shops, and the soft glows resembled fireflies hovering in the sheets of snow. The glows also highlighted the metal spires that adorned the corners of practically every building and made the sharp, slender points look like swords made of molten gold, silver, and bronze. In a way, the spires *were* swords, since they represented Bellona's gladiator history and tradition, just like the seven spires that topped the palace did.

I was still clutching the jewelry I'd taken from Maeven's chambers, and I laid the watch, the signet ring, and the pendant on top of the wall. I traced my index finger over the coined woman's face, then stared down at the Retribution Bridge and the plaza on the far side of the river.

The dead geldjagers were still strung up on the scaffolding, and the snow had started to crust their black cloaks. I wondered if the DiLucris had realized that their geldjagers were dead yet and that they wouldn't be able to fulfill whatever contract they had with the Mortan king. I hoped so. I wanted the DiLucris to realize how spectacularly they had failed, and I especially wanted them to worry about how I was going to strike back against them.

My gaze flicked from one dead magier to the next until I finally focused on Lena, the girl whom I'd so badly wanted to be a Blair.

That mix of anger, shame, and embarrassment scorched through me again, making my cheeks burn, despite the snow.

I'd told myself over and over again not to get my hopes up, but I'd done it anyway, and the DiLucris had thoroughly crushed them. No, not the DiLucris—the Mortan king. *He* was the one who'd most likely hired them, and he was probably the one responsible for the Blair rumor and everything that had followed, including this terrible, terrible ache in my chest.

Footsteps crunched through the grass behind me, and the hard, sharp smell of blood mixed with coldiron filled my nose, along with a faint, fruity tang. Serilda walked up beside me. She was clutching two empty glasses, and a bottle was tucked under her arm.

"A crown for your thoughts?" she murmured. "Or perhaps some cranberry sangria to drown them?"

"I'll take the sangria."

Serilda grinned and set the glasses on the wall. She eyed the jewelry that I'd arranged there, but she didn't comment on it. Instead, she opened the bottle and poured the sangria. I grabbed one of the glasses and *clink*ed it against hers. We both took a drink.

The sangria hit my tongue like a ripe honey cranberry exploding in my mouth, sweet and tart at the same time, with faint notes of apricot and just a trace of bright, tangy orange. Cranberry sangria was a popular drink during the winter months, served ice-cold, and I took another sip, savoring the intense flavor, along with the pleasant warmth that started pooling in my stomach.

Serilda and I sipped our sangria in comfortable, companionable silence for several minutes.

"What are you doing out here so late?" I finally asked.

She shrugged. "I couldn't sleep, so I decided to roam through the palace, soak up the quiet, and clear my head. It's a ritual of mine. You?"

"The same."

We fell silent, and I once again stared down at Lena's body.

Serilda tracked my gaze, then studied me over the rim of her glass. "You're still thinking about what happened with the geld-jagers. Not the attack itself, though. You're upset because the girl wasn't a Blair."

"Did your magic tell you that?"

Serilda was a sort of time magier who saw possibilities, all the ways that people might act in the future and all the consequences those actions might have.

She shrugged again. "My magic, and the fact that I know you, Evie. You tried to hide it, but I could see the hope on your face as soon as Xenia told you that another Blair might still be alive."

I sighed. "Was it really that obvious?"

"Only to me."

I eyed her. "You didn't say much during our planning for the plaza meeting. Did you know the rumor wasn't true? That the whole thing was a trap?"

"I thought it was more likely a trap than not, but I *always* think that way. It's one of the reasons I've lived this long. I also knew that you had to see it for yourself." She paused. "But you weren't wrong to hope."

"What do you mean?"

Serilda stared out into the snowy night, her blue eyes dark and dreamy. The scent of magic swirled around her, although the wind quickly whipped it away. "Because I think there really *is* another Blair out there somewhere," she murmured. "Maybe even more than one. I don't know who or where they are. My magic won't let me see them. It just whispers to me about them."

Once again, a bit of warm, sweet honey hope oozed through me. I let myself feel that hope for a moment before ruthlessly quashing it and latching on to the other emotion that it roused in me—cold, cold rage.

Serilda stared out into the dark, snowy night a moment longer, then blinked and shook her head. "I'm sorry. I wish I could be more help."

"You've been plenty of help. You brought me sangria." I toasted her, then drained the rest of the fruity liquid and set my empty glass aside. Time to get down to business.

"I already asked Auster to increase the number of guards patrolling the city plazas, and he and Xenia have their spies searching for more information about the geldjagers. Now we need to talk about how we're going to respond to this latest attack."

Serilda snorted and waved her glass toward the bodies hanging in the plaza. "I think you *responded* quite clearly."

I shook my head. "That was only the beginning. I mean how we're going to respond during the Regalia."

"What do you have in mind?"

I gestured at the silver signet ring and the gold-coin pendant lying on the wall. "Maeven, the Bastard Brigade, and now the DiLucri bounty hunters. The Mortan king just keeps sending people to kill me."

"So?"

"So I'm tired of always being the one on the defensive. We need to beat the Mortans at their own game, and the Regalia is the perfect opportunity. The Mortan king and the DiLucris will be there, maybe even Maeven too. No doubt they'll try to assassinate me again. Whatever they do, however they come at us, we need to strike back at them even more viciously. We need to end the threat they represent to us, to Bellona, once and for all."

Serilda's eyes narrowed with understanding. "You want to kill the Mortan king during the Games."

"I want to fucking *crush* the king." I slammed my fist down on top of the wall. "I want to take away every little thing he cares about, no matter how small it is. I want to hobble him, break him, and yes, I especially want to bloody kill him. But only *after* he's felt some of the pain that I have. He crushed my hope, my heart tonight, with his damn Blair rumor, and I want to crush his in return."

My words echoed out into the night air, although the wind and snow quickly drowned them. But they couldn't douse the cold, cold rage flowing through my veins with every beat of my heart.

"Diante told me earlier that I needed to do more of *that*." I gestured at the dead geldjagers. "And she is absolutely right. I have to go on the offensive, and I can't think of a better way to do that than by assassinating the Mortan king during the Regalia."

"How do you want to kill him?" Serilda asked, ever practical about such matters.

I shrugged. "Shoot an arrow into his throat. Poison his wine. Bash in his skull with a brick. I don't care how he dies, only that he does."

"Very well," she replied. "We'll start working on it tomorrow. Auster, Cho, and I can talk about arrows and the like. Xenia and Sullivan will probably have some ideas about potential poisons. And I'm sure that Paloma would be quite happy to bash in the king's skull with her mace."

I sighed. "And that's the problem. I want to kill the king, but I don't want to lose anyone doing it. His death doesn't mean more to me than your lives. I want you to know that."

Sympathy filled Serilda's face. "I *do* know that, just as you know that we would all give our lives for you, for Bellona. Don't worry, Evie. We'll find a way to keep you from having to make that choice."

My gaze flicked over the many spires that decorated the city rooftops, the ones gleaming like freshly sharpened gladiator swords. I already knew of one way to potentially kill the Mortan king, although I didn't mention it, given the inherent dangers. That way, the traditional Bellonan way, would be my last resort, a card I would play only if all else failed.

Perhaps it wouldn't come to that, but if it did, then it would be *my* choice, *my* decision, *my* sacrifice as queen. And I would make it just as gladly as Serilda and the others would lay down their lives for me.

Serilda tipped back her glass, draining the rest of her sangria. Then she grinned and poured us both some more of the sweet liquid. She handed my glass back to me, then *tink*ed hers against mine again.

That one crystalline note rang out loud and clear, summoning up that phantom music in my mind again. I listened to the rhythm and started thinking about the best ways to deal with my enemies.

"Well, then, there's only one thing left to say, my queen," Serilda purred, her grin taking on a hard, sharp edge. "Let the games begin."

PART TWO

GAMES PEOPLE PLAY

chapter seven

The morning of the first day of the Regalia dawned bright and clear, and I stood at the top of a rocky ridge at the edge of the Bellonan camp. Sullivan, Paloma, Serilda, Cho, Auster, Xenia. My friends were standing in a line with me, and we were all staring out at the spectacle before us.

The Summanus River emptied into a large natural harbor that stretched all the way over to Fortuna Island, where the cold, churning river currents mixed with the warmer ones of the Blue Glass Sea. Ships of all shapes and sizes were anchored in the harbor, and my gaze moved from one vessel to another, studying the flags they were flying.

Wide, flat barges bearing the Floresian royal crest of a golden horse running through an equally golden wheat field. Sleek, skinny ships displaying the Vacunan symbol of a green volcano with a trickle of red lava running down the side and a plume of black smoke rising above it. The large Ryusaman vessels with their thick paper sails and dragon crests done in rich jewel tones. The much smaller Andvarian ships with their snarling gargoyle faces. And finally, the Ungerian vessels with their many flags and figureheads, all of which bore fearsome ogres.

People moved all along the decks, tugging on ropes, trimming sails, and calling out to each other. Small boats surrounded many of the ships, and folks were rowing toward the massive port that lined this side of Fortuna Island. No one wanted to miss the opening ceremonies, and the smell of everyone's collective eagerness drifted over to me on the steady breeze, along with the mix of fresh and salt waters from the river and the sea.

Captain Auster had said that the ships and the kingdoms they represented were anchored in their usual spots and that everything was proceeding as normal in the harbor. Everyone seemed to be clinging to the status quo—for now.

I had never been to the Regalia before. Back when I was just Lady Everleigh, I hadn't been an important enough royal for Queen Cordelia to bring me, and I hadn't had the money to attend on my own. Instead, every time the Regalia had rolled around, I had stood on the Seven Spire lawn and watched the procession leave Svalin, desperately wishing that I was skilled enough at, well, *anything*, to be part of the festivities. I had also been on the lawn when the procession returned, once again watching from afar and wistfully wishing that the people were cheering for my victory.

Now my childhood dream had come true, and I was finally here—but I wasn't so sure that was a good thing. If I hadn't been queen, I would have been thrilled to see the competitions. But I *was* queen, and the Regalia was my most important test to date.

More eyes would be on Bellona—on *me*—than ever before. Royals, nobles, merchants, and wealthy citizens from the other kingdoms would all be watching, waiting to see what mistakes I made, and if I was strong enough to survive those mistakes. They would study my every word, smile, and gesture, silently judging me the whole time, as they decided whether or not to align with me and do business with Bellona.

Nervous butterflies flapped in my chest, but I swatted them away. Nerves were one of the many things that a queen couldn't afford to indulge in.

Several guards moved along the ridgeline, thrusting tall flags into the ground to formally mark this as the Bellonan camp, as was the tradition on the Regalia's opening morning. The flags would stand here for the next three days until the Games ended and we returned home to Svalin.

Or until I was killed, whichever came first.

Most of the flags featured my midnight-blue crown-of-shards crest on a light gray background, but a few other symbols were mixed in as well. One flag featured Serilda's crest—a black swan with a blue tearstone eye and beak on a white background—while another featured a snarling green ogre face with gold eyes on a gold background that was Xenia's crest.

Xenia was staying here in the Bellonan camp, but she was a cousin to the Ungerian queen and would also be advising her other majesty during the Regalia. I eyed my friend, but her face was calm, although the ogre on her neck had its amber eyes narrowed and lips puckered in thought. I wasn't quite sure how Xenia would divide her duties—and especially her loyalties—during the Games, but if anyone could dance to the tune of two mistresses, it was her.

The guards finished with the flags, bowed to me, and stepped back. I nodded my thanks, then looked out over the harbor again.

"I don't like this," Captain Auster muttered, breaking the silence. "I don't like this one bit. I never have."

"Why not?" I asked. "You've been to the Regalia several times."

He shook his head. "And I always worry about my queen

being assassinated here, more so than at any other place, especially with all the other royals and their guards lurking around. And I am especially wary of this Regalia, given everything that's happened over the past year."

Auster was right. I would have even fewer friends on Fortuna Island than I did at Seven Spire, and I had to be prepared for anything. Someone *always* wanted to kill the queen, even here, during this time of celebration, competition, and supposed goodwill between the kingdoms.

Oh, yes. I would most likely have to deal with assassins during the Regalia. But I had my own plans to kill the king, so I focused on the opposite side of the river—on Morta.

A similar ridge jutted up from the landscape there, but no flags lined the edge, and no tents dotted the flat, grassy plateau in the distance.

"Any sign of the Mortans?" I asked.

"No," Cho replied. "They haven't arrived yet."

"They're cutting it a bit close, aren't they?" Sullivan asked. "The Games start in less than three hours."

"Well, I can't kill the king if he's not bloody *here*," I growled.

Before we'd left Seven Spire, I had told everyone my determination to go on the offensive and assassinate the king during the Games before he could do the same to me. They had all offered their support, especially Paloma, who had volunteered to use her mace to bash in his skull, just like Serilda had predicted.

I wasn't going to let my friend do something so risky, but we had come up with several potential plans to kill the king. Still, all our plotting would be for nothing if he didn't actually attend the Regalia.

Still frustrated, I turned to Serilda. "What do you see with your magic? Anything to do with the Mortans?"

Her blue eyes grew dark and dreamy, and the smell of magic filled the air as she looked out over the water at Morta.

After several seconds of silent contemplation, Serilda frowned and shook her head.

"It's too early to tell. Right now all I see is darkness. It's almost like a . . . wave rising up, getting ready to drown us all." She dropped her hand to her sword, as if the blade would protect her from the horrible vision. "A wave that could swallow us, and everyone else here, and all of Bellona."

"See?" Auster muttered. "I told you that I didn't like coming to the Regalia."

Paloma clapped him on the shoulder. "Oh, cheer up, Auster. The Regalia is just another arena, and we'll win this fight, just like we have all the others."

She grinned at the older man. After a moment, Auster's lips turned up into a small smile.

"Don't forget that you do have some allies," Xenia chimed in. "My cousin the queen arrived late last night. She's most eager to finally set eyes on the great Everleigh Blair."

I made a face. There was nothing *great* about me, except perhaps the fact that I had survived this long, which I often thought had more to do with blind luck than any outstanding skill on my part. But sometimes luck was all you had, and I was determined to make the most of mine.

"You've already been reporting to your cousin?" Serilda snorted. "That's quick work, even for you."

Xenia bared her teeth at the other woman, as did the ogre on her neck. "That's because I deal in facts, not vague visions like you do."

Serilda's hand curled a little tighter around her sword, while Xenia's fingers did the same to her ogre cane, as though each woman wanted to battle the other. In some ways, the two of them couldn't be more different. Serilda was a soldier first, always ready, willing, and eager to dispatch Bellona's enemies with her sword, while Xenia was a spy, more apt to undercut her opponents than face them openly. Still, underneath all their sniping, I thought they had a lot of mutual respect for each other.

I had certainly learned a lot from both of them. Serilda had taught me how to physically fight for and win my throne, while Xenia's lessons about dealing with the nobles had helped me keep my crown.

"Well, I agree with Xenia," Cho chimed in. "I think you'll have far more allies than you expect, Evie. Everyone knows how greedy and ambitious the Mortan king is, and no one wants to see their people killed and their lands invaded by him. That includes Ryusama."

Xenia arched an eyebrow at him. "Sounds like I'm not the only one who's been busy. Did *your* cousin the queen tell you that?"

Like Xenia, Cho was related to royalty, a fact that I had only learned as we'd been planning our trip to the Regalia. He winked at her. "Oh, I never reveal my sources."

Xenia huffed, but she smiled a little at his teasing.

"Well, we know that the Andvarians are with you," Sullivan said. "Heinrich and Dominic are attending the Regalia, along with Rhea."

King Heinrich was Sullivan's father, Crown Prince Dominic was his half brother, and Rhea was the captain of the Andvarian royal guards and Dominic's unofficial consort. Heinrich and I had agreed to a new treaty between Bellona and Andvari a few months ago, and it was nice to know that I could count on his support as I tried to convince Unger and the other kingdoms to align with us against Morta.

"Don't worry, highness," Sullivan continued. "We're all here standing shoulder to shoulder with you. So let the Mortans come, and the DiLucris, and all your other enemies. Because none of us are going anywhere."

His blue eyes blazed with conviction and determination, and the smell of his rosy love washed over me. He would stand with me until his dying breath, just as I would do the same for him and the rest of my friends.

I grabbed his hand and squeezed his fingers. "I love you for that." I looked at the others. "I love *all* of you for that, and I'll do my very best to protect you."

That was the vow I had made to myself during the Seven Spire massacre, after Vasilia had killed almost everyone I had ever known and cared about, and it was the vow I had repeated to myself every single day since then. So far, I had kept it, and I had no intention of breaking it during the Regalia, not even to try to assassinate the Mortan king.

They all nodded at me. Sullivan. Paloma. Serilda. Cho. Auster. Xenia. I stared at them a moment longer, then turned to face my people.

While my friends and I had been talking, everyone in the Bellonan camp had been gathering in the open field behind us. Guards, servants, nobles, merchants, competitors, spectators. All shapes, sizes, and stations were represented in the crowd, and thousands of people had traveled from all across Bellona to watch and compete in the Games.

I strode forward and stopped in front of them. Slowly, the crowd quieted, and everyone focused on me. I looked from one face to another.

Calandre and her sisters clutching pennants with my crown-of-shards crest that they'd sewn themselves. Fullman and his son Tolliver, both wearing sour expressions, still un-happy that I'd nixed Tolliver from the Tournament of Champions. Diante and her grandson Nico, shooting smug, superior looks at the other two nobles. And dozens and dozens of other nobles, servants, guards, and gladiators I knew from my time at both Seven Spire and the Black Swan arena. All gathered here to represent Bellona and cheer on their fellow countrymen and -women.

I stared out at the sea of happy, excited faces and breathed in the scents of everyone's collective honey hope and sour, sweaty eagerness. An unusual combination, but a pleasant one today.

I glanced at Auster, who nodded. Even though I had never been to the Regalia before, this was part of our Bellonan tradition, and Auster had schooled me on what to do and say. So I drew in another breath, then let it out, and pulled the sword from the scabbard on my belt. The tearstone blade glinted a dull silver in the early morning sunlight, as did the two bracelets on my wrists.

I rubbed my thumb over the blue crown-of-shards crest embedded in the hilt, letting the sharp points dig into my skin. Then I drew in another breath, tightened my grip on my sword, and swept it out to the side as I performed the perfect Bellonan curtsy. I held the curtsy for several seconds, showing my respect for everyone who had gathered here, and all the work they had done to make this moment possible, then slowly straightened and spread my arms out wide.

"Bellonans!" I said, my voice ringing out over the field. "Welcome to the Regalia!"

The crowd roared back, yelling, cheering, clapping, screaming, and whistling. Calandre must have made more pennants than I'd realized, because several people waved them in time to the wild, raucous cheers.

Despite all the dangers that waited for me on Fortuna, their excitement was contagious, and an electric hum of anticipation charged the air. I suddenly found myself wanting to grab a pennant, snap it back and forth through the air, and cheer at the top of my lungs. My people had worked hard for weeks, months, years to hone and perfect their skills, and they deserved this chance to shine in front of the other kingdoms.

"Are you ready to show off your finest goods and amazing creations? Are you ready to display your skills and magic? Are you ready to battle in the arena for the glory of our applause? And most of all, are you ready to show everyone that Bellonans are the smartest, strongest, fiercest people on this continent?"

My words whipped the crowd into a frenzy, and their yells, cheers, claps, screams, and whistles reached a frantic, fevered pitch. The noise went on for more than a minute before they finally calmed down.

"Then let's show them all that and more!" I screamed, stabbing my sword high into the air. "To battle! To glory! To victory!"

"Battle! Glory! Victory!" everyone screamed back. "Battle! Glory! Victory! Battle! Glory! Victory!"

They kept screaming those three words over and over again, each one louder than the last. I soaked up the crowd's enthusiasm, pouring it into my mind and especially into my heart. No matter what happened during the Regalia, I would never forget this one perfect moment, when we were all united, and anything seemed possible, even the death of the Mortan king.

With my sword still raised high in the air, I turned around and marched across the field. Fortuna waited in the distance, as did my allies and enemies alike.

The Regalia had officially begun.

CHAPTER EIGHT

I wound my way down the stone steps that led from the ridge to the waterfront plaza below. Paloma, Sullivan, and Captain Auster stayed close to me, while Serilda, Cho, and Xenia trailed behind us, along with several guards and the chattering crowd.

Our route took us by a fountain shaped like a miniature version of Seven Spire that bubbled in the center of the plaza. People rushed past the fountain, across the plaza, and onto the wide stone drawbridge that stretched from Bellona across the water to Fortuna Island.

I waited for the bulk of the crowd to move past, then went over to the bridge, along with my friends and guards. Just like the seven bridges in Svalin, this one also had a name—Perseverance. A similar bridge stretched from the Mortan side of the river over to the island. Auster had told me that it was called Power. Of course it was.

Fierce-looking gladiators were carved into the Bellonan bridge's solid stone walls, while an alternating pattern of swords and shields was inlaid in the walkway flagstones. The bridge was only a few feet above the waterline, and the tearstone span shifted from light gray to dark blue and back again. The changing colors matched the sparkling surface of the water and almost seemed to move in time to the rolling waves.

By this point, most of the Bellonans were already halfway across the bridge, but I slowly walked along it, studying Fortuna Island as it came into focus.

Stone and wooden docks lined much of the golden, sandy shoreline, and fishermen were rowing and sailing their boats back to the island, having already secured their first catches of the day. My nose crinkled at the stench of fish, blood, and guts mixing with the fresh and salt waters.

The docks opened up into a series of stone plazas filled with wooden carts, and I could hear the merchants shouting and hawking their goods all the way over here. Beyond the plazas, a wide boulevard stretched out in both directions, and carts, carriages, and wagons jostled along the cobblestones, almost as if they were in a race to see who could circle the island the fastest.

The far side of the boulevard was lined with shops and houses, all painted in vibrant colors—bright reds, sunny yellows, summer blues. Black slate tiles covered the buildings' steep, sloping roofs, along with black wrought-iron weather vanes that looked like arrows pointing up at the stone steps that had been carved into the hills above. People were already climbing the steps, heading to the plaza on the very top of the island where the Games would be held.

My friends and I reached the opposite side of the bridge and headed onto the island. I'd only taken about three steps forward when a man planted himself in front of me.

He looked to be in his mid-thirties, with hazel eyes and black hair that gleamed with an oily sheen. A neat, trimmed mustache lined his upper lip, and his teeth were very square and blindingly white against his tan skin. He was wearing a short white jacket over a white tunic and sandy brown leggings and boots. Gold thread scrolled down his jacket sleeves, and the gold buttons on the front glimmered as though they had just been polished. The buttons were all stamped with a familiar symbol—a woman with coins for her eyes and mouth.

Standing next to him was a woman who looked to be in her late twenties, just like me. She too was wearing a short white jacket and tunic over brown leggings and boots, although her clothes were adorned with far less gold thread. She was quite lovely, with bright hazel eyes, tan skin, and golden hair that was pulled into a fat braid that trailed over her shoulder. An exquisite choker made of tiny gold coins ringed her neck, each separate piece stamped with the coined-woman crest.

Several guards dressed in sandy brown tunics, leggings, and boots flanked the man and the woman. That same coined-woman crest glittered in gold thread in the center of the guards' tunics, and each one had a sword with a gold hilt holstered to their brown leather belts.

"And here's the welcoming committee," Auster muttered, dropping his hand to his own sword.

The man in the white jacket bowed to me. "Queen Everleigh. Welcome to Fortuna. I am Driscol DiLucri, and this is my sister, Seraphine." He gestured at the woman.

I'd heard of Driscol, the current head of the DiLucri family and thus the Mint. Technically, no kingdom owned Fortuna, and the island was supposed to be a neutral site, not only for sailors and merchants, but for the Regalia as well. However, given all the gold and goods that flowed from the ships, through the Mint's doors, and back out again, the island more or less belonged to the DiLucris, who had long ago established their own guards, laws, and taxes.

The DiLucris might be a sort of royal family, but they did one thing differently than the Blairs, Ripleys, and all the others—the strongest, smartest, and cleverest person of each generation led them, instead of the firstborn. It was an unusual arrangement, but one that seemed to work well for the DiLucris, given their continued prosperity. Still, I'd heard rumors that the leadership battles were particularly ruthless—and that the bones of more than one DiLucri littered the bottom of the harbor.

"I am the head of the Regalia committee," Driscol continued.

Since the Regalia was always held on their island, the Di-Lucris were in charge of most of the preparations, although the kings and queens still had a say in how things were done. Despite the DiLucris' supposed neutrality, everyone knew that certain Regalia favors and advantages could be had—for the right price.

"Hello, Driscol, Seraphine. Thank you for such a warm welcome," I replied, following the standard protocol script.

Seraphine curtsied, while Driscol bowed and smiled, but there was no warmth in his expression, only white teeth. I could also clearly smell his hot, peppery anger. No doubt by now he had heard what I'd done to his geldjagers, whose bodies would slowly rot on the scaffolding outside Seven Spire until I returned from the Regalia.

"Most of the other royals have already arrived. If you will follow us, my guards will escort you to the arena for the opening ceremonies." Driscol smiled at me again, then strode away, with Seraphine and his guards following along behind him.

Paloma, Sullivan, and Captain Auster sidled a little closer, forming a protective semicircle around me. Auster was still clutching his sword, while Paloma's hand drifted down to the mace on her belt. Sullivan flexed his fingers, ready to reach for his lightning, should the need arise.

I glanced over my shoulder. Xenia was clutching her cane, while Serilda, Cho, and the Bellonan guards had their hands on their swords. Everyone was ready for trouble.

I headed after Driscol, and the others fell in step around and behind me.

Driscol, Seraphine, and their guards crossed the plazas and waited for us to catch up at the boulevard. We crossed that as a group and wound our way up the stone steps.

As we climbed, Driscol played the part of the pleasant host, pointing out fountains, buildings, and other interesting landmarks, and giving us an abbreviated history lesson about the island and its people. Seraphine remained silent, a bland, bored expression on her face.

Driscol stopped at one of the landings and gestured over at an enormous building perched at the end of the boulevard several hundred feet away. "And that, of course, is the Fortuna Mint."

I had been concentrating on the people moving across the plazas, along the boulevard, and up and down the steps, keeping an eye out for potential assassins, so I hadn't paid much attention to the surrounding buildings. But now that Driscol had pointed it out, I realized just how large the Mint was and how it completely dominated this part of the island.

The three-story structure was fashioned out of gleaming white marble that made it look like a huge square opal that had been set into the surrounding tan stone. Small bits of metal had been inlaid into the wide, fluted columns that supported the building, adding to its glowing luster. I squinted into the sun. No, not just metal—gold coins. Thousands and thousands of coins curled up and around the columns like gold ribbons before spreading out across and completely covering the wide, flat band of stone that topped the structure like a crown on a king's head.

"And then we have Lady Fortuna herself, our famous coined lady and our ancestor who first founded the Mint." Pride rippled through Driscol's voice as he gestured toward the building again.

A large fountain stood in the open space in front of the

Mint. The fountain's round base was made of the same tan stone as the surrounding plazas and boulevard, but the statue in the center looked like it was solid gold. The statue was easily more than forty feet tall and the embodiment of the DiLucri family crest—a woman with coins for her eyes and mouth.

Water rose and fell in small jets in the base of the fountain, but not a single drop touched the woman's golden skin. Her head was tilted back, and her arms were stretched upward in what was probably supposed to be a strong, triumphant pose, but I couldn't help but think that the woman—Lady Fortuna—was silently pleading with the gods to release her from her golden torment and give her real eyes to see with, as well as an actual mouth to voice her shrieking rage.

"Isn't she magnificent?" Driscol asked, clearly fishing for a compliment.

I held back a shudder. "The fountain is a bit garish for my tastes. Then again, I've never understood some people's need to flaunt their wealth."

Driscol's nostrils flared with anger, although Seraphine's expression remained calm. The DiLucri guards tightened their grips on their swords at my pointed insult. My friends did the same, ready to defend me. I gave Driscol a cold, flat look. I wasn't afraid of him or his men, and I wasn't going to pretend that he was anything other than an enemy.

After a long, tense moment, Driscol forced himself to smile at me again. "Let's continue our journey."

He started climbing the steps again. Seraphine and the guards followed him, and my friends and I brought up the rear.

Five minutes later, we trudged up a final set of steps to another large stone plaza lined with wooden carts and merchants selling everything from winter hats and gloves to brightly colored flags and pennants to replica weapons. Throngs of people milled around, moving from one cart to the next, and the sticky-sweet scents of cornucopia, liquored fudges, flavored ices, hot spiced toddies, and other treats filled the air.

But I only had eyes for the arena.

It loomed like some great stone kraken chained on top of the island. The arena was even larger than the Mint and made of the same gleaming white stone, although it didn't feature all the garish gold coins. It was easily one of the biggest structures I had ever seen, with level after level spiraling higher and higher into the air. Driscol didn't offer any tidbits of information about the arena, but I knew that it was called the Pinnaculum because winning here was supposed to be the very pinnacle of achievement.

A steady stream of spectators were climbing the steps that ringed the outside of the arena, carrying their food, drinks, and flags, while many of the competitors were gathered around the tables perched in front of the wide archways carved into the bottom level. Signs had been erected telling the competitors which table they needed to report to in order to find out when and where their event was being held. A hundred conversations trilled through the air, along with snorts of laughter and squeals of excitement.

Everyone was eager for the Games to begin.

My stomach twisted into knots thinking about what—and who—might be waiting inside the arena, but there was no turning back. I had to be strong now, not just for myself and my friends, but for all the Bellonans here and back home who were counting on me.

So I lifted my chin, squared my shoulders, and strode forward to meet my enemies.

My friends and I followed Driscol, Seraphine, and the guards through one of the archways and into the Pinnaculum. In many ways, it was like the Black Swan arena back home in Svalin—a wide circular space with hard-packed dirt that was cordoned off by a stone wall with several iron gates set into it.

Behind the wall, a wide walkway let people move from one section to another, while several sets of stairs led up to the stone bleachers that encircled the entire arena. The bleachers were rapidly filling up, as were the large boxes embedded at different points in the various levels. Many of the boxes featured cushioned chairs and shaded awnings, along with servants standing by with food and drink. That was where those with money, power, magic, and influence would sit and watch the Regalia, as well as play their own games with each other.

Flags from each one of the seven kingdoms lined the very top of the open-air arena, including one that featured my midnight-blue crown-of-shards crest on a light gray background. To my surprise, an eighth flag was also in the mix—one that boasted the gold face of the DiLucris' coined woman on a white background. The colorful cloths snapped back and forth in the steady breeze, making the crests seem like living things, as though the shimmering symbols were spectators watching, waving, and approving of all the action below.

"The royal box is this way," Driscol said.

He strode forward, along with Seraphine and their guards.

A hand touched my elbow, and I glanced over at Serilda. For a moment, we stared at each other, then her hand dropped, and she slipped away from our group. In an instant, she had pulled up the hood of her black cloak and vanished into the crowd.

My gaze flicked to the DiLucris and their guards, but none of them seemed to have noticed Serilda leaving. I moved forward, following them, along with the rest of my friends.

Driscol, Seraphine, and their men went about halfway around the arena before heading for the bleacher steps. He climbed them very slowly, stopping to smile, wave, and call out to several people, while Seraphine bobbed her head in greeting. But Driscol wasn't the only one that folks noticed.

"Look! Over there! It's the Bellonan queen!"

"Is that really her?"

"Of course it is! See her tearstone sword!"

Snatches of conversation drifted over to me, and people started calling out and waving. Even though I wanted to duck my head, hurry up the steps, and escape the unwanted attention, I forced myself to smile and wave back, as if I truly were the grand, regal queen they were all expecting, instead of just the royal stand-in who had unexpectedly wound up with the crown. Try as I might to resist the notion, I still sometimes thought of myself that way.

Driscol frowned, as though he were annoyed that I had more admirers than he did, and he quickly moved on. We wound up on a wide, rectangular terrace carved into the middle of the bleachers. Black wrought-iron railing cordoned off the area from the surrounding boxes, and dozens of people were already milling around, admiring the spectacular view of the arena floor below.

Driscol nodded at the two guards stationed at the terrace entrance and swept past them, as did Seraphine. I lifted my chin a bit higher and followed.

Several tables covered with platters of food had been pushed up against the far end of the terrace, along with carts covered with carafes of teas, juices, wines, and more. Dozens of minor royals, nobles, and advisors were gathered in that area, piling their plates high with fresh fruit, cheeses, crackers, scones, danishes, and other nibbles, while servants flitted around, fetching goblets full of kiwi and mango juices.

Conversations and laughter pealed through the air, but it wasn't all fun and games. Guards dressed in their kingdoms' uniforms stood in small groups all around the terrace. The opening ceremonies might supposedly be a peaceful gathering, but none of the royals were taking any chances with their safety.

Auster had sent a small contingent of men on ahead to the arena, and I nodded at the Bellonan guards, who snapped to attention at the sight of me.

The centerpiece of the terrace was a single round table covered with a simple white cloth and flanked by seven wooden chairs. None of the chairs featured any crests or markings, but there was one for the leader of each kingdom. An eighth chair, with the coined-woman crest carved into the top, was also squatting at the table. It seemed as though Driscol planned on sitting with the royals.

I paused, not quite sure what to do, but Cho touched my shoulder before striding forward and loudly clearing his throat, getting everyone's attention.

"Announcing Her Royal Majesty, Queen Everleigh Saffira Winter Blair of Bellona!" His voice boomed out like thunder, and everyone turned to stare at me.

I fixed a pleasant smile on my face, took a step forward, and stopped, letting everyone get a good, long look at me. The pause also gave me time to pick the other kings and queens out of the crowd.

King Eon Umbele of Vacuna was a fire magier with a tall, thick body and muscled arms. His eyes were a deep dark brown, while his black hair was cropped close to his skull and just a shade lighter than his ebony skin.

Eon was talking with Queen Ruri Yamato of Ryusama, a slender morph with a dragon's face made of emerald-green scales glimmering on her left hand. Ruri's black hair was sleeked back into a bun, all the better to show off her green eyes, high cheekbones, and golden skin.

A few feet away, King Cisco Castillo of Flores, a plant magier, was perusing the grapes on his plate with a critical gaze. He was short and stocky with a barrel chest that was slowly giving way to a paunchy stomach. His hazel eyes and bronze skin gleamed in the morning sunlight, as did his dark brown hair, which was pulled back into a low ponytail.

Eon, Ruri, and Cisco were all in their fifties, and each had been comfortable in their rule for quite some time. Given favorable enough terms, I would like to align with all of them, but their kingdoms weren't critical to my plans.

The person whose support I needed the most was Queen Zariza Rubin of Unger, a morph who was easily the most recognizable and notorious of all the royals. She was about ten years older than me, in her late thirties, and quite stunning with golden amber eyes and beautiful bronze skin. Zariza was famous for her dark red hair, which cascaded halfway down her back. Each strand was perfectly curled and had a high, glossy luster, and the ogre face on her neck boasted the same long, vibrant red hair.

Zariza was sipping a glass of Ungerian apple brandy and studying me with a neutral expression. Not welcoming, but not hostile either. Xenia was my friend and a fixture in my court, but I had never met Zariza, and it seemed as though she was far more reserved than her cousin. Or perhaps she didn't want to warmly acknowledge me and tip her hand about the Unger-Bellona alliance that we had secretly been negotiating for months.

I glanced around the rest of the terrace, studying the mix of lesser royals, nobles, advisors, servants, and guards. Concern filled me.

The Mortan king wasn't here.

I didn't see anyone wearing the Mortan crest or colors, not so much as a single guard. Even though the Mortans hadn't set up camp on their side of the river yet, I had still expected them to be at the opening ceremonies, which were supposed to start within the hour.

I wasn't the only one searching for them. Several people kept looking down at the arena floor, as if they were wondering when—or even if—the Mortans would arrive. But the Mortans would *never* skip the Regalia. Their warriors, magiers, masters, and athletes won far too many competitions for them to do that. So why weren't they here yet? Their absence only increased my concern about what the Mortan king might be plotting.

I kept glancing around the terrace, and I finally spotted two friendly faces—King Heinrich Ripley and his son Dominic. Sullivan's father and older half brother.

The two men put down their breakfast plates and walked over to me. Heinrich and Dominic were both dressed in black tunics, along with black leggings and boots, and the Ripley royal crest—a snarling gargoyle face—was stitched in black thread on their gray jackets. They both had the same dark brown hair, blue eyes, tan skin, and lightning magic that Sullivan did, although I had always thought Sullivan was by far the most handsome and powerful. Then again, my opinion was a little biased.

"Everleigh!" Heinrich said in a warm voice, grasping my hands. "It's so good to see you again!"

"And you too, Heinrich." I squeezed his hands in my own. "You look well."

And he truly did. A few months ago, Heinrich had been near death, thanks to the amethyst-eye poison that Dahlia, his long-time mistress and Sullivan's mother, had been slipping into his evening tea. I'd used my immunity to cleanse the foul magic from his system, and Heinrich now seemed fully recovered, healthy and strong again. At least when it came to his body, although I knew that the sting of Dahlia's betrayal would always linger in his heart.

I turned to the crown prince. "And you also look well, Dominic."

"Hello, Everleigh." He smiled, then leaned forward and kissed my cheek before drawing back.

I glanced around the terrace again. "Where's Gemma?"

Heinrich and Dominic exchanged a glance.

"She's back home with Alvis and Grimley," Dominic said in a smooth voice. "She wanted to come, of course, but we thought it would be better if she stayed at the palace. Just in case the Regalia turns out to be more . . . exciting than usual."

He smiled again, but the sharp scent of vinegary tension wafted off him. Dominic must be worried that the Mortans would try to kill him and his father again during the Games. I didn't fault him for taking precautions with his daughter's safety.

"And Rhea?" I asked.

Dominic looked to his right, and a much wider, far more genuine smile softened his face. "Here with me."

I followed his gaze over to a woman standing next to the wrought-iron railing along the front of the terrace. She was wearing black boots and leggings, along with a gray tunic with a gargoyle face done in black thread over her heart. Several gray crystal pins held her shoulder-length curly black hair back from her face, showing off her topaz eyes and ebony skin. In addition to being beautiful, Captain Rhea was also a fearsome warrior, and a dagger hung from her belt, along with a sword with three rubies set into the hilt to augment her own impressive strength magic.

Rhea was speaking with a short woman wearing a black jacket with red buttons who was part of the Ungerian contingent. The Andvarian captain noticed me and waved. I returned the gesture.

"I'm glad that Rhea is here to watch over you," I said. "And I'm especially glad that Gemma is far away and safe at Glitnir.

The poor girl already survived one massacre. She doesn't need to be in the middle of this circus too."

Heinrich and Dominic both grimaced, their faces tight with tension. Prince Frederich Ripley had died during the Seven Spire massacre, and they had almost lost Gemma during it as well, so they knew how dangerous royal gatherings could be.

"Where are the Mortans?" I asked in a low voice. "Why aren't they here yet?"

"I've been discreetly asking around, but no one seems to know," Dominic replied. "No one has spotted any activity on the Mortan side of the river. No servants or guards approaching, no tents being set up at their usual campsite, nothing like that. There's no indication that the king is anywhere near Fortuna."

"He'll be here," Heinrich said in a dark tone. "He *never* misses the Regalia, and he won't pass up this chance to remind us just how much we should all fear him. And he'll want to get a look at you in person, Everleigh. Especially since you keep killing all the assassins he sends after you."

"Lucky me," I muttered.

Heinrich gave me a sympathetic look, while Dominic waved over a servant, who handed each one of us a tall, frosty glass of kiwi mimosa. I discreetly smelled the drink, but I didn't sense anything that shouldn't be there, so I took a sip. The tart taste of the kiwi exploded on my tongue, along with the fizzy bubbles of the champagne. It was a perfect, refreshing way to start the gathering.

Over our drinks, Heinrich and Dominic filled me in on their conversations with the other royals and nobles, along with the gossip and rumors they'd heard. Most of it was typical stuff. Polite small talk and inane chitchat about the weather, the Regalia, and the upcoming yuletide season, as well as a few salacious whispers about various scandals. Nothing important, but that didn't surprise me. Serilda and Xenia had told me that nothing of consequence usually happened until the first of the royal balls, which was being held tonight.

As I listened to Heinrich and Dominic's tales, I kept looking around, searching for the Mortans. And I wasn't the only one who was on edge because they weren't here.

Captain Auster was standing a few feet away with the Bellonan guards, his hand on his sword, suspiciously eyeing anyone who came near me. Paloma was doing the same thing, her fingers resting against her mace handle. Xenia was sipping a mimosa and speaking with some of the Ungers, but she was still clutching her cane. Cho was chatting up a servant, trying to convince the other man to hand over his entire tray of pastries, but he too kept glancing around. Sullivan was speaking with Rhea, but he also kept looking out over the arena.

The Mortans might not be here, but the other royals were, so I shifted my focus back to them, and the cliques that were already forming. Heinrich and I were standing together and were already publicly, openly aligned, as were Eon and Ruri. The Vacunan king and Ryusaman queen were old allies, given their kingdoms' relatively close proximity and isolation from the rest of the continent, and they usually sided with each other rather than with anyone else. They kept a close watch on Morta and the other kingdoms, but their impressive navies kept their enemies at bay.

Cisco was standing off by himself, still perusing the grapes on his plate, while Zariza kept sipping her brandy, seemingly bored by this whole affair.

I hoped that Eon, Ruri, Cisco, and Zariza would align with me and Heinrich, with Bellona and Andvari, against the Mortans, but there was no way to tell. The other kings and queens had courts full of nobles and merchants to appease, just like I did, and it would be hard for them to justify aligning with me, especially if the Mortan king offered them some lucrative new trade agreements. In the end, each king and queen would do what was best for their own people. I just hoped they realized that the Mortans were a threat to us all.

I also kept an eye on Driscol as he flitted from one royal or noble to the next, shaking hands and exchanging greetings. Even among all the perfumes and colognes on the terrace, I could still smell his sour, sweaty eagerness. He didn't approach me, though, and I didn't seek him out. I wasn't making any deals with him, and his precious Mint could sink into the bloody sea for all I cared.

Driscol finished his rounds, drained the rest of his kiwi mimosa, and handed the empty glass off to a servant. I expected him to plunge back into the pack of royals to schmooze some more, but instead he walked over to Seraphine, who was chatting with some Floresian nobles. Driscol whispered something in his sister's ear, then glanced up.

At first I thought he was checking the weather, but only a few white, puffy clouds dotted the cerulean sky. No rain or snow would ruin the festivities, although the air was a bit chilly, but that was typical for this time of year.

Still, Driscol kept staring upward as though he were expecting a lightning bolt to drop from the sky or something else equally momentous to happen. What did he know that the rest of us didn't—

A loud, sharp, violent *screech* tore through the air, and several shadows fell over the terrace, blotting out the sun.

My head snapped up, and everyone on the terrace and in the surrounding boxes and bleachers stopped what they were doing and peered upward as well. I shielded my eyes with my hand so that I could better see.

A legion of strixes soared into view above the arena.

My eyes widened, and my breath caught in my throat at the beautiful, terrible sight. Every single one of the strixes was fully grown, with bodies that were bigger than Floresian horses. Their dark purple feathers gleamed, while the onyx tips on the ends whistled through the air like arrows searching for a target.

One, two, three . . . I couldn't tell exactly how many strixes were hovering overhead, and I stopped counting after the first dozen. But every single one of them was carrying a rider wearing midnight-purple armor and clutching a silver spear.

The Mortans were finally here.

CHAPTER NINE

The strixes continued to hover above the arena, their purple wings pumping hard and fast to keep them aloft in their loose, arrow-shaped formation. The people gathered in the surrounding boxes and bleachers gasped and yelled, and many in the crowd pointed up at the strixes and their armor-clad, spear-wielding riders. Despite my surprise and wariness, even I had to admit that the creatures' aerial prowess made for an impressive sight.

Sullivan stepped up beside me, his fingers flexing, and the scent of his magic filled my nose. He was ready to blast the strixes and their riders with his lightning if they made any threatening move toward me. Paloma sidled up on my other side, along with Captain Auster. They both had their hands on their weapons, and they too were ready to defend me. Behind them, the Bellonan guards snapped to attention as well.

Everyone else on the terrace was still staring up at the strixes and their riders, but I looked over at Driscol. The corners of his lips twitched up into a smug, satisfied smile. He had known *exactly* what the Mortans were planning, and he had probably helped them set it up. That's why they had arrived so late. The Mortans had wanted all the other royals and nobles—along with everyone else in the arena—to see just how strong they were.

I glanced around, clocking the other royals' reactions. Eon and Ruri were both frowning, apparently not caring much for the Mortans' theatrics. Good. That gave me a bit of hope they might align with me.

Cisco's lips were puckered in thought, and the stench of cherry lust wafted off him. The Floresian king was obviously wishing he had his own strixes on which to make such a grand entrance. Bellona and Flores had never been particularly friendly, and Cisco would probably be amenable to whatever the Mortans proposed, as long as it benefited him, despite the fact that they had killed his cousin Lord Durante.

Zariza kept sipping her brandy, seemingly more interested in it than the creatures and riders, and the ogre on her neck also wore a bored expression. She was hard to read, and I couldn't tell what she was thinking.

In contrast, Heinrich and Dominic were open books. They both had their arms crossed over their chests and were glaring up at the creatures and riders. The Andvarians had as little love for the Mortans as I did, given how many of their countrymen had died during the Seven Spire massacre and the recent assassination attempt on Dominic at Glitnir.

"I'd like to blast those bastards out of the sky for everything they've done to you, highness," Sullivan growled. "For everything they've done to us, to our families."

His hand twitched, and a bit of blue lightning sparked on his fingertips. The same power flashed in his eyes, and hot, peppery anger blasted off him in waves.

I touched his arm. "I feel the same way, but we both know we can't do that. We can't start a war. Not here, not now, with so many innocent people around. We need to beat the Mortans at their own game, remember? That's our plan, and we need to stick to it."

He stared at me, a muscle ticking in his jaw, even as more peppery anger surged off him. After a few seconds, he curled his hand into a fist, snuffing out his magic. I squeezed his arm, and we both turned our attention back to the sky.

Given the number of strixes, I couldn't tell where the Mortan king was—or if Maeven was here. I hoped she was. I might be plotting to kill her brother, but I also wanted to continue my long game with her.

The rider at the very front of the formation lifted his fist and then dropped it in a sharp motion. One after another, the creatures and their warriors plummeted to the ground, landing on the hard-packed dirt of the arena floor. The crowds in the boxes and bleachers yelled, cheered, clapped, screamed, and whistled, impressed by the aerial acrobatics, and several people on the royal terrace politely applauded, although most were far too refined, snobby, and self-important to deign to show any true, raucous emotion.

Still, everyone loved a good show.

The strixes landed in the same arrow formation they'd shown in the air, with the riders still atop their respective creatures. The first rider raised his fist again and let out a loud, earsplitting whistle, and the other riders steered the strixes into two rows. The Mortans were really going all-out with their show.

One of the strixes hopped forward and stopped in the open space between the two rows, and that rider looked around, as if checking to make sure that everyone was in their proper place. Once he was satisfied, the rider dismounted, and a servant rushed forward to help the man take off his golden helmet, along with his dark purple riding coat.

My breath caught in my throat. That had to be the Mortan king.

Behind him, a few other people also dismounted from their strixes and removed their own helmets, along with their riding coats. One of them was a woman with golden hair.

Maeven.

"She actually showed up," I whispered. "She's actually *here*."

Sullivan, Paloma, and Auster crowded in closer to me. I glanced across the terrace. Cho and Xenia had also spotted the king and Maeven. They both looked as tense as I felt, but Cho nodded at me. He and the others would be ready to move should the Mortans try to kill me.

The Mortan king took his sweet bloody time handing his helmet to a servant, stripping off his riding gear, and slipping into a new jacket. Only when he was properly attired did he deign to stride across the arena floor.

The crowd, of course, loved his long, drawn-out entrance, and they cheered wildly as he waved at first one section, then another. People also started tossing flowers and other trinkets from the bleachers down onto the arena floor.

Chains of white daisies, bundles of purple gladiolas, and crowns of blue laurels sailed through the air and landed on the hard-packed dirt, along with pennants and small stuffed strixes. Auster had told me that it was a Regalia tradition to shower gifts upon the gladiators after their bouts as a way for the audience to show its appreciation. Apparently, the people thought the Mortan king was also worthy of such high regard, although he didn't bother to pick up any of the items.

I looked past the king and scanned the section of bleachers closest to him. A bright flash of metal caught my eye. A figure wearing a black cloak with the hood pulled up over their head was lurking in the center of a pack of people near one of the gates set into the arena wall. The figure raised a black-gloved hand, and that bit of metal flashed again.

An instant later, an arrow zipped out of the crowd, zooming straight toward the Mortan king.

For one bright, shining, wonderful moment, I thought the Mortan king was going to die right there on the arena floor.

He must have somehow sensed the arrow, because he whirled in that direction. Large purple hailstones exploded out of his fingertips and *punch-punch-punch*ed into the arrow, reducing it to splinters a second before it would have slammed into his throat.

People gasped, and a stunned silence dropped over the arena. No one seemed to know for certain what had just happened, although all the guards on the royal terrace snapped to attention, ready to defend their own kings and queens in case any more arrows came zipping out of the crowd.

The Mortan king casually flexed his hand, causing more hailstones to streak out of his fingers and up into the sky. Then he whipped up his other hand and sent a bolt of cold purple lightning shooting out at the hailstones, shattering them in midair. Bits of purple ice rained down all around him, although he summoned up a breeze to make sure that none of the pellets actually touched him.

The Mortan king did that same hailstone-lightning sequence over and over again, adding in howling gusts of wind so that the ice showered different parts of the arena. I'd known that he was a weather magier, but I hadn't realized just how much raw power he had.

The crowd roared, apparently thinking it was all just part

of the show, and more flowers, pennants, and stuffed animals sailed through the air. No more arrows came shooting out of the crowd, though, and several Mortan guards flanked their king, forming a protective ring around him.

My heart dropped. Serilda had failed.

As per our plan, she had slipped away from our group and taken up a position in the crowd in hopes of getting a shot at the Mortan king when he arrived. I didn't see her black cloak anymore, although a dozen Mortan guards had moved away from their strixes and were hurrying through the nearest gate. Worry twisted my stomach, but there was nothing I could do to help Serilda now.

The Mortan king shot another bolt of cold lightning up into the sky, then lowered his hand and strode forward. Anger spiked through me, along with more than a little bitterness. My assassination attempt hadn't so much as ruffled his hair.

The smell of orange interest filled the air, and I was suddenly aware of just how many people on the terrace were staring at me. Royals, nobles, advisors, servants, guards. The spectators might think the king vanquishing that arrow had been an act, but everyone here knew about Bellona's troubles with Morta. No doubt they were wondering if I was the one who'd just tried to kill the king—and how I would react to the fact that my mortal enemy was still alive.

I was wondering that myself.

This wasn't the first time I had been confronted by someone I despised, but I still had to work very hard to keep my face blank and my hands from clenching into fists. Now was *not* the time to show any emotion, even though being so close to my enemy after spending the past year battling him from afar made my blood boil. Paloma always claimed that I was a gladiator at heart, and I had never felt like more of one than at this moment. I itched to draw my sword, charge down to the arena floor, and bury my blade in that bastard's rotten heart, just like a true gladiator would. But I couldn't do that.

Queens didn't have the luxury of blind bloodlust.

The king and the rest of the Mortan contingent finally made it over to this side of the arena and started climbing the bleacher steps. The other royals on the terrace held their positions, while all the guards remained vigilant. Sullivan was still standing by my side, and Auster and Paloma moved even closer to us. They too were ready to act should the Mortans decide to retaliate against me.

Driscol abandoned all pretense of neutrality and scuttled over to the terrace entrance, eager to greet the late-arriving royal, and making it clear whose pocket he was in. Seraphine glided along behind him, still looking vaguely bored.

Driscol's actions made me even more curious about the geldjagers that he'd sent to Svalin. Once again, I wondered if he'd dispatched them of his own volition or on the Mortan king's orders. And exactly who had the geldjagers been planning to turn me over to? Driscol? The Mortan king? Someone else?

The Mortans reached the terrace, and the king strode forward without waiting for his guards or the rest of his entourage. Then again, from what I'd just seen, the king didn't need anyone to protect him.

Driscol stepped forward and held his arms out wide. "Welcome! Welcome! It is once again my honor to host you and your countrymen at the Regalia."

The Mortan king brushed by Driscol, ignored Seraphine, and swept across the terrace with long, confident strides, as though he owned it, the arena, and everyone inside it, including the other royals. He stopped and turned in a slow circle, scanning the area. The king eyed Eon and Ruri, along with Cisco, although he didn't bother to greet any of them. He studied

Zariza a moment, then did the same to Heinrich. And finally, the king did something most surprising—he walked over to me.

Sullivan, Auster, and Paloma all tensed, but I broke free of their protective formation and strode forward. I had to show everyone that I wasn't afraid of him, starting this very second, or I would lose the Regalia before it even started. Being strong was even more important now that my assassination plot had failed.

The two of us met in the middle of the terrace, and I finally came face-to-face with my despicable, dangerous enemy—Maximus Mercer Morland Morricone, the king of Morta.

Maximus studied me from head to toe, and I did the same to him.

He was a tall, muscled, handsome man in his late forties, with tan skin and a thick mane of golden hair that was still perfectly styled, despite his recent ride on the strix. He had the amethyst eyes that I'd come to associate with the Morricone royal family, although his were particularly dark, more black than purple. He also had the same high cheekbones, pointed nose, and heart-shaped lips as Maeven. I had always thought Maeven's was a cold beauty, but the king's features were so sharp and angular that it seemed like you would cut your hand if you so much as brushed your fingertips across his skin.

I dropped my gaze to his clothes. Every royal here was dressed in some sort of finery, myself included, but Maximus's midnight-purple tunic, black leggings, and boots were easily the most impressive of all the garments. Thick seams of gold thread scrolled up his sleeves before spreading out across the front of his tunic and morphing into the Morricone royal crest—a large, fancy cursive *M* surrounded by a ring of strix feathers.

A gold signet ring bearing the same crest gleamed on his finger, but that was his only jewelry. He wasn't carrying any visible weapons. Not a sword, not a dagger, not even a knife sticking up out of one of his boots.

Then again, he didn't need a weapon, since he absolutely *reeked* of magic.

The hot, caustic stench of magic clung to Maximus's skin like an invisible sheen of smoke, along with a harsh note of coppery blood, and I had to twitch my nose to keep from sneezing. Even then, the stench kept burning and burning in my nostrils, and I could actually *taste* the coppery tang of his power on my tongue, as though I had a mouthful of blood. The aroma made me sick to my stomach, but I focused on it, analyzing everything about the odor, about *him*. As far as I could tell, there was nothing else to his scent—just blood and magic.

Maeven was extremely strong in her lightning magic, but her brother was an even more powerful weather magier. No wonder she was so afraid of him. Power and cruelty made for a very dangerous combination, and Maximus seemed to have an abundance of both.

Still, the more I breathed in the stench of his magic, the more I could feel my own power rising up in response. My cold, hard immunity wanted to lash out and crush every last drop of hot, stinking, coppery magic crackling through his body. Perhaps I would get the chance to do that before the Games were over.

I bloody hoped so.

"Queen Everleigh," Maximus said in a low, smooth, silky voice. "At long last, we finally meet."

"Maximus," I replied in a cool, clipped tone, deliberately using only his name and not his title.

He arched a perfectly sculpted golden eyebrow, and amusement flickered across his face. My slight didn't bother him at all. He kept studying me with his hard amethyst eyes, and I got the impression that I was nothing more to him than an annoying spider, one who kept skittering just out of his reach, despite his repeated efforts to squash me under his bootheel.

I expected him to make some snide comment about the assassination attempt. Like everyone else on the terrace, he had to suspect that I was behind it, given what he had done to the rest of the Blairs. But instead of confronting me, Maximus gestured for the other Mortan royals to step forward. There were four of them.

The first was a man about my age, late twenties, who was the spitting image of Maximus. Same golden hair, dark amethyst eyes, tan skin, and sharp, angular features. He too was wearing black leggings and boots, but the Morricone royal crest was done in silver instead of gold on his dark purple tunic, denoting his lesser status. I had never seen him in person before either, but I still knew who he was—Mercer, the king's oldest son and the Mortan crown prince.

Mercer sneered at me. I drew in a breath, tasting his scent. He too reeked of hot, caustic lightning, although the aroma was much weaker and without the bloody note that clung to his father. Mercer was powerful, but not nearly as strong as his father.

The second royal was also a man in his late twenties, with the same golden hair, tan skin, and amethyst eyes as his other relatives, although his features were a bit softer, making him far more handsome. He too was dressed in a dark purple tunic, although the Morricone royal crest was just a small symbol stitched in silver thread over his heart. Nox, one of the king's legitimate nephews.

Nox also sneered at me, but his expression quickly wilted under my cold glare, and he shifted on his feet. The last time I'd seen Nox had been the night of the royal challenge, when I'd killed Vasilia on the Seven Spire lawn. He had seen me shove my sword through my cousin's traitorous heart, and he at least had the common sense to be wary of me.

Nox's gaze flicked past me, and his eyes widened and his face paled. Auster stepped forward and stared at the younger man, his hand curled around his sword. The captain hated Nox even more than I did for his role in Queen Cordelia's death. Nox had also tortured Auster for months after the Seven Spire massacre.

I looked at Auster, who bowed to me and stepped back. He might want to kill Nox, but he would never disobey his queen, and I had given Auster strict orders not to touch Nox. Not yet.

I turned my attention to the other two Mortan royals. To my surprise, one of them was Leonidas, the teenage boy I'd spoken to through the Cardea mirror at Seven Spire. He was dressed in a light purple tunic, but the royal crest didn't adorn his clothes, further confirming my suspicion that he was a bastard, just like his mother was.

Leonidas stared at me, a worried look on his face, as though he was still concerned that I would announce to everyone that I had spoken to him through the mirror. I might still do that, but only when it benefited me the most, and now was not that moment.

And then there was the fourth and final Mortan royal, a woman in her mid-forties. Her golden hair was sleeked back into a high, elegant bun, and the perfect amount of understated makeup brought out her pale skin and amethyst eyes, along with the rest of her beautiful features, which were as familiar to me as my own face. She was quite a bit thinner than I remembered, although her face was finally free of the ugly mark that had marred it for so long from where the king had backhanded her after one of her failed attempts to murder me.

She was wearing a lovely lilac-colored gown, and a silver choker studded with amethysts ringed her neck. Two matching cuffs glinted on her wrists, while a ring gleamed on her index finger. All the gems reeked of magic, as did the woman herself.

Maeven, the bitch who'd orchestrated the Seven Spire massacre.

Icy rage surged through me, and once again my inner gladiator longed to draw my sword and ram it into her heart, before using the blade on Nox, Mercer, and Maximus. But I forced down my rage, just as I had the rest of my emotions.

This was supposed to be a civilized meeting, and I would not be the first one to break protocol and reveal it for the sham it truly was. Maximus had thwarted my assassination attempt, and I couldn't afford another failure right now. Once you started losing at courtly games, it was hard to stop the bleeding, much less get back onto your feet and actually win anything.

"I'm sure you know my son Mercer and my nephew Nox," Maximus said, breaking the silence.

"Of course." I kept staring at Maeven. "I know all the Morricone royals. Even the bastards like Maeven and Leonidas."

Maeven blinked, clearly surprised that I knew her son's name, and her fingers twitched as though she wanted to grab his shoulder and shove the boy behind her to protect him from me.

"Why, I'm probably more familiar with the bastard Morricones than anyone else," I continued in a light, pleasant voice. "After all, I've encountered *so* many of them over this past year."

Everyone on the terrace tensed. Gossip spread faster than the clap at my court and all the others, and everyone realized that I was talking about how many members of the Bastard Brigade I had killed. I might not be able to wound the Mortans with my sword, but I could still cut them to pieces with my words. Or at least try to.

"Well, perhaps you'll have the opportunity to meet even more of them." Mercer sneered at me again. "Sooner than you think."

The tension thickened, squeezing around the terrace like an invisible fist. The crown prince had just threatened my life. How sweet. Still, I took note of his words. He had just confirmed that the Bastard Brigade was lurking around somewhere, which meant that the Mortans were already plotting against me, just like I was them.

"I look forward to it. I'm sure I'll have just as much fun with them as I have with all your other relatives so far." I gave him a razor-thin smile. "Unless, of course, some legitimate Morricone wants to *meet* with me. Now, that would be a refreshing change."

Several people gasped at my returning Mercer's threat with one of my own, while others eased back, trying to get clear in case a fight actually did break out between me and the crown prince.

Anger stained Mercer's cheeks a bright red, and his right hand curled into a fist. The stench of magic surged around him, as though he were an instant away from blasting me with his lightning. Mercer glanced over at his father, clearly asking for permission. Maximus gave him a cold, flat stare, and Mercer's anger wilted like a flavored ice on a hot summer day, along with the scent of his magic.

Driscol cleared his throat and stepped forward, putting himself in the very dangerous space between me and the Mortan king. "Come. Sit. Eat. Relax. Let us enjoy the opening ceremonies. We've prepared a magnificent welcome spread . . ."

He kept chattering, trying to diffuse the situation. Maximus stared at me another moment, then followed the other man over to the buffet tables. Mercer smirked at me and headed after his father. Nox scuttled after them. The tension eased, and several servants and guards let out audible sighs of relief.

It seemed as though Maximus was going to completely ignore my attempt to kill him, and everyone was eager to follow his lead. By pretending nothing had happened, he was telling everyone how little he thought of the assassin's arrow and whomever had arranged it—me. More anger sizzled in my chest. My plotting didn't frighten him in the least.

Leonidas glanced at me, then at his mother. Maeven made a small shooing motion with her hand, and the boy hurried over to one of the buffet tables, although not the same one as Maximus, Mercer, and Nox.

Maeven started to join her son, but I moved forward and blocked her path.

"Hello, Maeven," I purred. "I'm so glad you're here. We haven't chatted much recently."

Her lips puckered, but she didn't respond. Maeven stepped to the side, and I let her sweep past me and head over to Leonidas, who was piling pastries on a plate.

Everyone returned to their previous conversations, although they all kept shooting glances at me and the Mortans. I eyed the other royals. Heinrich and Dominic were both grinning, but Eon, Ruri, Cisco, and Zariza all wore far more reserved expressions. They were still waiting to see what might happen between Maximus and me.

I grabbed another kiwi mimosa from a passing servant and toasted the other royals. Only Heinrich and Dominic returned the gesture, but that didn't surprise me. I tilted up the glass and took a long drink, but the sweet, fizzy liquid did little to drown the bitter taste of defeat in my mouth.

I glanced around the terrace. Cho was watching Maximus and Mercer, while Auster was glaring at Nox. Xenia had sidled up to Zariza and was murmuring in her cousin's ear, while Sullivan and Paloma stepped forward and flanked me again.

"That actually went better than I expected," Paloma said.

"How so?" I asked.

She shrugged. "Well, for one thing, the Mortans didn't try to kill you. And we didn't have to fight our way out of here."

"True," Sullivan agreed. "But even the Mortans wouldn't be so bold as to try to assassinate another royal in plain view of the entire arena."

He grimaced, as did Paloma. We all knew I had just tried to do that very thing and how easily Maximus had brushed it aside.

"Sorry, highness," Sullivan murmured.

More bitterness surged through me, but I quashed the emotion. Now was not the time to dwell on my failure. Instead, I eyed Mercer, who was glaring at me while a servant poured him a glass of wine. Maximus was deep in conversation with Driscol, who kept glancing at me.

"They might not attempt to assassinate me here, but they'll definitely try to kill me again the first chance they get," I murmured, a dark and deadly promise creeping into my voice. "We might have lost this battle, but we still have a war to win."

CHAPTER TEN

Driscol fluttered around, flapping his hands and announcing that it was time for the opening ceremonies. The kings and queens headed toward the round table in the center of the terrace, with everyone else sitting at smaller tables or standing along the back wall.

Sullivan and Dominic ended up at a table together, along with Paloma and Rhea. Xenia took a seat with some Ungers, while Auster remained standing with the Bellonan guards. Cho left the terrace. Still no sign of Serilda anywhere in the arena. She must have decided to head to our rendezvous point rather than risk returning to the terrace. Worry filled me, but Serilda could take care of herself, and I just had to trust that she would be okay until she could rejoin us.

I would have much rather remained with my friends, but I took a seat at the center table with the other royals. I sat down in the first chair I came to, one that had its back to the railing and the rest of the arena, making it the worst seat. Too late, I realized my mistake and that I wouldn't be able to see the opening ceremonies without craning my neck and looking back over my shoulder. But my ass was already in the chair, and it would have been a bigger error to try to take a better seat from someone else, so I stayed put.

Heinrich sat to my left, with Eon beside him. Zariza took the seat to my right, with Ruri on the other side, and Cisco beyond her. Maximus took the chair directly across from mine, the one with the best view of the arena. Naturally. That left one empty seat, the chair with the coined woman engraved in the top, and Driscol scurried forward and plopped down in it.

According to Xenia, this table was supposed to be for kings and queens only, but Driscol clearly wanted a seat here—literally and figuratively. The only way for that to happen would be for all the kings and queens to formally recognize Fortuna as its own kingdom and the DiLucris as a royal family, something the DiLucris had been trying to achieve for decades. Perhaps that was what Maximus had promised Driscol—that Morta would support the DiLucris in their relentless quest to officially establish their own kingdom.

Servants deposited platters of fresh fruit, cheeses, crackers, and pastries on the table, along with tiny chocolate-cherry and vanilla-orange sweet cakes. A second group of servants handed out plates, silverware, and napkins, and poured mugs of warm spiced apple cider. I drew in breath after breath, tasting the subtle aromas emanating from the food, as well as the steam wisping up from the cider, but I didn't smell or sense any poison.

Sullivan was right. The Mortans wouldn't be so bold as to try to murder me on the terrace. After we left the arena, though, it would be open season on me, especially since I had already tried to kill Maximus. But I was safe enough for now, so I sipped my cider and downed several cakes, enjoying the mix of the rich chocolate with the tart cherry, and the lighter, smoother vanilla with its bright pop of orange.

The other royals, along with Driscol, downed their own

food and drinks, as did the minor royals, nobles, and advisors at the surrounding tables. No one spoke, and the only sounds were the soft scrapes of forks and knives on dishes, along with the occasional clatter and clang of a servant refilling some-one's mug.

The silence stretched on and on, and the tension grew in commensurate measure. Everyone glanced at their neighbors, as well as the kings and queens, but no one dared to speak. I kept my mouth shut and concentrated on my food. This was yet an-other game, and I wasn't going to be the first one to give in and break the quiet.

But that didn't mean I still couldn't take control of the situation.

An idea occurred to me, one that would fix my previous mis-take in choosing this awful seat with no view and hopefully have the added bonus of annoying Maximus. Two strixes, one stone. I popped another chocolate-cherry cake into my mouth, then got to my feet.

The other kings and queens froze, their mugs and forks hovering in midair. They all looked at me, as did everyone else. No doubt some of them expected me to pull my sword and charge around the table toward Maximus in some reckless assassina-tion attempt, but I had set that game aside—for now. Instead, I picked up my chair, turned it around so that it was facing out toward the arena, and sat down, deliberately putting my back to the Mortan king.

Ostensibly, I made the move so that I would have a better view of the opening ceremonies, but I was silently declaring that Maximus didn't scare me, and everyone could see the motion for the insult it truly was.

Behind me, someone sucked in a surprised breath, and I got the impression that it was Driscol. Of course. As our esteemed host, he would want to keep the slights and insults among the royals to a minimum, and he especially wouldn't want me or anyone else to do or say anything to anger Maximus. But I was a queen, and Driscol was not, and he had no power over me whatsoever.

Once again, the silence stretched on and on. Every quiet second that ticked by filled my heart with even more malicious glee. I might not have killed Maximus yet, but insulting him was still extremely satisfying.

Beside me, Heinrich got to his feet. He paused a moment, staring at Maximus, then turned his chair around, lined it up with mine, and sat down in it, also putting his back to the Mortan king. Heinrich grinned at me, and I winked back.

To my surprise, another chair scraped away from the table. Zariza didn't even bother to stare down Maximus. Instead, she fluffed out her long, glorious red hair, then spun her chair around, lined it up with mine, and sat down, facing out toward the arena along with Heinrich and me.

"You're right, Everleigh," Zariza said in a loud, silky voice that carried across the terrace. "The view is *so* much better from this angle."

Not exactly a ringing endorsement, but it seemed as though I'd impressed her enough to get her to join my little rebellion. That, or she simply wanted a better view of the ceremonies. Hard to tell.

More chairs scraped back from the table, and Eon and Ruri also moved their seats so that they were sitting in a straight line with Heinrich, me, and Zariza. A few seconds later, Cisco joined them. That left Maximus and Driscol as the only ones still actually sitting at the table.

Several more seconds ticked by in silence. I couldn't see what Maximus was doing, but I could clearly smell his pungent onion annoyance, along with more than a little hot, peppery anger. He didn't like being upstaged and ignored.

Driscol cleared his throat. "Come, King Maximus. Let us

move your chair over to the designated spots so that you have the best view possible."

He was trying to spin it as though moving the seats had been planned all along, but his voice was soft and weak, and it was easy to tell that he didn't even believe his own lie.

Maximus murmured his agreement, and Driscol carried the king's chair to the far end of the line, positioning it a few feet away from Cisco's. Driscol started to fetch his own chair, but Maximus waved him off.

"That will be all."

Driscol visibly bristled at the curt dismissal, but he swallowed his anger, bowed his head, and headed over to the table where Mercer, Nox, Leonidas, and Maeven were sitting. Driscol started to take a seat there, but Mercer grabbed the empty chair, pulled it closer, and put his boots up in it. The Mortan crown prince crossed his arms over his chest, leaned back in his seat, and sneered at the other man.

Driscol bristled again, but he finally gave up and took a position next to Seraphine, who was standing with the DiLucri servants along the back wall.

I didn't bother to hide my smug smile as I reached back and grabbed my cider off the table. Everyone was watching me, including Sullivan, so I raised my mug in a silent toast to him. Sullivan grinned at me just like his father had. I smiled back, then turned around, facing out toward the arena again.

Without saying a word, I had wrested away some of Maximus's power and mystique and had shown everyone that I wouldn't be bullied, cowed, or intimidated by the Mortans.

Maximus might have avoided my assassin's arrow, but I had still come out ahead in this opening round of the Regalia.

Still basking in my small victory, I focused on the arena floor, where the opening ceremonies were about to begin.

Three large wooden rings, each one about a foot high, had been set into the hard-packed dirt, while thick cables had been strung up at varying heights and anchored to tall wooden platforms that rose more than a hundred feet into the air. Rectangular bales of hay lined the arena's circular wall, along with enormous balls, hoops, and other props. Black wrought-iron poles were also spaced along the wall, each one topped with a small lit cauldron. The flames danced, and the smoke curled through the air, mixing with the crowd's sour, sweaty eagerness.

Everyone was ready for the show to start.

A familiar figure pushed through one of the gates in the wall and strode out to the center ring. Cho looked as dashing as always in his white ruffled shirt and black leggings and boots, and Calandre had made him a special red tailcoat covered with tiny gold dragons to mark the occasion. Performers from every kingdom participated in the opening ceremonies, but choosing the ringmaster was an honor that passed from kingdom to kingdom, and this year it was Bellona's turn.

Cho had been absolutely thrilled when I'd selected him, but in my mind there was no other choice, since he was by far the best, most entertaining and enthusiastic ringmaster I'd ever seen. But I was also making a pointed statement by choosing him. Cho and Serilda had been exiled and outcast from Seven Spire years ago, and I wanted everyone to know that they were back home where they belonged.

Cho turned around in a circle, holding up his hands and asking for quiet. The crowd did as he commanded and slowly fell silent, but he kept his hands up, smiling wide, as did the dragon face on his neck. I'd never seen either one of them look so happy before, not even when they were eating sweet cakes. This was Cho's moment to shine, and he and his inner dragon were fully enjoying it.

"Lords and ladies, high and low!" Cho's deep voice boomed out like thunder. "Welcome to the opening ceremonies of the Regalia Games!"

The crowd roared in response, their cheers, yells, claps, and whistles so loud that the collective sound seemed to shake the entire arena.

Cho kept his hands raised a few seconds longer, soaking up the excitement and adulation, then lowered his arms to his sides and dropped into a formal Ryusaman bow. He held the bow until the crowd had finally quieted down. Only then did he straighten up and offer everyone another wide smile.

"Let's start the show!" he yelled.

Loud, raucous calliope music sounded, dozens of performers rushed through the gates, and everything started happening at once. Acrobats tumbled into view, while wire walkers darted out onto the cables overhead, doing their own handstands and somersaults. Morphs shifted into their other larger, stronger shapes, jumping through hoops, balancing on poles, and doing other amazing tricks, while magiers juggled balls of fire and ice, tossing them back and forth to each other at dizzying speed.

Many of the performers were from the Black Swan, of course, but I had also chosen performers from several other Bellonan gladiator troupes, including the Blue Thorns, the Scarlet Knights, and the Coral Vipers. Each performer was wearing the colors, costumes, and crests from their respective troupes, representing the best of Bellona. The gladiator tradition had been born in Bellona, and it was a part of our history, our culture, in a way that it wasn't for the other kingdoms.

The Bellonan troupes mixed beautifully with the performers from the other kingdoms, and together they put on a dazzling show. The crowd appreciatively oohed and aahed at every flip, dip, spin, and twirl, and the acrobats, wire walkers, morphs, and magiers pushed themselves to go faster, higher, and bigger with their impressive tricks.

I cheered and clapped along with everyone else. The lively music, the colorful costumes, the bright flashes of magic, the crowd's appreciative roars and delighted gasps. They all combined into a thrilling spectacle. *This* was what I had always longed to see when I'd dreamed of attending the Regalia, and it was just as exciting and wonderful as I'd imagined.

The performance also reminded me of the night when I had first snuck into the Black Swan arena to see the troupe's opening show in Svalin. If someone had told me back then that I would be sitting here now watching the Regalia as the queen of Bellona, I wouldn't have believed them. No, I would have laughed in their face and said they were crazy for thinking that I could ever rise so high.

But I had risen this high, and I was determined to stay here, despite all my enemies.

Forty-five minutes later, the acrobats finished their tumbles, the wire walkers climbed down from their platforms, the morphs changed back into their human shapes, and the magiers snuffed out their magic. The performers clasped hands and took several well-deserved bows, while the crowd cheered.

Finally, the performers left the arena floor, and workers streamed inside and started arranging the hay bales, archery targets, and other props for the competitions taking place this afternoon.

The first day of the Regalia was largely a skills challenge, with prizes awarded in everything from archery to spear-throwing to sprinting. Today was merely a warm-up for the Tournament of Champions, the most anticipated event, which would begin tomorrow morning. Much like this first meeting of the royals was merely a tease for bigger, bloodier, deadlier things to come.

Now that the opening ceremonies were over, that tense, heavy silence dropped over the terrace again, although it was quickly broken by Maximus, who let out a loud, exaggerated yawn, as if he'd been supremely bored. Maximus yawned again, handed his empty mug off to a servant, and turned his chair to the side so that he was facing the other royals, who were all still in line with me.

"Queen Everleigh," he said. "Your gladiator troupes put on a charming little show. With the help of the Mortan troupes, of course."

Charming little show? It had been *magnificent*, and he had been just as entertained and enthralled by it as everyone else had, despite his yawning. He was just trying to dismiss my people, and me along with them.

But two could play this game, so I shrugged as if his words didn't bother me. "Yes, they did. I'm quite proud of them. We should all be proud of our people for setting aside their differences to give us such a wonderful treat."

The other royals murmured their agreement.

Maximus's eyes narrowed. He didn't like them taking my side, not even in something as small and insignificant as this. "Yes, well, I will be even prouder when my warriors win their competitions, as well as the Tournament of Champions."

"Who are you putting forth in the tournament?" Cisco asked, a bit of envy creeping into his voice.

Most Floresians were more farmers than fighters, and none of them had ever won the tournament. Unlike the Mortans, who had won many times, as had the Bellonans.

"Mercer, of course, along with several of my most highly skilled guards," Maximus replied. "Any one of them could win, although Mercer will most likely prevail. He is the defending champion, after all."

I glanced over at Mercer, who was drinking a mug of cider,

his feet still up in that chair. His chin lifted, and his eyes gleamed with pride at being singled out by his father.

"Tell me, Everleigh," Maximus said. "Who are you presenting in the tournament?"

I gestured at Paloma, who was still sitting with Sullivan, Dominic, and Rhea. "My personal guard, Paloma, among others. She's quite formidable."

"She does look strong," Zariza agreed. "And she's an ogre morph. Everyone knows that ogres are the best warriors."

I eyed her, wondering if she was being sarcastic, but she seemed sincere. At least about ogres being the best warriors.

"Your choice surprises me," Maximus said.

I knew it was a trap, but I couldn't help but ask the inevitable question. "And why is that?"

He shrugged. "I fully expected *you* to participate in the tournament, Everleigh. You Bellonans do so love your barbaric gladiator tradition, and several Bellonan queens have taken part in the past. What better way to celebrate that storied history than by having the current queen participate in the Tournament of Champions?" His words were innocent enough, but a clear challenge rippled through his voice.

Worry churned in my stomach. Had Maximus somehow guessed one of my assassination plots? The thing I intended to use only as my last resort? I studied him, but his expression was more mocking than knowing. He didn't suspect that part of my long game. Not yet.

Why would Maximus care if I participated in the tournament? The bouts were only to first blood, and not to the death like in black-ring matches. Or perhaps he thought I could have an unfortunate *accident* in the arena, were I to face Mercer or some other Mortan fighter.

I didn't rise to his bait. "Unfortunately, I haven't had nearly enough opportunity to train for something as vigorous as the tournament."

It was a flat-out lie, since I trained with Serilda every single day, something she had insisted upon, even after I had become queen. I was extremely grateful for Serilda's skill and ruthlessness in knocking me on my ass time and time again, since that continued training had saved my life more than once over the past several months.

Maximus opened his mouth, no doubt to belittle and mock me again, but I cut him off.

"Besides, my thread master worked far too long and hard for me to ruin my Regalia wardrobe with blood, sweat, and dust. Why, she would kill me herself for that," I drawled.

The other royals politely laughed at my joke. Everyone except for Maximus, but I didn't care if he laughed. If I had my way, he'd be screaming before the Games were over. Him, Maeven, and the other Mortans, and Driscol along with them.

I stared at Maximus, silently daring him to challenge me again, but he decided to retreat—for now. He stood up and waved to his entourage. Mercer, Nox, Maeven, and Leonidas all shot to their feet and hurried over to flank him.

"Forgive me for leaving so early, but we flew directly here from the capital this morning, and it was a long, tiring journey." Maximus looked at me. "Made even more so by my spontaneous display on the arena floor."

This was the first time he had alluded to the assassin's arrow, and everyone on the terrace tensed. Maximus kept staring at me, but not a flicker of emotion crossed my features. Diante had been right back at Seven Spire. That skill had already come in handy during the Regalia.

"But I suppose it's a king's duty to give the people a show," Maximus continued. "I hope everyone was pleased with my little weather performance."

I had to hold back a derisive snort. No, I had not been *pleased* to see exactly how much magic he had. I hadn't thought Maximus would be easy to kill, but the depths of his power were forcing me to rethink my plots for eliminating him.

"Either way, I want to rest up for the kronekling tournament tonight," he finished.

As part of the Regalia, the kings and queens held a competition among themselves—kronekling, a card game that was played in front of all the other royals, nobles, and advisors. The game was always held during the opening-night ball, and it often set the tone for the rest of the Regalia, as the winning royal earned bragging rights that often bolstered their kingdom's competitors to even greater feats of athletic and magical prowess.

"Oh, yes," I replied. "I'm sure it will be a game that none of us will ever forget."

Maximus eyed me a moment longer before waving his hand at Driscol, indicating that the other man could finally approach His Royal Majesty again. The two of them spoke in low voices for several seconds before Driscol nodded and stepped back.

Maximus crooked his finger at first Mercer, then Nox, gesturing for the two younger men to follow him. He didn't acknowledge Maeven or Leonidas. He didn't even *look* at them as he left the terrace, and I realized that he hadn't introduced them earlier, or called their names, or done anything to indicate that he was even remotely aware of their presence. It was like his sister and her son were as invisible to him as the servants were, and he only noticed the pair whenever he wanted them to fetch him something. An interesting—and insulting—family dynamic.

Mercer sneered at me again, then followed his father. He didn't acknowledge Maeven or Leonidas either. Nox shot Maeven a guilty look and hurried to catch up with his legitimate relatives.

Maeven held her position on the terrace, her face calm and impassive, but a muscle ticked in her jaw, and hot, peppery anger blasted off her body. She didn't like being ignored by her brother, especially not in front of so many rich, powerful, important people. Leonidas stood quietly beside his mother, ducking his head and doing his best to remain as small and invisible as possible.

Once again, I felt a surprising amount of sympathy for the boy. Unlike his other relatives, he didn't seem to be an overtly bad sort, although I wondered how long that would last. Sooner or later, Leonidas would have to become as ruthless as his other relatives, if only to survive their petty games and deadly power struggles.

Maeven noticed me staring at her son, and she put her arm around his shoulders, bent down, and whispered something in his ear. Leonidas nodded, then left the terrace, heading after Maximus, Mercer, and Nox, although the three of them had already vanished into the crowd at the bottom of the bleachers.

That left Maeven standing all alone. Once again, I was tempted to draw my sword, close the distance between us, and bury my blade in her heart, but I tamped down the urge. I couldn't kill her. Not here, not now.

But I could certainly add to her humiliation.

I was still clutching my empty mug, so I got to my feet and toasted Maeven with it. "To family," I called out. "Isn't it wonderful?"

At my obvious mockery, chuckles rang out from several people, including Heinrich and Zariza, who were still sitting beside me.

Maeven's nostrils flared, her amethyst eyes glittered with anger, and hot pink streaked across her cheekbones, but she didn't respond. Instead, she whirled around and stormed off the terrace. I watched her go with a thin smile on my face.

Maximus might still be breathing, but I had definitely won this round in my ongoing battle against Maeven.

CHAPTER ELEVEN

With Maximus gone, the other kings and queens said their goodbyes and left.

Heinrich was among the last to go, and he squeezed my arm before following Dominic off the terrace. Several guards flanked them, including Rhea, who had her hand on her sword. She might be Dominic's unofficial consort, but she was also the captain of the Andvarian guards, and she was totally focused on protecting her king and prince. I wasn't the only royal the Mortans wanted to kill.

I waited until the Andvarians had walked down the steps and disappeared from sight before leaving the terrace. Sullivan, Paloma, and Captain Auster formed a loose, protective semicircle around me, with the Bellonan guards behind them. Xenia had already left with Zariza and the Ungers, while Cho was still down on the arena floor, helping the workers get ready for the afternoon competitions.

My friends and I quickly walked down the bleacher steps, circled around the arena wall, and stepped through one of the open archways and back out onto the plaza. Auster sent the guards on ahead to scout our route and report back if there were any signs of trouble. No one spoke until we had left the plaza and the crowds behind and were heading down the hillside steps toward the waterfront.

"Well, that went better than I expected," Paloma said, repeating her earlier sentiment.

I snorted. "Why? Because no one tried to kill me over cider and sweet cakes?"

She grinned. "That is a marked improvement from what usually happens whenever we leave Seven Spire."

I rolled my eyes, but I couldn't disagree.

"Yes, it did go well," Auster murmured, his head swiveling from side to side, examining everyone around us. "Perhaps a little *too* well."

"What do you mean?" Sullivan asked.

Auster rubbed his thumb over the hilt of his sword as if the motion was helping him organize his thoughts. "Maximus had enough guards and strixes to take control of the arena and try to kill anyone he wanted to, including Evie and the other royals. So why didn't he? Especially after our failed assassination attempt."

"Maybe Evie surprised him by striking so quickly. Or maybe he realized that there would have been an all-out riot if he'd tried to assassinate the other royals," Paloma said.

"That's certainly true, but Maximus isn't concerned with things like riots. He doesn't care who he has to slaughter to get what he wants," Auster replied. "He's never brought so many men and strixes to the Regalia before. He has something planned, something bigger than just killing Evie."

"Perhaps he brought the strixes so his guards could fly across the river and try to assassinate Evie in the Bellonan camp," Sullivan suggested.

"That thought has crossed my mind," Auster muttered.

"Mine too," I added. "When we get back, post more guards around the camp perimeter and tell them to keep their eyes on the sky. I also want your men to track the Mortans' movements. I want to know how the king and his entourage are getting from their camp to the island and back again. Just because Maximus survived one arrow doesn't mean that we can't try to kill him with another one."

"Yes, my queen," Auster replied.

But there was nothing my friends and I could do about Maximus or his plots at the moment, so we walked on. Eventually, we reached the boulevard at the bottom of the steps. Auster had led us down a different route than what we'd used climbing the hill, and we had ended up close to the Fortuna Mint.

We crossed the boulevard and went over to the plaza on the opposite side. It was just after noon, and the area was filled with people browsing the wares the merchants were enthusiastically hawking from their carts, eating bags of cornucopia, and strolling along the waterfront and admiring the picturesque view of the harbor.

We weaved in and out of the crowd, watching for trouble and heading toward our rendezvous point with Serilda—the gold coined-woman statue that loomed up in front of the Mint.

Serilda wasn't here yet, so Auster, Paloma, and Sullivan meandered over to the merchants' carts, trying to look casual, while I stopped at the base of the fountain, as though I were admiring the enormous figure in the center of the water.

The bright noon sun made the woman—Lady Fortuna—gleam as though she were made of liquid gold that was about to start oozing everywhere, while the coins in her eyes and mouth looked like tears that were about to start dripping down her face. If only she would melt away and take Driscol DiLucri and his Mint with her, then I imagined that the island would be a far happier and safer place, especially for me. But wishes were useless, especially to queens, so I turned away from the statue.

In the distance, I spotted Serilda weaving her way through the crowd and heading toward the statue. She had gotten rid of her black assassin's cloak, along with the bow she'd used, and she looked like her normal self again.

I had only taken a few steps toward her when I realized that someone was going to try to kill me.

I wasn't quite sure what tipped me off. Everything was the same as before. The merchants hawking their wares, some people eating and shopping, others strolling along the waterfront.

Slowly, I noticed that several of the merchants and shoppers were more interested in watching me than in selling and buying things. Oh, they all looked harmless enough, but they couldn't quite hide their interest, and every last one of them had their hands on the weapons belted to their waists. My nose twitched. Even more telling, they all reeked of magic.

My hand dropped to my sword, and my gaze flicked left and right, wondering which fake merchant or shopper would attack me first. The assassins sidled away from their carts and the goods they'd been admiring, but they didn't head toward me. Instead, they stalked toward my friend.

The assassins weren't here to kill me—they were here to murder Serilda.

For a split second, confusion filled me. I was so used to assassins trying to eliminate me that it hadn't occurred to me that my friend could be a target too. Then my mind kicked back into gear.

"Serilda!" I screamed. "Look out!"

I hadn't even finished speaking before Serilda drew her sword, whirled around, and sliced her blade across the chest of one of the men creeping up behind her. That man screamed and tumbled to the ground, but Serilda was already spinning around to face the next assassin.

I yanked my sword free of its scabbard and charged in that direction.

"Evie!" Paloma shouted behind me. "Evie! Wait!"

But I couldn't—*wouldn't*—wait. I had to help Serilda.

One of the assassins was stationed behind a cart filled with paper bags of cornucopia, and he rushed around it and raised his sword high, determined to bring it down on top of Serilda's head. She was engaged with another fighter, so instead of shouting a second warning, I threw myself into the space between Serilda and the assassin.

His sword clanged into mine, and a familiar sulfuric stench wafted off the metal. My nose twitched. His blade was coated with wormroot poison. These people weren't messing around, and they definitely wanted Serilda dead.

The assassin growled and drew his sword back for another strike, but I moved to the side and tripped him. The man stumbled past me, and I spun around, lifted my sword, and sliced my weapon across his back, all in one smooth move.

That man fell to the ground screaming, and I stepped up and drove my blade into his neck. He screamed again, then went limp. I growled, yanked my sword free, and turned to find a new enemy to fight.

Most of the assassins continued to focus on Serilda, but some of the others rushed over and engaged Paloma, Sullivan, and Auster. My friends drew their own weapons, and the harsh *clash, clang,* and *bang-bang-bang* of metal hitting metal rang across the plaza like bells pealing together.

People screamed and staggered back, not sure what was

happening. Merchants hunkered down behind their carts, shoppers dropped their bags, and parents grabbed their children and pulled them close. Fresh oranges, toy balls, and other goods hit the cobblestones and rolled every which way like marbles, and more than a few folks slipped on them in their panic, crashing into some of the carts and sending even more merchandise flying through the air and then raining down onto the ground.

"The queen!" I heard someone yell in the distance. "We have to get back to Queen Everleigh!"

The Bellonan guards who had been scouting up ahead must have seen the chaos, although I doubted they would be able to force their way through the crowd before the fight was decided—one way or another.

Two female assassins peeled off from the group surrounding Serilda and charged in my direction. One was a magier, who threw a ball of fire at me, while the other was a morph, who shifted into a fearsome ogre with jagged teeth and sharp talons. I avoided the fireball, which exploded against the front of the cornucopia cart. The magier's fire instantly ignited the paper bags, and the smell of charred corn and burned sugar clouded the air, along with smoke from the smoldering cart.

I headed toward the magier, but the ogre swiped out at me, and I had to lurch back to avoid her razor-sharp talons.

Merchants, shoppers, parents, and children were still screaming and running around the plaza, but they had all gotten away from the center of the fight. I spotted several DiLucri guards dressed in brown tunics mixed in with the crowd, but they held their positions, letting people run past them, instead of rushing forward to try to break up the battle. No doubt Driscol had told his guards not to intervene in the assassination attempt on Serilda.

I thought of how Driscol had been whispering to Maximus

right before the Mortan king had left the terrace. So this was what they'd been plotting. Driscol must have noticed Serilda slipping away from the Bellonan entourage in the arena earlier and realized that she was the one who'd fired that arrow at Maximus. But instead of attacking me, Maximus had decided to hurt my friend, even though Serilda had only been following my orders. Anger once again twisted my stomach, along with more than a little guilt. *I should have been the king's target, not Serilda.*

The ogre morph snarled and came at me again, although I managed to sidestep her a second time. The ogre ran right past me and plowed into the still-smoldering cornucopia cart. The wood splintered apart at the brutal impact, and red-hot embers shot into the air like fireworks. The ogre screamed with rage and used her long black talons to rip apart what was left of the cart.

If she had been a regular mortal, I would have charged forward and sliced my sword across whatever part of her I could reach. But I wasn't nearly as strong as the morph, who could easily crush my skull like a ripe melon, and I couldn't let her put her hands on me. One sharp *wrench* or vicious *pop,* and I would be dead.

The stench of magic filled my nose, and another ball of fire streaked toward me. I dodged this blast just like I had the first one, and the fire hurtled through the air and exploded against the stone railing that cordoned off the plaza from the water below. People screamed and stumbled even farther away from the fight.

I whirled back around to the magier, who screamed with frustration and summoned up another ball of fire. A few feet away, the ogre morph waded through the still-smoking remains of the cornucopia cart, heading toward me again.

I tightened my grip on my blade and watched them come, trying to figure out how to kill at least one of them without letting the other attack my blind side. But they were coming at me from two different angles, and I was at risk of either getting incinerated by the magier's fire or clawed to pieces by the morph's talons—

An idea popped into my mind. I stared at the fire sparking in the magier's hand, then at the morph's talons. Maybe I didn't have to get close to kill them. Maybe I didn't have to touch them at all.

It was a risky plan, but I forced myself to stop moving and widen my eyes, as though I were suddenly overwhelmed at the thought of facing two enemies at once.

The magier took the bait. She screamed in satisfaction and hurled her magic at me. After all, a stationary target was so much easier to hit than a moving one. The ogre realized that the fire was on its way, and she skidded to a halt.

The magier had put even more power into this ball of fire, and the flames burned bright and hot as they shot through the air like an arrow zooming toward a target.

But she wasn't the only one here with magic.

I reached for my own immunity, pulling my power up, up, up, and then pouring it down, down, down, so that the invisible strength of it coated my hands, along with my tearstone sword. Then, at the very last moment, right before the magier's fire would have slammed into my chest, I snapped up my sword and used the flat of the blade, along with my immunity, to bat the fire away from me and directly into the ogre morph.

My theory was right—a stationary target *was* so much easier to hit than a moving one.

The fire punched into the ogre's chest, and she lit up like an orange fluorestone—this tall pillar of intense light and heat. The ogre might be strong, but she was still susceptible to fire. She screamed and screamed and slapped at her body with her hands, trying to snuff out the flames, but they washed over her with incredible, unstoppable force, and it was already too late.

Her hoarse, pain-filled shrieks abruptly cut off, and she crumpled to the ground. The fire kept burning her body, though, the flames hungry for every morsel of meat and bone they could consume, and the stench of her fried flesh and singed hair hung in the air like a cloud of death.

My stomach roiled, but I focused on the magier, who was already summoning up another ball of fire to throw at me—

Blue lightning streaked through the air, slamming into the magier's chest and knocking her back against one of the wooden carts—and the fishing spear lying on top of it. The metal spear punched through the magier's back and all the way out her chest, killing her instantly. The burning ball of magic slipped through her fingers, hit the ground, and exploded against the front of the cart, which was filled with fresh fish. The magier's fire instantly charred the fillets, and the stench of the fried fish mixed with the ogre's still-burning flesh.

My stomach roiled again, but I looked over at Sullivan.

"Highness!" he yelled. "Behind you!"

I whirled around. Another woman was charging at me. I blinked in surprise. Where had she come from? She hadn't been part of the group stalking Serilda. I whipped up my weapon to attack her, but this new assassin must have been a mutt with speed magic because she was much, much quicker than I was.

The woman snarled and sliced her dagger across my left forearm, opening up a deep, jagged gash. I hissed with pain and staggered away. The woman executed the perfect spin move and lunged toward me again, trying to cut me with her dagger a second time.

I snapped up my sword, putting the blade in between us, but the woman was strong as well as fast, and she forced me backward. My boots slid across the slick stones, and she shoved me until the backs of my knees hit the edge of the fountain with its garish gold woman. I tensed my legs and barely managed to stop her from sending me over the rim and down into the fountain's pool of water.

The woman snarled again, trying to use her superior strength to cut through my defenses, but I braced my heels against the base of the fountain and tightened my grip on my sword, keeping it in between us.

"Fortuna favors her ladies," the woman hissed in my face. "And you *will* be ours, Everleigh Blair. One way or another."

I had no idea what she was babbling about, or who *they* were, but since her dagger was inches away from my heart, now didn't seem like the time to mention my confusion.

The woman opened her mouth, probably to hiss more dire warnings, but I snapped up my free fist and drove it into the side of her head. My unexpected punch threw the woman off balance, and she stumbled away from me—and straight into Paloma's mace.

My friend stepped up and rammed her mace into the assassin's back. Paloma put her considerable strength behind the blow, and the mace's spikes sank deep into the woman's body. She screamed and arched back, throwing up her arms and unintentionally mimicking the pose of the coined-woman statue looming above us. Paloma growled, ripped the mace out of the woman's back, whirled all the way around, and slammed it into the base of her skull.

The assassin froze like she was a puppet and Paloma was now pulling her strings. She stared at me, even as blood welled up out of her mouth and ran down her face.

Paloma ripped her mace out of the woman's skull and shoved her away. The assassin hit the cobblestones at my feet, blood already pooling underneath her body.

I lowered my sword and let out a breath, trying to slow my racing heart. Over the past year, I had been attacked by my fair share of assassins, but this one had come closer to killing me than most. And the strange things she'd said . . . I still had no idea what to make of those.

Paloma stepped over the woman's body and stopped in front of me, while Sullivan hurried over to me as well. I looked them both up and down, but they seemed fine, except for the blood on their clothes.

I made sure that it wasn't their blood, then glanced at Auster, who had been battling assassins a little farther away. He too seemed fine and headed in this direction. Finally, my gaze focused on Serilda. Bodies littered the ground all around her, cuts and bruises dotted her face and hands, and blood covered her clothes, but she was still in one piece and limping this way.

A relieved breath escaped my lips. Everyone was more or less okay, and my friends and I had survived another attack.

Normally, the thought of how close we had all come to dying—*again*—wouldn't have bothered me. At least not until tonight when I was asleep, and the battle started haunting my dreams like so many others did. But for some reason, the sight of the last assassin's blood oozing across the stones made me sick to my stomach, and I had to resist the urge to vomit.

Now that the battle was over, the other people in the plaza tiptoed forward, staring at the smoldering carts, the dead bodies, and especially me and my friends in the center of it all. The Bellonan guards finally broke through the crowd and flanked us, but they couldn't shield me from people's words.

"Is that the Bellonan queen?"

"Is she hurt?"

"I wonder who tried to kill her."

"It had to be the Morricones. Everyone knows how much their king hates Bellonans, especially the Blairs . . ."

The speculation and the comments went on and on. Each one made more and more guilt flood my body, adding to the sick sensation in my stomach. Maximus had been trying to kill someone else for a change, although he'd only gone after Serilda because of me. Once again, I thought of Diante's words back at Seven Spire. She was right. I would much rather put myself in danger than be the cause of it for my friends.

Auster reached my position, although he kept glancing around, scanning the crowd for other threats. "There could be more of them. We need to leave."

I slowly slid my sword back into its scabbard. The light tear-stone blade suddenly seemed strangely heavy. "Okay. Just give me a minute to get my breath back—"

"What is the meaning of this?" A voice rose up from the direction of the Mint. "Out of the way! Get out of the way!"

People stepped aside, and Driscol hurried in our direction, along with the DiLucri guards who had stood by and watched the battle. Seraphine trailed along in their wake, as calm and serene as ever.

Driscol stopped a few feet away from me. His gaze flicked from one dead assassin to the next, his face getting redder and redder all the while. He was probably embarrassed that they had failed, just like the geldjagers he'd sent to Bellona had failed.

He fixed his angry gaze on me. "What is the meaning of this? This is supposed to be a peaceable island!"

I stared him down. "Then perhaps you should tell that to the assassins who tried to kill my advisor. Oh, wait. You can't because they're all *dead*."

Driscol opened his mouth, probably to yell some more, but Seraphine glided forward and touched his arm.

"Now, now, Driscol," she cooed in a soft voice. "The only thing that truly matters is that Queen Everleigh and her friends survived and the assassins didn't."

Driscol eyed her, and she looked right back at him, that bland smile still firmly fixed on her face. The two of them must have reached some silent understanding, because he nodded, and some of the redness leached out of his face. "You're right, sister. You always are."

It was like a beauty taming a beast in some old fairy tale. Seraphine smiled at him again, and he turned back to me.

"Please forgive me, Queen Everleigh," Driscol said, a faint groveling note in his voice. "I meant no disrespect."

He sucked in another breath, as if to expand on his fake apology, but my cold, disbelieving glare must have made him think better of it because he clamped his lips shut.

In the distance, I could see more guards streaming out of the Mint and heading in our direction. In another minute, Driscol would have enough men to surround me, my friends, and the Bellonan guards. It was definitely time for us to leave, but for some reason I remained rooted in place, standing in the shadow of the coined-woman statue. My breathing had finally slowed down, although my heart kept pounding and pounding, even as this strange lethargy spread over me.

"Evie," Paloma said in a low, warning voice. "You're bleeding."

I glanced down. The gash that the last assassin had sliced into my left forearm was oozing blood, and the drops hit the cobblestones like soft scarlet coins. *Plop-plop-plop-plop.*

I had been so focused on just staying alive that I hadn't realized exactly how deep and gruesome the wound was—or that it was poisoned.

Perhaps it was the overpowering stench of the ogre's fried flesh and singed hair still filling the air, along with the acrid aroma of the charred fish, but I hadn't sensed the poison on the assassin's dagger. Otherwise, I would have tried harder not to let her cut me with the blade.

The poison had a harsh, coppery scent, along with a cold note, as if someone had somehow mixed blood and frost together. It was an unusual aroma, and the poison didn't have a caustic burn like wormroot that would tell me exactly how strong it was—or how quickly it might kill me.

That strange lethargy swept over me again, stronger than before. Even worse, my forearm had gone numb, and I couldn't even feel the deep, throbbing sting of the gash anymore. I had to do something to counteract the poison right now, before it spread up my arm, across my chest, and over to my heart.

So I ignored the lethargy as best I could and reached for my own magic, pulling it up just like I had when I'd been fighting the magier and the morph. Only this time, instead of coating my hands and sword with it, I forced all the cold, hard power into the cut on my forearm.

I stared at the gash and imagined my immunity like an invisible fist closing over the deep cut. More and more blood welled up out of the wound, turning into a steady stream that slid down my skin, hit my bracelet, and dripped off the silver thorns. The sight and smell of so much of my own blood made me nauseous and light-headed, but that was okay, because it meant that my power was working and pushing the poison out of my body. I gritted my teeth, reached for even more of my immunity, and forced it into the wound.

I wasn't sure how long I stood there, watching the blood leave my body. It couldn't have been more than a few seconds, although it seemed like an hour, due to the lethargy still creeping through my veins.

I drew in another breath, and the stench of the poison tickled my nose again. Copper and cold, blood and frost. I frowned. I had smelled this poison before. I *knew* that I had. I could feel the answer in the bottom of my brain, like a fish swimming along a riverbed. Oh, yes, the answer, the memory, was down in there somewhere, but I was too tired to bring it up to the surface right now . . .

"Evie?" Paloma said again.

Sullivan must have heard the concern in her voice. He cursed and lunged forward, probably to clamp his hand over the wound to stop the bleeding, but I waved him off.

"Grab the dagger from the last assassin, the one who cut me," I whispered to him. "Be careful. The blade is poisoned."

The scent of anger blasted off him, along with worry, but he whirled around, hurried over, and scooped the dagger up off the ground.

Paloma stayed by my side, her amber eyes wide, as were those of the ogre on her neck. "Wormroot?" she whispered, fear rasping through her voice.

Paloma had once been poisoned with wormroot by a jealous rival gladiator, so she knew how painful and horrible it felt.

I shook my head. "I don't think so."

"Amethyst-eye?"

That was the poison Dahlia had used to try to kill Heinrich at Glitnir a few months ago.

I shook my head again. "No."

"Then what?" Paloma asked, more worry filling her voice.

I started to tell her that I couldn't remember exactly what poison it was, but another wave of lethargy swept over me, much stronger than before. All the strength left my body, and the last thing I saw before I hit the cobblestones was the gold statue of Lady Fortuna looming above me.

CHAPTER TWELVE

I was lying on my side, curled up in a little ball, still feigning sleep.

It was well after dark now, and blackness cloaked the woods around the clearing, except for where the patches of snow lightened the ground and frosted the tree branches. Behind me, the campfire had burned down low, taking its warmth along with it, and a chill had soaked into my bones, despite the blanket and the cloak covering my body. Or perhaps the chill had more to do with how much danger I was in.

Some time ago, Rocinda and Caxton had finally quit plotting to sell me to the highest bidder and had lain down next to the fire. Caxton had been steadily, loudly snoring for several minutes. Every once in a while, Rocinda would let out a soft breathy sigh, indicating that she too was asleep.

I wouldn't get a better chance to escape. I didn't know who they were working for or where they wanted to take me, but I wasn't going to be anyone's slave, toy, or whatever horrible thing they had in mind. I'd already lost my parents, my home, and everything I had ever cared about. I wasn't losing my freedom too.

It was the only thing I had left.

So I sat up, careful not to rustle my blanket, and glanced over at my would-be kidnappers.

Caxton was lying on his back with his arm thrown up over his head. The deep, throaty snores rumbling out of his mouth matched the lumbering rise and fall of his chest. He was definitely asleep. Rocinda was on her side, turned away from me, and curled into a ball, much like I had been. Her chest also rose and fell in a steady rhythm, and she too appeared to be sleeping.

Now or never.

I pushed the blanket aside, stripped off the borrowed cloak, and got to my feet, making as little noise as possible. I also kept my hand in my dress pocket, my fingers still curled around the dagger hidden there. Despite my furtive movements, my would-be kidnappers remained asleep.

I eyed Rocinda's and Caxton's knapsacks a few feet away. I could use their supplies in the woods, but I didn't dare try to steal the bags. Not when they were lying within arm's reach of Caxton. I'd rather escape with my life than die for a wheel of cheese and some dried fruit.

I stayed where I was a moment longer, but Caxton kept snoring and Rocinda remained still. Keeping my eyes on them, I stepped back, putting my boot down on the ground—

Crunch.

My boot cracked through a patch of ice, the sound seeming as loud as a trumpet blaring. I froze, but Caxton and Rocinda didn't move. It didn't look like I had woken them, so I let out the breath I'd been holding and kept going.

Step by step, I backed away from them, as well as the dwindling heat and light of the campfire. My heart hammered, and my breath puffed out in shallow, frosty clouds, but I made it to the edge of the clearing. All I had to do was slip into the trees and then I could start running. I still didn't know where I was or where I was going, but hopefully, I could get far enough away that they wouldn't bother to chase after me—

A soft fluttering sound caught my ear. I froze again. My gaze snapped over to the campfire, but Caxton and Rocinda were in the same positions as before. I glanced around the rest of the clearing, but I didn't see anyone else.

So who—or what—had made that noise?

The soft fluttering sounded again, and again, and I realized that it was coming from the box Caxton had tied to one of the pines. The black cloth draped over the box was moving back and forth. At first I thought the wind was ruffling the fabric, but then I noticed that the air was completely still.

Something was inside the box.

I hesitated, torn between slipping into the trees and going over to the box. I didn't want the noise of the fluttering cloth, along with whatever was inside the container, to wake Caxton and Rocinda. But in the end, all that mattered was my escape, so I crept closer to the trees.

The cloth fluttered again, a little louder and more violently than before. I froze yet again. The cloth stilled, and I let out another breath and tiptoed forward.

The cloth fluttered for a third time. But instead of dropping back down into place, the black fabric kept snapping to and fro, as though whatever was inside could sense my leaving.

By this point, the entire box was vibrating, along with the attached rope, and bits of snow were flaking off the surrounding tree branches and plop-plop-plopping onto the ground. It wouldn't be long before larger chunks of snow and ice started slipping off the branches, making the limbs snap upward and scrape together. The resulting noise would most likely wake my captors, which meant that I had to shut up whatever was inside that bloody box before it ruined my chance to escape.

I ground my teeth at the delay, but I changed direction and sidled toward the box. Luckily, Caxton had tied the box on a low branch, and he had just draped the cloth over the container without bothering to tie it down. I glanced over at the campfire again, but he and Rocinda still appeared to be sleeping, so I turned back to the box.

I took hold of one corner of the black fabric and gently pulled it down, revealing a small container made of coldiron bars. It wasn't a box, it was a cage, with a small creature trapped inside.

A caladrius.

My breath caught in my throat, and the black cloth slipped from my fingers and floated down to the snowy ground. Despite the danger, I couldn't help but lean forward and peer through the bars.

The caladrius's tiny, owlish body was only a little bigger than my hand. Its feathers were a lovely snow-white and tipped with arrowlike points of light gray, while its beak and talons were a darker, smoky gray. The contrasting colors gave the creature an ethereal air, and its wings seemed to glow like an opal memory stone in the black night.

I had seen caladriuses in menageries, but I'd never been this close to one before. Those creatures had had broken wings and other injuries that made it impossible for them to survive in the wild, but this creature didn't seem to be wounded. So why was it in a cage?

The answer came to me an instant later. Caxton and Rocinda must be planning to sell it, just like they were me. Anger filled me, along with sadness.

The caladrius had been huddled in the back of the cage, but it hopped forward and peered at me through the bars. The creature crept closer and fluffed up its feathers, as if it were making sure it had my full attention. Then it leaned toward me so that its bright eyes were level with mine.

Help me.

The two words whispered through my mind like wind softly blowing over a field of wildflowers. I jerked back in surprise. My boot crunched on another patch of ice, but I kept staring at the caladrius.

Had the creature just . . . spoken to me?

No, of course not. That was silly. As far as I knew, caladriuses didn't talk, and only mind magiers could whisper thoughts to someone. Still, the creature was making me uneasy, so I took another step back. I needed to get out of here before Caxton and Rocinda woke up, not waste my time mooning over a pretty bird.

The caladrius let out what sounded like a soft resigned sigh. Its head drooped, along with its feathers, and it seemed to shrink, becoming even smaller than it already was. The creature realized that I was abandoning it, and its dusty resignation washed over me. The scent cut me deeper than a sword through my heart.

I couldn't leave the caladrius here to become someone's pet—or worse, to be carved up for its magic. Some people thought eating caladrius meat or ingesting powders made from the creatures' feathers, beaks, talons, and bones could cure illnesses, increase a person's magic, and bring good luck. The creatures were protected in Bellona, but they had been hunted to almost extinction in other kingdoms like Morta.

I glanced over at Caxton and Rocinda again, but they were still sleeping, so I tiptoed back over to the cage. The tiny, owlish bird perked up and cocked its head to the side, studying me. For the first time, I noticed that its eyes were a lovely gray-blue that shifted color, going from light to dark and back again, thanks to the campfire's low flames.

Caladriuses often nested in tearstone mines, and some legends claimed that the birds had dug into so much tearstone that it had turned their eyes the same unique color. Last winter, several caladriuses had nested in my father's mine, and we had often scattered toasted sunflower seeds and dried bits of bloodcrisp apples on the cavern floor for the creatures to eat.

Thinking about my dead father made my heart ache again, but I pushed the emotion and memories aside, bent down, and studied the small padlock on the cage. The simple metal contraption reeked of magic. Rocinda must have coated the lock with her fire power so that the caladrius couldn't use its hard beak to peck the metal to pieces and free itself.

I grimaced, knowing how much this was going to hurt, but I wrapped my hand around the padlock anyway. Orange-red fire spewed out from between my fingertips, and I quickly brought my other hand up, covering the flare of flames as best I could.

My immunity roared to life, and I focused my power on the lock, chipping away at the magic that held it together. Rocinda's fire burned and burned, trying to eat through my immunity and blister my skin. I gritted my teeth again and reached for even more of my magic, forcing it to smother the fire like an invisible blanket.

A few seconds later, the last of the flames were snuffed out. I sighed with relief and pulled down on the base of the metal. Rocinda hadn't bothered to actually lock it with a key, and the clasp slid free. I unhooked the padlock and slid it into my pocket, right alongside my hidden dagger.

I glanced over at Caxton and Rocinda again, but they hadn't moved, so I cracked open the cage door. The metal squeaked a bit, making me wince, but I opened it the rest of the way.

I stepped back, expecting the caladrius to immediately fly out, but it stayed where it was, still staring at me with its bright eyes.

"Go on," I whispered, waving my hand. "You're free."

The caladrius shuffled forward to the front of the cage. It fluffed out its white feathers again, lifted its wings, and took off. The creature was much faster than I expected, and it quickly darted across the clearing and disappeared into the trees. I watched it go with a smile on my face.

As soon as the bird vanished, I realized that the clearing was eerily quiet—and that I didn't hear Caxton snoring anymore. Dread filled me, and I whirled around, hoping that he and Rocinda were still asleep—

The two bounty hunters were standing right in front of me.

Caxton's hands were curled into fists, while Rocinda was clutching a knife. My nose twitched. The hot, peppery scent of their combined anger filled the clearing.

I started to bolt into the trees, but Caxton was fast as well as strong, and he used his mutt magic to grab my arm and yank me back.

"Where do you think you're going?" he growled.

I opened my mouth to stammer out some lie, but Caxton slapped me across the face. Pain exploded in my left cheek, and white stars winked on and off in my eyes.

"Stupid girl." He sneered. "You should have saved yourself instead of the bird."

Caxton shoved me toward Rocinda, who grabbed my hand and sliced her knife across my palm, opening up a deep cut.

I yelped with pain and raised my other hand to hit her, but Rocinda shoved me back, and Caxton's strong arms clamped around me from behind. I struggled with all my might, but I couldn't break his tight, bruising grip. I couldn't move my arms at all, not even to try to reach for the dagger still hidden in my dress pocket.

But the longer and harder I struggled, the more tired I felt—so very, very tired. I glanced down at my palm, which was

dripping blood. I could feel magic pulsing through my veins,
right alongside the sharp sting of the cut.

Rocinda's knife had been poisoned.

No, I thought. Not poisoned. The two of them had gone to
far too much trouble to feed me earlier just to kill me now, even
if I had freed the caladrius. They still wanted to sell me, which
meant . . . which meant that . . .

I was having trouble focusing through the fog suddenly
clouding my mind. Somehow, I forced myself to look at
Rocinda, even though she seemed very far away and was
growing more distant by the second.

"What . . . did you . . . do . . . to me?" I rasped out the words,
even though my tongue felt numb and heavy in my mouth.

Rocinda brandished her knife, making the sharp edge of
the blade gleam in the dying light of the campfire. "This? Oh,
it's just a little trick we use to keep our guests docile while we
transport them to their new homes. Say goodbye to Bellona, little
girl. Because this is the last time you're ever going to see it . . ."

Rocinda kept spewing threats, but I couldn't concentrate on
her words. That fog rose up in my mind stronger than before, and
I fell down into its dark gray abyss . . .

My eyes fluttered open. At least, I thought they fluttered
open. It was hard to tell, since all I could see was a solid wall of
gray. It took me a few moments to realize that it wasn't a wall,
but rather the curve of a tent swooping upward toward a large
crown-of-shards crest done in bright, glittering silver thread in
the center of the canvas ceiling.

A relieved breath escaped my lips. This was my tent, which
meant that I was off the island and back on the Bellonan side of
the river, where it was . . . Well, I didn't know that *safe* was the
right word. *Safer,* perhaps. Complete, utter, total safety would
always be forever out of my reach as long as I was queen.

But since I was currently safer, I wiggled my fingers. The gash on my left forearm was gone, and the clean, lemony scent of soap and magic that lingered on my skin indicated that Aisha, the head of my bone masters, had healed me. I didn't sense the poison coursing through my veins anymore, although I still felt tired and very, very stiff, as though I'd been frozen alive and was only just now thawing out.

I didn't know if being poisoned had triggered my nightmarish memory, or if my memory had helped me figure out what the poison was, but I now knew what the DiLucri assassin had dosed me with—blue sperren, the same drug Rocinda had given me all those years ago.

But the strange thing was that blue sperren wasn't usually fatal. No, it was a paralytic that just made people think you were dead. Combine that with the assassin's strange words, and how she had seemingly come out of nowhere to join the battle at the very end, and I got the sense that *I* had been her intended target.

The other assassins had all rushed toward Serilda, but that last woman had hung back and waited for an opportunity to focus on me and me alone. And since she had dosed me with blue sperren, her attack hadn't been meant to result in my death. At least, not immediately, not right there on the plaza.

I had assumed that Maximus had hired Driscol to send the geldjagers after Serilda, but now I was starting to think there were other forces—other people—at work who had a far different agenda regarding me than the Mortans did. I just wasn't quite sure what that agenda was yet.

It was probably something far worse than a quick death, though.

I drew in a breath, and several other familiar scents filled my nose. Cold, clean vanilla with a hint of spice. Peony perfume and wet fur. Blood mixed with coldiron. My friends were here.

I was lying in my bed against one wall of the tent, so I sat up, pushing aside the blankets. Sullivan, Paloma, Serilda, Cho, and Captain Auster were standing by the entrance, talking in low voices to a woman with short black hair, hazel eyes, and ebony skin. Aisha, the bone master. The scent of their collective worry filled the tent, as sharp as knives stabbing into my nose. They probably thought that I'd been dying, instead of just being paralyzed.

They didn't realize that I was sitting up, and I was so tired that I didn't feel like getting to my feet, so I cleared my throat. They all whipped around.

"Highness!" Sullivan rushed over and dropped to a knee beside me. "You're awake!"

"Of course I'm awake." My tongue still felt heavy and numb, so my words slurred a bit. "Why wouldn't I be awake?"

Aisha also hurried over, bent down, and peered at me, a worried look on her pretty face. "We weren't sure if you were ever going to wake up. I healed the cut and did my best to cleanse the poison from your system, but you were so stiff and pale, and your lips were so blue . . ." Her voice trailed off, and more worry blasted off her, drowning out her clean, lemony scent.

"It's okay, Aisha." I smiled. "You did your job, and I'm much better now. See?"

I tried to get up, but my legs buckled, and I would have fallen, if Sullivan hadn't reached out and steadied me.

"Take it easy, Evie," he murmured, helping me sit down. "Just take it easy."

He only called me *Evie* when he was truly, deeply concerned, and his hands tightened on my arms as if he wanted to pull me close and never let me go.

After a moment, Sullivan cleared his throat, dropped his hands from my arms, and went back down on his knee beside me. His blue eyes searched mine, and I reached up and cupped his face, stroking my thumb over the prickly stubble that darkened his jaw.

"I'm fine," I whispered. "Truly."

He smiled, but worry still sparked in his gaze like a wildfire that refused to be extinguished.

Aisha took hold of my wrist and checked my pulse before peering at my face. "Amazing," she murmured. "Ten minutes ago your lips were as blue as sapphires, but now they're back to their normal color. The poison, whatever it was, seems to be completely gone from your body. I didn't think that I was going to be able to heal it, to heal *you*."

She shook her head. "The assassin must not have used the proper dosage."

Sullivan, Paloma, Serilda, Cho, and Auster didn't say anything. They knew that my immunity was what had truly saved me. Aisha didn't know about my power, although she might guess after this episode.

"Or perhaps your healing magic was stronger than the poison," I lied in a light, unconcerned voice. "Either way, I owe you my life. Thank you, Aisha."

She bowed her head. "It's my job, my queen."

"And you do it very well, especially considering how difficult I so often make it."

Aisha politely laughed at my joke, but I could almost see the questions spinning around in her mind as she tried to figure out how I had really recovered. She promised to check on me later, then left the tent.

As soon as she was gone, Paloma dropped her hand to the mace on her belt. "We should forget about our other plans, sneak into the Mortan camp tonight, and bash in Maximus's head," she growled. "Maeven's too, and whomever else we can find."

"I agree with your sentiment, but that would be foolish," Auster rumbled in a far more reasonable tone. "There's no way we could sneak a large force into the Mortan camp, much less get close enough to Maximus to kill him. The Mortans are sure to be on high alert now after our earlier attempt in the arena."

His voice was calm and even, without a hint of accuasation, but everyone looked at Serilda. The scents of her peppery anger and minty regret burned my nose and matched my own emotions.

Serilda stepped forward and dropped into a traditional Bellonan curtsy in front of me. "I'm sorry, my queen," she said in a low, strained voice. "I don't know what happened. I coated the arrow with wormroot and aimed it at Maximus's throat in case he was wearing any armor under his clothes. All the arrow had to do was scratch him, and the poison would have killed him."

I still wasn't sure how Maximus had sensed the arrow streaking toward him, given all the people and chaos in the arena, but Serilda had done everything I had asked, and I reached out and squeezed her hand. "It's not your fault. Perhaps it's mine for not coming up with a better plan. I thought we could beat the Mortans at their own game and take Maximus by surprise by attacking right away, but I was wrong."

Serilda squeezed my hand back, then rose to her feet. "It was a good plan. It almost worked."

Unfortunately for me, *almost* wasn't good enough when it came to the Mortan king.

"So what do we do now? Even if we did somehow get close enough to attack with our weapons, Maximus could always kill us with his weather magic," Cho pointed out. "He could easily bludgeon us with his hailstones the same way he did that arrow. Or freeze us to death with his cold lightning."

We all fell silent, contemplating those horrible possibilities. I leaned back against the pillows, trying to ignore how tired I still felt.

"Maximus isn't the only one we need to worry about," I said. "We need to be careful of Driscol too."

"Why?" Paloma asked. "Driscol is just Maximus's lackey. We all saw the two of them whispering on the terrace. We all know that Driscol is working for the Mortans instead of being neutral like he's supposed to be."

"I agree that Maximus probably told Driscol to send those assassins to kill Serilda in the plaza."

"But?" Serilda asked.

"But just because Driscol is working for Maximus doesn't mean that he's not playing his own game and furthering his own agenda," I said.

"What do you mean?" Cho asked.

"Maximus might have wanted those assassins to kill Serilda, but I don't think that's what Driscol ordered them to do. At least, not the last woman, the one who cut me. I think she was trying to capture me, just like the geldjagers tried to in Svalin."

Auster frowned. "Why would you think that?"

I gestured at my healed arm. "Because she used blue sperren. If she had truly wanted to kill me, then her dagger would have been coated with wormroot or amethyst-eye or another deadly poison, like some of the other assassins' blades were. Blue sperren can be fatal, but more often than not it just paralyzes people until you give them the antidote."

"Blue sperren," Sullivan muttered. "Of course. Helene told me about it once. I should have recognized it as soon as your lips turned blue."

Helene Blume was a childhood friend of Sullivan's and a powerful plant magier, so it made sense that she had encountered blue sperren.

Serilda's eyes darkened, and the scent of her magic gusted around her. "Evie's right," she murmured. "I don't think that last assassin wanted to kill you. Not unless you gave her no other choice. Otherwise, she would have rushed at you sooner and tried harder to immediately cut you down. But what was Driscol planning to do with you?"

"Ransom?" Auster suggested. "Maybe he wanted to trade Evie for a quick payday. Maybe he got greedy and thought his men could kill Serilda and kidnap Evie at the same time."

"The DiLucris already have plenty of gold," Paloma pointed out. "Their whole bloody Mint is covered with coins."

"Maybe they wanted to sicken Evie so we would turn to them for help," Serilda suggested. "Maybe they thought we would be stupid enough to let her out of our sight. Maybe they hoped to steal her away in the confusion. Or maybe Driscol thought Maximus would give him an even greater reward if he brought her to the king alive. The possibilities are endless."

"Endless, maybe, but they all end pretty badly for me," I muttered.

"I can make Driscol talk," Sullivan snarled, blue lightning crackling around his clenched fists. "Get him to confess his scheme."

"It wouldn't do any good," I replied. "Fortuna is like a kingdom unto itself, and the DiLucris are well protected on their island. Besides, they'll be expecting us to retaliate, and Driscol will be even more well guarded now. We can't afford to go to war with both the DiLucris and the Mortans at the same time, especially not this far from home. No, we stick to our original plan of trying to kill Maximus. He's still the biggest threat to us, to Bellona. He might have escaped our first trap, but we can set another one for him."

My friends fell silent, but the scent of their collective dusty resignation slowly filled the tent. They knew that we couldn't strike back at the DiLucris. Not without making the situation even more dangerous.

"Well, Driscol and Maximus and whatever they're plotting are problems for tomorrow," Auster said. "I need to send a messenger over to the island to tell the other royals that you're too ill to attend the ball."

"Oh, I'm still going to the ball."

Paloma, Sullivan, Cho, and Auster looked at me with surprise, but Serilda nodded, a thoughtful expression on her face. Her magic must have already told her that I still planned to attend. Well, that and the fact she knew how stubborn I was.

Sullivan surged to his feet and threw his hand out, gesturing at the bed I was still sitting on. "Twenty minutes ago, you were unconscious. You should forget about the ball, stay here, and rest."

"Believe me, I would much rather spend the evening in bed, but I have to attend the ball, and I have to participate in the kronekling tournament. If I don't go, then everyone will realize just how close that last assassin came to killing, kidnapping, or whatever she was trying to do to me."

No one responded, but once again the collective scent of their worry filled the air.

"I need to show Maximus, Driscol, and everyone else that I'm fine, and that it takes more than a fight with a few assassins to hurt me. I can't show *any* sign of weakness. Otherwise, Maximus and Driscol will just keep sending assassins until one of them gets lucky and finally kills me. We need to make the bastards think twice about coming after me again. We need to make them hesitate. That's the only way we're going to get an advantage over them."

Sullivan's lips pressed together into a tight, unhappy line, but he didn't argue. Neither did Paloma, Serilda, Cho, or Auster. They all knew how important this was.

"I'm going to the ball," I repeated. "So go get Calandre so she can help me get ready."

CHAPTER THIRTEEN

Calandre didn't like the thought of my going to the ball either, but she and her sisters prepared me for the evening.

The thread master outfitted me in a beautiful gown made of
light gray silk. The dress had a boat neck and sleeves that stopped
at my elbows to show off the silver bracelets—gauntlets—on my
wrists. Two large crisscrossed swords done in bright silver
thread glittered in the center of the bodice, while the same sword
pattern circled the small band around my waist before spreading
down and covering the long, full skirt. The sword pattern could
also be seen in sparkling silver thread on the closed toes of my
gray sandals.

"I modeled the swords on your dress after the ones on the
Seven Spire columns," Calandre said in a proud voice. "I wanted
you to take some of our gladiator tradition with you to the ball."

I smoothed my hands down the skirt. "It's beautiful."

Calandre beamed at me, then stepped back so her sisters
could do their part. Cerana curled my black hair into loose, pretty
waves, while Camille covered my eyes with shimmering silver

powder and liner and added some deep plum-colored berry balm to my lips.

Once they finished, I studied my reflection in the mirror over the vanity table. Cerana and Camille had done a masterful job, and not a trace of paleness remained in my face from the blood loss or the poison. Perhaps knowing that I looked better made me feel better as well, because the last dregs of my lethargy finally, fully vanished.

I thanked Calandre and her sisters, then shooed them out of the tent. When I was sure they were gone, I went over to a wooden jewelry box sitting on one of the tables. I opened the top and pressed on a button hidden inside the purple velvet lining. A secret drawer popped out of the bottom of the box, revealing a small glass vial. I held the vial up to the light, studying the clear liquid inside.

Wormroot.

Sullivan had distilled the poison before we'd left Seven Spire, and I had tucked it away in this jewelry box, which had belonged to Maeven. It had seemed like an appropriate hiding spot, given that she had used the same poison to murder the Blairs.

Auster was right. As a group, we couldn't get close enough to cut down Maximus with our weapons, but perhaps I, as the queen, could do the deed on the sly. I would much rather risk myself than my friends again, which was why I wasn't going to tell them that I was carrying the wormroot. Perhaps an opportunity would present itself for me to poison the king during the ball. My fingers curled around the vial. I hoped so.

I slipped the poison into my dress pocket, then stepped outside where my friends were waiting.

Sullivan was sporting dark gray leggings and boots, along with one of Calandre's designs—a short, formal light gray jacket with silver buttons that featured the same sword pattern as my dress. An actual sword dangled from his belt, along with a dagger.

Paloma was wearing a dark green tunic with gold thread stitched in a jagged zigzag pattern that looked like teeth circling her neck and eating down her sleeves. Her blond hair was done up in a lovely crown braid, while golden shadow and liner brought out her amber eyes. Her mace dangled off her belt like usual.

Serilda was dressed in a white tunic with a black swan stretching across her chest, along with white leggings and black knee-high boots. Her blond hair was slicked back from her face, and black shadow ringed her blue eyes. She too was wearing her usual sword and dagger on her belt.

Cho had changed into a fresh ringmaster's uniform of a red jacket over a ruffled white shirt. He didn't have a weapon, but he didn't need one. As a dragon morph, he could easily shift into his other, larger, stronger form and be more than a match for any enemy.

Captain Auster was sporting a sword, along with a light gray jacket that featured my crown-of-shards crest done in silver thread over his heart. Several guards also wearing gray jackets and swords waited in the distance.

Sullivan took my hand and pressed a kiss to my knuckles. "You look lovely, highness," he whispered in a husky voice.

He straightened, and I smoothed my hands down the front of his jacket, feeling the heat of his body radiate out into mine. "You look pretty handsome yourself."

I drew in a breath, letting his vanilla scent sink deep into my lungs. Sullivan grinned, his eyes as bright as blue stars.

Captain Auster cleared his throat. "Anytime you're ready, my queen."

I took Sullivan's arm and headed toward the steps that led from our campsite down to the river. We quickly made our way across the plaza with its Seven Spire–shaped fountain and over to the Perseverance Bridge. I stopped and gestured at Auster, who strode forward.

"Keep half the guards here at this end of the bridge. When we get over to the island, post the remaining guards at that end of the bridge," I said.

Auster frowned. "But I was going to send them all with you. To ensure your safety during the ball."

I gave him a grim smile. "Nothing can ensure my safety. We could take a hundred guards, and the Mortans would still try to kill me. Besides, I can't afford to appear scared, frightened, or worried. Not tonight when everyone will be watching. So no legion of guards."

Auster didn't like it, but he gave me a reluctant nod.

"I also can't afford to get trapped on the island," I continued. "I want the guards stationed at both ends of the bridge to make sure that we can get back across the river to Bellona after the ball."

Auster nodded again. "As you wish, my queen."

The captain ordered some of his men to take up their position here, while the rest of us stepped onto the bridge. Auster and the remaining guards followed us.

The sun was setting, and the golden rays had turned the tearstone expanse the same dazzling light gray as my dress, while the surface of the water gleamed like a bed of moving, sparkling sapphires. Farther out, the ships in the harbor bobbed up and down on the waves, and their colorful crested flags snapped to and fro in the cool, steady breeze.

Despite the lovely, picturesque scene, I couldn't help but notice the shadows slowly creeping over everything. Or perhaps those were simply reflections of my own dark thoughts about the danger that waited for us on the island.

Still, it was a pleasant walk, and my friends chatted back and forth, telling me how the Bellonans had done in today's Regalia events. My countrymen and -women had acquitted themselves quite nicely, winning and placing in several competitions for the cook, thread, plant, metalstone, and other masters. Nico, Diante's grandson, had won the archery tournament, one of the day's big events. I made a mental note to congratulate him and his grandmother the next time I saw them.

We were almost to the end of the bridge when I noticed a ship anchored all by itself near the middle of the harbor. It was a relatively small vessel, the kind I would expect to be much closer to shore, given the violent waves that sometimes rocked the water. Even stranger than its location was the fact that it wasn't flying any flags, and no sailors were working on deck. It almost seemed like the ship was deserted, although someone would have had to sail it out to its current location. Maybe the crew and the passengers had gone over to the island to cap off the Regalia's opening day by celebrating in the gaming and pleasure houses. Either way, the ship wasn't a threat, since it was so far away from the bridge, so I put it out of my mind.

We stopped at the opposite end of the bridge so Auster could give a few final orders to the guards. Then we left them behind and stepped onto the island.

The plazas and the boulevard had been crowded during the day, but they were absolutely packed with people this evening. The sour smell of wine and other spirits filled the air, and the crowd was much more raucous than before. The winners of the day's events were celebrating their victories, while the losers were drowning their sorrows.

My friends and I kept an eye out for trouble, in case Maximus or Driscol had sent more assassins, but no one approached or seemed to be watching us, and we left the waterfront behind and climbed the steps to the top of the island.

Captain Auster led us to the plaza that surrounded the

Pinnaculum arena, then headed into a nearby series of gardens filled with flowers, trees, benches, and fountains. A few minutes later, we stepped onto a new path, and the gardens fell away, revealing a castle looming up from the landscape.

"And this," Auster muttered, "is the DiLucris' not-so-humble home."

The DiLucri family castle was made of the same glowing white stone as the Mint, but it wasn't nearly as large or covered with garish gold coins. This was a far more tasteful, elegant structure, with gleaming windows, fluted columns, and other bits of artistry. The floors and wings led up to several slender towers, each one topped with a white flag that featured a gold coined-woman crest. More flags were planted along the cobblestone walkway that led to the castle.

We fell in with the steady stream of people heading toward the castle. Since this was a royal ball, everyone was dressed in formal jackets, gowns, and glittering jewels, although nothing too large or ostentatious. Calandre had told me that the jackets, gowns, and jewels would get more elaborate, colorful, and expensive as the Regalia went on, with everyone saving their most dazzling items for the third and final ball.

Still, the lords, ladies, and jewels weren't nearly as impressive as the castle. White marble floors polished to a high gloss. Paintings and mirrors in gold frames. Chandeliers made of sparkling crystals. Something glittered, glistened, and gleamed everywhere I looked, and almost as much wealth was on display here as there was in Glitnir, the Andvarian royal palace.

But it was easy to tell that this castle belonged to the DiLucris, given all the images of the coined woman. The crest was carved, emblazoned, and stamped onto almost everything, from the floors to the walls to the frescoes that stretched across the ceilings. Something that was perfectly normal, as many royals, nobles, and merchants proudly displayed their crests, including myself with my own crown of shards. But the longer I stared at the symbols, the sorrier I felt for the woman depicted in them. It almost seemed like the coins in Lady Fortuna's eyes and mouth were slowly growing larger and larger and threatening to swallow her up completely until there was nothing left of her features but a golden gleam.

Paloma noticed me eyeing the furnishings. "The DiLucris really like their crest, don't they?" she murmured. "Well, I think it's creepy. That poor woman seems like she's screaming and pleading with the gods to free her, only no one can hear her cries due to all that suffocating gold." She shuddered, and the ogre on her neck scrunched up its face in displeasure.

We walked on and eventually reached the grand ballroom. The large rectangular area was made of the same glowing white stone as the rest of the castle, although the ceiling was a round dome with milky panes of glass held together with thick golden seams. Banners featuring the royal crests of each one of the seven kingdoms dangled from the second-floor balcony that wrapped around the ballroom, while a single, much larger white banner bearing the DiLucris' gold coined woman dropped down from the crystal chandelier in the center of the ceiling.

A faint, steady *tinkle-tinkle-tinkle* caught my ear, and I noticed a white stone fountain in the corner. This fountain was a smaller version of the one in front of the Mint, and it also featured a golden statute of Lady Fortuna with her arms held upward. Only instead of water, gold coins spewed out of the woman's lips, as well as dripped out of her eyes like tears. And not just Fortunan coins. I spotted dragon-stamped Ryusaman coins, as well as those bearing Ungerian ogres, Andvarian gargoyles, Mortan strixes, and Bellonan swords.

Tinkle-tinkle-tinkle. The incessant sound of all those coins softly clattering together made me shiver. I'd never thought that was a particularly sinister sound until right now.

My friends and I must have been among the last to arrive, because hundreds of people had already filled the ballroom. Some wandered along the buffet tables, picking and choosing various delicacies, while others stood in small groups, sipping champagne and other spirits while they gossiped. Servants moved around, fetching whatever was required, while guards stood along the edges of the room.

It was easy to pick the other royals out of the crowd, given the clusters of people hovering around them. My gaze moved from one royal and entourage to the next. Eon, Ruri, Cisco, Heinrich, Zariza. All the other kings and queens had already arrived—except for Maximus.

The Mortan king wasn't here, and neither were Mercer, Nox, or Maeven. Maximus must be waiting to make a grand entrance just like he had in the arena. I wondered if he would plow one of his strixes down through the glass ceiling and land in the center of the ballroom. Probably, given his enormous ego.

"So, highness," Sullivan murmured. "Who do you want to attack first?"

I scanned the ballroom. "Well, since the Mortans aren't here yet, let's go visit our esteemed host."

Sullivan grinned, and we headed in that direction.

Driscol DiLucri was holding court in the center of the ballroom. He was wearing a short white jacket over a white tunic and sandy brown leggings and boots, just as he had been earlier, although these garments featured even more gold thread and buttons. Driscol was talking loudly and gesturing wildly with a glass of champagne, telling some story.

Seraphine was standing beside him, also holding a glass of champagne, and looking vaguely bored. A long white gown flowed around her body like watery silk, and her only jewelry was the same choker of gold coins that she'd worn to the opening ceremonies. Her simple, understated elegance made her look as regal as a queen standing next to her garish jester of a brother.

Driscol spied me heading toward them. He froze for a moment right in the middle of his story, then finished it with a rush of words and a weak laugh. He whispered something to Seraphine, who shrugged. She seemed as unimpressed by my arrival as she was by everything else.

At my appearance, murmurs rippled through the crowd, and the nobles standing around Driscol fell back, although they watched us with great interest.

"Queen Everleigh," Driscol said. "I didn't expect you to attend the ball, given the . . . unpleasantness in the plaza earlier."

I gave him my brightest, most dazzling smile. "Oh, Driscol. It takes more than a few assassins to stop me from attending a royal ball. I've grown rather used to people trying to kill me and my friends. The perils of being queen." I let out a hearty chuckle, as though I found the whole situation highly amusing.

Driscol glanced at Seraphine, who responded by taking a sip of her champagne. She didn't offer him any help, so he focused on me again.

"Well, I'm so glad that you could attend." He waved his hand. "Please, get something to eat, drink, anything you like. The kronekling tournament won't start for another half hour. Now, if you'll excuse me, I need to greet my other guests."

Driscol gave me a tight smile, then hurried away, with Seraphine gliding along behind him.

"Spread out and see what gossip you can pick up about the attack," I murmured to my friends. "I'm going to speak to the other royals."

Being queen was about far more than just plotting to kill your enemies. I had come to the Regalia with a three-pronged attack in mind to accomplish three separate things: crush the king, advance Bellona's fortunes, and manipulate Maeven.

The first part of my strategy might be focused on assassinating Maximus, but the second part—showing strength and cleverness and securing alliances with the other royals—was equally important and what I needed to concentrate on tonight.

Paloma, Serilda, Cho, and Auster all headed off in different directions, but Sullivan stayed by my side and offered me his arm again.

"Allow me to escort you, highness. After all, it is my duty as your consort."

"Duty?" I sighed. "You make it sound exactly as miserable as it's going to be."

"Well, there are other, private duties I enjoy far more." His teasing tone and the wicked glint in his eyes made my stomach clench in anticipation, as well as cut through some of my dread and worry.

I stepped closer to him and stared up into his blue, blue eyes. "Perhaps we can discuss those duties in greater detail later on tonight."

His eyes brightened. "Count on it, highness."

As much as I would have loved to drag him into some shadowy corner of the castle and kiss him senseless, I had my own duty to attend to, so I plastered a smile on my face and strode forward.

My meeting with Driscol must have attracted more attention than I'd realized, because sharp whispers and sly comments surged through the ballroom, trailing after us like sharks racing after a school of fish.

"Look! The Bellonan queen is here!"

"Wasn't she attacked earlier?"

"I thought she was dead."

That last comment made me grimace, but I forced my smile back up into place, and Sullivan and I walked on.

A few feet away, Eon and Ruri were talking and sipping

champagne. Eon was wearing a short-sleeve, floor-length green robe, along with gold sandals. Gold bangles set with emeralds, rubies, and other gems were stacked up on his wrists, and a gold machete dangled from his wide gold belt. My nose twitched. The scent of magic wafted off each and every one of his jewels. Emeralds to increase his speed, rubies to augment his strength, and so on. The aromas swirled together into one thick blanket of power, but the strongest one was the scent of Eon's own fire magic, which smoldered like a hot ember.

Instead of a gown, Ruri was sporting black boots and tight black leggings that showed off her strong, slender figure, along with a ruffled white shirt topped with a knee-length emerald-green jacket covered with dragons done in gold thread. An exquisite gold ring shaped like a flying dragon stretched across all four of her left fingers, and her inner dragon's face of emerald-green scales was once again clearly visible on that same hand.

The Vacunan king and the Ryusaman queen were both loosely surrounded by nobles from their own kingdoms, as well as their consorts. Eon's wife, Jari, was a beautiful woman with a shaved head, hazel eyes, and ebony skin who was almost as tall as Eon was, while Ruri's husband, Riko, had silver hair, gray eyes, and golden skin. The dragon's face on his neck had a combination of silver and golden scales.

I tipped my head to the king, the queen, and their respective consorts. "King Eon, Queen Ruri. So lovely to see you again. As well as your stunning companions. Jari, Riko."

The two consorts smiled at me, and I returned the gesture.

"It's lovely to see you again as well, Queen Everleigh," Eon rumbled in his deep, gravelly voice. "We weren't sure whether you were going to attend."

"Especially after that unpleasantness down by the waterfront earlier," Ruri added in a much lighter tone.

I was getting tired of everyone referring to the assassination attempt as mere *unpleasantness,* but I forced myself to smile even wider. "Yes, well, it takes more than a bit of unpleasantness to keep me down for long."

Eon had one of his servants fetch a glass of champagne for me, as well as one for Sullivan, and we chatted with the two other royals, along with their consorts. We talked about the Regalia, the weather, and all the other usual polite, inane chitchat one would make at a ball.

"I wish to extend my condolences on the deaths of Queen Cordelia, Princess Madelena, and everyone else who was lost at Seven Spire," Eon said, finally getting down to business.

Ruri murmured her agreement.

"Thank you." I drew in a breath to steady my nerves, then launched into my verbal attack. "I wanted to speak to you both about the massacre. Namely, how we can prevent it from ever happening again."

Ruri frowned. "What do you mean?"

"Maximus was behind the Seven Spire massacre. His relatives carried it out on *his* orders. In a single afternoon, Mortan assassins almost wiped out the entire Blair royal family, and Maximus tried to do something similar to the Ripleys in Andvari a few months ago. It wouldn't surprise me if he turns his attention to Vacuna and Ryusama next."

Both rulers blinked in surprise. They hadn't expected me to speak so frankly, so harshly, at a royal ball, but I didn't have time to tiptoe around and follow proper protocol. I needed to secure their help as soon as possible before Maximus tried to kill me again.

"Surely the attack at Seven Spire was an unfortunate, isolated incident," Eon said, trying to be diplomatic.

I gave him a flat stare. "I was there, Eon. I witnessed that horrible day, and there was nothing unfortunate or isolated about it. The Seven Spire massacre was a carefully planned attack on the Blair family, on Bellona. And for the most part, it succeeded. The Mortan conspirators and their turncoat guards slaughtered my cousins with no hesitation and no remorse. Men, women, children. No one was spared."

Eon didn't have a response to that, but Ruri gave me a thoughtful look, as did the green dragon on her hand.

"We've all heard about the Seven Spire massacre," she murmured. "I imagine that's one of the reasons why you tried to have Maximus killed right after he landed in the arena."

Even though I had been expecting one or both of them to mention the earlier incident, I still had to work very hard to keep from showing any emotion. The spectators might have thought that the arrow had been a lark, or part of some act, but Ruri and Eon knew better. Then again, queens and kings were more cognizant about people trying to kill them.

Still, I had no alliance or friendship with either one of them—not yet—and I knew better than to be loose with my words and brag about what I'd done. Not that there was anything to brag about, since my assassination attempt had failed.

"Maximus was attacked before the opening ceremonies, and my friends and I were besieged by assassins afterward," I replied in a neutral tone. "You can both draw your own conclusions about the incidents and how they might impact your own safety during the Regalia."

Eon remained silent, but Ruri spoke up again.

"My conclusion is that I might have done the same, should such a terrible tragedy have befallen my family," she murmured, and the dragon on her hand peered up at me with what seemed like sympathy.

She had given me an opening, so I stepped even closer to the two rulers, letting them see exactly how serious I was. "The Morricones have *always* been a threat to the other kingdoms.

Maximus has *always* wanted more land, magic, and resources. At Seven Spire, he showed exactly how far he's willing to go to get what he wants. He won't rest until he has control of all seven kingdoms."

They didn't say anything, but the scent of their collective worry filled my nose. They didn't disagree with me. They couldn't because they'd had the same dark thoughts themselves. Kings and queens always had to worry about someone trying to take their thrones. It was the only way they survived for any length of time.

"What are you proposing?" Ruri asked.

I looked at the dragon on her hand, then up at her face, speaking to both of them. "I want you and Eon to align with me, with Bellona. I want you to promise aid if Morta ever attacks or invades Bellona or Andvari."

Both royals frowned at each other, then looked at me again.

"And why should we agree to such a deal?" Eon asked. "How does it benefit *us*? Bellona does not have a large navy, and Andvari doesn't have one at all. So how can they help us? We have our own problems. Pirates, sea monsters, and the like."

"I don't have many ships, but I have other resources," I countered. "Coldiron, timber, fluorestones, coal. Things your kingdoms have in limited supplies. You help me, and I help you. It's as simple as that."

"Vacuna and Ryusama have helped each other for centuries," Ruri pointed out. "And our two kingdoms have flourished together. So why upset that balance? Why should we help Bellona? Or Andvari?"

"Because if you don't, and Maximus continues on his current path, then he will conquer both Bellona and Andvari, and maybe Unger too. And when he finishes with us, he will turn his gaze to your kingdoms. You might think the sea will shield Vacuna and Ryusama from Morta. And it might, for a time. But that water is not nearly deep or wide enough to thwart Maximus's ambition and greed."

Eon still looked doubtful, but agreement flashed in Ruri's green eyes. Then again, Ryusama was much closer to Morta than Vacuna was.

I sensed an opportunity to sway them, so I kept talking. "The Mortans attacked my queen, my family, in our palace, in the very *heart* of Bellona. And they will do the exact same thing to you the second they get the chance. The Mortans will slaughter you, your consorts, and your children without a second thought. So think about that when you lie down to sleep tonight—if you can sleep at all."

My dire warning delivered, I respectfully bowed my head to the king and queen, along with their consorts. Sullivan offered me his arm again, and the two of us strolled away.

"What do you think?" I asked.

He turned his head so that he could see the two royals. "They're talking to each other. They both look worried, as do their consorts. If nothing else, you gave them something to think about."

Well, it was a start and probably the best I could hope for tonight, so we moved on.

King Cisco of Flores was wearing a long tan coat over a light green tunic and tan leggings and boots. A large pendant of a gold horse with topaz eyes running through a topaz wheat field hung from a thick gold chain around his neck, and several gold rings also shaped like horses and studded with emeralds and rubies adorned his fingers, almost as if animals were galloping across his knuckles. The scent of beauty, strength, and other glamours wafted off the jewels.

Cisco was a cousin to Lord Durante, who had tried to save Princess Madelena, his pregnant wife, during the Seven Spire massacre, although Vasilia had eventually killed them both. Several months ago, I had sent Cisco a letter expressing my condolences for Durante's death, but he had not responded.

I stopped and nodded at Cisco, trying to engage him in some benign communication. The Floresian king stared at me a moment, then deliberately turned his back, indicating that he didn't want to speak to me.

A few nobles gasped at the obvious insult, but I kept my pleasant smile fixed on my face, as though Cisco's snub didn't bother me. Right now it was a minor annoyance. Flores might have wheat fields and grape vines galore, but they didn't have much of an army. I didn't need an alliance with Flores as badly as I did with Vacuna, Ryusama, and especially Unger, so I swept past Cisco.

Our next stop was Heinrich, Dominic, and Rhea, who were standing close to the buffet tables. The two men looked quite handsome in their dark gray jackets, while Rhea was absolutely stunning in an emerald-green gown that highlighted her strong, beautiful curves.

The captain might have dressed up for the ball, but she hadn't abandoned her duties any more than Paloma and Auster had. Two daggers were holstered to the thin silver belt that circled her waist, and I was willing to bet that she had at least two more strapped to her shins underneath her long skirt. Several Andvarian guards were also lurking nearby, ready to spring into action if anyone threatened their king and prince.

"Finally, some friendly faces," I drawled.

Heinrich, Dominic, and Rhea all laughed at my joke, but their chuckles quickly faded away, and their faces grew watchful and serious again.

"I see that Cisco openly snubbed you, but that was to be expected," Heinrich murmured, studying the other king over the rim of his champagne glass. "He's always been jealous of

Bellona's mines and timber, and he never got along with Cordelia. That old fool is so desperate and greedy for the things he doesn't have that he doesn't realize Maximus is planning to take away everything he does have."

"But Eon and Ruri spoke to you at length," Dominic said. "How did that go?"

I shrugged. "I asked them to align with us and told them the Morricones will murder us all if they don't. We'll see if they take my warning to heart."

"An alliance would have been much easier to come by if your assassin's arrow had found Maximus's throat earlier," Heinrich murmured. "Bold of you to attack him so soon. Even I didn't expect that from you, Everleigh. I think it earned you quite a bit of respect with everyone, even Cisco."

Heinrich studied me with sharp, shrewd eyes, but once again I kept my face blank, neither confirming nor denying that I had anything to do with the attack on Maximus. Heinrich might be my friend, but I didn't want to put him in a position where he had to lie to the other royals or his own people.

A courtier came up and whispered something in Heinrich's ear, and he moved off to speak with the man. That left Sullivan and me standing with Dominic and Rhea.

I didn't want to dodge any more awkward questions, so I turned to the other woman and changed the subject. "You look beautiful."

"As do you." Rhea smoothed down her skirt. "It's nice to get dressed up, although I would much rather be wearing my sword and fighting leathers."

"You'll be wearing both of those all day tomorrow during the tournament." Dominic curled his arm around her waist. "And I will be cheering you on the whole time."

Rhea nudged him with her elbow. "You'd better cheer, if you know what's good for you."

Dominic pulled her a bit closer. "Oh, I certainly do," he said in a low, husky voice.

She nudged him again, but her eyes were warm and luminous, and the scent of their rosy love for each other swirled through the air.

Sullivan discreetly pointed his finger to the side. "Xenia's waving at us."

I glanced in that direction. Xenia was standing with Zariza, and she tapped her silver ogre cane on the floor in a clear indication that we should come over there *right now*. Sullivan and I both wished Rhea good luck in the tournament tomorrow, said our goodbyes to Dominic, and headed over to the Ungers.

I hadn't seen Xenia since she had left with the Ungers after the opening ceremonies, but she looked lovely in a dark green velvet gown patterned with tiny ogre faces done in silver thread. Her amber gaze swept over me from head to toe, and the ogre on her neck peered at me as well, as though they were both making sure I was okay after the plaza attack. She must have been satisfied that I was all right, because she relaxed a bit, and the ogre's worried expression smoothed out as well.

I nodded at Xenia, then turned my attention to her cousin.

Even among the many beautiful women here, Queen Zariza was in a class by herself. She looked absolutely stunning in a green gown that brought out the deep, rich color of her glorious red hair, which cascaded in loose waves past her shoulders. The slits in the bottom of the gown offered teasing glimpses of her long, toned legs, while the deep, plunging neckline showed off her cleavage to its maximum effect.

A thick gold chain ringed her neck, along with a gold pendant shaped like a snarling ogre face that was bigger than my palm. Emerald eyes had been set in the ogre's face, along with glittering diamond and ruby teeth, as though the creature had just taken a bloody bite out of someone. The ogre rose and fell and seemed to stare at me with every breath Zariza took, as did the morph mark on her neck.

"Queen Zariza, Lady Xenia." I tipped my head to them. "You both look lovely."

"I always look lovely," Zariza said in a matter-of-fact tone.

"I'm sure you think so."

The words popped out of my mouth before I could stop them. Xenia grimaced, while Zariza arched an eyebrow at me.

I hadn't meant to be quite so catty, but I couldn't apologize. If Zariza thought I was some meek little thing, some weak queen who cowed at an angry look or a stinging rebuke, she would never align with me. No, I needed to be just as bold as Zariza herself was, insults and all.

"I'm so glad we're finally getting a chance to talk," I said, preparing to launch into the same speech I had given Eon and Ruri. "We both know that the Mortans are a serious threat—"

"Is it true that you're a dancer?" Zariza asked, cutting in and cutting me off.

I blinked, surprised by the change in topic. I had expected some pointed questions about my attack on Maximus, not an inquiry about my dancing skills.

"Oh, it's true," Xenia smoothly answered for me. "Why, earlier this year, Everleigh performed the most beautiful rendition of the Tanzen Freund that I have ever seen."

"Even more beautiful than the one I did for your sixtieth birthday a few years ago?" Zariza challenged.

"Yes," Xenia said without hesitation. "You stumbled in the final section, remember? Queen Everleigh did not. Plus, your hand movements were terribly sloppy. I taught you better than that, but apparently you had forgotten all my lessons. Everleigh did not."

I grimaced, really wishing that she would stop saying my name. I didn't know what game Xenia was playing with her cousin, but hot, peppery anger blasted off Zariza, and the amber eyes of her inner ogre narrowed to thin slits. I might have insulted the queen, but Xenia had enraged her.

The Ungerian queen eyed her cousin a moment longer, then looked at me. "Tell me, Everleigh. Do you also know the Tanzen Falter?"

I had to bite my tongue to hold back a groan. Xenia had said that Zariza would challenge me to perform the Tanzen Falter during the Regalia. I just hadn't thought it would be at one of the balls in front of everyone. I should have known better, though. The Ungers loved dancing as much as they did fighting. To them, they were one and the same.

"Why are you asking her that?" Xenia said in a sharp tone, once again answering for me, and obviously steering the conversation in the direction she wanted it to go. "What do you expect? That Everleigh will agree to perform the dance right here and now?"

Zariza took a sip of her apple brandy, then used the glass to gesture around the ballroom. "We have a dance floor, musicians, and an audience of Ungers to judge the competition. That's all we need."

Xenia's lips pressed together, as though she were most unhappy, but she reeked of smug triumph. Zariza was doing exactly what the older woman wanted. The two of them seemed to have a very strange relationship, one that was a mix of competition and affection, much like Xenia's was with Serilda.

"You must forgive Zariza," Xenia said. "She's so used to getting her own way that she doesn't realize we aren't in Unger right now."

Zariza sniffed, dismissing her cousin's argument, then focused on me again. "Regardless, my point remains the same. So, Everleigh, will you perform the Tanzen Falter? That way, we can settle this silly nonsense about who is the best dancer once and for all."

More smug satisfaction rolled off of Xenia, but I bit back another groan. Why couldn't someone, *anyone*, just bloody align with me because it was the right thing to do? But no, we royals had to duel with cutting words and dirty looks. And now, apparently, another bloody dance. I wondered if Zariza would try to have me executed if she won, as was the Ungerian tradition. Probably not, given the fact that Paloma and Captain Auster were lurking nearby. Well, that was something, I supposed.

Still, if I was going to dance to Zariza's tune, then I was getting something in return. Something other than sore, tired, aching feet.

"Very well. I will perform the Tanzen Falter—on one condition."

Zariza arched her eyebrow again. "What?"

I looked at the ogre on her neck, then at her face, just like I had done with Ruri earlier. "If I win, then you will publicly, formally align Unger with Bellona and Andvari right here and now in front of everyone."

Zariza arched her eyebrow even higher, then glanced at her cousin.

Xenia shrugged, although she couldn't quite hide her grin. "I told you she was bold. You're the one who suggested the dance. It is only fair that Everleigh suggest the prize."

Zariza sniffed again. "And what do I get if *I* win?"

I racked my brain, trying to come up with something significant that wouldn't be seen as an insult, given what was at stake on her side. Desperate, I glanced at Xenia, who shrugged. She might have set this up, but she couldn't help me with the prize. Still, the longer I stared at Xenia, the more I thought about

Castle Asmund, her home, where I had performed the Tanzen Freund. An idea popped into my mind.

"I'll give you Winterwind, my family's estate in the Spire Mountains. It's not too far from Unger. You could turn it into a summer retreat, if you like." I didn't mention the fact that the property had been in ruins ever since the Mortans had killed my parents.

"A summer home in Bellona." Her face brightened. "I like the sound of that. Deal."

She stuck out her hand, and we shook on it. I started to let go, but Zariza tightened her grip and stepped closer.

"I hope you can dance as well as my cousin says," she purred. "Otherwise I'm going to be very disappointed in you, Everleigh."

I wasn't sure whether the words were a threat, but I decided to respond in kind. "Oh, you're going to be disappointed—when you lose."

She blinked, as did the ogre on her neck. Both narrowed their eyes, and they studied me more closely, as though they were truly seeing me for the first time.

"Oh, yes," Zariza purred again. "This is going to be *fun*."

For the third time in as many minutes, all I could do was bite back a groan.

CHAPTER FOURTEEN

Zariza strode out to the center of the room, clapped her hands, and announced that she was commandeering the area for the Tanzen Falter.

Driscol looked absolutely shocked that someone would dare usurp his ball, and he kept opening and closing his mouth, as if he didn't know what to say. Zariza's pronouncement also wiped the vacant smile off Seraphine's face, and her lips puckered, as though she'd bitten into something sour.

My nose twitched. This was the first time I'd seen Seraphine show any real emotion, and I could smell her hot, peppery anger all the way across the room. She was royally pissed that Zariza had taken over the ball. Interesting. I would have expected Driscol to be the angriest, since he was the head of their family, but he seemed lost more than anything else, and he kept glancing at his sister, as if she could somehow stop this.

But there was no stopping Zariza. The Ungerian queen ignored the DiLucris, ordered the floor to be cleared, and went over to talk to the musicians.

Sullivan and I were still standing next to Xenia, and Paloma and Auster came over to us, as did Serilda and Cho.

I crossed my arms over my chest and gave Xenia a flat look. "You said that Zariza would challenge me to perform the Tanzen Falter during a private meeting. Not that you were going to manipulate us into dancing at a royal ball. This is *not* what we discussed."

Xenia shrugged. "I didn't manipulate anything. I merely suggested something that Zariza was already considering. She always challenges someone to dance during one of the balls, and I figured that it might as well be you."

"Wonderful."

She ignored my sarcasm. "Besides, this was the easiest and most expedient way to get your alliance. Especially since people keep trying to kill you. Don't you want Unger's support before you die?"

I sighed. As much as I hated to admit it, she had a point, and the chances of me making it through the Regalia alive were not good.

"Please tell me the penalty for losing this dance isn't immediate execution," Paloma said, glancing over at Zariza, who was still talking to the musicians.

"Nope," I replied. "Just the loss of my family's home."

"Ah," Paloma said, her voice as matter-of-fact as Xenia's had been. "A bargain, then."

Despite the fact that it was in ruins, the thought of losing Winterwind still filled me with despair, but Paloma was right. Losing a home was far better than losing my life. But in some ways, the stakes were much, much higher than if we had been dancing to the death. Gaining an alliance with Unger would help protect Bellona and all her people—including myself—from the Mortans.

Cho glanced at Xenia, then me. "So this is the dance she's been teaching you for the last several weeks."

"Teaching?" I snorted. "More like beating it into me with her bloody cane."

Xenia twirled her cane out to the side and dipped into a small curtsy before straightening. I gave her a sour look.

"Well, no matter the stakes, Zariza looks like she wants to win." Auster eyed the other queen, who was now stabbing her finger at the musicians, giving them order after order.

Zariza stabbed her finger at the musicians a final time, then strode out to the center of the ballroom. She made several sharp shooing motions with her hands, and people shuffled back, creating an opening around her.

Once Zariza was satisfied that there was enough room, she stepped out of her heels and scooted them off to the side. Then she planted her hands on her hips and raised her eyebrows, clearly daring me to step forward.

"Here we go again," I muttered.

But Xenia was right. This was the quickest, easiest, and least dangerous way to get what I wanted, so I stepped out of my own sandals and strode to the center of the dance floor. The other royals, nobles, advisors, servants, and guards tiptoed forward, trying to get the best view possible. I glanced around, but I didn't see Maximus, Maeven, or any of the Mortans. Well, at least they wouldn't be here to see me humiliate myself, if it came down to that.

I stopped about five feet away from Zariza and dropped into a traditional Bellonan curtsy. She responded with an Ungerian curtsy. Then we both straightened and raised our hands into the first position.

Zariza grinned, and the smell of her smug satisfaction swirled through the air. The Ungerian queen thought that I couldn't possibly beat her, especially not at her own kingdom's dance and tradition.

Anger sparked in my heart that she wasn't taking me seriously, and I latched on to the emotion. Zariza might be Xenia's cousin and a queen in her own right, but nobody dismissed me, and I was going to enjoy wiping that smirk off her face.

Winning was *always* the best revenge.

So I smiled back at her, showing even more teeth than the ogre on her neck was.

Showtime.

The opening strains of the music began. Zariza stared at me, and I looked right back at her.

Unlike the Tanzen Freund, which was to demonstrate friendship, the Tanzen Falter was a competition, pure and simple. The two dancers stared at each other while performing, and then, at the end, the audience decided the winner by clapping and cheering for the person they thought had done the best rendition. Whoever got the loudest and most enthusiastic applause won. Not an exact method, to be sure, but it was fair enough.

The music swelled like a tidal wave slowly rising, and Zariza lifted her arms a little higher, getting ready for the first section. I did the same.

And then we danced.

Almost immediately the music ramped up from a slow, sonorous waltz to a fast, lively reel. Zariza quickened her movements, and I did the same, never taking my eyes off her, not for a single second.

We both rose up on our toes and lifted our arms. Then, just as quickly, we snapped our arms down and rocked back on our heels in unison. The sounds of our bare feet touching down rang out like two swords clanging together, and the battle began in earnest.

That first loud, resounding *slap* of my feet on the floor unlocked my mind, and all the movements and steps of the

Tanzen Falter came rushing back to me. I had always loved dancing, and despite the high stakes, I was determined to fully enjoy this moment—and give everyone here a show they would never forget.

As the dance went on, my smile grew more genuine, and I lost myself in the rise and fall of the music, the ebb and flow of the steps, and the twists and turns of my arms, hands, and fingers flying through the air.

Up, down, right, left, twirl, twirl, twirl . . .

Point the right toe, then the left . . .

Then hop, hop, hop, hop . . .

We moved from the first section of the dance and into the second, then the third, then the fourth. The one good thing about the Tanzen Falter was that it was much shorter than the Tanzen Freund, only seven sections instead of thirteen, although the pace was much, much quicker. My endurance was exceptional, given all the long hours I had spent training and sparring with Serilda over the past several months, but even I found the dance to be extremely tiring.

Sweat quickly beaded on my temples and gathered in the small of my back underneath my gown. My cheeks felt hot, as did my feet, which started throbbing from my slamming them down onto the floor so many times. But I didn't care that I didn't look cool, queenly, and regal. No, all I cared about right now was *winning.* And not just to secure my alliance. I wanted to win for *me,* and for Xenia too. Because I had put the time, energy, and effort into learning the dance, and I wanted to show my excellent teacher that I had thoroughly mastered her lessons.

The longer we danced, the more I realized that I just might be able to triumph after all.

Somewhere around the middle of the second section, Zariza's smug smile slowly started to wilt. Somewhere around the third section, it vanished altogether, and by the fifth, it had been replaced with an intense frown as she concentrated on her own steps.

She was sweating, just like I was, but I could also smell her surprise. She hadn't thought that I knew the dance so well, or that I could keep up with her, or that I could match her move for move for move. She'd expected this to be an easy victory, but I was proving her wrong with every slap of my feet, twirl of my body, and slice of my hands through the air.

Zariza might not be smiling anymore, but I certainly was, and I even started humming along to the music, although no one could hear the soft sounds but me. Well, I thought no one could hear, but Zariza's amber eyes narrowed in anger. Her morph magic let her hear me humming, something she didn't have the breath or energy to do, and it further frustrated and infuriated her.

As the dance went on, the Ungers started enthusiastically clapping in time to the quick beat, just as they had the night I'd performed the Tanzen Freund. I laughed and kept dancing, letting the rhythm of the music sweep me away from everything else. All my worries about Maximus and Maeven. All my concerns about Bellona and her people. All my small, lingering fears, doubts, and insecurities about whether or not I was a strong queen, a good queen, a true Winter queen.

At this moment, there was nothing but the music and the dance.

Zariza also kept dancing, although her steps were now half a second slower than mine, which were still perfectly in sync with the music. My smile widened. That half a second might not seem like much, but it was going to trip her up at the very end.

And it did.

The seventh and final section of the dance was the fastest and hardest one of all, with more sharp toe points, elaborate hand movements, and prolonged twirls than all the other sections combined. I moved through the very last section, my feet flowing, my arms floating, and my body flying through the patterns, and Zariza's slight lack of speed finally caught up with her.

She started to twirl around, but her toes weren't in exactly the right position, and she wobbled, just a bit. At first I didn't think that her slight hiccup was even noticeable to the crowd, but gasps surged through the ballroom, all of them coming from the Ungerian contingent. The Ungers loved dancing just about more than anything else, so of course they had spotted her small mistake. Zariza growled in frustration, while I kept going, dancing and humming as though I hadn't seen or heard anything but the music.

That was the final twirl, and the dance ended a few seconds later with Zariza and me facing each other again, our arms and bodies in the same position as in the very beginning.

The music faded away, but Zariza and I kept staring at each other. This time, I smirked, knowing that I had won. She glowered back, but a sheepish expression slowly crept over her face. She curtsied to me, much lower than before, acknowledging my victory, then straightened. I returned the gesture with a low, respectful curtsy of my own.

Zariza waved to the crowd. Everyone politely clapped, but the Ungers weren't nearly as enthusiastic as they should have been. They had seen her mistake, even if everyone else hadn't.

She stepped back, and it was my turn to wave. The applause was just as polite for me, but the Ungers were much more enthusiastic, and everyone could hear that I was the clear winner. Still smiling wide, I dipped into another curtsy, acknowledging the applause and savoring my victory.

Zariza signaled to the musicians that they could take a break, and everyone started milling around the ballroom again, eating, drinking, and gossiping, although many folks kept glancing at the two of us, wondering how one queen would handle being defeated by another.

Xenia stepped up to Zariza's side, while Sullivan did the same for me. Paloma flashed me a thumbs-up, and Auster, Serilda, and Cho all smiled at me. Then the four of them slipped back into the crowd to see if they could pick up any more gossip about the plaza attack, the Mortans, or anything else notewor-thy. The longer the ball went on, the more people would drink, and the looser their tongues would become.

Zariza tipped her head to me. "You dance exceptionally well." She paused. "For a Bellonan."

"As do you." I also paused. "For an Unger."

The other queen eyed me, as did the ogre face on her neck. Then she threw back her head and laughed, long, loud, and deep, and her inner ogre chimed in with its own silent chuckles.

Zariza smiled. "Xenia also warned me about your biting tongue. I think you wield it even better than you dance."

Xenia shrugged. "I told you not to underestimate her."

"Yes, well, I won't make that mistake again," Zariza mur-mured. "Regardless, you clearly won the dance, Everleigh. Congratulations."

I tipped my head to her, acknowledging her grace in defeat. Then I held out my hand. "And our alliance?"

Perhaps it was gauche to bring up my prize mere minutes after beating her, but I hadn't danced so bloody long and hard for nothing. Besides, Xenia was right. I needed to secure Zariza's support before the Morricones or the DiLucris tried to kill me again.

Zariza stared at my outstretched hand. For a moment, I won-dered if I'd made a mistake in asking so soon, but she stepped forward and took my hand in hers. "From this moment forward, Unger and Bellona are allies. Until the mountains crumble to ash."

"Until the mountains crumble to ash," I said, repeating the traditional Ungerian phrase.

And then we shook on it, officially sealing our alliance—

"I must congratulate you both on such a masterful performance." A low, silky voice slithered through the air. "It truly was something to see."

Startled, Zariza dropped my hand and whirled around.

Maximus was standing in front of us, with Mercer by his side, and Nox and Maeven lurking behind them.

The Mortans had finally arrived.

At the sight of the Mortans, faint murmurs rippled through the crowd, and several people sidled closer to us, not so subtly trying to see and hear everything that was happening.

Like many men in attendance, Maximus was wearing a short, formal jacket. The Morricone family crest—that fancy cursive *M* surrounded by a ring of strix feathers—was done in gold thread over the place where his heart would be, if he actually had one.

The crest was fairly large, about the size of my palm, and gleamed like liquid gold, as though it were ink that had somehow been stamped onto the midnight-purple fabric. Gold buttons boasting the same symbol marched down the front of his jacket. No weapons dangled from his black leather belt, but he once again reeked of magic.

Mercer and Nox were dressed the same way, although the crest on Mercer's jacket was much smaller, only about the size of a coin, while the one on Nox's jacket was done in silver thread instead of gold. The Morricone crest didn't adorn Maeven's much lighter, lilac-colored gown, and it wasn't engraved into her silver choker studded with amethysts, her two matching bracelets, or the ring that gleamed on her index finger.

My hand slid into my dress pocket, and my fingers curled around the vial of wormroot hidden there. My plan had been to dose Maximus's food or drink with the poison, but now that he was standing right in front of me, I wondered if I could leap forward, close the distance between us, and smash the glass against his smug face.

Probably, but there was no guarantee the poison would kill him that way, and the Mortan guards lurking nearby would almost certainly cut me down. It wasn't worth the risk. No, I would bide my time and see if a more feasible opportunity presented itself.

Zariza tossed her long red hair over one shoulder, as though the Mortans' sudden appearance already bored her. "Why, Maximus," she drawled. "You finally decided to grace us with your presence."

"I had some business to attend to before the kronekling tournament," he replied. "But I'm so glad the two of you were able to entertain everyone with your little . . . demonstration."

I clutched the vial of poison in my pocket even tighter to help me resist the urge to lunge forward, wrap my fingers around the king's throat, and squeeze the life out of him. But my anger didn't go unnoticed, and Mercer smirked at me, as did Nox. I glanced at Maeven, expecting her to sneer at me as well, but her face was absolutely blank.

She was far too worried to mock me right now.

The sharp scent of her concern rolled off her body, burning my nose with its unexpected intensity. What was Maeven so worried about? It wasn't like I could give in to my dark desires, grab someone's weapon, and try to kill her and her murderous brother in the middle of the ballroom.

Several Mortan nobles, servants, and guards were lurking behind Maeven, and I studied them all in turn, trying to pinpoint the source of her worry. Leonidas, her son, wasn't here, but that wasn't terribly unusual. The ball was a time for the adults to plot, scheme, and gossip, and few children attended, even among the royals and their respective broods. Still, the longer I studied Maeven, the more worried I became.

"Oh, yes. My only reason for existing is to entertain people in your absence," Zariza drawled again, her voice even more mocking. "You might not have found our dance interesting, but perhaps you'll be more invested in the outcome."

Maximus hesitated, sensing it was a trap, but his curiosity got the better of him. "What outcome?"

"The new alliance between Unger and Bellona," Zariza purred. "It will be quite lucrative for both our kingdoms, as well as for Andvari. All three of us are united now."

Her sly words punched Maximus in the face, shattering his smooth, smug facade. His jaw clenched, his nostrils flared, and anger sparked like matches in his dark amethyst eyes. Mercer and Nox sidled away from their king, but Maeven held her position, looking back and forth between her brother and me.

It took Maximus a few seconds to tamp down his ire enough to speak. "Such an alliance is quite . . . *unwise*," he said in a cold, clipped voice. "Unger would be *much* better served aligning with Morta, rather than Bellona."

Everyone could hear the underlying threat in the king's voice. I held my breath, wondering if Zariza would back out of our deal moments after it had been struck. Beside me, Sullivan tensed, as if he were thinking the same thing.

I opened my mouth to say . . . something, but Xenia discreetly shook her head, so I shut my mouth and kept quiet. Besides, Maximus had threatened Zariza, not me, so this was between Morta and Unger.

Zariza smiled at the king, but the expression was all teeth, as was the one of the ogre on her neck. "Eon and Ruri might be across the sea and able to turn a blind eye to your actions, and Cisco might be so desperate to align with you that he overlooks his own cousin's murder, but I will do no such thing."

Maximus lifted his chin. "I have no idea what you're talking about."

"Oh, I think you do." Zariza tilted her head to the side, making her glorious red hair fall prettily over her shoulder. "It's very hard to forget giving the order to massacre a royal family in their own palace."

Shocked gasps surged through the crowd around us. Those gasps, whispers, and murmurs quickly spread even farther out into the ballroom, like waves rippling along the surface of a pond.

As far as I knew, this was the first time anyone had openly accused Maximus of orchestrating the Seven Spire massacre, and Zariza couldn't have chosen a more public setting. The news would be all over the castle within minutes. By midnight it would have spread to every part of the island, and by morning it would have started making its way through the ships and camps and out into the kingdoms beyond.

All eyes turned to Maximus. That muscle ticked in his jaw again, and he practically smoldered with barely restrained anger. He didn't like someone so loudly pointing out his despicable crime.

"Now, I might be willing to ignore such a horrific travesty were you to offer me something to make it worth my while," Zariza continued. "After all, that is what royals do. We plot and scheme and wheel and deal to raise up our own kingdom and people above all others."

"What's your point?" Maximus said through gritted teeth, neither confirming nor denying her accusation, much like I had done with the other royals and their questions about my assassination attempt on him.

"Unfortunately for you, my dear beloved cousin Xenia was one of the people your minions tried to murder at Seven Spire." Zariza gestured at the older woman, and Xenia stepped up beside her.

"We all know that the Morricones don't really value family. Otherwise, you would treat your bastard relatives much better." Her gaze pointedly flicked to Maeven for a moment before she focused on the king again. "But you shouldn't have included *my* family, *my* blood, in your plans. That was a mistake, and it's going to cost you dearly."

Maximus opened his mouth, probably to deliver some threat, but Zariza cut him off.

"From this day forward, Unger will align itself with Bellona and Andvari," she said in a loud voice that boomed through the ballroom. "An attack on one of us is an attack on all. Until the mountains crumble to ash!"

"Until the mountains crumble to ash!" Every single Unger in the ballroom repeated the traditional phrase, their voices ringing out just as loudly as hers had.

Zariza smirked at Maximus again, then scanned the ballroom. At first I wasn't sure who she was searching for, but her gaze settled on Heinrich, who was still standing near the buffet tables, holding a glass of champagne.

"Well, Heinrich?" Zariza called out. "How do you feel about our new alliance?"

All eyes turned to Heinrich, who stepped forward. The Andvarian king looked at Zariza, then Maximus, and finally me. A wide grin split his face, and he pressed his fist to his heart and bowed low to first Zariza and then to me before straightening.

"Until the mountains crumble to ash," he said, toasting us both with his glass. "And our enemies are dead and buried."

More murmurs rippled through the crowd, although silence quickly fell over the ballroom again.

"Thank you, Heinrich," Zariza replied. "I knew I could count on you to express the proper sentiment."

He grinned and toasted her with his glass a second time.

Zariza turned back to Maximus and arched an eyebrow, silently daring the Mortan king to threaten her again.

"You've made your choice, Zariza," he said in a cold voice. "Unfortunately for you, it's the wrong one. Don't say that I didn't warn you."

Maximus spun around on his bootheels. People scurried out of his way, and he stormed across the ballroom and disappeared through one of the archways that led deeper into the castle. Mercer and Nox followed him, but Maeven stayed in the ballroom with the rest of the Mortans, all of whom looked and smelled just as worried as she did.

Still basking in her triumph, Zariza waved her hand. "Heinrich had the right idea. This calls for a toast."

A servant rushed forward, and Zariza plucked two snifters of Ungerian apple brandy off the man's tray. I finally loosened my grip on the vial of poison in my pocket and took one of the glasses from her. Xenia and Sullivan grabbed their own drinks.

"To our new alliance," Zariza murmured.

"To our alliance," I repeated.

She *clink*ed her glass against mine, then threw back her brandy like it was water. I took a much more modest sip, enjoying the sweet, crisp apple flavor and then slow cinnamon burn in my stomach. Xenia and Sullivan also *clink*ed their glasses together and started sipping their brandy.

I thought about everything that had just happened, then toasted the Ungerian queen with my glass. "Well done," I murmured. "That was a truly masterful performance. One of the best I've ever seen."

"I have no idea what you're talking about." Zariza signaled for another brandy.

I waited until the servant had handed her a fresh glass before I spoke again. "Oh, don't be so modest. You really had me sweating there for a while, especially during the dance."

Sullivan frowned. "What are you talking about, highness?"

"I'm talking about the fact that Zariza was *always* going to align with me. The dance, insulting Maximus, it was all just a show for her nobles and everyone else."

Zariza pouted a moment, but then a sly smile slowly curved her lips. "What gave me away?"

"Part of it was how eager you were to confront Maximus. Your eyes practically lit up with glee when you saw him," I said. "And then there was your speech about family. Few people can speak so eloquently and viciously on the fly, so you had to have been thinking about exactly what you were going to say for quite some time."

Zariza shrugged, conceding my points.

"But I still don't understand why you told Xenia to teach me the Tanzen Falter, or why you challenged me to perform it here."

She shrugged again. "I did that for *me*. Xenia, Halvar, and Bjarni told me about you dancing the Tanzen Freund at Castle Asmund. I wanted to see for myself how good you really were. I also wanted to see whether you would rise to the challenge, or do the polite thing and throw away the dance so that I could win, regardless of the stakes."

"Would you have preferred that?"

She let out a low, amused laugh. "Fuck politeness. You won fair and square. You outdanced me, which is something very few people can do."

I grinned. I was starting to like the Ungerian queen. "You're right. Fuck politeness. And fuck the Morricones."

Zariza grinned back at me. "I'll definitely drink to that."

She *clink*ed her glass against mine again, and we both sipped our brandy, celebrating our new alliance.

CHAPTER FIFTEEN

A series of bells chimed, signaling the start of the kronekling tournament. Everyone in the center of the ballroom stepped back, while the servants brought out two tables, along with several chairs.

The royals huddled with their respective entourages, and my friends and I ended up in the corner, next to one of those annoying fountains that kept spitting out gold coins.

"Now, remember," Cho said. "Watch the other players for nervous tics and tells. That's half the battle of winning kronekling. Along with counting cards." He winked at me.

Xenia might have schooled me in the Tanzen Falter, but Cho was the one who'd spent hours reviewing kronekling rules and strategies with me. The dragon morph loved the card game as much as he did sweets, and we'd played hand after hand with Sullivan and Serilda, most of which he won. Of course I had played kronekling before, but only casually, and the pressure to win had never been so high.

"Oh, leave her alone," Serilda said. "Evie is going to do fine."

"Did you see that with your magic?" I asked, not quite joking. "*Please* tell me you saw that with your magic."

"I don't have to see it with my magic. You're smart and a quick thinker and ruthless when it comes to winning. You'll do fine. Now go out there and make Bellona proud."

Xenia, Paloma, and Auster nodded their encouragement, while Sullivan kissed my cheek.

"I would wish you luck, highness," he murmured. "But Serilda's right. You don't need it."

I flashed him a grateful smile, then strode forward and took my place at one of the tables.

Eon, Heinrich, and Zariza filled the remaining three seats at my table. Maximus was at the other table, along with Ruri, Cisco, and Driscol. Even though he wasn't a royal, it made sense for Driscol to join the game, since you needed four people to play. Perched at each table was a dealer wearing DiLucri colors.

The two dealers grabbed their decks and started sliding cards across the wooden surfaces, which featured squares embossed with gold crowns and silver swords. A hush fell over the ballroom as we all picked up our cards to see our first hand of the night.

Kronekling was played with a regular deck with four suits—crowns, coins, hearts, and swords—and cards ranging in value from two to ten, along with kings, queens, and jacks. But what made kronekling different from a more common game like rummy were the four extra cards in the deck. Two of them were jokers and utterly useless, but the other two cards—a gold crown and a silver sword—were the most important ones in the game. The gold crown, or geldkrone, could trump any other card, while the silver sword, or silberkling, was the second-most powerful and capable of trumping every card except the geldkrone.

Each one of the four players was dealt twelve cards, while

the dealer put the last four cards from the deck in a stack called the armory. After each player looked at their cards, they could decide whether they wanted to bid for the right to look at the cards in the armory. Your bid was the number of points you thought you could make off your hand. The higher the number, the more difficult it was to achieve the point total.

Whoever bid the highest won the armory and got to add the cards they wanted from it to their hand while discarding the ones they didn't want. Whoever won the last round of the hand won the armory and whatever points those four cards were worth.

The goal of kronekling was to accumulate as many or even more points than you had bid. If you succeeded, you got to keep all the points you had earned, as did all the other players. If you failed, the amount you originally bid was subtracted from your total.

The overall goal was to accumulate the most points in seven hands. Tonight, after the first seven hands, the people with the two highest point totals at my table would face off against the top two point-getters at the other table. Then those four people would play seven more hands to determine the final winner.

I had a decent hand to begin—two tens, a queen of swords, a queen of hearts, and a king of coins, along with a mix of lower, numbered cards.

Eon won the armory, announced that the trump, or leading suit, was crowns, and played the geldkrone. Then we went around the table, with everyone laying down their lowest crown card, not wanting to give him any more points than necessary. Eon swept those cards up, set them off to the side, and then played the silberkling. Once again, everyone gave him a crown card.

Next, Eon played a two of crowns, which Zariza trumped by playing her king on it. Then she changed suit, throwing down a king of hearts. Around and around the table we went, laying cards down one after another and trying to accumulate as many points as possible.

Eon won the first hand, since he accumulated more points than he had bid, and we started a new one. This time, I had the geldkrone, along with a couple of kings and queens, and I bid on the armory and easily won.

And on and on it went. Finally, after seven hands, the cards were set aside, and the points were totaled. Zariza had amassed the most points, while I had come in second, so the two of us moved on to play the winners at the other table—Maximus and Driscol.

The crowd applauded politely for both the winners and the losers, and all the players got to their feet. There would be a brief break for refreshments and to let the finalists gather their thoughts, as well as decide exactly what they wanted to risk losing during these last seven hands.

During the first part of the tournament, we had just played for points and the right to move on to the second round. But at the final table, each royal was expected to offer up a prize, creating a cache of treasures that would go to the overall tournament winner. According to Auster and Xenia, anything from gold and jewelry to fine wines to rare books could be used as prizes. The item—or items—didn't necessarily have to be large or extravagant, although the objects had to have some special meaning to their royal.

Paloma handed me a small blue velvet bag. "Are you sure you want to bet these?"

I hefted the bag, listening to the faint *clink-clink-clink* of the items rattling around inside. "Yes. I might as well get some use out of them."

"What do you think Maximus is going to bet?" Sullivan asked.

"I have no idea. It could be almost anything."

The steady *squeak-squeak-squeak* of wheels caught my attention, and Mercer and Nox appeared, along with a young servant pushing a large silver cart in front of him. Maeven was trailing along behind them.

Two large coldiron cages were perched on the cart. At first I wasn't sure what they were for, but then the cart rattled closer, and I spotted the gleam of purple feathers behind the metal bars. My breath caught in my throat.

Those cages contained strixes.

Was Maximus going to bet one or both of them during the final round of the tournament? Well, that would certainly be unique. Although I wondered why he would gamble with something so precious. Losing the strixes, the national symbols of Morta, would not set a good tone for Maximus and might dishearten his people for the rest of the Games.

Another series of bells chimed, indicating that it was time for the final round. I sat down at the single half-moon-shaped table in the center of the ballroom. Zariza sat down next to me, with Driscol on the other side of her, while Maximus took the seat across from mine. A dealer sat down at the table as well, facing the four of us.

People tiptoed forward and leaned over the second-floor balcony, eager to see the final seven hands, and an expectant hush fell over the ballroom.

Servants stepped forward, offering drinks. Zariza took another apple brandy, while Driscol grabbed a whiskey, but I didn't get anything to drink. A servant approached Maximus, and I eyed the glasses on her tray. The wormroot poison was still nestled in my dress pocket. Perhaps I could somehow slip it into whatever drink he chose before the next round of the tournament began.

The king waved off the servant, dashing my hopes, then

reached inside his jacket, drew out a small glass vial, and popped the cork out of the top.

The vial contained a light gray-blue powder that featured small purple flecks. My nose twitched. I could clearly smell the powder, which contained notes of chalky dust and sweet lavender. I recognized the scents—crushed tearstone mixed with amethyst-eye poison.

The Morricones were known for the strange brews they concocted to dispatch their enemies, and Maximus himself was rumored to be a tinkerer, with a workshop that featured all sorts of deadly and unnatural horrors. But I'd never heard of anyone combining tearstone with a known poison. What was he up to?

Still holding the vial, Maximus turned in his seat and poured the powder into a large gold goblet studded with amethysts that was sitting on the cart. If Maximus was knowingly ingesting amethyst-eye poison, then I doubted the vial of wormroot in my pocket would have much effect on him. I bit back a frustrated curse. Once again, the Mortan king had thwarted my plan to kill him with minimal effort.

Maximus set the empty vial aside and grabbed a gold dagger off the cart. I tensed. What was he going to do with the blade?

Beside me, Zariza tensed as well, while Driscol shifted in his seat, looking uncomfortable, as if he knew exactly what was coming next and didn't much care for it.

Maximus must have sensed my confusion, because he looked over at me. "Don't worry, Everleigh. We'll start playing in a few minutes. Just as soon as I have my nightcap."

Nightcap? The servants had already offered us drinks, so what was he talking about?

Maximus studied the strix in the cage closest to him. The longer the king stared at the creature, the more the scent of the bird's fear filled the air. The poor creature seemed to be practically paralyzed with it.

Maximus snapped his fingers. Mercer and Nox were standing beside the cart, and they both stiffened at the sound, as did Maeven, who was lurking a few feet behind them. Maximus snapped his fingers again, and the young servant slowly shuffled forward and opened the cage.

I expected the strix to try to fly away, or at least lash out with its sharp wings, beak, and talons, but Maximus flicked his hand, and purple lightning shot out from his fingertips and zoomed into the cage, stunning the strix.

Several people in the crowd gasped. It was a small, controlled, precise display of magic, and much weaker than the lightning bolts Maximus had shot off in the arena, but I could still sense the pure force in the cold blast. It was another reminder of just how much power he truly had, more power than I had ever sensed from any other magier, including Maeven.

The king waited a moment, making sure that the creature was dazed, then reached into the cage and pulled out the strix as easily as a child grabbing a piece of candy from a dish.

The strix was little more than a baby, and only about the size of a large chicken, so Maximus was able to hold it with one hand. He studied it a moment longer, then set it back down on the silver cart, arranging the creature so that its head dangled off the edge.

Then he lifted the gold dagger in his other hand. I sucked in a ragged breath. Even though I could guess what was coming next, it was still so fucking *gruesome* that I didn't quite believe it was happening.

Maximus reached over and quickly, casually slit the strix's throat.

The poor, dazed creature died without making a sound. Maximus set the dagger on the gaming table, even though it dripped blood all over the gold crowns and silver swords embossed on the wood.

For a moment, nothing happened, and stunned, horrified silence filled the ballroom. Then that young servant grabbed the gold goblet off the cart, stepped forward, and held it down and out so that the strix's blood drained into it. I could have sworn I heard every single drop hit the side of the goblet.

Plop-plop-plop-plop . . .

The process didn't take long, no more than a minute. Then, when the steady flow of blood had slowed to a trickle, Maximus waved his hand, and the servant stepped forward and placed the blood-filled goblet on the table in front of the king. That was when I noticed the boy's black hair and light purple tunic.

Not just a servant—Leonidas.

The boy didn't look at me or anyone else, but his face was pale, and the scents of ashy heartbreak and dusty resignation rolled off him in wave after wave. He hadn't liked what his uncle had done any more than I had.

Leonidas stepped back and glanced over at the second cage on the cart. The scents of his heartbreak and resignation increased tenfold, and I realized that the second strix was a much larger creature, one that I had seen before.

Lyra, Leonidas's strix.

Shock jolted through me, along with sick understanding. This must have been what the boy had wanted to save Lyra from by trying to send her through the Cardea mirror.

Maeven was standing a few feet behind her son, and she moved forward and clamped her hand on Leonidas's shoulder, as if to remind him that he couldn't save his beloved strix. I stared at her, wondering how she could let such a horrible thing happen to her own child. For once, she wouldn't meet my accusing gaze, although I could smell her anger, along with her sharp minty regret.

The sight of an innocent creature being slaughtered filled me with disgust, along with cold, cold rage. I turned my harsh glare back to Maximus, who stared me in the eyes, picked up the gold goblet, and lifted it to his lips.

Was he actually going to . . . The idea was so horrible that I couldn't bring myself to actually think it through, although it happened anyway.

Maximus tipped up the goblet and drank the strix's blood.

He slurped it down like it was a hot, fruity toddy. He kept his eyes on me the whole time, and I couldn't look away. It was just that fascinating and horrible and sick and disgusting.

Maximus kept drinking . . . and drinking . . . and drinking . . . until he had drained the last drop of the strix's blood out of the goblet. Then he lowered the empty glass and grinned, showing off his bloodstained teeth, and the coppery stench of his blood-drenched breath drifted across the table to me. Hot, sour bile rose in my throat. I managed to choke it down, although I couldn't stop from shuddering in revulsion.

"Ah," he murmured, placing the goblet on the table. "That's always so refreshing. I'll have another round later on. Now, shall we start the game?"

Start the game? We had never *stopped* playing the fucking game.

I sucked in a breath to tell him exactly what a vile monster he was, and a familiar scent tickled my nose, even stronger than the coppery tang of the strix's blood.

The stench of magic.

My nose twitched. I discreetly drew in another breath, tasting the air, and I noticed that the blood and the magic had the same coppery notes. Strixes had magic, just like gargoyles and caladriuses did, so it made sense that their blood would contain the same power that the creatures themselves did.

Power that Maximus had just slurped down.

The stench of magic clung to him like a second skin, along with the blood on his breath, and a sudden influx of power sparked in his eyes, like fireworks exploding over and over again.

Shock blasted through me. Not only had Maximus proven what a heartless bastard he was by drinking the strix's blood, but he had actually *absorbed* the creature's magic.

I shouldn't have been so surprised. After all, I could destroy magic, so it made sense that someone else might be able to channel it. In a way, Maximus and I were like two sides of the same coin, connected and yet completely opposite at the same time.

Perhaps absorbing the strixes' magic was Maximus's own personal mutt skill, the same way that throttling magic was mine. Perhaps he was even a magic master, like I was. Or perhaps his was a unique family trait passed down through the generations of Morricone kings and queens, the same way that Winter and Summer magics had been passed down through the Blair royal family.

Or maybe, just maybe, the Morricones' power had *always* come from the strixes.

Legends said that the Blairs had dug so much tearstone out of Seven Spire that it had turned our eyes the same gray-blue color, and some of my cousins had thought our ancestors mining the stone was the ultimate source of our power, the thing that had triggered all the magic in our family. Just like Andvarian stories claimed that the Ripleys were the first family to ever befriend gargoyles. Maybe one of Maximus's ancestors either bonding with or killing strixes was the reason why Morricones' eyes were the same purple as the creatures' eyes and feathers.

Most magiers, morphs, masters, and mutts augmented their power with jewels filled with magic and other glamours, but some people believed that wearing the bones or eating the flesh of certain creatures, like caladriuses, increased their own magic. I'd thought those were just silly legends, but apparently not in Maximus's case.

And he had drunk more than just the strix's blood.

My gaze flicked to the empty vial sitting on the cart, the one that had been filled with crushed tearstone and amethyst-eye poison. Tearstone could absorb and reflect back magic, and I was betting that a certain dose of the poison could do the same thing. Maximus must add the powder to his foul cocktail in order to help him soak up and then wield as much power as possible.

I wondered if he could also sense magic like I could. If that was the case, then Maximus had probably felt the power in the wormroot poison coating Serilda's arrow, which had let him blast the projectile to pieces. It was probably a good thing I hadn't tried to dose Maximus with the vial of wormroot in my own pocket. Instead of killing him, I might have inadvertently made him stronger.

However, perhaps the most disgusting and disheartening thing was that Maximus had only consumed about a cup of blood. He could have easily siphoned off that much of the strix's blood without killing the creature. But no, he had slaughtered the strix outright. Just because he could. Just because it amused him. Just because he wanted to show us all how cruel he truly was.

I wondered how many strixes died on a regular basis to satisfy the Mortan king's lust for power. One a month? A week? Every single day? The potential numbers horrified and disgusted me. And were strixes the only creatures he slaughtered? Or did he somehow do the same to gargoyles, despite their stone skins? And what about caladriuses? They had even more magic than strixes and gargoyles. Then there was the biggest question of all.

Did he do it to *people*?

There had long been rumors of slavery, labor camps, and

other horrors in Morta, and I couldn't help but think that those atrocities were linked to Maximus's monstrous appetite. No wonder Maeven was afraid of him. No wonder all the Mortans were afraid of him.

Even if Maximus didn't kill people to take their magic, there was still a human cost to his cruelty. I looked at Leonidas, who was still standing beside the cart. His hands were clenched into tight fists, and he was staring at the cage that held Lyra as though he wanted to rush forward, free the bird, and run away with her. No doubt he did, knowing what a gruesome fate awaited her before the night was through.

No wonder the boy had tried to get Lyra to hop through the Cardea mirror. He had known that it was the only way to save her from *this*. At least at Seven Spire, she would have had a chance to escape, and even if she had been killed or captured, no one at my palace would have tried to drink her blood.

The dealer cleared his throat, finally breaking the horrified silence. "It's time to place the prizes on the table for the final round."

Driscol went first, and his prize turned out to be a gold chest filled with gold coins, all of which featured the Fortuna Mint's coined-woman crest. "Ten thousand gold crowns," he said in a subdued voice.

Extravagant, but not unique or surprising. A murmur rippled through the crowd that was equal parts appreciative and disappointed.

Zariza was next, and she unhooked the gold chain from around her neck and placed the gold ogre pendant with its emerald eyes and diamond and ruby teeth in the center of the table next to Driscol's chest.

"It's nothing much," she declared. "Just a little bauble I had made for the Regalia."

Laughter rang out, along with loud claps and whistles. The jewels alone in that little bauble were easily worth more than Driscol's gold.

Now it was my turn, and I opened the blue velvet bag Paloma had given me, tipped the contents into my hand, and laid them out on the glossy wood. Zariza studied the items curiously, although Driscol's face paled in recognition.

"A bronze pocket watch, a gold pendant, and a silver signet ring?" Maximus said, a sneer creeping into his voice. "I didn't realize Bellona was so poor these days. You could have at least brought something with some jewels in it."

Several agreeing murmurs sounded. I ignored them.

"Oh, it's true that they don't have nearly as much monetary worth as Driscol's chest and Zariza's bauble, but their sentimental value is priceless." I paused a moment for dramatic effect and tapped my finger on the pocket watch. "This belonged to my tutor Ansel, who poisoned my father with wormroot. He was killed by a weather magier named Marisse outside Winterwind, my family's estate. Marisse tried to kill me too, but I stabbed her to death with my father's dagger."

Surprised gasps rang out. I ignored them and kept going, gesturing at the gold-coin pendant. "This was hanging around the neck of Lena, a geldjager who died just last week." I stared at Driscol. "Lena and her compatriots foolishly thought that they could come to my capital and threaten my people. They were wrong, and their bodies are currently hanging in a plaza across the river from Seven Spire."

More surprised gasps sounded. I kept staring at Driscol, whose face got a little redder with each passing second. The scent of his anger grew in direct proportion to the mottled flush staining his cheeks.

Driscol opened his mouth and leaned forward as if to curse me, but Seraphine quickly, smoothly stepped up and laid her hand on his shoulder. For a moment, I thought he was going to shake her off, but she tightened her grip, digging her long white polished nails into his shoulder. Driscol slowly choked down his anger, clamped his lips shut, and leaned back in his chair. Seraphine loosened her grip and glided back into the ring of spectators around the table.

When I was sure that Driscol wasn't going to interrupt me, I tapped my finger on the silver signet ring. "But out of all my little trinkets, this ring is my favorite because it belongs to one of the people responsible for the Seven Spire massacre. Now, that person isn't dead yet, but if I have my way, she will be very, very soon, along with her family."

I glanced at Maximus a moment, then pointedly fixed my gaze on Maeven. Not a flicker of emotion showed on her face at my accusation and threat, but I could smell her hot, peppery anger.

Maximus glanced over his shoulder at his half sister. Maeven's face remained impassive, but her peppery anger quickly melted into coppery fear. Mercer and Nox sidled away from her, but Leonidas actually shifted closer to Maeven, as if he wanted to shield his mother from Maximus. Brave, stupid boy.

The king faced the table again. "I didn't realize that Everleigh was going to tell us bedtime stories. How quaint."

Laughter pealed out all around the ballroom, but I shrugged it off, along with his mocking words. "Not bedtime stories. More like lessons from the past—and promises of things to come."

The king stared at me, and I looked right back at him. Just like his sister, Maximus didn't show any visible emotion, but I could smell his anger and annoyance. He didn't care for my theatrics, even though they were far less digusting than his own.

Maximus might have drunk the strix blood for its power, but he'd also done it to try to intimidate me. I needed to match his viciousness, lest everyone here think me weaker than him.

I wasn't going to slaughter an innocent creature, but I had no qualms about displaying the remains of my dead enemies. The trinkets and my so-called *stories* were yet another way to remind him and the other royals that they trifled with me—and Bellona—at their own peril.

The dealer cleared his throat again, interrupting the tense silence. "King Maximus," he said in a low, deferential voice. "What are you offering as your prize?"

Instead of answering the question, Maximus picked up his gold goblet. He started to take a drink but then realized it was empty. He set it down and flapped his hand in a sharp, annoyed motion over at the cart where Lyra was still sitting in her cage.

The bastard wanted another bloody nightcap.

No one immediately moved to do his bidding, so Maximus turned around in his seat and glared at his entourage. That prompted Mercer and Nox to spring into action. Mercer stepped forward and plucked Maximus's dagger off the table, while Nox headed toward Lyra's cage.

Leonidas's hands clenched into even tighter fists, and he moved forward as though he was going to step in between Nox and his beloved strix, but Maeven latched on to her son's shoulder again, holding him in place.

Leonidas stared at his mother, a silent plea in his eyes, but Maeven didn't do or say anything. After a few seconds, the boy's head dropped, and his shoulders slumped in defeat.

Lyra must have sensed his anguish, because she let out a couple of low, sad notes. Perhaps it was my imagination, but it almost sounded like she sang the word *goodbye*. The mournful cries, along with the overpowering scents of her dusty resignation and Leonidas's ashy heartbreak, stabbed into my heart like three separate swords, cutting me to pieces.

But what could I do? How could I stop Maximus from kill-

ing the strix? I looked at the king, then at Leonidas, then at
Lyra in her cage. No answers there, so I dropped my gaze to the
gaming table. Driscol's chest of gold, Zariza's ogre pendant,
and my trinkets gleamed in the center of the wood, and the
answer suddenly came to me.

"Why not put up the strix as your prize?"

At the sound of my voice, everyone looked at me, including Maximus, who swiveled back around in his seat to face me
again. His golden eyebrows creased together, as if he were truly
surprised by my suggestion.

"The strix is not available," he said.

"Why not? It belongs to you, doesn't it? Can't you do whatever you like with it?" I gestured at his empty goblet. "That's
certainly the impression you gave earlier."

My voice took on a loud, sneering note, and a few snickers
sounded. Maximus's eyes narrowed, and once again he practically smoldered with anger. He didn't like being mocked.

"Besides, I've always wanted my very own strix," I continued
in a lighter voice, as though the creature's fate didn't matter to
me at all. "I always thought they were *so* much more interesting
than ponies, and now I finally have a chance to win one. Surely
you wouldn't deny me that childhood dream?"

I gestured at the other items on the table. "Especially when
you have an opportunity to win so much more in return."

He stared at me, speculation filling his face. Maximus was
wondering if I really wanted the creature or if I'd figured out
his dirty little secret, that he planned to drink the strix's blood
to absorb its magic. No, the creature might not have as much
monetary value as Driscol's gold or Zariza's bauble, but it was
priceless to Maximus, the same way my trinkets were priceless
to me. The Mortan king didn't want to risk giving up a single
drop of the strix's blood and the power that it contained.

"How much is a strix worth?" I asked, further goading him. "I'll happily put up the cost—in gold. We'll think of it as a bonus prize for the winner."

Some low whistles sounded, along with several appreciative claps. It was a more than generous offer, and one that Maximus couldn't turn down without arousing suspicion about what was so special about this particular strix. But he still tried to weasel out of the corner that I'd just twirled him into.

"You couldn't handle a strix, Everleigh," he said. "They're quite vicious unless properly trained."

I gave him a thin smile. "Anything can be vicious when it's stuffed in a cage. I'll manage. Now, name your price."

"Yes, Maximus," Zariza chimed in. "Do tell us what this strix is worth to you."

He shot her a sour look, but he had run out of excuses. "Ten thousand gold crowns."

It was a small fortune and far more than what the strix was actually worth, if you could ever truly put a price on a creature's life.

I leaned back in my seat and gave an airy, dismissive wave of my hand. "Done."

Maximus's eyes narrowed again. "You have ten thousand gold crowns? *You*, personally? We don't gamble with our kingdom's coffers here, Everleigh. And if you don't have the money to pay for the strix, then it can't be used as a prize."

Ah, so that was his scheme. But it wasn't going to work.

"Oh, yes," I purred. "I have ten thousand gold crowns."

"How did *you* get your hands on so much money?" Driscol asked, an incredulous note in his voice.

"Haven't you heard? I won a black-ring gladiator match several months ago. I made sure that the purse was quite generous before I stepped one foot into the arena."

I glanced over and winked at Serilda. The troupe leader rolled her eyes, but she grinned back at me.

"Of course, I don't have the money with me at this very moment, but I'm sure the Fortuna Mint can extend me a line of credit."

Driscol looked at Maximus, who drew his index finger in a short line across the table. *No.* Driscol glanced over at Seraphine. After a moment, she nodded. *Yes.*

Driscol was clearly caught between the king and his sister— a very uncomfortable place to be. He dropped his gaze to the table again, as if staring at the gold crowns and silver swords in the wood would somehow get him out of this dilemma. Then he sighed and slowly lifted his head.

"The Mint will be happy to extend Queen Everleigh a line of credit," he mumbled.

His decision surprised me. He was so obviously, deeply in Maximus's pocket that I'd expected him to refuse and for us to continue our verbal duel. So had Maximus, given the harsh, angry glare he shot at Driscol, who slumped in his chair. Maximus also glared at Seraphine, but she remained as calm and cool as ever.

Fortuna favors her ladies. The female assassin had said that on the plaza earlier, and I was beginning to think that her words had far more meaning than I'd realized—and that there was much more to Seraphine than just a bland smile and a pretty face.

But I pushed her out of my mind and looked at the Mortan king again. "Excellent! Now that the stakes are set, let's play."

Maximus glowered at me, and I gave him another thin smile in return. We both knew that the game between us had only just begun.

CHAPTER SIXTEEN

Another expectant hush fell over the ballroom, and everyone leaned forward to watch this last game of the night. The dealer shuffled the deck and passed out the cards, which landed with raspy whispers against the gleaming wood.

Maximus leaned forward and picked up his cards. I hadn't played kronekling with him before, so I studied him carefully. The king had gotten his anger and annoyance under control, and no obvious emotion marred his features, but I could smell his sudden eagerness. He had a good hand.

I picked up my own cards, careful not to show any emotion either. My hand was okay, but it wasn't strong enough to bid on the armory, so I decided to play for points instead. Like most things, kronekling was a long game, and I was determined to win.

Maximus easily won that first hand, while Zariza took the second, and I won the third. Driscol didn't win any hands, but then again, he wasn't trying to. Instead, he played as if he didn't know the rules, foolishly giving away card after card and point after point, all to benefit Maximus.

Driscol was clearly trying to make sure Maximus won and

kept his precious strix. He probably thought it was the only way he could salvage whatever deal he'd made with the Mortan king. He might as well have just handed his cards to Maximus and let the king play them as his own. That's how badly and obviously Driscol was losing.

Zariza didn't like Driscol throwing the game either, and she glared at him.

"Are you really that bloody *stupid*?" she snarled at one point, when Driscol started to play a ten of coins on Maximus's king, instead of a lower-point card.

Driscol froze, his hand still on his card. He looked at the glaring ogre face on her neck, then slowly slid the card across the table and back into his hand. He hesitated, then laid down an eight of coins, giving Maximus two fewer points.

Zariza rolled her eyes. "Idiot."

People snickered. Driscol's face turned an interesting shade of red, but after that, he tried to be a little less obvious in his cheating.

It all came down to the seventh and final hand. Maximus, Zariza, and I had all won two hands each. Maximus had the most points, while I was in second. Zariza was still within striking distance in third, while Driscol was a distant, dismal fourth.

The cards were dealt. I wound up with a fairly even mix of suits and point values, along with the silberkling, the silver sword and second-highest trump. A decent hand, but not good enough to win outright, so I waited to see what the others would do.

Driscol passed on bidding, like always, but Zariza was very aggressive, and she and Maximus got into a bidding war for the armory. Maximus finally prevailed, but he had to bid an outrageous amount, and he would have to take back practically every single card in order to win. But if he did that, his point total would easily outstrip mine, and he would win the tournament, along with all the prizes, including Lyra, who was still sitting in her cage.

Maximus rifled through the armory, picking up a couple of cards and putting others back down. He once again smelled of eagerness, indicating that he had a good hand. "Trumps are swords."

I had to work very hard to hide my surprise. I'd expected him to pick another suit, but I had four regular sword cards, which meant that I probably had just as many trumps as he did, although mine were mostly low cards. But I did have one high card—the silberkling—and I suddenly saw a way I could use that one single card to win *everything*.

Maximus played his opening card, the geldkrone. I gave him my lowest trump, as did Zariza. Driscol, of course, gave him a ten. Idiot.

Around and around the table we went, with Maximus playing his trump cards, and trying to force either Zariza or me to throw down the silberkling, since Driscol would have foolishly given it away already. Maximus must have thought that once the silberkling was gone, the rest of his cards were good enough to win all the other rounds. The common strategy probably would have worked if I hadn't had just as many trumps as he did.

Zariza and Driscol both quickly ran out of trumps, and Maximus realized that I had the silberkling. So he changed his strategy and laid down a queen of crowns, trying to tempt me into trumping it and taking the points, but I had another plan, and I laid down a joker, a throwaway card. Zariza put down a king of crowns, winning that round and stealing those precious points away from Maximus.

Zariza realized what was going on and gave me a speculative look. Driscol blundered along just like he had through the rest of the game.

Zariza managed to win the next round with a jack of crowns, and I tossed her a ten of hearts, the highest card I had left besides the silberkling. Every point that Maximus didn't get furthered my own goal.

Maximus's lips pinched together, and his smug eagerness flared up into annoyance again. He won the next round, then took control of the game once more, using a combination of trumps and high cards to win those points. But with each round, the tension around the table grew and grew, and the smell of the crowd's collective curiosity filled my nose. They were all wondering why I hadn't played the silberkling yet.

Everyone except Cho.

I glanced over at the ringmaster. He'd taught me the strategy, so he knew exactly what I was doing, and the dragon on his neck winked at me in approval. I hid a grin and turned my attention back to my cards.

On the very last round, Maximus played the five of swords, his final trump. Zariza laid down a queen of coins, while Driscol offered up a ten of crowns. I leaned forward and laid my final card—the silberkling—on top of the others.

"Why, look at that," I purred. "I had a trump card left too. And since my trump is higher than yours, then all the cards in the armory are mine too. Let's see how many points you left in there for me to steal."

Maximus's lips pinched together a little tighter than before, and his nostrils flared in anger. I gestured at the dealer, who flipped the armory cards over and started calling out the points.

Maximus might have had a strong hand, but he'd still had to put four cards back into the armory. They were mostly low cards, but they slowly added up. That number, combined with my silberkling and the points Zariza had thrown me in the final hand, was just enough to ruin the Mortan king.

The dealer looked at Maximus. "I'm sorry, sir, but you didn't make your bid. That means you lose those points, and that our winner is Queen Everleigh."

The dealer cringed as he said the last few words, obviously afraid of what the king might do, but Maximus just sat there and stared at the cards as if he couldn't believe what had happened.

Surprised gasps rippled through the ballroom, but they were quickly drowned out by my friends, who started clapping and cheering.

"Yeah! Way to go, Evie!" Paloma yelled.

"Fantastic game, highness!" Sullivan chimed in.

"Well done, my queen!" Auster added. "Well done!"

Serilda and Xenia were also grinning and clapping, while Cho let out a loud, earsplitting whistle.

Smiling wide, I got to my feet and shook hands with Zariza. "Good game. And thanks for throwing me those last few points," I murmured. "That helped put me over the top."

Her amber eyes gleamed with satisfaction. "I'm just glad one of us beat that bastard at his own game."

I turned and shook Driscol's hand as well, but he was utterly deflated, and his fingers felt as cold and limp as a dead fish against mine. Finally, I faced Maximus, who was still seated.

"You shouldn't bid if you're not absolutely certain you can win," I said.

He didn't respond, but anger sparked in his eyes, and he smelled of rage. Most people probably would have taken their victory and left it at that, but I decided to rub his face in it some more.

"Well, it looks like I am now the proud owner of a strix," I drawled. "Tell me, does it have a name? Or do you just give them all numbers?"

Maximus slowly pushed back from the gaming table and stood up. His nostrils flared, a muscle ticked in his jaw, and the scent of his hot jalapeño rage blasted over me again, even stronger than before. Mercer, Nox, Leonidas, and Maeven all tensed, as did the other Mortans gathered around them.

For a moment, I thought Maximus was going to renege, but he jerked his head, and one of the Mortan servants pushed the cart over to my side of the table.

I leaned down and stared into the cage. Lyra stared back at me and quirked her head from side to side, as if she weren't quite sure what had just happened—and why she wasn't being butchered.

Maximus turned his angry glare to Zariza. "This is your fault. You deliberately gave her those points at the end."

"Of course I did." Zariza proudly tossed her long red hair over her shoulder again. "I got the idea from Driscol. Perhaps he's not such an idiot after all. And perhaps you should have played a better hand, Maximus, and not relied on your lead to see you through to the end."

His face darkened with even more anger, but she calmly took another sip of her brandy, then smirked at him over the rim of her glass.

Maximus's fingers twitched, as though he wanted to blast her with his magic, but he faced me again. He didn't so much as glance at Driscol, who let out a quiet sigh of relief.

"Enjoy your new pet, Everleigh," Maximus muttered. "For as long as you can."

Just like Zariza, I smiled in the face of his obvious threat. "Oh, I intend to."

The Mortan king stared at me a moment longer, then whirled around and stormed out of the ballroom.

Maximus disappeared through an archway, heading deeper into the castle. Mercer shot me a nasty look, as did Nox, and the two of them hurried after their king. Leonidas hesitated, clearly wondering what I was going to do with his beloved strix, but Maeven clamped her hand on her son's shoulder again and steered him after the others.

According to Auster's spies, the Mortans were riding strixes back and forth from their camp to the various Regalia events on the island. I wondered if Maximus would kill one of those creatures to take Lyra's place. I hoped not.

Cisco had already left the ballroom, but Heinrich, Dominic, and Rhea came over to congratulate me, as did Eon, Ruri, and their consorts. I smiled, accepting their well-wishes. They moved off, and my friends gathered around me again.

Cho let out a loud whoop, lifted me up and off my feet, and spun me around before setting me back down. "Now I know how Xenia felt when you beat Zariza at the Tanzen Falter earlier." He beamed at me, as did the dragon on his neck.

I squeezed his arm. "That's because you are a most excellent teacher, just like Xenia is."

Xenia sniffed. "A card game is not nearly as complicated as a dance."

Cho ignored her words, picked her up, and spun her around too. He set her back down, and Xenia snapped up her cane and poked him in the chest with it.

"Don't ever do that again, dragon," she warned.

Cho winked at her, as did the dragon on his neck. Xenia's lips twitched up into a smile that she couldn't quite hide.

"I'm so proud of you, Evie," Auster said, his voice raspy and his eyes suspiciously red and watery. "This is the first time a Bellonan queen has won the kronekling tournament in more than twenty years."

I stepped forward and hugged him tight before drawing back. Auster cleared his throat, blinked a few times, and schooled his face back into its usual stern expression.

"That was wonderful, highness," Sullivan murmured, kissing my cheek. "Absolutely wonderful."

"Well done, Evie," Serilda chimed in. "Very well done."

She smiled, but her blue eyes were dark and troubled, and she kept glancing at the archway that Maximus had gone through. I didn't ask her about the possibilities she was seeing with her magic. I didn't have to. I knew Maximus was already plotting how to retaliate for my humiliating him.

I might have won this round, but the true game between me and the Mortan king was far from over.

The kronekling tournament was the final event of the night, and everyone streamed out of the ballroom, left the DiLucri castle, and walked down the steps to the waterfront.

Some people headed over to the pleasure and gaming houses to extend their celebration, while others waited for rowboats that would take them back to their ships in the harbor. More than a few folks stumbled by, already drunk on whatever ale, liquor, or other intoxicants they could afford. Music and laughter rang up and down the boulevard, and every single building blazed with light.

Keeping an eye out for more assassins, my friends and I quickly made our way to the Perseverance Bridge, where Auster's guards were waiting. Together, we crossed the span, heading back over to the relative safety of the Bellonan side of the river.

Many of my fellow countrymen and -women were also on the bridge, moving from Bellona to Fortuna and back again. Some folks had already celebrated a little too much, and we passed a couple of people hanging over the side of the stone railing, violently vomiting into the water below.

"Remind me not to eat any fish while we're here," Paloma said.

The farther we walked along the bridge, the more Captain

Auster relaxed, as did the rest of my friends, and we slowed down to admire the breathtaking nighttime view. Strings of blue, white, red, green, and other colored fluorestones had been wrapped around the railings and masts of many of the ships, making the vessels look like they were swathed in bright electric spiderwebs. The glows spread out across the water, and the waves danced to and fro like liquid silver.

But there was one dark spot in the center of the harbor—the ship that I'd noticed earlier, the one without any flags, crests, or other markings. No pretty fluorestones were wrapped around its railing, and the vessel was totally dark. I squinted, but I didn't see anyone on deck, and no lights glimmered in the round windows below. The ship might as well have been a rock sitting in the water, for all the life and personality it showed. Curious. Very curious.

The thrill of beating Maximus was wearing off, and I was growing tired, so I followed my friends the rest of the way across the bridge.

We made it back to the Bellonan camp. Cheery music trilled through the air, and people were moving through the rows of tents, into the common areas, and back again, drinking, dancing, singing, and laughing. Everyone had thoroughly enjoyed the first day of the Regalia.

My friends split off to take care of their chores, while Sullivan and I stepped into my tent. Calandre and her two sisters were waiting to help me undress, and there was one other person—or creature—inside my canvas chambers.

Lyra.

The strix was still in her coldiron cage, which had been placed on a long table along one of the tent walls. Driscol's chest of gold coins and Zariza's ogre pendant also glimmered on the table. Camille and Cerana were bent down, peering through the bars at Lyra, who stared back at them, not moving a single feather.

"I see that you had an eventful evening," Calandre drawled.

"Oh, yes. I leave in a ball gown and come back with my very own strix. Why, it's like I'm living a fairy tale."

She laughed, while her sisters continued to stare at the strix. Lyra stared back at all of us, still not moving a single feather, although I could smell the creature's wariness and suspicion. She probably thought I was going to cut her throat and drink her blood like Maximus had done to the other strix. I shuddered at the thought. I could still smell the poor creature's blood in my nose—and the magic it had given the Mortan king.

"What are you going to do with it?" Calandre asked.

"I have no idea. I don't even know what strixes eat."

"Mostly rabbits, mice, and other small animals, just like gargoyles do," Sullivan said. "Along with seeds, bugs, and the like. But from what I've read, they mostly eat meat."

"Well, please ask the guards outside to fetch some meat. I don't want it to be hungry."

"Of course, highness. I'll go with the guards and see what we can find for the creature to eat." Sullivan nodded at me and left the tent.

Calandre and her sisters bustled forward, helping me out of the ball gown, pulling off my sandals, and cleaning what was left of the makeup off my face. Calandre laid out some nightclothes, but I slipped back into a regular tunic, leggings, and boots and cinched my weapons belt around my waist, just in case some new crisis arose before Sullivan returned.

Calandre and her sisters wished me good night, then left. Sullivan hadn't returned yet, so I walked over, bent down, and peered at Lyra.

She had been completely quiet and still while Calandre and her sisters had been moving around the tent. I waited, thinking the creature might squawk or let out some other sound now that it was just the two of us, but she remained in the back of her cage, with her body pressed up against the metal bars.

"I'm not going to hurt you," I said in a soft voice. "But I'm going to leave you in your cage for now, in case you have any ideas about flying across the river to Leonidas. I know that he's your human, and you're his strix, but going back will only get you killed. You saw what happened to the other strix. The same thing will happen to you if you try to return to Leonidas. Maximus won't let you get away again."

Lyra eyed me, but she still didn't make a sound. I knew that she could talk, but apparently she didn't want to talk to me. Couldn't blame her for that. I was a stranger, and she came from a land where most people weren't kind to her or anyone else.

"How about a compromise?" I suggested. "I'll open your cage to prove that I'm not going to hurt you. Just don't peck me to death in the middle of the night, okay?"

Lyra kept eyeing me, but she still didn't move or make any noise. I sighed, wondering if I was making a mistake, but I reached forward and wrapped my hand around the small padlock on the front of the cage.

Purple lightning exploded the second my fingers touched the metal.

In an instant, the cold blast of power congealed into hailstones with sharp, jagged edges. The pellets shot out from the padlock and *punch-punch-punch*ed into my palm like frozen, serrated hammers.

This magic was much more powerful than what Maximus had used to stun the strix at the ball, and the force of the blast knocked me back five feet. My immunity kept the hailstones from piercing my skin, although the hard, heavy blows still bruised my fingers.

The pellets dropped to the ground, but bolts of cold lightning kept crackling against my skin, making me hiss with pain. I quickly snuffed them out with my immunity, although the icy, stinging shocks still reverberated all the way up my arm. If anyone else had touched the contraption, their skin would have been horribly cut, bruised, and frozen all at once.

I wasn't surprised that Maximus had been petty enough to booby-trap the padlock, but he'd used far more power on it than I'd expected. Then again, who cared how much power you used on a simple lock when you could just drink strix blood and get some more? Magic was probably as common as water to Maximus, and I doubted he ever thought about how much he was truly using, since he had a seemingly endless supply.

I stepped forward, flexed my fingers, and grabbed the padlock again. My immunity was stronger than the remaining magic, and it soon fizzled away into a shower of hot purple sparks. I let out a breath, flexed my fingers, and wiped the sweat off my forehead.

"There," I said, unhooking the lock and setting it aside. "Now, if you want to get out, all you have to do is push the door open with your wing. Okay? Isn't that better?"

Lyra kept staring at me with big, bright, unreadable eyes. She seemed determined to remain still and stoic, so I sighed. Maybe she would warm up to me later.

I had started to turn away from her cage when Lyra's eyes widened, and she let out a loud *squawk*. I frowned, wondering what had suddenly excited her. I drew in a breath, and the stench of magic filled my nose.

That was all the warning I had before a dagger zoomed out of the shadows, heading straight for my heart.

CHAPTER SEVENTEEN

There was no time to duck, so I snapped up my hand and reached for my immunity, pretending that it was an invisible shield spreading out from my palm and covering my chest. Then, at the last instant, right before the dagger would have plunged into my chest, I flicked my fingers to the left and used my magic to knock the blade off course. The weapon flew through the air and stuck in the thick wooden support pole in the center of the tent.

My attacker growled in apparent frustration, and a slender figure wrapped in a midnight-purple cloak ran toward me. I didn't know how the assassin had gotten past the guards stationed around the Bellonan camp, much less into my tent, but it was going to be the last mistake they ever made. Determination surged through me. This assassin would die just like all the others had.

A hood covered the assassin's head and cast their face in shadow, but the dagger in their hand was clearly visible. The assassin swiped out with the weapon, but it was a weak, awkward, clumsy attempt. I spun out of the way, whirled around, and yanked my sword out of its scabbard.

The assassin hesitated, then grabbed another dagger from the folds of their cloak and came at me again. This strike was a little more deliberate and skilled, but the assassin didn't have my gladiator training, and I easily avoided the attack.

The assassin lurched past me, and I stuck my foot out, tripping the figure, and sending them crashing to their knees. The assassin hit the ground hard, and both daggers skittered out of their hands and tumbled end over end along the ground.

I hurried forward, grabbed the assassin's shoulder, and yanked them to their feet. Then I churned my legs, forcing the figure across the chambers until their back slammed up against the center support pole. I started to shove my sword into the assassin's throat, but the figure jerked to the side, and their hood slid down, revealing their features. Black hair, amethyst eyes, young frightened face.

Leonidas.

I cursed and managed to stop my swing, my sword hovering an inch away from the boy's neck. "What are you doing here? Why are you trying to kill me?"

"I-I-I—" he stuttered.

I moved forward so that the point of my sword rested in the hollow of his throat. "Spit it out, or I will pin you to this pole like you're a butterfly in a collection."

"I-I-I didn't want to!" he said, his voice a low, panicked whisper. "I didn't want to come here. I didn't want to hurt you. Not after you saved Lyra."

"But you came here anyway," I snarled. "Why? To kill me so you could take back your strix?"

Leonidas's eyes widened. "No! Of course not! You won her fair and square. Besides, she'll be much safer with you than she would ever be with me."

Lyra let out a loud *squawk*, clearly disagreeing. I eyed the strix, wondering if she might burst out of her cage to defend

Leonidas. I was surprised she hadn't done that already, but the strix remained behind the bars, so I turned back to the boy.

"If you didn't come for Lyra, then why are you here?"

Leonidas wet his lips. "Uncle Maximus made me come. He was furious that he lost Lyra in the kronekling tournament, and he knows that I'm the only one she'll listen to. He told me to come here, kill you, and bring Lyra to him."

I could hear the underlying threat in his words. "Or else?"

He wet his lips again. "Or else he would hurt my mother. And me too."

Maximus had once hit Maeven because she'd failed to kill me, and I had seen the dark, ugly impression his ring had left behind on her face. I had also seen how he snapped his fingers at Mercer and Nox and ordered them around like they were his servants instead of his son and nephew. And of course I knew how disposable the members of the Bastard Brigade were to him. But I hadn't thought the Mortan king would be so heartless as to order a teenage boy to kill me, even if that boy was another one of his bastard relatives. Just when I thought Maximus couldn't surprise me anymore, he sank to an even lower level of depravity.

I couldn't keep myself from asking the obvious question. "Hurt you how?"

A shudder rippled through his body, and the scent of ashy heartbreak surged off him, along with strong notes of pain, anger, and misery. The emotions were even sharper than my sword at his throat.

"You don't want to know," he whispered.

No, I didn't want to know. Given what Maximus had done to that strix earlier, I could well imagine the horrible tortures he would coldly inflict on whoever displeased him.

"So your uncle sent you here to kill me," I murmured. "Well, you did a poor job of it, since my sword is at your throat."

Leonidas lifted his chin and straightened a bit, despite the blade at his neck. "I don't care what you do to me. But please, *please* don't hurt Lyra. She didn't know I was coming, and she has nothing to do with any of this. So don't hurt her. Please?"

Well, at least he was polite, even if he had tried to kill me. But the boy was right. The strix had nothing to do with Maximus.

"I'm not going to hurt Lyra. I would never do anything like that. But what about your mother? Does Maeven know about this?"

Leonidas shook his head a tiny bit. "I don't think so. Uncle Maximus summoned me to his tent and gave me the daggers and the mission himself. Mercer was there, but my mother wasn't, and I didn't see her before the guards escorted me out of camp and across the bridge to Fortuna."

Of course she hadn't been there. Maximus wouldn't have wanted Maeven to try to stop him from sending her son off to die.

I had already killed several members of the Bastard Brigade, strong, seasoned adults who had a lot more training and magic than Leonidas did. Maximus had to know that I would most likely best the boy, but he had sent his nephew here anyway. Why? Did he want Leonidas dead for some reason? But if that was Maximus's goal, then why not just cut the boy's throat like he had the strix's earlier?

Or maybe Maximus simply wanted me to live with the guilt of killing the boy. Although as soon as I had that thought I dismissed it as ridiculous. Maximus didn't feel guilt, and he wouldn't expect others to indulge in the emotion, especially not a queen like me.

The Mortan king could have had any number of reasons for sending the boy here to die, but Leonidas's familiar features and amethyst eyes made me think about Maeven.

Maybe Maximus wanted to punish Maeven for failing to kill me so many times before. Maybe he was even hoping that my killing Leonidas would enrage Maeven enough that she would finally figure out a way to successfully murder me.

Dahlia had said that Maeven loved her children, and this evening Maeven had shown far more worry and concern for Leonidas than I'd expected.

After all these months of battling the bitch, I could finally do something to hurt Maeven the way she'd hurt me. I could finally take something away from her the way she'd taken so much away from me.

I could kill her son and send his body back to her in bloody pieces.

Maybe I was a horrible person for even thinking such an awful thing. Maybe the mere idea made me just as cruel and heartless as Maximus. But the longer I looked at Leonidas, the more I could hear the screams of Isobel, the cook master who'd been like a second mother to me, along with Cordelia, Madelena, and my murdered cousins ringing in my ears, and the more I could see Maeven smiling while the turncoat guards cut down everyone on the Seven Spire lawn, including the children.

So many dead, bloody, broken children.

Leonidas must have seen the play of emotions on my face, because he straightened a bit more. "I don't care what you do to me," he repeated. His voice didn't waver, but I could smell his dusty resignation. "But please don't hurt Lyra. Please?"

His last word came out as a low, ragged whisper, and tears filled his eyes. The tears, along with the sharp scent of his worry, made me think that he wasn't crying for himself, but rather at the thought of all the horrible ways I could torture his beloved strix.

In that moment, I realized that I couldn't do it.

I couldn't kill this boy in cold blood, not even after he'd halfheartedly tried to kill me. That was a line I just couldn't—

wouldn't—cross, not even to get my much-desired revenge on Maeven.

I let out a tense breath, backed away from him, and lowered my sword. "I'm not going to hurt you or Lyra."

Leonidas stayed stiff and frozen up against the support pole. Suspicion filled his face. "But you thought about it."

"Yes. I thought about it."

He frowned and cocked his head to the side. The quizzical look and bobbing motion reminded me of how Lyra had studied me earlier. The strix was still in her cage, peering through the bars at us.

"Then why didn't you go ahead and kill me? Uncle Maximus would have. So would Mercer and Nox." He paused. "And my mother. None of them would have hesitated."

"I know. But that's not the kind of person, not the kind of queen, I want to be."

As soon as I said the words, I realized how true they were—and how wrong I had been about my Regalia strategy.

An assassin's arrow and wormroot poison were Mortan games. I might be able to engage in such plots, but my heart wasn't truly in those sorts of sly machinations, which was one of the reasons my efforts to kill Maximus had failed so far.

I needed to change my strategy to play to *my* strengths. That meant focusing on the things Serilda and Xenia had taught me—how to fight and how to spy. That's how I had won my crown, and that's how I would keep it, along with my life.

"My mother would say that makes you weak," Leonidas said in a chiding, singsong voice, as if he were repeating something he'd been told many times.

"I am not *weak*," I snapped. "I will do what I must to protect myself and my kingdom. But there is a difference between being strong and being cruel, and killing you would just be cruel."

Leonidas's frown deepened, as if he couldn't understand why I wasn't killing him anyway, despite my explanation. Then again, I doubted the boy had seen anything other than cruelty in his life, so I couldn't blame him for not understanding the concept of *not* indulging in it.

Leonidas opened his mouth, probably to ask another question, but then his eyes widened, and the scent of his surprise washed over me.

That was all the warning I had before I was attacked—again.

My gladiator training, survival instinct, or maybe even luck took over, and I whirled to my right, barely avoiding the knife that whistled past my body. I whipped up my sword and turned to face my enemy—

And ran straight into someone's fist.

Well, I supposed it was less about my running into their fist and more about them actually hitting me, but pain exploded in my jaw, my feet flew out from under me, and I landed hard on my ass. White stars winked on and off in my eyes, and everything blurred. I blinked and blinked, trying to focus and ignore the ache that radiated out from my jaw and pounded up into my skull.

Two men and a woman were looming over me, their black cloaks marking them as Fortuna Mint geldjagers. One of the men was grinning and cracking his knuckles. He must have been the one who'd hit me, and he had some mutt strength, judging from the pain still rippling through my face.

"Stay down." He sneered. "Or I'll put you down again."

I started to scramble to my feet, but he slammed his fist into my face again. This time, my whole body snapped back against the ground, including my head, and I groaned as a fresh wave of pain exploded in my skull.

"That's enough, Jerome," the woman said. "We need her alive, remember?"

Jerome cracked his knuckles again. "I think you mean mostly alive, Kenna."

She shrugged. "You know what I mean. Now get her up."

Jerome leaned down. I had managed to hang on to my sword, so I lashed out with it, trying to cut him, but it was a weak, awkward blow. Jerome wrested my weapon away and flung it across the tent.

The tearstone blade banged into the table where Lyra was still sitting in her cage, then dropped to the ground. The strix didn't make a sound at the sudden bit of violence, but her eyes narrowed, and the razor-sharp onyx tips on the ends of her feathers tilted up.

Jerome grabbed my arm and yanked me to my feet. Then he spun me around, pulled a knife off his belt, and held it up against my neck. "You yell, scream, or do anything that I don't like, and I will slit your throat, orders be damned."

I had to crinkle my nose to keep from sneezing at the rotten, oniony stench of his breath. Ugh. That was even worse than the blade at my neck.

"Take it easy," the other man piped up. "She's worth too much to kill."

"Shut up, Darron," Jerome growled. "You're not in charge. I am."

Darron glared at the other man, lifted his sword, and moved forward, but Kenna stepped in front of him and held up her hand.

"Forget about who's in charge," she hissed. "Let's get her out of here before the guards come back and find us—"

"Leave her alone," a voice growled.

Kenna and Darron whirled around, as did Jerome, who spun me around with him. Leonidas was standing in front of us, his hands clenched into fists.

"Let her go," he said. "Now."

Silence dropped over the tent. Jerome and Darron stared at the boy, but Kenna sidled toward him.

"Hello, Leonidas," she crooned. "Your Uncle Maximus sent us to help with your mission."

The smoky lie of her words filled the air. Maximus hadn't sent her. At least, not to help the boy. I opened my mouth to tell Leonidas as much, but Jerome dug his knife into my neck. The blade nicked my skin, making me hiss with pain and blood trickle down my throat.

"Keep your mouth shut," he snarled.

Leonidas glanced at me, but Kenna sidled forward another step, drawing his attention.

"Your Uncle Maximus sent us to help you," she repeated. "And he wanted us to give you a message."

"What message?" Leonidas asked.

She smiled, but her eyes glinted with a dark, dangerous light. "That he doesn't tolerate weakness—or especially failure."

She snapped up her arm and threw her knife at him. Kenna's aim was true, and the blade was going to plunge into Leonidas's heart—

The knife stopped a foot away from the boy.

Kenna frowned, wondering what was happening. So did Darron, and Jerome jerked back in surprise, dragging me along with him. My nose twitched. Instead of Jerome's horrible onion breath, the scent of magic now filled the air.

Leonidas's power.

The three geldjagers couldn't smell the boy's magic, but they finally noticed the power crackling in his eyes, making them burn a bright, eerie violet. They all froze.

"You shouldn't have lied." Leonidas gave Kenna a grim smile. "Uncle Maximus *never* sends anyone to help me—only kill me."

He waved his hand, and the knife hovering in the air in

front of him flew right back at her. The blade punched into Kenna's chest, and she yelped with pain and toppled to the ground.

"Kenna!" Darron shouted.

He too drew a knife off his belt and threw it at Leonidas, who also stopped this weapon in midair with his magic. Darron rushed at the boy, raising his sword to attack. Leonidas's eyes widened, and he lunged forward and plucked the knife out of the air, bringing it up just in time to block Darron's sword.

Their fight distracted Jerome, who lowered the knife at my throat a few inches. With one hand, I grabbed his arm and wrenched it and the blade away from my neck. With my other, I rammed my elbow back into his stomach. Jerome let out a loud *oof!* of air and staggered away. He tripped over a chest full of clothes and tumbled to the ground.

I yanked my tearstone dagger off my belt and charged forward. Leonidas and Darron were locked together, their blades seesawing back and forth. Leonidas might have magic, but the geldjager was much stronger, and he was slowly inching his sword toward the boy's throat.

I couldn't let the boy die, not after he'd tried to save me, so I buried my dagger in Darron's back. He screamed, and I yanked out the blade, drew his head back, and slit his throat. He crumpled to the ground, bleeding out.

I looked at Leonidas. "Are you okay—"

A hand dug into my hair, making me yelp, and Jerome yanked me back and threw me down. My head snapped against the ground again, and more white stars exploded in my eyes.

Jerome stepped over me, drew back his fist, and punched Leonidas in the face. The boy groaned and toppled to the ground, and Jerome kicked him in the ribs. Leonidas started coughing, trying to get his breath back after the hard, brutal blow.

"Weak Mortan brat," Jerome growled. "No wonder the king wanted us to kill you."

I blinked the stars out of my eyes again, tightened my grip on the dagger still in my hand, and staggered back up and onto my feet.

Jerome's hands clenched into fists, and his lips twisted into an angry sneer. "You really think you're going to stop me with that dagger?"

Behind him, the cage door *creak*ed open, and two purple eyes gleamed like matches burning in the dark.

"I don't have to stop you," I said, my words slurring a bit. "Lyra's going to do it for me."

Jerome frowned. "Who the fuck is Lyra—"

With a loud shriek of rage, the strix flew out of her cage, zoomed across the tent, and drove her body straight into Jerome's. The geldjager slammed into the ground, landing flat on his back. Lyra hopped up onto his chest, snapped her beak forward, and buried it in his throat like it was a sword she was wielding.

Jerome tried to scream, but all that came out was a choked, bloody gurgle.

Lyra threw her head back, flexed her wings, and let out a loud, triumphant cry. Then she started raking her talons across Jerome's body, cutting through his clothes and opening up deep, bloody gashes across his chest and stomach. In less than ten seconds it was over, and Jerome died without making another sound.

When she was sure Jerome was dead, Lyra hopped across the ground to Leonidas, who was clutching his bruised ribs. She gently nuzzled her head against his free hand, and Leonidas reached out and hugged the bird to his side.

"Good girl," he rasped. "Good girl."

Lyra's feathers puffed up with pride, and she snuggled closer to the boy. Leonidas didn't seem to notice the blood coating her beak and talons. Or if he did, he just didn't care that Lyra was smearing it all over him.

"What's going on?"

"Was that a strix scream?"

"The queen! Check on the queen!"

More and more shouts rose up outside the tent. Lyra's cries had been sharper and louder than the general camp revelry and had alerted the Bellonan guards that something was wrong.

Instead of lunging to his feet and trying to run away, Leonidas sighed and slumped back against one of the support poles, with Lyra still by his side. "You should have gone ahead and killed me. Your people will tear me apart for this. And Lyra too."

The strix let out a sharp *caw!* and flexed her wings, as if ready to take on anyone who dared to threaten Leonidas.

"My only regret is that I can't save the others," the boy continued. "I should have found some way to open their cages before I came here."

"Others? What are you talking about?"

Leonidas sighed again. "The other strixes that Uncle Maximus brought to the Regalia."

I frowned. "You mean the ones the guards flew into the arena?"

The boy shook his head. "No. The *other* strixes. The ones that Uncle Maximus . . ." He didn't finish his thought, but he didn't have to.

My stomach roiled at the idea, but I pushed my disgust aside and forced myself to think about the king's actions. Surely there was only so much blood and magic Maximus could drink and absorb at one time. So why bring that many creatures to the Regalia?

Unless . . . he was planning to unleash all that magic.

He's never brought so many men and strixes to the Regalia before,

Auster's voice whispered in my mind. *He has something planned, something bigger than just killing Evie.*

Auster had said that after the opening ceremonies, and we'd taken precautions to make sure we wouldn't be taken by surprise by the Mortan guards on their strixes. But if Maximus slaughtered more strixes, then he could potentially amass enough magic to blast through our defenses, leaving his men and their strixes free to swoop down and decimate the ranks of my guards.

He could potentially wipe out the entire Bellonan camp, which would leave him free to do something even worse—invade my kingdom.

"Where are these strixes?" I asked in a sharp voice.

Leonidas sighed for a third time. "In their cages. In our camp. On the Mortan side of the river."

"Could you draw me a map? Show me where they are?"

He shrugged. "I could, but your people are coming to kill me, so what's the point? I'll be dead soon enough, and so will those strixes."

I stared at the three dead geldjagers, thoughts and schemes whirling through my mind. Maximus had sent Leonidas to kill me, but he'd realized that the boy might fail, so he'd most likely told Driscol to send these assassins as backup. And not just to kill me, but Leonidas too.

But the assassins were Fortuna geldjagers, and they had wanted to kidnap me, rather than murder me. Once again, it seemed like the DiLucris were making promises to Maximus, but then ignoring his orders in favor of their own sinister plans.

Leonidas was right. Captain Auster would want to tear him to pieces for attacking me. So would Paloma, Sullivan, and the rest of my friends. It would be so easy to let them do whatever they liked to Leonidas, and Lyra too.

But once again, I couldn't—*wouldn't*—do that.

The boy had been trying to save his strix, as well as protect himself and his mother. If my own mother had still been alive, I would have done *anything* to keep her safe, even try to kill a queen.

No, I wasn't going to kill Leonidas—but I could still use him.

At the very least, I needed more information about the strixes that Maximus planned to slaughter. And that wasn't the only way I could use the boy. Maximus didn't realize it, but he'd just given me the perfect tool to further my long game with Maeven, a game that might let me crush the king at the same time.

I looked at Leonidas. "Do you trust me?"

"Of course not. Why would I trust you? You're the Bellonan queen." He frowned. "And why would you even want me to trust you? I just tried to kill you."

Well, at least the boy was honest. So I asked a different, better question. "Do you want to live? More importantly, do you want Lyra to live?"

He threw his hands up in frustration and confusion. "Of course I want Lyra to live." He eyed me, and his frown slowly deepened. "Wait. Why are you smiling like that?"

My smile stretched a little wider across my face. "Listen to me very carefully. Here's what we're going to do."

CHAPTER EIGHTEEN

I had barely finished telling Leonidas my plan when people started rushing into my tent.

Auster, Serilda, and Cho had their swords drawn, ready to battle any assassins, while Paloma clutched her mace, eager to do the same. Sullivan's blue lightning crackled on his fingertips. Even Calandre and her two sisters hurried inside, brandishing scissors to cut down anyone who was threatening me.

They all jerked to a stop at the sight of me calmly searching Jerome's pockets. I'd already patted down the other two geldjagers while I was talking to Leonidas, but they hadn't been carrying anything noteworthy. And none of them, Jerome included, was wearing a gold coined-woman pendant that would have marked them as working for the Mint. Driscol had corrected that mistake, at least.

"Oh," Paloma said, lowering her mace. "You killed them already."

"You sound disappointed."

She shrugged. "I could have used some practice for the tournament tomorrow."

I rolled my eyes. Of course she would say that. I finished searching Jerome's pockets and got to my feet.

"What happened?" Auster asked, his brown eyes fixed on Leonidas and Lyra, who were still sitting on the ground in the center of the tent. "And why is the Morricone boy here?"

"Yes, highness," Sullivan murmured, also staring at Leonidas, his magic still crackling on his fingertips. "What *is* the Morricone boy doing here? And why is that strix out of its cage?"

"Her name is Lyra. And she saved me, along with Leonidas."

My friends all gave me incredulous looks, but I told them what had happened. When I finished, Captain Auster summoned some guards to remove the assassins' bodies. Unfortunately, there was no platform or scaffolding on which to display them, like I'd done with the geldjagers in Svalin, so I told Auster to bury the bodies and be done with them. The captain left the tent, along with the guards.

Calandre and her sisters fluttered about, straightening up the mess left behind by the battle. They also found several long slits in one of the canvas walls from where the assassins had snuck into the tent, and they sewed up the holes.

While they worked, I answered question after question from Paloma, Sullivan, Serilda, and Cho about the attack.

Finally, I held up my hands, calling for quiet. "You're asking the wrong questions and thinking about the wrong things. It doesn't matter that Leonidas tried to kill me or that the geldjagers wanted to kidnap me."

"Then what does matter?" Cho gave me a curious look.

"How I react. And especially how we use it against Maximus and Maeven."

"So that's why you're keeping the boy alive," Serilda said.

She glanced over at Leonidas, who was still sitting with Lyra. The boy kept sliding his fingers down the strix's purple feathers in a quick, nervous rhythm. I could smell his worry, but I hadn't lied to him earlier. He was going to live, and so was Lyra.

I was going to protect them, but I was also going to use the boy to further my own goals. A good queen took advantage of every tool at her disposal, and Leonidas was going to help me undercut Maximus in a number of ways.

I smiled. "Oh, yes. I have something special in mind for the boy."

Paloma stared at me. "You know, Evie, I never thought that you looked or sounded particularly sinister until this very moment."

My smile slowly widened.

I left the Bellonan camp early the next morning.

Sullivan, Paloma, Serilda, Cho, Captain Auster, and several guards flanked me as I walked down the steps and headed toward the Perseverance Bridge. The only one missing was Xenia, who had spent the night on one of the Ungerian ships with Zariza. But there was a new addition to our troupe.

Leonidas.

The boy had spent the night in a tent with Lyra under a heavy guard. But other than the dread filling his face, he looked no worse for the wear.

I couldn't do anything about his dread, but I had kept my promise, and he and Lyra had not been harmed. The boy had been given a bath and fresh clothes, along with plenty of food and water, and Lyra had been offered several cuts of meat, which she had gobbled down.

The strix was now back in their tent, where Leonidas had told her to stay until he returned, and she had seemed content enough to hunker down inside her cage, although the boy had left the door open so she could hop around the tent if she liked. I'd told the guards not to bother the strix or try to stop her if she decided to leave camp.

My friends and I quickly reached the bridge and crossed it, heading back to Fortuna for day two of the Regalia. It was a lovely morning, cold, crisp, and sunny, and throngs of people were already streaming over to the island. The Tournament of Champions would kick off this morning, and everyone wanted to get to the arena early to get the best possible seat.

Despite the crowds, it didn't take us long to walk over to the island and climb the steps to the arena. I stopped at the edge of the main plaza, drinking in the sights, sounds, and especially the smells.

Many spectators sported painted faces and were enthusiastically waving pennants featuring the colors and crests of their favorite troupes and gladiators. The merchants were already hawking their wares, their voices ringing together in a chorus of commerce. The smoky sizzle of frying bacon mingled with the buttery, sugary scents of freshly made cornucopia and other decadent treats. I soaked up as many of the sights, sounds, and smells as possible, especially since I didn't know if I would actually live through the day.

Given my plans, I might not even make it until lunchtime.

Together, my friends and I headed toward the long tables that served as the registration area.

"This is where we leave you," Cho said, then looked at Paloma. "Are you ready for this?"

As ringmaster, he was announcing the tournament, while Paloma was competing. Cho was wearing his red ringmaster's jacket, while Paloma was dressed in light gray fighting leathers. She had a shield strapped to her forearm, and her mace was dangling from her belt.

"Of course I'm ready for this," she said, then glanced at me. "Aren't you going to wish me luck?"

"Luck is for fools and children," I replied. "Isn't that what you said to me in Xenia's dance hall last week?"

She rolled her eyes at my teasing, but I reached out and squeezed her bare muscled arm.

"You don't need luck," I said. "You are going to go into the ring and show everyone that you're not just the best gladiator in the Black Swan troupe or in Svalin, but that you are the best bloody gladiator in *all* the kingdoms. You are going to *win*, and you are going to look fierce and fabulous doing it."

A grin slowly spread across Paloma's face. "Queen Everleigh is getting pretty good at giving inspiring speeches."

I grinned back at her. "Well, I'm glad you think that I'm finally getting good at *something*."

She smiled at me a moment longer, then her face turned serious, and she stabbed her finger at me. "You'd better not die while I'm fighting, and you'd better be here to see me win."

"I won't, and I will. Promise."

Paloma and Cho headed over to the tables. Sullivan, Serilda, Auster, and I headed into the arena, with Leonidas sandwiched in the middle of us and the Bellonan guards.

We threaded our way through the crowd and climbed the bleacher steps to the royal terrace. Dozens of minor royals, nobles, advisors, and others were already milling around, laughing, gossiping, and enjoying refreshments. Driscol was speaking with a servant, while Seraphine was standing by his side, another blank smile on her face.

Eon, Ruri, Cisco, Zariza, Heinrich. All the other kings and queens were already here, including Maximus, and I was the last to arrive. Good. I wanted everyone to see my special guest.

Maximus turned toward our group, a sneering smile on his face. I didn't know what he had hoped or expected to see, but it definitely wasn't Leonidas standing next to me, and Maximus's smile vanished like a snowman melting in the sun. Maeven also turned around, wondering what her brother was staring at, and she stiffened in surprise. So did Nox, who was standing next to her. Mercer wasn't here, since he was competing in the tournament.

I ignored the Mortans and made a slow circuit around the terrace, greeting the other royals. Eon and Ruri were polite, Cisco was cold and dismissive, and Heinrich and Zariza were warm and welcoming. Nothing had changed from last night, including how angry Maximus was, anger that grew with every second I ignored him. Even though the scent of his hot, peppery anger burned my nose, I breathed it in over and over again.

I did so love the smell of my enemy's impotent rage.

Finally, I deigned to walk over to Maximus. Nox stepped up beside his uncle, but Maeven hovered a few feet away, as did Driscol and Seraphine.

"Hello, Maximus," I purred. "Isn't it a fine morning?"

He stared at me, and I smiled back, as if it were perfectly natural for his bastard nephew to be a part of my contingent. Everyone else had noticed Leonidas trailing along behind me, and whispers were already swirling about what I was doing with the boy.

Maximus frowned, clearly not understanding what I hoped to gain, but he couldn't contain his curiosity. "Is there a problem?"

I frowned back at him, as though I were puzzled. "Problem? Why would there be a problem?"

He gestured at Leonidas, who was standing behind me, right in between Sullivan and Captain Auster. "It seems as though you have my nephew in your custody."

"Leonidas? In my custody?" I laughed. "You make it sound like he's my prisoner. Quite the contrary."

"What do you mean?" Maximus asked in a suspicious voice. "Has something unpleasant happened?"

There was that damn word again, but I waved my hand. "Oh, some assassins infiltrated the Bellonan camp last night and tried to kill me, but of course they didn't succeed."

"Yes, I can see that," Maximus muttered, shooting a nasty look at Driscol, who visibly paled.

The Mortan king faced me again. "But that still doesn't explain what you're doing with my nephew. We were all quite concerned when we couldn't find him in our camp this morning."

I had to give him credit for saying the lie with a straight face, but Maximus had just given me the perfect opening to spin my own tale. "Actually, I wanted to talk to you about Leonidas and his actions last night."

"Oh, really?"

Maximus probably thought I was going to accuse him of sending the boy to murder me. So did Nox and Maeven, from the way they both tensed. Driscol looked nervous as well, although Seraphine was as calm as ever.

"Oh, yes." I looked around the terrace, making sure I had everyone's attention. Time to once again focus on the second part of my Regalia plan, showing strength and cleverness in front of the other royals. "Leonidas saved my life last night. Why, the boy is a bloody *hero*."

Silence dropped over the terrace, and everyone went utterly still. No one seemed to know what to do or say, including Maximus, who blinked in confusion.

"A hero?" he said. "I'm not sure what you mean."

I gestured at Leonidas, who shuffled up beside me. The boy's face was pale, and he looked like he might faint, so I patted his shoulder, trying to reassure him, then turned back to Maximus.

"Yes, a *hero*," I repeated. "You see, that strix I won during the kronekling tournament is actually Leonidas's strix. I didn't realize that, or I *never* would have taken it away from the boy."

Maximus kept blinking, still not sure where I was going with this.

"Leonidas came to the Bellonan camp last night to say good-bye to his beloved strix. Such a good boy, going to honor the outcome of the tournament, regardless of how much it hurt to lose his best friend." I glanced at Leonidas, but he didn't contradict my lies. "Anyway, Leonidas saw some assassins sneaking into my camp. He sounded the alarm, and he stopped the assassins from hurting anyone, including me."

Maximus frowned, as did Nox, but I focused on Maeven. Anger stained her cheeks a bright, hot pink, and her hands were fisted in her skirt. She didn't know what I was doing with her son, but she didn't like it. Too damn bad. This game was just getting started.

"I was so impressed with Leonidas's bravery that I've invited him to stay in the Bellonan camp for the duration of the Regalia as my special guest," I said, looking at the king again. "I hope that you'll agree, Maximus. I think it would be a wonderful way to foster better relations between our two kingdoms."

Maximus's eyes narrowed, and fury sparked in his dark purple gaze. He knew I was mocking him with Leonidas's failure to kill me. No doubt, as soon as he'd seen Leonidas, Maximus had thought I would tell everyone that the boy had tried to murder me. Then the Mortan king could have publicly denounced his nephew or perhaps taken him into custody to be executed at a later date. But I'd surprised Maximus by painting the boy as a hero, and he couldn't claim otherwise. Not without revealing that he'd sent the boy to try to assassinate me.

"Of course." Maximus said the words through gritted teeth. "I'm sure that my nephew will enjoy your hospitality."

I gestured at the buffet tables. "Leonidas, why don't you get something to eat? You look famished."

Leonidas actually looked sick to his stomach, but he shuffled over and started filling a plate with food, although I doubted he would eat any of it. Still, it gave him something to do, and it got him a little farther away from the rest of the Mortans.

"Enjoy the tournament," I said.

I smiled at Maximus again, then walked over and took a seat at the royal table. The other kings and queens slowly moved forward and took their seats as well. Eon tipped his head respectfully to me. Ruri did the same, and the dragon on her hand actually winked at me. Cisco remained as sour as ever, ignoring me, while Heinrich and Zariza were both grinning.

"Well done, Everleigh," Zariza whispered as she sat down beside me. "Very well done."

I shrugged. "Well, it's not as complicated as the Tanzen Falter, but I know how to dance around people like Maximus."

"Yes, you do." Zariza's grin slowly faded. "The only question now is, how will he retaliate?"

I glanced over at Maximus. Even though he was on the opposite side of the terrace, I could clearly smell his hot jalapeño rage. It was practically blasting out of his pores like lightning from a magier's fingertips.

Zariza was right. I had just kicked a nest of coral vipers. Now all I could do was wait and see how many of them slithered out and tried to kill me.

Five minutes later, Cho strode out to the center of the arena floor and used his booming voice to announce the start of the tournament. The crowd went wild, yelling, cheering, clapping, screaming, and whistling, and the scent of everyone's collective eagerness flooded the air. The other events and competitions were entertaining enough, but this was what everyone had come to see.

Since Mercer was the defending champion, he had the honor of participating in the first bout. Cho announced him, and the Mortan crown prince strode out to the middle of the arena.

Like all the competitors, Mercer was wearing traditional gladiator fighting leathers—a tight, fitted sleeveless shirt, a knee-length kilt, and flat sandals with straps that wound up past his ankles. His leathers were a dark purple, with the fancy cursive *M* of the Morricone royal crest stretching across his chest in silver thread. A silver shield that featured the same *M* was strapped to his forearm, and he was also carrying a sword with a silver hilt.

The Mortan crown prince held his arms out wide, soaking up the crowd's raucous cheers. Mercer turned around in a slow circle, then stepped into the center ring. The wooden ring had been painted a bright, glossy red, indicating that the bouts were only to first blood.

Cho announced Mercer's opponent, a man from Flores, and then started the bout.

The Floresian fighter lunged forward, but Mercer coolly spun away. Mercer could have whirled back around, sliced his sword across the man's exposed back, and ended the bout right then and there, but he danced around, avoiding the other man's attacks, and drawing out the fight like a cat playing with a mouse.

A few minutes later, Mercer sliced his sword across the man's chest, ending the bout.

Since the tournament was only to first blood, most of the competitors didn't wind up too badly injured, but the Floresian fighter screamed and crumpled to the ground at the deep, gruesome wound. Mercer loomed over the fallen man, sneering down at his victim, then raised his arms out to his sides, once again soaking up the crowd's cheers.

"That's my son," Maximus said in a proud tone, his voice booming across the terrace.

Most people politely clapped, acknowledging Mercer's victory, but I gave Maximus a disgusted look. He smiled back at me.

Cho rushed over to the fallen fighter, as did the bone masters who were waiting in the archways around the arena floor. They managed to heal the Floresian, then carried him out of the arena.

A few other bouts took place, and then it was Paloma's turn.

I surged to my feet, yelling, cheering, clapping, and whistling. Sullivan, Serilda, and Auster were cheering just as loudly as I was, and Heinrich and Dominic were clapping too.

Paloma looked up at the royal terrace and stabbed her mace into the air. Then she nodded to her competitor, who returned the gesture. Cho started the fight, and Paloma and the other gladiator charged at each other, much to the delight of the roaring crowd.

The other gladiator was a mutt from Vacuna with strength and speed magic, but he was no match for Paloma, who drew first blood less than two minutes later. She helped the man to his feet, then stood in the ring and stabbed her mace up into the air over and over again. I knew that my friend had missed being part of the Black Swan troupe, especially the arena fights, and I was glad she was getting this chance to enjoy the crowd's cheers again.

"Your guard is quite formidable," Zariza murmured. The Ungerian queen was still sitting beside me, sipping some apple brandy. "She reminds me of Amira."

"Is she one of your fighters?"

"No. Amira was Xenia's daughter."

Shock knifed through me, and I stopped clapping. "What do you mean *was*?"

Zariza shrugged. "Amira got involved with a boy that Xenia didn't approve of and foolishly ran off with him. Of course Xenia tried to track her down, but she couldn't find Amira, and no one has seen or heard from her in more than twenty years. We all assume she's dead, including Xenia."

"Why?"

"Because Amira would have contacted her by now. She might have made a mistake running off with that boy, but she loved Xenia too much to stay angry with her mother this long."

I glanced over at Xenia, who was standing with the rest of the Ungers. Paloma must have also reminded Xenia of her lost daughter, because the older woman was leaning heavily on her silver ogre cane, and the scent of ashy heartbreak rolled off her in wave after wave.

The longer I looked at Xenia, the more I was reminded of Paloma's own heartbreak over her missing mother, who had also vanished without a trace. Strange, that two ogre morphs would just disappear like that and leave their families behind.

"What did Amira look like?" I asked.

Zariza tapped her finger on her glass. "I was just a child when she vanished, so my memories are a bit fuzzy. The main thing I remember was that Amira had long, wavy golden hair that bounced and shimmered with every step she took. It was even prettier than mine." She pouted a bit, as did the ogre on her neck, as if neither one of them could imagine such a thing.

I thought back, trying to recall every single thing Paloma had ever told me about her mother. My friend was still stabbing her mace up into the air, and my gaze locked onto the weapon—*Peony*.

"Did Amira wear peony perfume?"

Zariza blinked in surprise. "Yes, she did. It was her favorite scent. How did you know that?"

More shock knifed through me, and theories and implications spun through my mind, although I kept my expression neutral. "Just a lucky guess. Xenia wears the same perfume."

As does Paloma. Although I didn't voice that thought.

Zariza's amber eyes narrowed. She didn't believe me, but she didn't have a reason to question me either.

Out of the corner of my eye, I noticed Serilda discreetly waving at me. "Please excuse me."

Zariza turned her attention back to the arena floor. I got to my feet and went over to Serilda and Sullivan, who were standing by one of the buffet tables. Auster was sitting nearby, keeping an eye on Leonidas, who was slowly, resolutely shifting food from one side of his plate to the other and back again.

"It's time," Serilda said in a low voice. "If you want to do this, then we need to leave now."

I nodded at her and looked at Sullivan. Worry filled his blue eyes, and I could smell his concern. He hadn't liked my plan, but he especially didn't like this part of it.

"Are you sure that you don't want me to come with you?" he whispered. "I could help."

"I know, but it will look suspicious if we all leave," I murmured back. "Besides, I need you to stay here. If things go wrong, you and Auster need to get Leonidas to safety, along with the rest of the Bellonans."

He reluctantly nodded, ceding to my wishes, but more worry sparked in his eyes. We all knew how dangerous this was, but it was the only way I could think of to weaken Maximus. I had to disrupt and sabotage his plans, just like Xenia had taught me. I had to protect my kingdom above all else, even my burning desire to kill the king.

"I want to congratulate Paloma on her win," I said in a loud voice for the benefit of anyone listening. "Serilda, follow me."

Serilda bowed her head and fell in step beside me. Together, the two of us crossed the terrace.

Our route took us past Maximus, who eyed me. But another Mortan was getting ready to fight, so he turned his attention back to the arena floor. Of course he did. Watching his gladiator advance in the tournament was far more important than whatever I might be up to. But his dismissiveness worked in my favor, and Serilda and I left the terrace without any interference.

We quickly made our way down the steps, then walked through one of the archways and back out onto the plaza. More people were moving through the area than before, but a large crowd was gathered in front of a nearby archway, and shouts rang through the air.

"Paloma! Paloma, sign my banner!"

"No! Sign *my* banner!"

"Paloma! You're the greatest gladiator ever!"

I caught a glimpse of my friend standing in the center of the crush of people, smiling and signing autographs. She was playing her part perfectly, and now it was time for Serilda and me to do the same.

"Let's go," I said.

We both stepped forward, but someone glided in front of me, blocking my path.

Maeven.

She had been on the royal terrace when Serilda and I had left, and she must have had to hustle to catch us. I wondered if Maximus had sent her or if she had sought me out on her own.

"Everleigh," Maeven said in a cold, if somewhat civil voice. "A word, please."

"At last," I drawled. "She speaks. Did you know that's the

first thing I've heard you say during the entire Regalia? I was beginning to think that Maximus had cut out your tongue."

Anger sparked in her amethyst eyes, but she didn't respond to my insult. Instead, she whirled around and stepped into the shadows of a nearby archway, apparently wanting some privacy. She must have come here on her own, rather than on her brother's orders.

Serilda's hand curled around her sword hilt, but I shook my head. Maeven wasn't foolish enough to try to kill me here, with so many other people around to see her do it and Serilda just itching to cut her down.

So I stepped into the archway and faced the other woman. Maeven glanced over at Serilda, who gave her a flat look and kept her hand on her sword. She wasn't going anywhere, so Maeven looked at me again.

"What do you think you're doing?" she hissed.

"Well, I was going to congratulate my friend on her victory. Until you so rudely interrupted me."

"My son," she hissed again. "What do you think you're doing with *my son*?"

"Nothing much," I replied in a dry tone. "Just saving him from being assassinated."

"What are you talking about? He was supposed to kill—" She bit back the *you* dangling on the end of her tongue.

"So you knew that Maximus sent Leonidas off to die last night." I shook my head. "And here I thought you actually loved your son. My mistake."

Maeven's lips pinched together into a hard, thin line. "My son is a fine warrior. Maximus didn't send him off to die."

"Oh, yes, he did," I snapped. "Leonidas might know how to fight, but I've spent just about every single day of the past year battling for my life. Who did you think was going to win?"

She didn't respond, which was answer enough.

"Besides, Leonidas told me that you weren't even there when Maximus and Mercer gave him the order, and I'm betting that you didn't even realize he had been escorted out of the Mortan camp until it was too late."

Agreement flickered across her face before she could hide it. So far, I hadn't had a chance to implement the third part of my Regalia plan and manipulate Maeven, but this was the perfect opportunity to continue my long game with her, the one she still didn't seem to realize we were playing.

"I've been watching you during the Regalia. All this time, all these months we've been battling one another, I thought you were this great leader, this important Morricone royal, but that's not the case, is it?" I said in a mocking voice. "You just follow your brother around and do whatever he says, along with Mercer and Nox."

"Maximus is the king," she replied in a cold, flat voice.

I snorted. "King? More like a bloody dictator. A king listens to his advisors, but not Maximus. He *never* listens to you. Why, he's barely even *looked* at you during the Regalia. I bet that he just orders you around, along with the other members of your Bastard Brigade. Funny, how I haven't seen any of them at the Regalia, just you and Leonidas."

I paused, hoping Maeven might say something reckless and give me a clue as to the location of the other members of the Bastard Brigade. She remained silent, so I continued with my taunts.

"You probably had to leave your bastard cousins back home in Morta. Or perhaps they're out on other missions, spying, thieving, and killing. Either way, Maximus didn't think they were worth bringing here. Why, I'm surprised that he brought *you*."

Maeven stepped a little closer, her hands clenching into fists. Magic crackled in her eyes, making them burn a dark, dangerous purple, but she held back her electric rage—for now. "You might be a legitimate royal, but deep down you're just a scared little girl playing dress-up. The only reason you're queen is because all the other Blairs are dead. Face it, Everleigh. *I* made you queen. You didn't earn that tearstone throne. You didn't earn *anything*."

Icy rage spiked through me, and I stepped closer to her. "You're right. I'm only queen because everyone else is dead. But so far, I've managed to hang on to my kingdom, my crown, and my life, despite all your plots and schemes and bloody assassins. Face it, Maeven. You could send a hundred members of your Bastard Brigade to kill me, and I would slaughter them just like I have all the others."

"You haven't managed to kill me yet," she said in a proud voice.

I shrugged. "Maybe you're just a little stronger or smarter or luckier than your brethren. I don't know, and I don't care, because you don't fucking *matter*. Only Maximus does. You said it yourself—*he's* the king. You're just the serving girl who cleans up his messes and takes out his trash. I'm surprised he doesn't make you empty his chamber pots too."

More magic sparked in her eyes, and the scent of her hot jalapeño rage blasted through the air. A muscle ticked in her jaw, and I got the sense that she was seconds away from snapping up her hands and blasting me with her magic, Maximus's plans and orders and everything else be damned.

I could have insulted her again and pushed her over the edge. I could have suckered her into attacking me, then used my immunity to throttle her magic long enough for Serilda to bury her blade in the bitch's back. Oh, yes, at long last, I could have finally killed Maeven.

But I decided not to.

Because I wasn't finished playing my long game with her, and it was a game I desperately needed to win for the sake of my kingdom. So, as much as it pained me, I pushed down my own thirst for revenge and thought of how I could best manipulate her into doing what I wanted.

"And here's something else to think about," I said in a much calmer voice. "Something your dear brother obviously didn't tell you about Leonidas's mission."

Maeven blinked at the unexpected change in topic, and some of the dangerous magic leaked out of her eyes. "And what would that be?"

"Leonidas wasn't the only assassin Maximus sent to my tent last night. There were three others. DiLucri geldjagers."

"So what?"

I paused again, drawing out the moment to give my next words even more impact. "So those other three assassins weren't there just to murder me. They had orders to kill Leonidas too, if I hadn't already disposed of him."

Her eyes widened in surprise, although she quickly schooled her features into a more neutral expression. She shook her head. "No. You're lying. Maximus would never—"

"Would never what? Send your son to murder me, and then send assassins to kill the boy so he couldn't tell anyone about his orders?" I laughed. "Please tell me you're not that naïve—or stupid."

Maeven didn't respond. We both knew she wasn't that naïve or stupid, just like we both knew there was nothing she could do about her brother trying to have her son murdered.

"I told you once before that you didn't have to follow Maximus," I said in a serious voice, without the mocking tone. "That you could leave Morta, go somewhere else, and start a new life. Maybe it's finally time for you to do so—for your son's sake."

"I don't have to go anywhere," Maeven hissed. "Once I finally kill you, all will be forgiven."

"How many times have you tried to kill me now? Four? Five? I've honestly lost count. But what makes you think you can succeed in the future? Face it, Maeven. You are *never* going to kill me. Not you, and not your Bastard Brigade. And if you can't kill me, then that makes you useless to Maximus. Or maybe . . ." I let my voice trail off.

"What?" she growled.

"Or maybe Maximus was planning to sacrifice Leonidas all along. Maybe he thought the death of your son at my hands would finally motivate you enough to kill me."

She didn't respond, but her scent took on a speculative, smoky aroma, and agreement flickered in her eyes. We both knew Maximus was cruel enough to do something like that.

"What are you planning to do with Leonidas?" she asked. "If you hurt him—"

I laughed, cutting off her threat. "*Me?* Hurt *him?* Please. Maximus has already threatened to kill his beloved strix and sent the boy on a suicide mission. There's hardly any way left for me to torture your son."

I paused again. "Although I'm sure that I can come up with *something.* Or perhaps Serilda can. She's had far more experience at that sort of thing than I have."

"I'd be happy to help, my queen," Serilda chimed in, her hand still on her sword.

Maeven shot her an angry glare, but Serilda merely arched an eyebrow in response.

"The more I think about it, the more I realize that Maximus practically handed me your son on a silver platter," I drawled. "I could torture Leonidas for days, weeks, months, and your precious king wouldn't lift a finger to save your son, his nephew, his own flesh and blood. That should tell you exactly how much regard Maximus has for you and Leonidas—none at all."

More agreement flashed in Maeven's eyes, and her scent took on a note of dusty resignation.

"Run or die, Maeven. Those are your only two choices. I hope you make the right one. For Leonidas's sake, of course."

Truth be told, Maeven had a third choice, the one I'd subtly been trying to get her to make for months now. I wondered if that other option had occurred to her yet, but of course I couldn't ask without tipping my hand about what I was really up to.

"You're playing a dangerous game, Everleigh," Maeven said, although her voice contained far less venom and bite than before. "And it's one you're going to lose, along with your crown, your life, and your beloved kingdom."

I smiled in the face of her dire prediction. "We'll see about that."

I mockingly tipped my head to her, then stepped out of the archway, leaving my enemy behind to stew in her own thoughts.

CHAPTER NINETEEN

Serilda fell in step beside me, and we walked about thirty feet from the archway before slipping behind one of the carts that lined the plaza. The merchant glanced at us, but when she realized we weren't interested in buying her flavored ices, she started hawking her wares again.

Serilda and I both peered around the cart. In the distance, Maeven stalked out of the archway, her hands clenched into fists and her head swiveling from side to side. I didn't know if she was searching for us, or perhaps checking to make sure no one had witnessed our little tête-à-tête, but I could still smell her hot, peppery anger, even above all the other scents swirling through the plaza.

She didn't spot us, and her fists slowly relaxed. Maeven smoothed her hands down her skirt, as if trying to get her raging emotions under control. Then she headed back inside the arena, disappearing from sight.

"Did you enjoy insulting Maeven?" Serilda asked.

"Oh, I thoroughly enjoyed it, but insulting Maeven wasn't the reason I talked to her."

Serilda arched her eyebrow again.

"Okay, so it wasn't the *only* reason I talked to her," I corrected. "I also wanted to tell her the truth about Maximus, especially how her beloved brother views her and her son."

"And what do you want her to do with that truth?"

"The only thing she can."

Serilda frowned, her eyes darkened, and the scent of her magic gusted over me, as if she were using her time magier power to consider my cryptic words. I wanted to ask what possibilities she saw, and if my long game with Maeven would ever come to fruition, but I didn't want to jinx my plan, so I kept quiet.

Serilda shook her head, her eyes cleared, and the scent of her magic vanished. "Come on. Your little talk with Maeven has put us behind. We need to hurry."

We moved away from the cart and headed deeper into the crowd. People were talking, eating, laughing, and drinking, and no one gave us a second look. Paloma was still signing banners, flyers, pennants, and more, but Serilda and I strolled past her and headed to another archway. This opening was much smaller than the others, only wide enough for two people to walk through at a time. A man was lurking in the shadows, although he stepped forward when Serilda and I slipped inside the opening.

"Finally," Cho muttered. "It's almost time for me to introduce the next gladiators. I thought I was going to have to leave this here for you to find."

He shoved a black knapsack into Serilda's hands. She flipped open the top and drew out a long purple cloak, which she tossed over to me. I draped the cloak around my shoulders, covering up my blue tunic with its silver crown-of-shards crest.

"I want you to know those cloaks were hard to get," Cho said.

Serilda rolled her eyes. "Hard to get? All you had to do was swipe them from one of the dressing rooms and bring them here. Besides, how many times have you told me what a master thief you are?"

"Only when it comes to stealing sweets," he said. "And only because I can make the evidence disappear."

He winked at her. Serilda rolled her eyes again, but she was smiling as she yanked a second purple cloak out of the knapsack and settled it around her own shoulders, covering up her white tunic with its black-swan design.

She shook the knapsack, and the soft *clang-clang-clang* of metal hitting metal rang out. "What else is in here?"

Cho shrugged. "Some extra weapons and a hammer. I thought they might be useful."

Serilda nodded and hoisted the knapsack onto her shoulder.

"I still think that I should come with you," Cho said. "I could help."

"I know you could, but the more people who go, the riskier it is," I replied. "Besides, you're the tournament ringmaster. It would look suspicious if you suddenly disappeared."

Cho didn't like being left behind any more than Sullivan had, but he turned to Serilda. He hesitated, then reached out and touched her arm. "Be careful."

Serilda's face softened, and she laid her hand on top of his. "To the end."

"To the end," he repeated in a low voice.

The two of them studied each other a moment longer, then they both dropped their hands and cleared their throats, pointedly not looking at each other. I had never quite understood their relationship and why they weren't together when it was so painfully obvious they loved each other. Perhaps that would change when we defeated Maximus.

If we defeated Maximus.

Serilda and I pulled up the hoods on our purple cloaks, covering our heads. Cho went deeper into the archway, disappearing from sight. Serilda and I waited a few seconds, then slipped out of the shadows and stepped back into the crowd.

We made our way across the plaza and over to the steps and quickly walked down to the waterfront. Only this time, we didn't go to the Bellonan bridge like usual.

We went to the Mortan one.

Auster had been right when he'd said that we couldn't get a large contingent of men across the bridge without attracting attention, but Leonidas and the geldjagers had slipped into the Bellonan camp last night, and I was hoping Serilda and I could do the same to the Mortan one now.

We stopped near a cart close to the Mortan bridge. The span was roughly the same size and shape as the Bellonan bridge, although it was made of dark gray granite instead of tearstone, and the fancy cursive *M* of the Morricone royal crest was carved into the railing and flagstones, instead of Bellonan gladiators and weapons.

A couple of guards wearing Mortan purple were standing on either side of the bridge entrance, but one was eating a bag of cornucopia, while the other was flirting with a giggling girl selling stuffed strixes from a nearby cart. The guards weren't paying any attention to the streams of people coming and going on the bridge.

"Are you sure you want to do this?" Serilda asked. "This is your last chance to turn around. Because once we cross that bridge, we might not come back."

I thought of how Maximus had so casually slit that strix's throat during the kronekling tournament last night and all the magic he had absorbed from the creature's blood. The memory made me sick to my stomach.

"I told you back at Seven Spire that I was tired of playing defense. This is my chance to finally go on the offensive. Besides, we have to take away Maximus's supply of magic if we have any chance of assassinating him before the Regalia ends. It's worth the risk. Let's go."

Serilda dropped her hand to her sword. I did the same, and the two of us headed for the Mortan bridge.

Despite our purple cloaks, I still expected the guards to stop us and demand to know where we were going. But the two men were busy eating and flirting, and they didn't even glance at Serilda and me as we walked past them and stepped onto the bridge.

No one on the bridge gave us a second look either, except for one man who saluted us with his tankard. He was clearly drunk on the contents, and my nose crinkled at the sour stench of ale that wafted off his body.

He blinked, and recognition sparked in his bloodshot eyes. "Hey, aren't you the Bellonan—"

Serilda shoved the man, making him stumble backward and flip up and over the bridge railing. He landed with a loud *splash* in the water below and came up blubbering for air. My heart leaped up into my throat, wondering what he would say next.

"My ale!" he wailed. "You made me spill my ale!"

"Let's go!" Serilda hissed, dragging me forward.

I glanced back over my shoulder at the guards, but they were laughing and pointing at the waterlogged man. I let out a tense breath, and we hurried onward.

It didn't take us long to reach the far end of the bridge, but I hesitated a moment before stepping off it and putting my foot down onto the plaza beyond. A Bellonan queen on Mortan soil. I couldn't even *imagine* the last time that had occurred, and I half expected the ground to crack apart and swallow me whole. But of course that didn't happen, and we walked on.

In many ways, the Mortan side of the river was identical to the Bellonan one. The plaza featured a fountain, although this one was made of black marble and shaped like a strix with its wings spread wide, as if it were about to rise up out of the water basin and take flight. And just like on the Bellonan side of the river, a series of steps led up to a high ridge where the Mortans had pitched their tents. Serilda and I quickly climbed the steps, crossed the grassy field, and kept moving forward.

Straight into the Mortan camp.

The front common area featured tables and chairs, along with wooden stands where merchants were selling meats, cheeses, wines, and ales, as well as purple pennants bearing the Morricone royal crest. Everything a person needed to properly enjoy the Regalia.

Guards ambling around, servants rushing to and fro, a few nobles lounging in the sun and drinking wine. This part of the Mortan camp was eerily similar to the Bellonan one, but it was much quieter here, and I didn't hear any music or laughter. I wondered if those things were reserved for Maximus like everything else seemed to be. Probably, knowing his ego. Or perhaps people simply didn't want to risk making too much noise, lest they draw their king's attention—and ire.

"My lady!" one of the merchants called out, using a glass filled with red liquid to gesture at me. "May I interest you in some cranberry sangria?"

Once again, my heart leaped up into my throat at the sudden outburst, but I sidestepped his arm, ducked my head, and kept walking.

"Who was that?" I heard another merchant say behind me.

I glanced over at Serilda, whose hand was on her sword, ready to whirl around and cut down the merchants if they had recognized me.

"No idea," the first merchant replied. "My lord! My lord! May I interest you in some cranberry sangria?"

I let out a relieved breath, and we hurried on.

The wooden stands gave way to rows of small tents made of light purple canvas that were the servants' quarters. A teenage girl wearing a kitchen apron stepped out of one of the tents right into our path. She glanced at us, and her eyes widened. For the third time, my heart galloped up into my throat.

The girl bowed her head and dropped into a curtsy. "My ladies," she murmured.

Serilda waved her hand, dismissing the girl, who scurried off.

I wiped a sheen of sweat off my forehead. "Maximus doesn't have to send any more assassins. My heart is going to give out before we even reach the strix cages."

"Forget about your heart. You're going to die of a Mortan sword to the gut if we don't keep moving," Serilda hissed back.

She grabbed my arm and pulled me forward again.

The servants' section was largely empty, so Serilda and I were much more noticeable here. More than once we had to stop and hunker down behind one of the tents until a wandering guard had passed by, although most of them were far more interested in eating, drinking, and ogling the servant girls than keeping an eye out for potential danger. Then again, this was Mortan soil. No one in their right mind was stupid enough to come here and make trouble.

No one except me.

Serilda and I slipped deeper into the Mortan camp, moving as fast as we dared, our hands on our weapons. Given their dark purple canvas and fine furnishings, the second section of tents belonged to the wealthy Mortan nobles and merchants, although they too were largely empty.

The third section of tents were the same light purple as the servants' quarters, but the racks of swords and shields set up in between the canvas walls indicated that this was where the guards stayed.

Serilda and I picked up our pace, so that we were practically running. My heart started pounding again, and I sucked down breath after breath, even as my gaze darted around, searching for the slightest hint of movement. But we didn't run into any guards, and we slid behind one of the tents to get our bearings.

Up ahead, beyond the guards' quarters, I could see a fourth and final ring of tents—including the midnight-purple one that belonged to Maximus. It was the largest tent by far in the whole encampment and was topped with an enormous flag featuring the Morricone family crest in glittering gold thread on a midnight-purple background.

I eyed the tent, but two guards were standing at rigid attention by the entrance. Even if we could sneak past the guards, Maximus probably had enough magic to overcome any poison or other deadly trap I might leave behind in his quarters. I would have to be content with my other scheme.

"Where are they?" Serilda asked.

I glanced around, comparing our surroundings to my memories of the crude map Leonidas had drawn for me last night. "The strixes are kept on the west side of camp, close to the trees. Apparently the guards let them out to stretch their wings every now and then, so as not to be too cruel to them."

Serilda snorted. "Having a brief taste of freedom and then being forced back into a cage is probably crueler than never having any freedom at all."

I couldn't argue with that.

We crept forward to the edge of the tents. A grassy field stretched out before us. Leonidas was right.

The strixes were here.

Many of the older, larger creatures had metal collars around their necks with chains that were attached to wooden posts, as though they were horses waiting to be ridden. Leonidas had said that these strixes were trained to obey only Mortan soldiers and that they would tear Serilda and me to pieces with their beaks and talons if we tried to free them.

No matter how much I wanted to, I couldn't save these strixes—but I *could* save the ones that Maximus planned to slaughter for their magic.

Those creatures were housed in coldiron cages stacked up on top of each other at the far end of the clearing. The cages were the same size as Lyra's, and the strixes inside looked to be about the same age as her—not babies, but not full-grown adults either. My nose twitched. And unlike the older, larger birds, every single one of those strixes reeked of magic.

"So that's how he chooses them," I muttered. "Of course. I should have guessed."

"What are you talking about?" Serilda whispered, still eyeing the adult strixes tied to the wooden stakes.

"See the smaller strixes in the cages? Maximus plans to kill those for their magic, just like he killed that poor creature during the ball."

"How do you know those are the right birds? Did Leonidas tell you?"

"He didn't have to." I tapped my nose. "I can smell how much magic they have. Each one of those birds is practically dripping with power. Maximus must be able to sense magic as well as absorb it. He must go through the rookeries in Morta and pick out the strixes that have the most power. He's not slaughtering them at random. He's choosing the ones that can give him the most magic."

I had thought that the Mortan king couldn't possibly disgust me any more, but I was wrong. All those beautiful strixes, locked in cages, waiting to have their throats cut whenever Maximus snapped his fingers, just so he could have even more magic. Heartless, greedy bastard.

I started to sprint over to the cages, but voices floated through the air, and a couple of guards rounded the opposite side of the tent we were hiding behind. I scuttled backward and hunkered down next to Serilda.

We both drew our swords, and my heart pounded yet again. Had the guards seen me? If so, we would have to take them down as quickly and quietly as possible and hope no one heard the noise and came to investigate.

I tightened my grip on my weapon and waited. Beside me, Serilda did the same thing.

The guards came closer . . . and closer . . . and closer . . .

And walked right on by our position.

I let out a breath I didn't even realize I'd been holding. The two men crossed the clearing and stopped by the strix cages, gesturing and talking to each other.

"We need to get rid of them," I muttered. "Right now."

Serilda sheathed her sword and set her knapsack on the ground. "Leave that to me. Stay here."

She vanished around the other side of the tent, while I held my position. A minute later, Serilda reappeared about fifty feet away and boldly sauntered over to the two guards. She'd gotten a glass, along with a bottle of wine from somewhere, and she listed back and forth as though she were already deep into her Regalia celebration.

"Hellooo, boys," she called out.

The guards whirled around, and Serilda raised her glass and staggered in their direction. At first the guards watched her approach with suspicious frowns, but the closer and more wobbly she got, the more their frowns melted into leering appreciation, especially since Serilda had thrown back her purple cloak and unlaced the top of her tunic to show off her cleavage.

I had never seen Serilda be anything other than a tough, hard-nosed warrior, and it was startling to see this slightly softer side of her—even if it was just for the guards' benefit.

She reached the guards, smiled, and offered one of them the empty glass in her hand. The two men hemmed and hawed a few seconds, but one of them grinned and reached for the glass.

Serilda smiled and handed it to him. Then she snapped up the wine bottle and slammed it into the side of his head.

The guard's eyes rolled up, and he dropped to the ground unconscious. The other guard yelped in surprise, but Serilda whirled around and slammed the bottle into the side of his head as well, and he too dropped to the ground.

The second the men were down, I grabbed Serilda's knapsack, left the shadow of the tent behind, and sprinted across the clearing. Serilda tossed her bottle aside, and we hurried over to the cages.

There were more than a dozen cages, each one containing a strix, and the hot, caustic stench that filled the air indicated that Maximus had booby-trapped every one of these cages with his magic. He was probably the only one who could open the padlocks without being severely injured. He wouldn't want Mercer, Nox, or Maeven to drink strix blood to increase their own magic—if they could even stomach the idea.

I passed over the knapsack, and Serilda drew out the hammer that Cho had mentioned earlier.

"Do you want me to smash the locks?" she asked.

"Not unless you want to get bludgeoned with hailstones and frozen with cold lightning. I'm going to have to use my immunity to snuff out the magic on each lock."

"Can you do that without getting hurt?" Serilda asked in a worried voice.

"We're about to find out." I pushed up my tunic sleeves, stepped forward, and reached for the first padlock.

Purple lightning sparked to life the second my fingers touched the metal.

I gritted my teeth against the cold, jolting pain, reached for my immunity, and snuffed out the magic. To my surprise, it was much easier to do than it had been on Lyra's cage last night. Maximus hadn't used nearly as much magic on these locks, and no hailstones shot out from the metal to bruise and cut my hand. He probably thought no one would be stupid enough to try to steal his strixes from his own camp.

I was exactly that stupid. More than that, I *wanted* to do it. Not just to save the creatures from a pointless, gruesome death, but also to hurt the king. Sometimes a small slice in the arena could sting much more than a deeper wound, and I wanted Maximus to feel as much pain as he had inflicted on me over the past year.

One by one, I wrapped my hand around the padlocks and snuffed out the magic on them. Serilda came along behind me, undoing the clasps, yanking off the locks, and opening the doors.

It didn't take me long to extinguish the magic on the last lock, but we had another, unexpected problem—the strixes weren't moving.

"Why aren't they flying away?" Serilda muttered. "Don't they realize that we're trying to save them?"

I remembered how the first, doomed strix had stared resolutely at Maximus during the ball. It had known that it couldn't escape, so it hadn't even attempted to fight back or fly away. Maximus had broken its spirit, and it had given up all hope of avoiding its bloody, brutal fate. These creatures all had that same dull, lethargic look, and they all smelled of dusty resignation, even now, with their cage doors standing wide open.

I bent down and waved my hand at the strix inside the closest cage. "Come on," I cooed in a gentle voice. "We're not going to hurt you. We want you to fly away and be free."

The strix kept staring at me with dull, blank eyes, and it didn't even twitch its feathers at the sound of my voice. Well, if it wouldn't come out on its own, I would have to reach inside and get it. The creature would probably stab me with its beak, but I had to try. So I pushed my sleeve up higher and started to reach inside—

Caw! Caw-caw-caw! Caw!

Serilda and I both whirled around. At first I thought one of the adult strixes had realized what we were doing and was crying out a warning, but then I noticed that the *caw*s were coming from a nearby tree branch—and that Lyra was making the noise.

"She was supposed to stay in her tent!" Serilda hissed.

Apparently the strix had had other ideas. Then again, Leonidas had said she would listen only to him.

Lyra leaped off the tree branch and landed right in front of the cages. She spread her wings out wide and *caw*ed at the other strixes again.

"Leave! Fly! Now!" Perhaps it was my imagination, but I thought I heard the sharp snap of commands in her singsong voice.

Her loud *caw*s finally roused the other creatures out of their dull, resigned state, and they quirked their heads from side to side, staring at Lyra. I wondered if the strixes knew each other the way that people did. Grimley and the other gargoyles at Glitnir had recognized each other, and I was betting the strixes did too.

Either way, Lyra's appearance perked up the other strixes, and they began ruffling their wings, as though they were about to take flight. I started to reach forward and rattle the cage in front of me to further encourage them when another, smaller flutter of movement caught my eye. I looked to the right. I hadn't noticed it before, but a final cage was sitting off to the side all by itself, almost buried in the tall grass.

I squinted into the sun. This cage was smaller than the ones that housed the strixes, and the creature inside seemed smaller too, with feathers that were white instead of purple—

My breath caught in my throat. It was a *caladrius*.

I had wondered if Maximus killed other creatures for their magic, and now I knew that the answer was a sick, resounding *yes*. Even worse was the fact that the caladrius absolutely *reeked* of magic, more than the strixes did. The tiny, owlish bird had more raw power than all the other creatures combined, and I couldn't help but think that Maximus had brought it here to use for something special.

Like murdering me and my friends.

The Mortan king had already tried to have me assassinated during the Regalia, and the caladrius must be his backup plan, his final secret weapon if all his other plots and schemes failed. I thought back to the opening ceremonies when Maximus and his guards had flown their strixes into the arena. Maximus had said that they had ridden the creatures all the way from the Mortan capital, which meant they could easily ride them from here all the way to *Svalin*.

I had already been worried about Maximus invading Bellona, and I had left Halvar and Bjarni behind at Seven Spire to hold the palace until I returned. With the caladrius's magic, Maximus could kill me and my friends, destroy our encampment, and fly to my capital. Halvar, Bjarni, and the palace guards would put up a fierce fight, but they wouldn't be able to counter the king's magic, and Maximus would eventually take the palace—and the rest of Bellona along with it.

I wasn't a time magier like Serilda, so I never got glimpses of the future, but I could see it all unspooling clearly in my mind, as if I were watching images from a memory stone. Right now I knew that the fate of my whole kingdom hinged on freeing this one small creature from Maximus's clutches.

"Keep trying to get the strixes out of their cages," I said.

"Evie!" Serilda hissed. "What are you doing?"

I ignored her, ran over to the final cage, and crouched down. The caladrius was tiny, smaller than my palm, and its feathers were completely white, without any ribbons of gray, indicating that it was little more than a baby. Its eyes were light gray too, without any hint of blue that older birds had.

"Hey, there, little fella," I said, cooing to the caladrius the same way I had to the strixes. "Let's get you out of that nasty cage."

I reached out and grabbed the padlock. The second my fingers touched the metal, I wished they hadn't.

Maximus had put more magic on this one lock than on all the strix cages combined, and purple lightning exploded around the metal, along with a flurry of hailstones. The cold blast tried to freeze my skin, while the sharp, hard pellets blasted against my palm, and I had to choke down a surprised shriek.

But I wasn't leaving the creature behind, so I gritted my teeth, wrapped both hands around the padlock, and poured my immunity into it. A few seconds and several violent, chilly shocks later, the lightning sizzled out in a shower of sparks, and the last of the serrated hailstones dropped to the ground.

I unclenched my teeth, raised a shaking hand, and wiped the sweat off my forehead. Then I leaned forward, opened the lock, and tossed it into the grass before yanking open the door on the front of the cage.

"Come on," I cooed again. "You're free."

To my surprise, the caladrius immediately hopped forward to the edge of the cage, perhaps because it was a baby and hadn't been held captive as long as the strixes had. I cautiously held my hand out, trying to show that I wasn't going to hurt it. The caladrius studied my fingers for a moment, then bent down and rubbed its tiny head against my hand just like a cat would.

"That's a good boy." I don't know why, but for some reason I thought it was a male, although I couldn't tell for sure.

The caladrius rubbed its head against my hand again, then straightened up and hopped out of its cage. The second it was clear of the metal bars, it spread its small wings as wide as they would go and took flight. The caladrius wobbled a bit, as though it wasn't used to flying, but the bird made it to the trees and disappeared into the thick tangle of branches.

I sighed with relief. The caladrius was gone, as was the threat it represented. Maximus could have more of the creatures hidden somewhere else in camp, but at least I'd gotten rid of this obvious, immediate danger—

"Oh, fuck this," Serilda growled.

I surged to my feet and whirled around just in time to see my friend lift her hammer and bang it against the side of one of the cages.

"Leave! Fly! Now! Before it's too late!" she yelled.

The banging hammer finally startled that strix and all the others out of the last of their dull lethargy. With a series of loud *caw-caw-caws*, the creatures hopped out of their cages and took flight in an explosion of sound and feathers that made Serilda duck. A strix zoomed by me, and I ducked too.

The creatures soared up into the bright blue sky. Lyra let out another fierce *caw,* lifted her wings, and flew up to join them. I watched them go with a smile on my face. The strixes' wild cries faded away, but they were replaced by other, far more worrisome sounds.

"Hey! The strixes are free!"

"We need to catch them!"

"Hurry! Hurry! Hurry!"

More and more shouts rose up, and I whirled around. In the distance I could see guards running through the maze of tents, heading this way. Those men were all shouting and stabbing their fingers and weapons up into the air, but the second they spotted the two unconscious guards, they would realize we were here. We needed to be out of camp before that happened, or we would never leave Morta alive.

Serilda shoved the hammer back into her knapsack and drew her purple cloak around her shoulders again. She also pulled the hood up over her blond hair, quickly morphing back into just another Mortan spectator. I did the same with my own cloak.

"Evie!" Serilda hissed again, heading back toward the tents. "Move! Now!"

I watched the strixes fly away for another moment, then hurried after her.

chapter twenty

Serilda and I abandoned all pretense of stealth and ran through the Mortan camp as fast as we could.

We hadn't seen many guards on our way in, but now they were *everywhere*. Running, shouting, brandishing their weapons. Most of them were focused on getting to the strix cages, so they didn't pay any attention to us.

Most, but not all.

Serilda and I darted down an aisle and ran straight into two guards heading the opposite direction.

"Hey! You're not supposed to be here!" one of the men yelled, and reached for his sword.

Serilda stepped up and coolly punched that guard in the face, knocking him unconscious, while I darted forward and slammed my sword hilt into the other man's temple, dropping him as well. The second the guards were down, we jumped over their prone forms and hurried on.

Luckily, we didn't run into any more guards, and we broke free of the tents and made it back to the grassy clearing at the front of the ridge. More guards, merchants, and servants were yelling and running around here, but no one seemed to realize what was going on. Serilda and I sheathed our weapons and used the cover of the chaos to sprint down the steps to the waterfront, cross the plaza, and head toward the bridge.

I thought we might run into trouble trying to get onto the Mortan bridge, but all the guards stationed down here had gone up to the campsite, instead of cutting off the bridge as a potential escape route. Serilda and I slowed down to a quick walk, trying to blend in with the other people crossing the span.

"Don't look back," she muttered. "Only guilty people look back."

I did as she commanded, although my shoulders were tense and I expected a blade to punch into my back at any moment.

It seemed to take *forever* to cross the bridge, although it couldn't have been more than a couple of minutes. We walked by the two guards we had passed earlier. Both men were shading their eyes with their hands and peering up into the sky, as though they were trying to see where the strixes had gone. Serilda and I bowed our heads and scurried by them without stopping.

The second we were back on the island and out of sight of the bridge, Serilda ducked behind a merchant's cart, ripped off her purple cloak, and stuffed it into her black knapsack. I did the same, and my cloak disappeared into the bag too.

"Hurry, hurry!" Serilda whispered as she slung the knapsack over her shoulder. "We have to get back to the arena. We've already been gone too long."

The two of us raced up the hillside steps as fast as we could, but it was still slow going, given the crowds. Several minutes later, we finally reached the plaza, threaded our way through the throngs of people, and ducked into the same shadowy archway as before.

Cho was pacing back and forth in the small opening, and he looked up at the sound of our quick footsteps. He rushed over to us, took the black knapsack from Serilda, and slung it over his own shoulder.

"What did we miss?" Serilda asked.

She wasn't even winded, but I was sweating, sucking down breath after breath, and trying to ignore the throbbing stitch in my side and burning ache in my legs from running up so many bloody steps.

"Most of the tournament," Cho replied. "The final bout is set to start in less than an hour."

"Please . . . tell me that . . . Paloma . . . is in . . . the final," I rasped between gulps of air.

Cho grinned. "She easily advanced. She did everyone at the Black Swan proud." His grin faded. "Paloma is fighting Mercer."

Serilda let out a soft muttered curse.

"What's . . . wrong . . . with that?" I rasped again. "Paloma . . . can beat him . . . just like . . . she beats . . . everyone else."

Cho shook his head. "Mercer has a nasty habit of severely wounding his opponents, even if the match is only to first blood. You saw what he did to that Floresian this morning. During the last Regalia, Mercer almost killed the other gladiator he was fighting for the title, even though that man was also a Mortan."

The scent of his worry washed over me, but Cho shook his head again, as if pushing the emotion aside.

"I'll watch out for Paloma as best I can," he said. "You two need to get back up to the royal terrace before the final bout. If you don't, Maximus will be even more suspicious than he probably already is."

Cho hoisted the knapsack a little higher on his shoulder and headed into the arena. Serilda and I left the archway and stepped out onto the plaza. By this point, I had gotten my breath back, although I wasn't looking forward to climbing up the bleacher steps to the royal terrace. I started to head in that direction, but Serilda held out her arm, stopping me.

"Wait," she said. "We need something to explain why we've been gone so long. This way."

She dragged me over to one of the merchant carts and bought several bags of cornucopia. She shoved the bags at me and went over to another cart, this time buying some cinnamon candy apples. Then she changed direction, heading toward a cart that sold winter hats, gloves, and scarves. And then she went to another cart, and then another one.

By the time Serilda finished, several bags bulging with sweet, savory, and fried treats filled my hands, blue crystal pins were stuck in my hair, and a dark blue wool scarf with the word *Bellona* flowing down it in silver thread was wrapped around my neck.

Despite our rush, I enjoyed seeing all the handcrafted items and the pride shining in the merchants' faces as they showed off their goods. It was definitely the most fun I'd had at the Regalia so far. I would have loved to stay longer and chat with folks about what inspired them to create their crafts, but Serilda led me back into the arena.

My stomach rumbled, reminding me that it had been hours since breakfast, so I dug my hand into one of the bags, grabbed a couple of clusters of cornucopia, and stuffed them into my mouth.

Rich, buttery popped corn. Dried bits of bloodcrisp apples. Toasted slivers of almonds. Crunchy sunflower seeds. All of it brought together by drizzles of dark chocolate and sticky-sweet salted caramel. I quickly polished off that bag and dug into another one.

"I like this idea," I mumbled, trying to walk, talk, and chew at the same time.

"I bought the food and everything else to explain why we were gone so long, not for you to actually eat it," Serilda replied in a snide voice.

"Well, I *do* need to keep up appearances. Besides, who buys cornucopia and doesn't eat it?" I grinned and popped another cluster into my mouth.

Serilda rolled her eyes, but she dug her hand into her own bag of cornucopia and started eating the clusters of popped corn, dried fruit, and toasted nuts and seeds.

While we munched on our treats, we made our way up the bleacher steps and back to the royal terrace.

I wasn't the only one who had left to roam around and sample the best of what the Regalia had to offer. Eon and Ruri were both sipping dark ales, while Cisco was eating fried fruit pies topped with vanilla-bean whipped cream and Heinrich was munching on a bag of cornucopia.

Zariza was examining a box of chocolates, and she studied the entire assortment before finally selecting one and popping it into her mouth. The ogre face on her neck chomped along with her, although its fierce features quickly crinkled with comical disgust. She must have picked a chocolate that her inner ogre didn't like. A moment later, Zariza's face crinkled as well. She didn't like that flavor either.

Maximus was lounging in his chair, sipping a glass of champagne, and it didn't look like he had moved the entire time I'd been gone. Nox was sitting next to him, also sipping champagne, but Maeven was once again standing near the back of the terrace, closer to the servants than her royal relatives.

Maximus didn't deign to look at me. Neither did Nox, but Maeven stared at me. I mockingly tipped my head to her, then headed over to where Sullivan was standing with Dominic.

Sullivan broke away from his brother and met me halfway. He smiled, reached out, and waggled the end of my scarf. "Looks like you had fun shopping on the plaza."

"Oh, I could have stayed down there for *hours*," I replied. "But I wanted to come back and see Paloma win."

A few people had sidled forward to hear our conversation, but apparently the idea that I'd just been shopping bored them, and they sidled away and returned to their previous gossip.

Sullivan dropped the end of my scarf. "How did it go?" he asked in a low voice only I could hear.

"Leonidas was right. Maximus had more than a dozen strixes that he was planning to slaughter."

Leonidas was slumped in the same seat as before and staring fixedly at the table, as if he were a statue frozen in place. Auster was a few feet away, keeping an eye on the boy while he talked with Xenia.

I glanced over at Maximus, making sure he was still ignoring me, then pitched my voice even softer and lower. "He also had a caladrius in a cage."

"A caladrius?" Worry filled Sullivan's face. "They have even more magic than strixes do. Gargoyles too."

"I know. The caladrius was just a baby, but I think that Maximus was going to cut its throat, drink its blood, and take its magic, just like he did to that strix during the ball."

More worry filled Sullivan's face. "With that much power, he could do almost *anything*. Kill a dozen people with a single blast of lightning. Crush solid stone to splinters. Even knock this entire terrace right out from under us."

"Or flatten an encampment and everyone in it," I whispered back.

Understanding flashed in his eyes. "You think he was going to use the caladrius against you, against Bellona."

"Yes. Otherwise, why bring it all this way from Morta and risk losing it?"

Sullivan hesitated, as though he didn't want to give voice to his thought, but he finally said the words. "Do you think he has more of them? More caladriuses?"

I glanced over at the Mortan king, who was still sipping

champagne and talking to Nox. "I don't know. But I hope not, for all our sakes."

Down below, Cho strode out to the middle of the arena floor to announce that the final bout of the tournament was starting. Everyone on the terrace took their seats, as did the people in the bleachers.

No one wanted to miss the championship fight.

The crowd quieted, and a low, rolling drumbeat rang out. The sound went on and on and on, and everyone leaned forward, eager for what was coming next.

"And now," Cho called out, his voice booming through the arena, "our first finalist and the reigning champion. Prince Mercer Maximus Morland Morricone of Morta!"

Cheers erupted, and people yelled, screamed, clapped, and whistled for Mercer, who strode forward and lifted his arms out to his sides, just like he had during the first bout this morning. The prince was wearing the same dark purple fighting leathers as before, and his silver shield and sword gleamed in his hands.

On the terrace, Maximus rose from his seat, smiling and clapping. Nox did the same, and the rest of the Mortan contingent clapped along, as did Maeven, although she didn't look nearly as thrilled as everyone else did.

Mercer stepped into the center ring and started swinging his sword, warming up. Cho ignored him and turned toward the opposite end of the arena.

"And our challenger, Paloma the Powerful of Bellona!"

Paloma appeared and strode to the center of the arena. She was wearing her light gray fighting leathers, with her silver mace in her hand and her silver shield strapped to her forearm.

I surged to my feet, as did Heinrich and Zariza, who were

sitting beside me again, and we all yelled, clapped, screamed, and whistled at the top of our lungs. Sullivan, Serilda, Auster, Xenia—they all joined in, and our cheers were among the loudest in the arena.

Paloma looked up at us, grinned, and stabbed her mace into the air. The she dropped it to her side, stepped into the ring, and faced Mercer.

Cho held up his hands, asking for silence. "This is the final bout to determine the winner of this year's Tournament of Champions and the best gladiator in all the kingdoms. This fight is to first blood only. Remember that."

Cho looked at the fighters. Mercer predictably sneered at him, but Paloma merely nodded.

The ringmaster raised his hands again, and an expectant silence dropped over the arena. Ever the showman, Cho glanced back and forth between the two fighters, drawing out the moment for as long as possible.

"And begin!" he yelled, and stepped back out of the way.

Mercer snapped up his sword and lunged forward like he was going to charge Paloma, but instead of moving out of the way, she simply lifted her shield and waited for him to come, as though she wasn't worried about any attack he might make.

Her utter lack of fear, panic, and motion seemed to surprise Mercer, and he pulled up short and almost tripped over his own feet before he managed to right himself. Laughter rippled through the arena, and an ugly red flush stained Mercer's cheeks. Not the start the crown prince wanted, and he didn't appreciate the chuckles at his expense.

Mercer snarled and went on the offensive, lashing out with his sword. Once again, Paloma simply stood there and blocked his blow with her shield. Then she swung her mace, going on the offensive, although Mercer used his shield to block her blow.

And so the battle began in earnest.

Mercer and Paloma fought back and forth through the ring, hacking and slashing at each other with their weapons and blocking blows with their shields. It was an intense fight, and the two of them were evenly matched when it came to their skills. But as the fight dragged on, it became apparent that Paloma was stronger and had more endurance than the prince, and that he was going to wear out long before she did.

Mercer must have realized it too, because he changed tactics. He raised his sword as though he were going to swing it at Paloma again, but at the last moment he dropped his shield and snapped up his left hand.

The hot, caustic scent of his magic filled the air. I surged to my feet to scream a warning, even though I doubted Paloma would hear me over the continued roar of the crowd. But I was already too late.

Purple sparks erupted on Mercer's fingertips, and he blasted Paloma with his lightning.

The bolt hit her square in the chest and threw her back five feet. Paloma lost her grip on both her mace and shield and landed flat on her back in the center of the ring.

She didn't move after that.

Everyone in the bleachers leaped to their feet, and the noise grew more raucous than ever before. But I only had eyes for Paloma. Finally—*finally*—she pushed herself up onto her elbows. I let out a relieved sigh that Mercer hadn't killed her outright with that blast.

But the Mortan prince thought he'd found a way to win, and he snapped up his hand and blasted Paloma with his magic again. And then again, and then again, until Paloma was hunkered down on her knees like a wounded animal. Worry twisted my stomach, but there was nothing I could do to help her.

"Why isn't she morphing?" Zariza asked, still sitting beside me. "That's the only way she can beat him now."

"Paloma doesn't like to morph in front of strangers," I said.

"Well, she'd better do it now," Zariza replied. "Because that's the only way she's going to keep him from killing her."

Zariza was right. That first blast of magic had stunned Paloma, and Mercer easily could have stepped forward and sliced his weapon across her arm or leg, drawing first blood and ending the fight. But he hadn't done that, and it didn't look like he was going to stop blasting her with his magic until he had fried her to a crisp.

"Come on, Paloma," I muttered, even though she couldn't hear me. "Come on. Get up. Morph. Show that bastard how strong you really are."

But she remained huddled on the ground, and Mercer kept blasting her with his lightning.

I looked over at Maximus, who gave me a thin, satisfied smile. I wondered if he had told Mercer to use his magic to try to kill Paloma. Probably.

Mercer must have thought Paloma was dead, or maybe he simply needed a break from using so much magic for so long, because he finally released his power. His purple lightning vanished, and he lowered his hand to his side.

A hush dropped over the arena, and all eyes fell on Paloma, who was still hunkered down on her knees, with her arms wrapped around her chest, and her head almost touching the hard-packed dirt.

"Come on, Paloma," I whispered. "Get up. Morph."

Her right arm twitched.

I blinked, wondering if I was imagining the small motion, but her right arm twitched again. And then her left. I drew in a breath. The hot, caustic stench of Mercer's magic lingered in the air, but another scent was now flooding the arena, like a soft peony perfume mixed with just a hint of wet fur.

Paloma's scent. Paloma's magic. Paloma's power.

My friend remained hunkered down on the ground, but she quickly grew larger and larger. Muscles bulged in her arms and legs, while the ones in her back strained against her fighting leathers. Her braided blond hair took on a bright golden sheen, and long, sharp black talons sprouted on her fingertips.

Paloma slowly lifted her head. Her amber eyes gleamed with a fierce light, while jagged teeth now filled her mouth.

Everyone in the arena gasped, including me.

Paloma climbed to her feet, now several inches taller than normal, her entire body hard, thick, and strong with muscle. She loomed over Mercer, who took a step back, then another one. Paloma stared at him a moment, then walked over and picked up her mace. Then she crooked her finger at the prince in a clear challenge.

Mercer froze, as though he didn't know what to do, and a few titters of laughter rang out. The guffaws snapped the prince out of his stupor, and he raised his hand and blasted Paloma with his lightning again. But morphing had made her even stronger, and Paloma stood still and tall and absorbed this blast.

Mercer snarled and hit her again and again, but Paloma absorbed each and every one of his attacks. Finally, the Mortan prince ran out of magic. He lifted his hand to hit her again, but only a few sparks flickered on his fingertips. Paloma cocked her head to the side, a smile stretching across her face and showing all her many jagged teeth.

With a loud, thunderous roar, Paloma surged forward, raised her mace high, and smashed it down onto Mercer's left arm. Perhaps it was my imagination, but I thought I heard several audible *crack-crack-crack*s as his bones shattered.

Mercer screamed and tumbled to the ground, clutching his arm to his chest and writhing in agony. Paloma towered over him, making sure that he wasn't going to get back up, then held her mace out to the side where everyone could see it.

Several drops of blood—Mercer's blood—oozed off the spikes and spattered onto the dirt.

"And we have first blood!" Cho's voice boomed out, and he hurried forward, grabbed Paloma's arm, and lifted it high into the air. "Our new champion! Paloma the Powerful!"

The crowd exploded. The cheers, yells, claps, screams, and whistles thundered so long and loud that they seemed to shake the entire arena. People also tossed crowns of white daisies, purple gladiolas, and blue laurels down from the bleachers, along with Bellonan pennants and small stuffed ogres. In seconds the trinkets covered the arena floor like a colorful, fragrant carpet.

Paloma bent down and picked up one of the stuffed ogres. Her long black talons gently curled around it, and she straightened and lifted it high overhead, along with her bloody mace.

The crowd roared even louder. My friend stood in the center ring, still in her ogre form, her eyes wide and a huge grin on her face, soaking up the attention. She had more than earned it with that performance.

"Paloma! Paloma! Paloma!" I started yelling her name over and over again.

Beside me, Zariza and Heinrich took up the chant, along with Sullivan, Serilda, Auster, and Xenia. Soon it had spread throughout the arena.

Down below, Paloma kept her spiked mace raised high in the air. She stared up at the royal terrace, and her gaze met mine. Paloma grinned at me, then dropped into a perfect Bellonan curtsy. That only made the crowd cheer even louder, especially me and the rest of the Bellonans.

Paloma the Powerful, indeed.

CHAPTER TWENTY-ONE

The cheers and applause went on for quite some time before Paloma morphed back into her normal self and vanished into one of the arena tunnels. When she was gone, Cho signaled for the bone masters, who came forward, hoisted Mercer to his feet, and took him to be healed.

I looked over at Maximus, who was still in his seat, staring down at the arena floor with a stony expression. I drew in a breath, enjoying the hot, peppery scent of his anger.

Serilda stepped up beside me and handed me a glass of cranberry sangria. I *clink*ed mine against hers.

"To Paloma," I said.

"To Paloma," she echoed.

We both took a long sip, enjoying our friend's victory.

Now that the tournament was over, most people were getting to their feet and plodding down the bleacher steps. But two men were going against the flow and running up the steps as fast as they could—Mortan guards.

"Evie," Serilda said in a low, warning voice.

"I see them."

Serilda and I might have escaped from the Mortan camp, but the danger wasn't over. Sullivan sidled closer to me, while Auster tapped Leonidas on the shoulder and gestured for the boy to stand.

Maximus noticed the guards, and he watched their approach with narrowed eyes.

Maeven also spied the two guards, and she frowned, realizing that they wouldn't be moving so fast if they didn't have important news. She went over to Maximus and started to say something, but her brother snapped up his hand, telling her to keep quiet. He never took his gaze off the guards.

Maeven's lips pinched together, and she retreated a few steps, but I could smell her anger smoldering like a glowing ember that was trying to ignite into a full-fledged fire.

Nox was still sitting beside Maximus. He glanced up at Maeven and slowly, subtly scooted his chair away from the king. He didn't know what was happening, but he didn't want any part of it.

The two Mortan guards rushed onto the terrace. Unlike Nox, they didn't have the good sense to stop and judge their king's mood before approaching. Instead, the guards hurried forward, planting themselves in front of Maximus and cutting off his view of the arena below.

Maximus glared up at the two guards. "What do you think you're doing?"

The men realized their mistake, and they both immediately dropped to one knee.

"Your Majesty, I apologize for the interruption," one of the guards said. "But there's been an . . . incident at camp."

"What sort of *incident*?" Maximus asked.

The guard wet his lips and swallowed, as if nervous about delivering his news. I wouldn't have wanted to deliver it either. Beside him, the second guard scrunched down, like he was a tortoise trying to tuck his head back inside his shell to keep it from being bitten off by some larger predator. Maximus, in this case.

The first guard wet his lips and swallowed again, but he forced out the words. "It's your, um, pet strixes, sire. I'm afraid that they've all . . . escaped."

Well, that was a diplomatic way of putting things.

Maximus's face hardened. "What do you mean the strixes have *escaped*?"

"The cages are empty, Your Majesty. Somehow, the strixes escaped and flew away. We've sent guards on the older strixes after them, but so far we haven't been able to recapture any of your . . . pets."

Maximus tilted his head to the side and studied the guard, as though the other man were speaking some foreign language that he was trying to decipher. "And what about my other special pet?"

He had to be talking about the caladrius, judging from the way the guard's face paled and from the sweat suddenly shining on his forehead.

"I'm sorry, Your Majesty, but it also escaped."

The guard said the words in a rush and then grimaced, as though he expected Maximus to jerk forward and slap him.

The king remained in his chair, absolutely still and quiet, and the only visible sign of his anger was the muscle that kept *tick-tick-tick*ing in his jaw. I could smell his rage, though, and the hot jalapeño scent seared my nose with its fiery intensity.

Nox was still sitting beside the king, with Maeven standing behind him. Neither one of them moved, and I imagined they would have even stopped breathing, if they could have. They might not be able to smell Maximus's rage, but they realized exactly what was coming next, just like I did.

An eruption.

Maximus slowly rose to his feet. Nox stood up as well, although he scurried back to stand beside Maeven. The two guards stayed on their knees, both of them visibly sweating and shaking now.

"So all my strixes are gone, every last one of them, along with my other pet?" Maximus's voice was perfectly calm, smooth, and even, but the scent of his rage grew stronger with each passing second, and I had to crinkle my nose to keep from sneezing.

The other royals, nobles, advisors, servants, and guards were now staring at Maximus. All other conversation had ceased, and everyone was waiting to hear what was wrong—and to see how he would react.

"Well?" Maximus bellowed, when the guards didn't answer.

The first guard wet his lips yet again, and his voice came out as a low, trembling rasp. "Yes, Your Majesty. All your pets are . . . gone."

Maximus stared at the guard, his amethyst eyes practically glowing with anger. His nostrils flared, and his hands clenched into tight fists, although no magic crackled across his knuckles.

The guard eyed the king's fists. He swallowed again, then lifted his head and looked up at Maximus. "Don't worry, Your Majesty. I've already sent the riders out on the older strixes with the usual nets and ropes. The other birds couldn't have gotten far, especially since most of them are not yet fully grown."

The guard reeked of desperation, and he spat out the words one after another, almost as if he were trying to find the right combination of sentences that would cool the king's anger. He sucked in a breath and kept going. "We should be able to catch at least a few of them before the end of the day, but if we can't, we can always send back to the capital for more—"

Maximus snapped up his leg and kicked the other man square in the chest.

The guard let out a loud, strangled cry and crumpled to the floor. With one hand, he clutched his ribs, which were probably broken, but he held up his other hand in supplication, silently begging for mercy.

Maximus studied him with cold, dispassionate eyes, then stepped up and kicked him again. And then again, and then again . . .

The Mortan king kicked his guard over and over, viciously driving his boot into the other man's chest, arms, legs, even his face. The guard's nose broke with a loud, audible *crack* that rang across the terrace like a clap of thunder announcing the full extent of Maximus's rage.

That sound snapped me out of my shock, and I started forward to do . . . something, but Sullivan grabbed my arm.

"You can't stop it," he whispered. "That's his guard, not yours."

Guilt flooded my body, but he was right. I couldn't intervene, and neither could anyone else.

Everyone fell silent, and the only sounds were the steady *thud-thud-thud* of Maximus's boot and the guard's sharp, answering cries of pain. No one said anything, and no one moved to intervene. In less than a minute, it was over, and the guard lay dying on the terrace, struggling to breathe and choking to death on his own blood.

Maximus finally stopped his brutal assault and stared down at the guard with the same dispassionate expression as before, as though he were looking at a cut of meat in a butcher's shop instead of his fellow countryman. Then the king snapped up his hand and blasted the guard with his cold lightning.

Maximus was far stronger in his magic than Mercer was. The guard's head snapped back, and he didn't make another sound as the cold lightning zipped over and then froze his body. Brittle bits of ice flaked off his now-purple skin, and the chilly stench of his frostbitten flesh filled the air. Out of the corner of my eye, I saw Driscol clamp his hand over his mouth, as though trying to keep from vomiting at the horrible sight.

Maximus focused on the second guard, who was still kneeling on the terrace. The second man hadn't moved a muscle while Maximus had beaten and frozen his compatriot, but his left eye was involuntarily twitching in a nervous, jumpy rhythm, and the stench of his fear poured out of his pores, right along with his sour, nervous sweat. He thought the king was going to execute him too.

Maximus snapped his fingers. "Get up."

The second guard swallowed, but he did as commanded. That twitch in his eye picked up speed, and the rest of his body trembled in time to the quick beat.

"Return to camp, get on your strix, and find my fucking pets. Every last one of them," Maximus hissed in a low, dangerous voice. "Failure is *unacceptable*. Do you understand?"

The guard opened his mouth to answer, but not so much as a squeak of agreement escaped his lips.

"Do you understand?" Each word Maximus said was as sharp as a dagger slicing through the air.

The guard still couldn't bring himself to speak, so he bobbed his head instead.

"Then why are you still standing here?" Maximus snarled.

The instant the king finished speaking, the guard stepped over his fellow guard's body, sprinted across the terrace, and ran down the bleacher steps as fast as he could.

The quick, staccato rhythm of the guard's frantic footsteps faded away, and that tense, heavy silence dropped over the terrace again. Maximus seemed completely unconcerned by the silence and the shocked stares, and he sat back down in his seat as though nothing out of the ordinary had happened.

He glanced over at Nox and Maeven, but they both looked

back at him with blank expressions. Neither one of them said a word or moved a muscle, but I could smell their worry and fear. They didn't want to be the next victim of his wrath.

Maximus glanced around the rest of the terrace. Eon, Ruri, Cisco, Zariza, Heinrich. The other royals were regarding him with a mix of disgust and wariness, and the ogre on Zariza's neck was baring its teeth. Driscol still had his hand clamped over his mouth, although Seraphine seemed as calm as ever.

Everyone knew about Maximus's capacity for cruelty, something that he had reinforced by slaughtering the strix and drinking its blood at the ball. But killing one's own guard at such a public event was something that just wasn't *done*, not even among the most vicious royals. Everyone was staring at Maximus as if they had just now realized there was a rabid animal in their midst, instead of a reasonable, rational king.

I was glad that Serilda and I had been able to free the creatures, but more guilt filled me at the fact that my thwarting the king's scheme had cost an innocent man his life.

As if he could hear my dark thoughts, Maximus turned his cold gaze to me. I didn't know what he saw in my face. Disgust, probably, mixed with anger and guilt over the guard's death, but his eyes narrowed, and the scent of his rage intensified, so hot and strong that it felt like my nose was on fire. Maximus knew that I was the reason he'd lost his precious pets.

And he wasn't the only one. Maeven also frowned at me, but I lifted my chin and stared back at the Mortan king. Now was *not* the time to show any sign of dread, doubt, or especially weakness.

I was still holding a bag of cornucopia, so I grabbed a cluster, popped it into my mouth, and crunched down on it. Even though the sweet treat now tasted like blood and ash, I popped another cluster into my mouth and chewed and swallowed it before I spoke.

"Problems?" I drawled.

Maximus's jaw clenched, and his eyes narrowed even more. But after a few seconds, his tight features relaxed into a thin smile. "Nothing that can't be fixed. I always have contingency plans in place, in case things go wrong."

Contingency plans? What could he possibly have or do to replace the loss of all those strixes and their magic? Maybe Sullivan was right. Maybe Maximus had more strixes or even another caladrius stashed somewhere in the Mortan camp.

Maximus crooked his finger at Nox, who stepped forward. The two of them started speaking in low voices, with Maeven hovering nearby. The rest of the royals and nobles slowly returned to their own conversations, although everyone kept shooting wary looks at both Maximus and me.

I lowered the bag of cornucopia to my side. I'd lost my appetite for it, and the last few pieces I'd eaten had already soured in my stomach. I might have won this battle, but Maximus already had something planned for the next round between us, and I couldn't help but think that his next attack would be something far more vicious than what he'd just done to his own guard.

Ten minutes later, Maximus got to his feet and announced that he was returning to the Mortan camp to prepare for tonight's ball. The Mortan king didn't glance at me as he swept down the bleacher steps, but sour, sweaty eagerness rolled off him in waves. He was already putting his next scheme against me into motion.

Nox and the rest of the Mortans followed him, but Maeven stopped and looked at Leonidas. The boy started to go over to his mother, but she shook her head the tiniest bit, telling him to stay put.

Maeven had probably realized that Leonidas was the one

who'd told me about the strixes in the Mortan camp. No doubt Maximus would come to the same conclusion sooner or later, and he might take his anger out on the boy the same way he had on the guard, whose frozen, bloody body was still lying on the terrace.

Leonidas's face fell, but he stayed still.

Maeven smiled at him, then stared at me. Her eyes narrowed in a clear warning. Take good care of her son—or else.

I smirked back at her. Of course I would never hurt the boy, but she didn't need to know that.

Maeven stared at me a moment longer, then left the terrace. One by one, the other royals and their contingents also departed, until my friends and I were the only ones on the terrace. Sullivan, Serilda, and Auster gathered around me, and Xenia remained with us as well.

"You certainly made Maximus angry," Xenia said, eyeing the guard's body.

"Maybe too angry," Auster said in a low, worried voice. "There's no telling what he might do now."

"I know," I replied. "But at the very least, Serilda and I cut off his supply of magic. Maximus won't be able to have more strixes brought here before the Regalia ends tomorrow. So hopefully I've derailed at least some of his plans for me and Bellona."

"And what about your plans for him?" Sullivan asked. "Did you see or hear anything in the Mortan camp that would help us kill him?"

Serilda shook her head. "No. His tent was too well guarded to approach, and he'll increase security at the camp now, along with his own personal guard."

"Don't worry," I said, trying to reassure my friends. "We'll figure it out. We'll find a way to stop him before the Regalia ends."

Despite my strong, confident tone, I didn't really believe

my words, and neither did my friends. So far Maximus seemed to be untouchable, and we were running out of time to find a weakness that would let us destroy him. Of course, I could still implement the idea I'd had back at Seven Spire about how to kill the king, but I didn't want to do that unless I had no other options.

Either way, there was nothing else to do here, so we left the terrace and headed down to the arena floor, where Paloma and Cho were waiting for us.

I laughed, ran over, and hugged Paloma tight. "I'm so proud of you!"

She returned my hug, then drew back. "For kicking the ass of a royal piece of Morricone scum and winning the tournament? Of course you should be proud of me." Her voice might be matter-of-fact, but she was grinning, as was the ogre face on her neck.

"Not just for that," I said. "But for morphing in front of everyone. I know how hard that was for you."

Paloma's grin dimmed a bit, and the glassy sheen of tears filled her eyes. "I did it for my mother," she said in a low voice. "She always told me to be proud that I was a morph, an ogre, and I wanted to honor her."

"You know, you've never told me her name. What was it?" I made it seem like a casual question, but it was far more important than she knew, and so many things could change, depending on her answer.

Paloma plucked her mace off her belt and swung it through the air. "Amira," she said in a soft voice. "Her name was Amira."

Even though I'd been expecting—hoping—for that answer, shock still blasted through me. That was the same name as Xenia's daughter. Could Paloma's mother and Xenia's daughter be the same person? But that would mean . . . that would mean . . .

Paloma was Xenia's granddaughter.

As soon as the thought occurred to me, I realized it had to be true. There were just too many coincidences in their family histories, including how Paloma's mother and Xenia's daughter had both vanished without a trace. Plus, Zariza had said that Paloma reminded her of Amira, and I'd noticed myself how similar Paloma's morph mark was to Xenia's. But there was only one way to be sure, and that was to tell both my friends my suspicions.

"Is something wrong?" Paloma asked. "You have a really strange look on your face."

"I need to tell you something." I sucked in a breath. "It's about—"

"Paloma! Congratulations! I knew you could do it!" Auster stepped forward.

"Of course she did it," Xenia said, coming up to them. "She's an ogre morph."

Her voice had the same matter-of-fact tone that Paloma's always did, and the ogre on her neck grinned at the one on Paloma's throat. Golden amber eyes, bronze skin, razor-sharp teeth. The two morph marks were almost identical, except for the coppery hair that curled around the one on Xenia's neck, versus the blond hair on Paloma's mark. But the resemblance between them, as well as Xenia and Paloma themselves, became more and more obvious the longer I looked at all four of them.

I opened my mouth again, but Serilda and Sullivan came forward, also congratulating Paloma.

Seeing the wide grin on Paloma's face, as well as the one of her inner ogre, made me bite back my words. My friend had just won the biggest bout of her life, and I would let her fully enjoy her victory with no worries or distractions. I would tell her my suspicions later, when she was out of the spotlight and had more time to process them.

"Evie? Are you crying?" Cho asked, walking over to me.

Serilda had given him one of the bags of cornucopia she had bought, and he popped a cluster into his mouth and crunched down on it. Cho sighed with happiness.

I wiped the tears out of the corners of my eyes. "Just a little bit."

He frowned. "Why? Paloma won. You should be smiling and laughing, not crying."

"Don't worry. These are happy tears."

And they were happy tears—not only for Paloma's victory, but for the secret I planned on telling her and the gift I hoped it would be for both her and Xenia.

Cho held out his bag to me. "Well, if you really want to be happy, then you should have some cornucopia. It always makes me feel better." He winked at me.

I laughed and popped a cluster into my mouth. He was right. It did make me feel a little better.

We stayed in the arena celebrating Paloma's victory for the next half hour. We would have stayed even longer, but my friends and I had to get ready for tonight's ball. So we all congratulated Paloma a final time, then left the arena together.

To the casual observer, we probably appeared happy and relaxed as we crossed the plaza, walked down the steps, and made our way back to the waterfront. But everyone kept their hands on their weapons, and we all kept glancing around, searching for danger.

Auster was right. I had enraged Maximus, and he could strike out again at any time. But no assassins rushed out of the crowd to try to kill us, and we made it back to the Perseverance Bridge without incident.

Auster stopped and spoke to the guards at the end of the bridge. "Any problems? Has anyone unusual or suspicious gone over to the Bellonan side of the river?"

One of the guards shook his head. "No, sir. Just folks celebrating Paloma's victory."

He grinned at her, and a faint blush stained my friend's cheeks. She might be a Black Swan gladiator, but winning the Tournament of Champions came with a whole new level of attention, and people had been calling out, grinning, and waving at her during our trek across the island.

Auster questioned that guard and the others, but they hadn't seen anything out of the ordinary, other than the raucous celebrations from the Bellonans. So we stepped onto the bridge and headed back to camp.

The others relaxed a bit, thinking we were more or less safe now that we were off the island, but I kept glancing around, more and more cold dread trickling through my body.

I felt like we were being watched. At least, more so than usual. Everyone was always watching me, and now they were watching Paloma too. Still, my unease grew stronger and stronger the farther we walked along the bridge.

"Something wrong, highness?" Sullivan asked. "You've gone quiet."

I shook my head. "Just tired, I guess."

We were about halfway across the bridge when the hot, caustic stench of magic filled my nose. And not just a little magic—far more magic than I had sensed during the Regalia so far, even among the strixes and the caladrius in the Mortan camp.

I stopped in the center of the bridge and looked around, searching for the source of the magic and all the danger it represented. No one used that much magic unless they were trying to kill someone else, and I was betting that the person they wanted dead was me.

The Mortans were definitely here—but where?

I glanced around, but they weren't on the bridge ahead of us, and they weren't rushing up behind us either. I even craned my neck up, searching the sky, but I didn't see anyone riding a strix.

"Where are they?" I said, still looking around. "Where the fuck are they?"

"Evie?" Paloma asked. "What are you muttering about?"

I started to answer her when a flash of bright purple lightning caught my eye. I whirled to the right, and I finally realized where the Mortans were—and where they had been hiding all along.

The seemingly empty ship, the one I'd noticed when we'd walked across the bridge before, wasn't empty anymore. Now more than a dozen people stood on the deck, all facing this direction. And the ship itself had been sailed closer to the Bellonan bridge, although it was anchored off to the side of the span and was still several hundred feet away from our current position.

I squinted into the sun, desperately hoping I had just imagined that flash of lightning—but I hadn't.

Every single person on the ship's deck had their arms lifted out to their sides, and powerful purple lightning was streaking up out of their hands and gathering in the sky above like a bright electrified spiderweb.

And that was just the beginning.

In seconds, storm clouds had rushed in all around the lightning, and the dark, ominous mass cloaked the island and cast everything in an eerie, purplish shadow. The wind picked up, howling around us like a pack of greywolves, and more and more lightning blasted up out of the magiers' hands and sizzled in the sky. The eerie purple streaks matched the power glowing in the magiers' eyes.

The members of the Bastard Brigade had finally shown themselves.

But those weren't just magiers on the ship—they were weather magiers, and they were all working together to create one massive, deadly storm.

The water in the harbor started to pitch, buck, and heave in time to the howling wind. One particularly large wave arced over the bridge railing and crashed down on the flagstones, soaking me to the bone. I gasped at the shock of the cold water and swiped my wet hair out of my eyes. When I could focus again, I realized just how much worse things had gotten in the space of those few seconds.

The weather magiers had quit sending their power up into the sky and were now moving their hands in unison. An instant later, a single enormous bolt of purple lightning streaked down and slammed into the harbor off to my right, in between their ship and where my friends and I were standing on the bridge. The resulting concussive *boom* was so loud that I couldn't hear myself think for several seconds.

But I could clearly see the water rising in the distance.

As soon as the lightning hit the water, the magiers began to move their hands in rapid unison, as though they were knitters stitching together an elaborate blanket. Except this blanket wasn't made of soft wool—it was comprised of cold, crushing water.

One wave lifted off the surface of the harbor, then another, then another. In an instant they had all gelled into a single wave, a solid line of water that just kept growing higher and higher and higher. Ten feet, twenty, fifty, a hundred. The wave just kept climbing and climbing and climbing, like it was somehow sliding up a staircase. The water also crackled with that eerie purple lightning, sucking up all the magiers' power and seemingly hungry for more, as though it were a living thing, a cold, wet kraken eager to gobble up everything in its path.

Including me.

I always have contingency plans in place, in case things go wrong, Maximus's snide voice whispered in my mind.

This had to be one of those plans. I'd taken away his pets, and he'd unleashed these weather magiers on me in return. Except the Bastard Brigade wasn't just trying to assassinate me.

No, this time Maximus was determined to kill us all.

CHAPTER TWENTY-TWO

Perhaps it was the cold water that had crashed over me, or the sheer size, scope, and audacity of Maximus's plan, but I stood there, frozen in place, eyes wide, completely dumb-founded, staring up at the wall of water that kept getting higher and higher and closer and closer to the bridge.

The other people on the bridge saw the wave too, and they started screaming and stampeding back to the closest end. But that wouldn't save them. The wave was almost as wide as the length of the bridge now, and the resulting crash would crush and drown everyone in the immediate vicinity, whether they were actually on the span or over on the Bellonan shore.

Unless I stopped it.

"Evie!" Sullivan yelled. "We have to get off the bridge!"

The howling wind drowned out his voice and swept his words away. He held out his hand, but I shook my head.

"No! Get behind me!" I shouted back. "Tell everyone to get behind me and hang on to the bridge railing! I'm going to try to stop the wave with my immunity! It's the only chance we have!"

Sullivan turned around, yelling out my instructions. Paloma

started toward me, but I shook my head and stabbed my finger at the railing behind me. She didn't like my order, but she reluctantly grabbed hold of the railing, right alongside Xenia. Serilda and Cho were hunkered down next to them, along with Auster and Leonidas.

The boy was clutching the railing so tightly that his knuckles stood out like white bruises against his skin, but his features were more resigned than frightened. He must have seen this sort of attack before, and he thought we were doomed. Maybe we were, but I was still going to fight until the wave hit me and the water pulled me under and drowned me for good.

Everyone else was looking at the wave, watching it come with a mixture of growing fear and dread, but to my surprise, Serilda was staring at me, instead of the rising water.

All I see is darkness. It's almost like a . . . wave rising up, getting ready to drown us all, her voice whispered in my mind. *A wave that could swallow us, and everyone else here, and all of Bellona.*

She'd given me that warning before the Regalia. I just hadn't realized how literal her words would turn out to be.

A faint bit of magic flared in Serilda's eyes, making them burn an even darker blue than usual, as if she were peering into the future and observing our fate. I wanted to yell and ask her what she was seeing, but there was no time. An instant later, the magic in her eyes vanished, and she gave me a single sharp nod. She was telling me that I could do this—that I *had* to do this, or we were all dead, along with scores of innocent people.

I strode over to the opposite side of the bridge, lifted my head, and stared up into the center of the wave. Purple lightning was still crackling through the water, so I opened my mouth and let the gusting air roll in over my tongue, tasting all the scents in it. There was only one—the hot, caustic stench of magic.

Every single member of the Bastard Brigade that I'd encountered over the past year had been strong in their magic, and
now that the weather magiers had combined their power, they
had gone from merely dangerous to seemingly unstoppable.
I didn't know if my immunity was strong enough to overcome
their collective power, but I had to try. So I kept tasting all the
magic in the air, trying to figure out how to destroy the tidal
wave that was still growing.

But the problem with so many magiers feeding their power
into the wave was that the magic wasn't focused in just one spot.
It was more or less evenly spread out through the whole length
of the water, just like the power was more or less evenly spread
out among the magiers. I might have been able to snuff out the
magic in one part of the wave, and make that section collapse,
but I wasn't strong enough to dissolve all the magic at once, and
the rest of the water would still hit us with its deadly, crushing
force.

So how could I possibly save my friends?

I looked over at the magiers, whose hands were still moving
back and forth in those sharp knitting motions. Even if I'd had
lightning, fire, or some other offensive magic, the magiers were
too far away for me to attack. Even Sullivan, with all his powerful
blue lightning, wouldn't have been able to reach the ship from
here, and especially not now with the gale-force winds gusting
around us and the water sweeping over the bridge railing and
slapping against our bodies.

Desperation filled me. I didn't want to die, and I certainly
didn't want my friends or all the other innocent people on and
around the bridge to die. But right now I didn't see a way to save
them, much less myself.

My gaze flicked from one thing to the next. The purple
lightning streaking through the water. The magiers moving

their hands. Their eyes glowing like amethyst stars as they fed more and more of their power into their horrible storm. And of course the tidal wave that just kept growing higher and larger with every passing second—

And I suddenly realized that this wasn't the first time I'd had to battle two enemies at once. During the assassination attempt on Serilda outside the Mint yesterday, I had faced down a fire magier and an ogre morph. I hadn't been strong enough to kill the morph on my own, so I'd used my immunity to trick the magier into doing it for me with her fire. Maybe I could do the same thing right now. Maybe I didn't have to destroy the wave and all the magic churning through it.

Maybe I just had to redirect it.

"Evie! Evie!"

Behind me, my friends screamed my name, although if they said anything else, I didn't hear it. I tuned out their frantic cries, along with the booming thunder and the wind howling in my ears.

Instead, I focused on the wave, timing my movements to it. As it grew higher and higher, I reached for my own magic, for my own immunity, pulling the power up and up and up, until the invisible strength of it was crackling around my hands like the purple lightning was streaking through the water. Then, when I had an iron grip on my power, I lifted my hands and planted my boots on the wet flagstones, bracing myself as best I could.

The magiers must have finally exhausted their collective power, because they all snapped their hands down at once, forcing the wave to start its inevitable deadly downward roll. A final crack of thunder roared through the air, and the concussive *boom* rattled everything, including the bridge. I bent my knees, bracing myself a little more, and held my ground.

I had often thought of my immunity as a gladiator's weapon, as a dagger to slice through someone else's power, or a sword to kill their magic completely. Now I thought of it as a shield, the largest and most important shield I had ever held. I pictured my immunity streaking out of my fingertips like gray and blue stars, and then those stars fusing together and arcing out into this enormous, invisible shield that stood between me, my friends, and the tidal wave rushing toward us.

"Come on!" I screamed, urging myself on. "Come on, come on, come on!"

I reached for even more of my magic. And more magic, and more magic still. Even though I couldn't actually see it, I still pictured the invisible force of my power going up, up, up, until it formed this strong, solid shield that completely covered me and my friends. And then I lifted that shield up into a defensive position, just like I would in a gladiator fight in the arena.

I had never tried to use so much magic before, had never tried to dig it out of myself like a miner chipping tearstone out of a cavern wall, but I reached and clawed and scraped up every last drop of power I had, every little shard of magic buried deep down inside me.

The wave arced higher still, blotting out the storm clouds overhead, and casting the bridge in almost total darkness. All I could see was the dark wall of water, along with those damned purple streaks of lightning zipping through it. I gritted my teeth and reached for even more magic, knowing that I had to hold the water back or we were all dead, and most likely Bellona along with us—

With a loud, booming, thunderous roar, the wave slammed down on the center of the bridge, right on top of me and my friends.

But the water didn't touch us—not a single fucking *drop*.

I looked up, but all I could see was the water churning and churning, desperately trying to batter through the invisible shield of my magic. My arms were still raised high overhead, with my fingers spread out wide, but my entire body was trembling and shaking from the effort of using so much of my own power to hold back so much violent, heavy, destructive force.

The water kept crashing down, down, down on top of my shield, even as the lightning inside the wave lashed out like a hot, caustic whip. Every blow knocked me back and threatened to break through my immunity, threatened to break *me*, and I ended up sliding all the way back across the flagstones until I hit the railing behind me. I would have flipped over it and plunged into the water below, dooming us all, but Paloma and Sullivan reached out and latched on to my legs, anchoring me to them and the bridge.

"We've got you, Evie!" Paloma screamed.

"Hold on, highness!" Sullivan shouted. "Hold on!"

I didn't have the strength to yell back. It was taking all my concentration, power, and focus to keep the water from crushing us.

But that much water couldn't just *stop*. It needed somewhere to go, and it started arcing up, up, up, getting ready to come crashing back down again. I wouldn't be able to shield us from a second blast, so with the last remaining scraps of my strength, I started pushing back against the water.

Well, I supposed I wasn't pushing back so much as I was changing the shape and position of my invisible shield. Instead of a round dome covering the bridge and protecting me and my friends, I imagined tilting the shield to the side, so that the water hit it and started arcing up again, forming another massive tidal wave.

Even though I wasn't tilting the shield all that much, it still took every ounce of my concentration. One degree of rotation too far, one second of inattention, one moment of hesitation, and the water would slip around the edge of the invisible barrier and flatten me, along with my friends.

So I focused on that shield like I had never focused on anything before in my life. Everything else fell away. My back pressing up against the railing. Paloma and Sullivan anchoring my legs. The shrieks and screams of everyone on the bridge. All I could see, hear, feel, taste, and smell was that crushing wall of water sliding up against my magic.

The wave arced up and up and up. Finally, when it reached its peak, I gritted my teeth, shoved my invisible shield forward, and threw the water away from us with all my might.

It was hard—so bloody fucking *hard*—but I pushed and pushed and pushed, shoving my invisible shield away from us, and all that damn water along with it.

The wave wobbled, but it didn't want to move, so I reached for even more of my magic, and pushed on the shield again, and then again, and then again, as though I were beating my fists against it, even though it was my own creation.

Slowly, the water started to tilt, but not quite enough, so I kept hammering at my shield, trying to push it and the massive wave away from us. I was almost out of power, and it was now or never. With a loud, primal scream of rage, I pushed on my shield one last time.

And the wave finally—*finally*—arced away from me and my friends.

The water kept moving, churning, seething, but it was now heading in the opposite direction. Even though the danger had passed, I kept my hands raised and my shield locked in place. I couldn't physically get my body to move at the moment, so I stood there and watched the wave roll away from the bridge and head exactly where I'd wanted it to go.

To the Bastard Brigade ship.

The weather magiers were still standing on the deck, and I thought I could almost smell their shock, horror, and fear at the sight of the wave zooming toward them. A few magiers turned and ran, probably to jump off the opposite side of the ship so they could try to swim to safety, even though that wouldn't save them.

The rest of the magiers snapped up their hands, desperately trying to summon their own magic to do something, anything, to keep the wave from killing them. But they didn't have enough magic or time, and a few seconds later the wave crashed down right on top of the Mortan ship.

Bull's-eye.

For several seconds there was just noise and spray and one concussive *boom-boom-boom* after another. The wave and the water seemed to go on and on and on . . .

Finally, the wave dissipated, although the water still churned, frothed, and bubbled, as though the entire surface of the harbor was quaking and shaking. I squinted, trying to see exactly how much damage I'd done.

The Mortan ship was gone—and so were the weather magiers.

No, that wasn't quite right. The ship wasn't gone so much as it was splintered into pieces, and broken bits of the wreckage bobbed up and down on the surface of the water like fishing lures. The largest piece of the ship that was left was the mainmast, and it quickly sank beneath the waves like an arrow that had been shot toward the bottom of the harbor.

I scanned the still-churning water, but I didn't see the magiers anywhere. The wave had probably crushed them against the deck, and their bodies were probably sinking to the bottom of the harbor along with the rest of the ship.

It was over. I had done it. I had saved us.

My body started violently shaking, and my arms went suddenly limp and numb and fell to my sides. I didn't have the strength to hold them up anymore. I didn't even *feel* them anymore, or my legs, and I would have crumpled to the flagstones if Paloma and Sullivan hadn't still been holding on to me.

Slowly, the water stopped its violent churning, although rip-
ples continued to shoot out in every direction, rocking the other
boats and ships anchored closer to the shorelines. It would be
quite some time before the harbor was completely calm again.
More wind blew over the bridge, but this was a natural breeze,
and not what the magiers had made, and it quickly swept away
the last of the ugly dark purple storm clouds.

The wind whispered away, and I was suddenly aware of this
strange loud buzzing in my ears. It took me a moment to realize that it was the screams and shouts of everyone on the bridge
and the people on the boats, ships, and shorelines who had witnessed what had happened.

A couple of bright purple sparks caught my eye, and I slowly
turned my head, looking back toward Fortuna Island.

Maximus was watching me.

The Mortan king was standing on a high rise along the
waterfront that offered him a clear view of the Bellonan bridge,
as well as where the Mortan ship had been. Despite the distance
between us, I could see the magic burning in his purple eyes. I
didn't know if he had fed his power into the wave along with the
other weather magiers', but he was clearly furious that his contingency plan had failed.

Mercer and Nox were standing next to the king, both of
them looking stunned, as if they didn't understand why their
bastard relatives were dead instead of me.

And then there was Maeven.

She too was standing on the rise, although she was slightly
apart from her male relatives, just as she had been during the
rest of the Regalia. Instead of being angry or shocked, Maeven
seemed contemplative, as though she were thinking about far
more important things than how I had survived this latest assassination attempt.

After a few seconds, she looked past me. I followed her gaze, and I realized that she was staring at Leonidas, who was still slumped against the bridge railing, cold, wet, and shaking just like everyone else was. I wondered if Maximus had told Maeven that he was going to kill Leonidas along with me. Probably. The Mortan king wouldn't let something as insignificant as his nephew's life stand in the way of murdering me.

Once Maeven was sure that her son was okay, she stared at me. Her features took on that contemplative look again, and she actually tipped her head. I wasn't sure whether she was mocking or congratulating me. Probably both.

Maeven turned and vanished from sight, but Maximus, Mercer, and Nox stayed on the rise, still staring down at the bridge. After a few seconds, Nox noticed that Maeven had slipped away, and he did the same. I wondered if they wanted to get away from the king in order to avoid his wrath. Probably a good idea.

Mercer was glaring at me, but I ignored him and focused on Maximus. His eyes were still burning with magic, and I could have sworn I could smell his hot jalapeño rage all the way out here on the bridge.

If I'd had the strength left, I would have lifted my hand and snapped off a mocking salute, just to piss him off even more.

Paloma and Sullivan let go of my legs and got to their feet, although they were both shaking, just like I still was.

"Evie?" Paloma whispered. "Are you okay?"

I didn't have the energy left to answer her. I glanced along the bridge. Serilda, Cho, Xenia, and Auster were all climbing to their feet. Leonidas was still sitting down, slumped against the railing, but the boy was in one piece, as was everyone else farther out on the bridge.

I looked toward the Bellonan end of the bridge. Everyone there was either climbing to their feet or standing in place, still shocked by what had just happened. But my countrymen all looked okay, and no one seemed to have gone into the water.

The only ones who had been drowned by the wave had been the ship full of Mortans.

"Evie?" Sullivan said. "Evie, talk to me."

I tried to smile at him, but I didn't have the strength left for that either. Instead, my legs finally gave way, and I pitched backward.

This time, I couldn't stop myself from collapsing. I heard my friends shout my name, but that strange buzzing filled my ears again, and the last thing I saw was the cold, wet flagstones rushing up to meet me.

CHAPTER TWENTY-THREE

The first thing I was aware of was the cold water slowly soaking into the side of my body.

I tried to squirm away, but it seemed to be everywhere. When that didn't work, I cracked my eyes open. That's when I realized that I wasn't lying in water at all, but rather on a pile of snow near a campfire that was slowly melting the icy crystals, hence the cold wetness that had soaked into my dress.

Everything came rushing back to me. Meeting Rocinda and Caxton in the woods. Hearing their awful plans for me. Freeing the caged caladrius. Caxton hitting me in the face, Rocinda cutting me with her dagger, and the poison on the blade spreading through my body.

The one good thing about lying in the snow was that the cold had soaked into my cheek, which wasn't throbbing quite as badly as before, although pain still rippled through my skull. I lay still and quiet, trying to figure out what was going on. We *were still at the campsite, since I could see the caladrius's empty cage hanging in the tree.*

Someone, Caxton probably, had stoked the campfire back up into a bright blaze, and the heat of it pressed against my back. I didn't see my enemies, so I listened, straining to hear above the soft popping and crackling of the fire, and trying to figure out exactly where they were . . .

"Did you signal the Mortans yet?" Caxton's voice cut through the quiet.

The sudden sound startled me, and I had to work very hard not to jerk in surprise.

Footsteps sounded, growing closer and louder, as though someone was leaving the edge of the woods and crunching back through the patches of snow toward the campsite.

"Yes." Rocinda's voice drifted over to me. "I just spoke to one of the bastard Morricones through the Cardea mirror they gave us the last time we brought them some strixes. They're very eager to get their hands on the girl."

"Who did you talk to?" Caxton asked.

"Someone named Maeven. I think she's one of the king's bastard sisters. I told her that the little Blair bitch doesn't seem to have any magic, but she didn't care. In fact, Maeven seemed even more interested in the girl after I told her that."

Panic filled me, and I had to fight the urge to jump to my feet and run away. They were going to take me to Morta? And sell me to one of the king's relatives? This was even worse than I'd feared. Slavery would be bad enough, but going to Morta was a certain death sentence.

My mother had told me all sorts of horror stories about the Morricone royal family—how much they hated the Blairs, how they coveted our tearstone mines, and especially how they were always brewing poisons and dreaming up new ways to try to kill us. I'd thought she'd just been trying to scare me into behaving, but Rocinda and Caxton's words seemed to confirm all those awful tales.

So how could I escape this gruesome fate?

My hands had been tied in front of my body with a thick, heavy rope. I tested the bonds, but the rope was far too strong to break. A sob of despair rose in my throat, but I choked it down. Now was not the time to give in to my fear and panic. No, I needed to be calm if I had any chance of surviving. And right now I desperately needed something to cut through the ropes.

I was still lying in the snow, and I glanced around, searching for a rock, a tree branch, or anything else I could use to either get out of my bonds or wield as a weapon. I didn't see anything, but a little bit more snow melted under my body, and something colder and harder than the ice dug into my hip.

My breath caught in my throat. It was the dagger my mother had given to me back at Winterwind. The blade was still hidden in my pocket. Rocinda and Caxton must not have searched me, and they didn't realize that I had a weapon.

Maybe I could escape after all.

Rocinda and Caxton kept talking, going over their route from Bellona, through Andvari, and over into Morta, but I tuned them out. They weren't paying attention to me, and I slowly shifted to the side, so that I was leaning more onto my back. Then I reached around and started working my hands down into my dress pocket.

It was hard, especially since my hands were tied, and I was trying to move my arms as little as possible, but I wormed my fingers into the opening. My dagger was still in there, and I managed to get one fingertip on it, then two, then three. Somehow, I pulled the dagger up high enough so that I could grab the hilt. Then, when I had a good grip on it, I started sliding it out of my pocket.

All I had to do was quietly slice through my bonds and wait for my enemies to go back to sleep. Then I could get up and run into the woods, and this time I wouldn't be stupid enough to stop for anything—

"I think our little friend is awake," Caxton said.

For a moment, I froze, but there was no time to waste, so I yanked the dagger free. I didn't have time to try to slice through my bonds, so instead I wrapped both hands around the hilt—

A rough hand grabbed my shoulder and rolled me over onto my back.

Caxton dropped to his knee and bent down over me. "What do you think you're doing—"

I whipped up the dagger and stabbed him in the chest.

Caxton screamed in surprise. He jerked back, and the blade slid free of his chest, but I kept my grip on it and shoved it right back into his body again, even deeper than before. He screamed again, then flopped to the ground beside me.

I scrambled up onto my knees, took hold of the dagger, and ripped it out of his chest, but he didn't scream again. Blood spurted everywhere, making my hands warm and slippery, but I plunged the dagger tip into the snowy ground, then put my hands up against the sharp blade, using it to saw through my bonds.

"Caxton!" Rocinda screamed.

Footsteps crunched through the snow, and the stench of magic filled the air. I looked up. Rocinda was running toward me, a ball of fire crackling in her hand. I went back to work on my bonds, sawing, sawing, sawing with all my might.

Snap!

The ropes finally broke apart. I didn't even wait for them to drop away from my hands before I grabbed the dagger out of the ground, but Rocinda was quicker than I was, and she hurled her fire at me. I lurched to the side, accidentally tripping over Caxton's body. The fire zoomed over my head, but I hit the ground hard, landing on my back again, and more pain bloomed in my face and skull. I pushed it away the best I could, but once again, I was too late.

In an instant Rocinda was looming over me, another ball of fire burning in her hand. "Maeven only told me to bring you to her alive. She never said that I couldn't melt your skin off first," she hissed.

The magier drew her hand back to blast me with her fire. I lifted my own hand, reaching for my immunity, even though I didn't know if I was strong enough to snuff out her power—

A shadow zoomed out of the trees and flew straight at Rocinda's face. She shrieked in surprise, and the fire slipped out of her hand and exploded against the ground, making the snow hiss as it instantly melted.

I scrambled to my feet. The magier whirled around to me, but the shadow came at her again, and I realized that it wasn't a shadow at all.

It was the caladrius.

The tiny, owlish bird kept attacking the magier, raking its sharp talons across her hands, arms, and face. Rocinda shrieked and staggered back, trying to summon up more magic to roast the bird in midair, but every time she raised her hand, the caladrius swooped down at her again.

In my hurry to get away from the magier I had dropped my dagger, and I fell back down to my knees, trying to find where the weapon had landed in the snow. The cold crystals stung my hands, but I kept digging and digging through the clumps of snow.

"Die, you damn bird!" Rocinda snarled.

I looked up just in time to see the magier hurl a ball of magic at the caladrius. Rocinda's aim was true, and the fire bloomed like a red-hot flower against the creature's snow-white wings, completely engulfing its body. The caladrius didn't make a sound as it dropped into the campfire.

A shrieking sob rose in my throat. Even though I had only seen the creature for a few moments, it was a shame that something so beautiful had been put in a cage. And now it was dead, just because it had tried to help me.

Icy rage filled me, freezing out my grief. My hand closed over the dagger, and I ripped it out of the snowdrift. Then I got to my feet and headed toward Rocinda.

The magier whirled around to me, another ball of fire popping into her hand. "Come here, girl," she snarled. "And let me cook you alive just like I did that damn bird."

But she didn't wait for me to come closer. Instead, Rocinda reared her hand back and threw her fire at me.

I could feel and smell the hot flames streaking through the air, and I grabbed hold of my immunity, coating my skin with the cold, hard power that perfectly matched the rage beating in my heart. The fire blasted against me, but I pushed back with my immunity, and the flames vanished without even touching my body, much less scorching my skin.

Rocinda blinked in surprise, but she threw another ball of fire at me. And then another one, and then another.

I kept my grip on my immunity, and I snuffed out all her magic. And the whole time, I kept stalking toward her at that same slow, steady, determined pace.

Finally, she stopped long enough to stare at me with wide eyes. "Why aren't you burned? Why aren't you dead?"

I screamed with rage and ran straight at her. Rocinda backed up, but this time she was the one who tripped over Caxton's body. She staggered to the side, still trying to get away from me, but before she could recover her balance, I surged forward and stabbed her in the chest.

Rocinda screamed and lifted her hand to blast me with her magic again, but I ripped the dagger out of her chest and sliced it across her throat. I didn't really know what I was doing, other than trying to hurt her, but I got lucky and the blade sliced cleanly across her neck.

Rocinda stared at me, choking on her own blood. Then her eyes rolled up in the back of her head, and she dropped to the ground, bleeding out all over the snow.

I stood over her, the bloody dagger still clutched in my hand, breathing hard. When I was sure she was dead, I slumped down to my knees, then plopped over onto the ground.

I didn't know how long I huddled there, staring dully at Rocinda's and Caxton's bodies. Right now I didn't have the strength to move, much less think about what I should do next—

Hoot. Hoot-hoot. Hoot.

My head snapped up, and I looked around the clearing, wondering who—or what—was making that sound. For a moment, I thought that maybe Caxton or Rocinda was still alive, but they were dead, so they weren't the ones making the noise.

Hoot. Hoot-hoot. Hoot.

The sound came again, and I realized that it was coming from . . . the campfire.

I looked in that direction, and I noticed that something was moving in the flames. At first I thought it was just a chunk of wood burning, but then I realized the object was shaped like a small bird . . .

The caladrius.

I gasped in surprise, wondering if my eyes were playing tricks on me, but they weren't. Somehow, the caladrius was still alive in the middle of the flickering flames.

My gaze darted around the clearing, searching for

something that I could wrap around my hand. But there was no time to protect myself, not if I wanted to save the creature, so I lunged over and stretched my hand out toward the fire. I grimaced, knowing how much this was going to hurt, but I shoved my fingers forward anyway.

The instant before my hand would have plunged into the fire, the caladrius twitched its wings, hopped out of the flames, and landed on my outstretched palm. I jerked back, and the caladrius shuffled around, its talons digging into my skin as it held on to my palm, but not unpleasantly so.

My shock wore off, and I slowly rose to my feet with the caladrius still perched on my hand. The creature ruffled its feathers, shaking the soot and ash off them. A few red-hot embers flickered around the bird, but its feathers were a pristine snow-white, and the caladrius seemed completely untouched and unharmed by the fire.

"How did you do that?" I whispered.

Magic.

I blinked. Had the caladrius just . . . talked to me again?

The creature kept staring at me, then raised its wing and pointed it to the right.

"That way?" I asked. "I should go that way?"

The caladrius bobbed its head and shuffled on my palm again.

My father had always told me that caladriuses had powerful magic, but I hadn't known they were strong and tough enough to survive a blast of magier power and then an actual fire. For the first time, I understood why Rocinda and Caxton— and whomever they had been working for—had wanted the creature for their own.

But it was a wild thing, and it deserved to be free, like all wild things did. So I lifted it up, staring into its gray-blue eyes.

"Thank you," I murmured. "For saving me."

The caladrius shuffled around again, bent down, and rubbed its soft head and feathers against my fingers. Then it spread its wings wide and took off, disappearing into the trees. I watched it go with a smile on my face.

But all too soon reality set in, reminding me that I needed to get out of here and find someone who would help me. So I headed over to Rocinda's and Caxton's knapsacks to see what I could take with me on my journey out of the cold, snowy woods . . .

My eyes fluttered open. For a moment, I thought I was still in the woods that awful night so long ago. But then I realized I was staring at the wall of a gray canvas tent, instead of the snow-dappled ground, and everything came rushing back to me.

Sneaking into the Mortan camp. Freeing the strixes and the caladrius. Sneaking back over to the island. Seeing Paloma win the tournament. Watching Maximus kill his own guard. Stepping onto the bridge and seeing the weather magiers' tidal wave . . .

I shuddered at the horrible memory of that wall of water rising up. Even among all the horrible things I had been through over the past year, that image would haunt my nightmares for the rest of my life.

Low voices sounded, and I glanced over to my right.

Paloma, Sullivan, Serilda, Cho, Xenia, Auster. My friends were gathered around a table that had been set up along one of the tent walls. I didn't see Leonidas, so the boy must be in his own tent. I wondered if Lyra had flown back here to find him. Probably.

My friends kept talking in soft voices. I lay still and listened to their conversation.

"We've gotten reports that the Mortans are massing on their

side of the river. Guards and strixes are lined up on the rise at the edge of their camp." Auster pointed to a spot on a map spread out on the table.

"Do you think the Mortans will actually fly across the river and invade Bellona?" Paloma asked in a worried voice.

"It's too early to say," Serilda murmured. "More likely, Maximus doesn't want us sneaking into his camp again. That's why he's making such a strong show of force."

"But what if you're wrong?" Sullivan asked. "What if he comes here and tries to kill Evie again? The strixes could easily fly across the river and swoop down into our camp."

"Then we'll fight the bastards off," Xenia replied. "Just the way we've been doing for months now . . ."

My friends kept discussing the movements of the Mortan soldiers and strixes, and the scent of their collective worry hung like a wet blanket in the air. But there was only one way to end this now—my plan of last resort.

Perhaps I had always known that it would come to this, ever since the Seven Spire massacre. After all, it was a grand Bellonan tradition and how my kingdom had been founded. It seemed fitting that I should defend it the same way all these centuries later.

As much as I wanted to rest, I couldn't let my friends deal with the fallout of Maximus's latest attack by themselves. Queens did not have the luxury of lounging around in bed, not even after they'd almost been assassinated—again.

"Well, I say that we forget our problems and go to the ball," I drawled, sitting up on the bed.

My friends whirled around at the sound of my voice, then rushed forward.

"Evie! Evie!"

"Are you okay, highness?"

"How are you feeling?"

The questions tumbled out of their mouths one after another, and their chatter made me smile. On the bridge, I had thought I would never hear their voices again, but here we were, all safe and sound, and I couldn't stop smiling at that.

"I'm fine. Really. No doubt thanks to Aisha and her healing magic." I looked around for the bone master, but she wasn't here.

"Aisha went to check on Leonidas," Serilda said. "The boy was still a bit shaken up, so she was going to make sure he was okay. Lyra flew back to camp. She's in the tent with him."

Good. I was glad the boy had a friend right now.

"Aisha was here, but she said that you were exhausted more than anything else," Cho chimed in. "She told us to let you rest, and that you would wake up when your strength returned."

I did feel extremely tired, but there was nothing Aisha or any other bone master could do about that. My body would just have to recover in its own time, even though time was something that was in short supply right now.

Auster gestured at the map again. "We were just talking about what course of action we should take next."

The others filled me in on what had happened. After I'd collapsed on the bridge, my friends had rushed me to the Bellonan camp, where Aisha had healed me as much as she could. Then Auster had sent his guards and Xenia had sent her spies back to Fortuna to watch the Mortan side of the river. So far, there had been no sign of Maximus, although Mortan soldiers and strixes had been spotted guarding their camp.

"As for the ship in the harbor, no one seems to know where it came from or who it belonged to, but we all know this was Maximus's doing," Auster said.

"Along with the members of the Bastard Brigade," Xenia added.

I thought of the weather magiers standing on the deck and

the terror on their faces when they'd realized that I'd turned their own tidal wave against them. "Did any of the magiers survive?"

Serilda shook her head. "No."

Xenia eyed the other woman. "How do you know?"

"My magic might not always be precise, but it is quite useful when it comes to this sort of thing," Serilda replied. "I could *see* the magiers' deaths the moment Evie pushed the water back in their direction. Believe me, no one on that ship survived, not even the rats."

"Well, the magiers being dead solves one of our problems," Cho said. "But we still have to do something about Maximus before he orders his men and their strixes to cross the river and invade Bellona."

Worry curled through my stomach, then drew itself into tight little knots. Maximus and I had a relatively even number of soldiers here, but his strixes would turn the tide in his favor, and he could potentially slaughter everyone in the Bellonan camp. Or worse, have his guards fly to Seven Spire and try to take the palace while I was stuck down here miles away.

I had to stop that from happening, which meant that I needed to give Maximus another target to focus on. So far, the two of us had been trading attacks and insults, but I had to give him a reason to play *my* game for a change, instead of going ahead with his own schemes.

I had used the lessons Xenia had taught me on being a spy to sabotage and undercut Maximus. Now it was time to turn to Serilda's teachings and be a soldier again.

Now it was time to fight.

"Evie?" Paloma asked. "What are you thinking about? You look worried."

I sighed. "That's because I *am* worried. But I know what we have to do. I know how we can stop Maximus."

"And how is that?" Xenia asked.

I told my friends my plan. Well, not all of it, but the most important part, the one I could actually control, and the one I needed their help with.

When I finished, they stood there in stunned silence. Then they all started shouting at once.

"No! You can't do that!"

"It's too dangerous."

"It's a stupid plan, since it mostly involves you getting yourself killed."

That last comment came from Paloma, who was never shy about telling me when she thought I was being an idiot.

I held up my hands, asking for quiet. "We have to stop Maximus here and now, and we especially have to give him a reason to keep all his guards and strixes here. This is our best option, our *only* option, and I think you all know that."

My friends didn't like it, but slowly, one by one, they nodded their agreement, although Sullivan gave me an anguished look that made my heart twist.

But heartache was something else queens didn't have the luxury of indulging in, so I threw back the covers and stood up.

"Go back to your tents and get ready." I gave them all a grim smile. "We have a royal ball to attend."

PART THREE

THE LONG GAME

CHAPTER TWENTY-FOUR

I called for Calandre and her sisters, and they helped me get ready for the ball.

Calandre had made me another gorgeous gown. It was similar to the one I'd worn last night, with a pattern of silver shields dotting it, and the fabric was a dark gray that almost looked blue, depending on how the light hit it. Cerana and Camille also worked their magic on my hair and makeup, hiding the pale exhaustion of my features with their dark liners, shadows, and berry balms.

When they had finished, I thanked them for their work.

Calandre dismissed her sisters, then looked at me. "Is there something else you need, my queen?"

I sighed. "Is it that obvious?"

She shrugged. "Only to those who can see the worry on your face. Which would probably be anyone who looks at you right now."

"I need you to make me one final outfit for the Regalia. I should have asked you to make it back at Seven Spire, but I was hoping that I wouldn't need it." I told her what I wanted. "What do you think? Is it possible on such short notice?"

Calandre stood still, digesting my request. She knew what it meant, and why I would wear such a thing. After several seconds, she nodded. "I can do it, even if I have to sew all night."

I reached out and squeezed her hand. "Thank you. And please, keep this to yourself." I grimaced. "Although I imagine that it will be all over the island and the camps soon enough."

"Of course." Calandre squeezed back. "Good luck, Everleigh."

"Thank you. I'm going to need it."

Calandre left the tent to get started on my project, and I stepped outside where the others were waiting. Sullivan, Cho, and Auster looked handsome in their formal jackets, Xenia was stunning in a long green gown, and Serilda was a vision in white. Paloma was wearing a green tunic patterned with gold ogre heads, and she looked fierce and beautiful.

Paloma and Xenia were talking, and the ogre faces on their necks were silently admiring each other. I hadn't had a chance to tell them my theory about Amira, but I would. If nothing else, the two of them would have each other, even if I didn't make it through the Regalia.

"You look stunning, highness," Sullivan said, pulling me away from the others.

"I know you don't want me to do this. But I also hope you know why I have to."

"I do, and I couldn't be prouder of you." His blue gaze locked with mine. "I told you once that you would be a wonderful queen. I just wish that the hard and ruthless parts didn't make me worry so much."

"Do you regret becoming my consort?"

"Not for one bloody second, highness," he said in a fierce voice. "Not for one bloody second."

He took my hand, leaned down, and pressed a kiss to my knuckles, his lips scorching my skin. He straightened and gave me a wicked grin. "Now, let's get you to the ball, so we can get on with the business of defeating Maximus. What do you say?"

I threaded my arm through his. "That sounds like an excellent plan."

We left the Bellonan camp with a large contingent of guards. We stopped at our end of the bridge, looking around to make sure Maximus hadn't set another deadly trap, but the plaza was deserted. Ships were still anchored in the harbor, but they were all close to shore, and I didn't see anyone standing on the decks, waiting to strike out at us. So we crossed the bridge and headed over to the island.

Crowds of people were moving along the waterfront, eating, shopping, and talking, but the mood was far more subdued than it had been this afternoon, and several folks eyed the water with suspicion, as if they thought it was going to suddenly surge up and drown them.

We left the waterfront behind, climbed the hill, and made our way to the DiLucri castle. Several guards were manning the open front gate, and they stopped talking at the sight of me and my friends walking toward them. One of the guards ran deeper into the castle, no doubt to tell Driscol and Seraphine that I was still alive.

We went to the grand ballroom in the center of the castle. The area looked much the same as it had last night. Polished white marble floor and walls. Crested banners hanging down from the second-floor balcony. Royals, nobles, advisors, and others clustered in groups, eating, drinking, and gossiping. The steady *tink-tink-tink* of gold coins dripping out of the Lady Fortuna fountains in all four corners.

Yes, everything looked more or less the same, but the people and the overall mood were just as subdued here as by the waterfront.

But the quiet didn't last for long.

One by one, people caught sight of me, my friends, and the Bellonan guards, and several shocked gasps surged through the ballroom. I strode forward and stopped in an open space, my face calm, my shoulders back and down, and my chin held high, letting them all get a good, long look at me. I wanted everyone to see that I was still in one piece and suffering no ill effects from the attack on the bridge.

I wanted them all to see *exactly* how strong Bellona was.

The loud gasps quieted to soft whispers that spread throughout the ballroom. In less than a minute, everyone knew that I was here. I held my position a few seconds longer, then strode forward toward the center of the ballroom where the other royals were.

They were split into two factions. Eon, Ruri, Cisco, Heinrich, and Zariza were together. Maximus was standing by himself, although Mercer, Nox, and Maeven were lurking behind him like usual. Driscol and Seraphine were here too, a few feet away from the royals.

The whispers had already reached the other kings and queens, who turned to stare at me. The musicians had been playing a soft, dreamy song, but Seraphine made a sharp motion with her hand. The music abruptly screeched to a stop, and the only sound was the steady *snap-snap-snap-snap* of my heels on the marble floor.

I stopped in the empty space between the other royals and Maximus. "Good evening. How is everyone?"

For a long, tense moment, no one spoke. Then Seraphine nudged her brother with her elbow, and Driscol stepped forward and gave me a tight smile.

"Queen Everleigh," he said, his voice much higher than normal. "How nice to see you looking so well, given all that . . . unpleasantness earlier."

"Unpleasantness?" I said, my voice as cold as ice. If I never heard that word again, it would be too soon. "It wasn't mere *unpleasantness*. It was an assassination attempt. Maximus sent his bastard relatives to try to drown me on my own bloody bridge."

More shocked gasps surged through the crowd, followed by furious whispers. It was one thing for everyone to suspect that the Morricones had tried to kill me again, but it was quite another for me to openly proclaim it, especially during a royal ball. Well, fuck protocol, and fuck being polite.

I was through playing everyone else's games.

Maximus stared at me, not at all concerned by my accusation. "You are mistaken, Everleigh. I have no idea what you're talking about. I certainly had nothing to do with that unfortunate incident in the harbor."

"Oh, cut the bullshit," I snarled. "It was you. It's always been *you*."

Maximus opened his mouth, but I didn't want to listen to his lies, so I stabbed my finger at him.

"*You* sent Maeven and Nox to Seven Spire to murder Queen Cordelia and assassinate the Blairs. Then, a few months ago, *you* ordered Maeven to try to kill Dominic and me at Glitnir. Just last week, *you* dispatched DiLucri geldjagers to Svalin to kill, torture, and wreak as much havoc as possible among my people. *You* sent assassins after Serilda on the plaza yesterday and then more into my camp last night after the kronekling tournament. And finally, this afternoon, *you* ordered the members of your Bastard Brigade to use their magic to create that tidal wave, which was designed to do one thing and one thing only—kill me and my friends."

Shocked silence dropped over the ballroom again, and no one moved or said anything.

I looked at the other royals. "I've told you what a threat *he* is to all of us." I stabbed my finger at Maximus again. "Maybe now you'll finally believe me. You all saw him execute his own guard just for delivering bad news. Imagine what he would do to a true enemy. Actually, you don't have to imagine anything, given that tidal wave he orchestrated against me."

Once again, no one moved or said anything, and the scent of everyone's collective worry, fear, and tension blanketed the air.

"You are mistaken, Everleigh," Maximus repeated, his voice as smooth and silky as ever. "I had absolutely nothing to do with those weather magiers, whomever they were."

I laughed. "Please. They were your *blood,* and now they're all fish food. But you don't care, do you? Even your relatives are just pawns that you use and sacrifice any way you want whenever you feel like it. All to give yourself a tiny bit more power."

The king didn't respond, but a muscle ticked in his jaw. My tirade was beginning to anger him. Good.

"Being here in the ballroom again, I can't help but think of that strix you slaughtered last night. At first I thought you did it just to be disgusting, but then I realized that you had an ulterior motive. You wanted the strix's magic, and you drank its blood so you could absorb its power."

More shocked gasps rang out, but I ignored them and kept staring at the Mortan king.

"You know, Maximus, I'm starting to wonder if you have any real magic of your own—or just what you take from others. You're not a true king. You're not even a common mutt. You're nothing but a sick, disgusting little *thief*."

I didn't know if Maximus had any magic of his own, and I really didn't care. All that mattered right now was goading him into agreeing to my proposal and having another chance to end him.

A flurry of whispers sounded at my harsh insults, and everyone started eyeing Maximus, clearly wondering if my words were true, and what magic—if any—the Mortan king had.

Mercer and Nox both looked pale at my exposing their king's secret, but Maeven studied her brother with a thoughtful expression.

My latest round of insults made Maximus go from merely being angry to being outright incensed. His purple eyes glowed with hate, his hands clenched into fists, and the scent of his hot jalapeño rage blasted over me in continuous gusts, like I was breathing in fire instead of the cool air.

"I would be careful, Everleigh," he said in an icy voice. "You are dangerously close to insulting me. And that is not a wise thing to do."

I arched an eyebrow. "Only close to insulting you? Well, then, let me make myself crystal clear."

I held out my hand. Serilda stepped up and passed me my sword. Everyone, including Maximus, tensed, but I held the sword up high and turned around in a slow circle, so that everyone could see it.

A couple of low murmurs sounded. A few people had already figured out what I was up to, including Maeven, who stared at me with the same thoughtful expression she'd given her brother a few moments ago.

I kept my sword raised high overhead as I looked out over the crowd of royals, nobles, advisors, servants, and guards. "Maximus has spent the past year trying to kill me, and he almost succeeded today. Royals trying to murder each other is nothing new, but he didn't just target me. How many people would have died on the bridge? Or on the shoreline? Hundreds, maybe even thousands. And this man, this so-called *king*, wouldn't have given a damn about any of those innocent people. Just like he doesn't give a damn about his subjects, not even his own flesh and blood."

Several people nodded, and more than a few murmurs of agreement sounded. Maximus heard them too, and even more rage sparked in his eyes. He didn't like my announcing his many sins. Too damn bad.

"Well, I say no more," I called out. "We must all hold Maximus accountable for his actions, and especially those of his bastard relatives, the ones who lie, cheat, and kill on his orders."

"What are you proposing?" Zariza called out.

I looked at the Ungerian queen. "There is only one way to settle this now."

"And how is that?" This time Heinrich asked the question.

I smiled, baring my teeth at everyone. "Through a royal challenge."

More shocked gasps surged through the crowd, but they almost immediately vanished, like candles being snuffed out by a cold, stiff wind.

I faced Maximus again. I raised my sword a little higher, then brought it down. Still keeping my gaze on his, I sliced the blade across my left palm, opening up a deep gash. Then I held my hand out and clenched it into a tight fist, so that my blood spurted out from between my fingers. The steady *plop-plop-plop* of my blood dripping onto the white marble floor seemed even louder than the coins still tinkling out of the fountains in the corners.

"I, Everleigh Saffira Winter Blair, queen of Bellona, challenge you, Maximus Mercer Morland Morricone, king of Morta, to a royal fight to the death."

My voice boomed through the ballroom just like the thunder from the magiers' storm had over the bridge. The last echoes of my voice and challenge quickly faded away, but no one moved or spoke.

Surprise flashed in Maximus's eyes. Even after his vicious attack on the bridge, he still hadn't expected me to do something so bold in return. Arrogant fool. He didn't realize that his plots were finished and that we were playing *my* game from here on out.

"Do you accept?" I asked, a loud, mocking sneer in my voice. "Or are you going to keep being a coward and sending others to try to kill me?"

My insult whisked away his surprise, and cold calculation filled his eyes. Maximus knew as well as I did that I'd twirled him into a corner with my challenge. He had to accept, or he would be confirming everything that I had just said about him—including how weak he truly was.

"I accept," Maximus said, his voice booming just as loudly as mine had.

Everyone started talking and yelling at once. I let them chatter on for several seconds, then held my sword up again, calling for silence.

"Excellent," I said. "Let's talk terms. Since we're at the Regalia, why don't we give the people a show?"

He frowned. "What do you mean?"

"Why not make the challenge the finale of the Regalia? Why not let the people gather in the arena to see who triumphs? Our ancestors did it all those years ago. Why not continue the tradition and finally finish what they started?"

He kept frowning, turning the idea over in his mind, even as more and more whispers of excitement and agreement surged through the crowd. Maximus's gaze cut left and right, and his frown deepened. He didn't like my idea, but once again I had twirled him into a corner, and he couldn't refuse, given the rapidly growing support for my suggestion. Proposing a more private battle now would make it seem like he was hiding something.

"Very well," he said. "We will fight at noon tomorrow in the arena. I'm looking forward to it, Everleigh."

I gave him a cold, thin smile. "As am I."

My challenge delivered and accepted, I whirled around and strode out of the ballroom, my bloody sword still clutched in my hand.

CHAPTER TWENTY-FIVE

My friends and I left the island and went back to the Bellonan camp to get ready for tomorrow.

I had Auster triple the number of guards on duty. Just because Maximus had agreed to the royal challenge didn't mean that he still wouldn't send more assassins to try to kill me beforehand. So Auster posted guards all around camp, as well as in the surrounding trees to keep an eye out for strixes, in case the Mortan king decided to attack from the sky instead of the ground.

While Auster dealt with the guards, my other friends and I gathered in my tent, studying maps of the island and debating the best, quickest, and easiest routes to get from here to the arena without running into another ambush. But there really wasn't one, and we finally decided to go to the arena the same way we had been for the last two days.

We also talked about what to do given the outcome of the challenge. Our own contingency plans, as they were.

"If Maximus kills me, then you have to find some way to kill him before he leaves the arena." I didn't want to ask my friends to risk themselves again, but I had to put aside their safety and think about what was best for Bellona.

Sullivan, Paloma, Serilda, and Xenia fell quiet, thinking about it.

"I'll do it," Cho said.

We all looked at him in surprise, especially Serilda.

"I'm the ringmaster, so I'll be on the arena floor anyway," he continued. "If Maximus wins, then I'll go over to lift his hand in victory like I would for anyone else."

"And then?" Serilda asked in a low, strained voice.

Cho shrugged. "And then I'll palm a dagger and cut his throat. And if that doesn't work, I'll morph and tear him to pieces with my teeth and talons. Either way, Maximus won't be expecting me to attack, and he won't leave the arena alive, not even if it costs me my own life. I promise you that, Evie."

Cho was talking to me, but his black eyes were fixed on Serilda, as were those of the dragon on his neck. Serilda stared at him a moment, then turned away, but not before I saw the glassy sheen of tears in her eyes.

"He's right," Xenia said in a sympathetic voice. "It's the best plan."

Serilda didn't say anything, but she gave a single sharp nod. When she looked at Cho again, her tears were gone, and she was once again a warrior ready to sacrifice anything for her kingdom, even the man she loved.

"And when Evie wins?" Paloma asked, refusing to accept anything less than my victory.

Her confidence made me smile, but I forced myself to focus. "Then we'll probably have to kill Mercer, Nox, and Maeven. No doubt Maximus will order them to try to kill me again, on the off chance that he loses."

My friends started throwing out ideas on how best to kill the Morricone royals, but I stayed quiet, thinking about Maeven. I wouldn't just be fighting Maximus tomorrow. I would be battling her too.

For the last few months, I had been playing my long game with Maeven, and tomorrow would probably determine whether I won or lost that battle, along with my life, in the arena. But I'd made my moves and played the long game as best I could. Now all I could do was wait and see what tomorrow brought—for everyone.

An hour later, we finished our plotting, and everyone left my tent to go to bed, except for Sullivan. I was still standing by the table full of maps, and he walked up beside me.

"A crown for your thoughts, highness?" he murmured.

"Just thinking about tomorrow, and all the things that could go wrong." I let out a low, bitter laugh. "Sometimes I feel like all I do, every single day, is think about all the things that could go wrong."

His gaze locked with mine. "And that is one of the things that makes you such an excellent queen."

"I don't know about that, but I try. I suppose that's all any of us can really do in the end, even Winter queens."

Sullivan stared at me, love and understanding filling his blue, blue eyes. I leaned forward and kissed him, breathing in his cold, clean vanilla scent. His arms snaked around me, and he kissed me back, even as the warmth of his body soaked into my own.

"Come to bed," he murmured.

I did, and we spent the next hour making each other forget about all the dangers waiting for us in the arena tomorrow.

Afterward, Sullivan drifted off to sleep, but I couldn't rest, so I got out of bed, put on some clothes, along with my sword and dagger, and left the tent. The guards stationed outside started to follow me, but I waved them off. I wasn't going far.

I ended up on the rise at the edge of the Bellonan camp. Down below, the Perseverance Bridge gleamed like a sapphire arrow pointing toward Fortuna, while the ships anchored in the harbor bobbed up and down like golden and silver fireflies dancing on the surface of the water. More lights gleamed on the island, although the Mortan side of the river was largely dark.

It was a cold, clear December night, and the moon hung like a silver shield in the black arena of the sky, surrounded by the bright, tiny drops of blood oozing out of the stars. I drew in a breath, tasting all the scents swirling through the air. The smoke from the campfires. The last lingering hints of grilled chicken, fish, and more from people's dinners. The frost slowly forming on the ground.

But above it all, I could smell this rich, dark scent—crushed stone mixed with cold dirt. The scent that was truly, uniquely Bellona.

I crouched down. Aisha had healed the gash in my left palm, so I dug my hands into the ground, moving past the grass and grabbing two handfuls of earth. Then I drew my hands up and inhaled deeply. The scent of stone and dirt flooded my nose again, bringing with it a sense of strength, peace, and above all, determination. I was fighting for this land and its people, so they could be safe, happy, and free, and I could never, ever forget that.

I let the dirt slowly trickle through my fingers, then got to my feet. I stared at the island in the distance again, then turned and headed back to my tent and Sullivan to get what sleep I could.

The next morning, I sat in front of the vanity table in my tent, staring at my reflection.

Calandre had made me exactly what I'd requested. She must have worked on the outfit all night, but she had kept her promise.

I was wearing fighting leathers similar to the ones I'd worn at the Black Swan arena—a tight, fitted sleeveless shirt, a knee-length kilt, and sturdy sandals with straps that wound up past my ankles. The leathers were a deep midnight-blue, and Calandre had stitched my crown-of-shards crest in glittering silver thread over my heart. My tearstone sword dangled off my belt, and my shield was sitting nearby, waiting to be strapped to my forearm.

Calandre's sisters had also done their part, painting my face to make me look like a swan. But not a black swan this time. That was Serilda's symbol. No, I was a tearstone swan, a Bellonan swan, a Winter queen swan.

Dark blue shadow rimmed my eyes in thick, heavy circles before tapering off to sharp points. Bright silver paint had been streaked over the blue, creating shard-like feathers. Blue and silver crystals had been glued at the corners of my eyes, and silver glitter had been dusted all over my neck, arms, hands, and legs. My black hair was pulled back into three knots that bristled with blue feathers, and for a final touch, my lips had been painted a dark blue.

I had started this journey as a gladiator, and I was going to finish it as one.

"Well, my queen?" Calandre asked. "What do you think?"

I looked up and smiled at her, along with Camille and Cerana, who were hovering nearby. "It's perfect. Exactly what I wanted. Thank you again for making it on such short notice."

Calandre bowed her head. "It's been my honor to serve you, and I look forward to doing so for many more years to come."

Her confidence surprised me. Warmth and gratitude flooded my heart, and I got to my feet, reached out, and hugged her.

I drew back. "Thank you. It has been an honor to have you as my thread master."

Calandre wet her lips, as if debating whether she should say what was on her mind, but she finally did. "I've already lost one queen to the Mortans. I would hate to lose another one."

She curtsied to me in the traditional Bellonan style, then left the tent with her sisters trailing along behind her.

I stared at my reflection a moment longer, then grabbed my shield and left the tent as well.

My friends were waiting outside. Sullivan. Paloma. Serilda. Cho. Xenia. Auster. The last time we had done something like this had been the night of Vasilia's coronation. I hoped that today went as well as that night had—and that I was able to save Bellona from the Mortans.

So many things needed to fall into place for that to truly happen, but I was more optimistic about my chances for success than I had been in months. Plus, my friends were here to see this thing through with me—even if it led to our deaths.

"To the end?" I asked in a soft voice.

"To the end," they replied back in unison.

"Then let's finish this."

My friends and I headed toward the rise at the edge of camp. Leonidas was also here, once again sandwiched in the middle of the large contingent of guards who flanked us. To my surprise, the boy had asked Auster if he could attend the royal challenge, although his face was pale, and I could smell his worry.

But perhaps the biggest surprise was that the people—*my people*—were waiting for me.

Nobles, competitors, merchants, servants, guards. Old, young, rich, poor, and everyone in between. They had all flocked to the plaza along the waterfront, and they all started yelling, screaming, and cheering when they saw me standing on the rise above them.

"Evie! Evie! Evie!"

The chant rang out over and over again, and people waved

pennants and flags, many of which featured my crown-of-shards crest. I felt like I was staring out at the living, beating heart of Bellona, and it was one of the most wonderful sights I'd ever seen.

This was what I had always secretly dreamed about when it came to the Regalia. The cheers, the excitement, the support. Now that it had come true, I realized that it was far more meaningful than just a childhood fantasy.

Even if Maximus killed me and my friends today, Bellona would live on through her people. And that thought brought me far more peace and comfort than anything else had over the past year.

"You should wave to your people, highness," Sullivan murmured.

His words roused me out of my reverie, and I lifted my hand, smiling and waving. The people cheered even louder. I kept right on smiling and waving as I wound my way down the steps and across the plaza.

As I headed toward the bridge, something else unexpected happened. The crowd of people closed in so that they surrounded me, my friends, and the guards, like a moving gladiator's shield.

"Don't worry, Evie!"

"We'll protect you!"

"No assassins are getting to you today!"

One after another, voices rose up in the crowd. Tears filled my eyes, but I blinked them away and smiled and waved again, thanking my people for their service. Then together, en masse, we crossed the bridge and headed over to the island.

The mood might have been subdued on Fortuna last night, but that was no longer the case. Thousands upon thousands of people had flocked to the island, and more folks were crammed into the plazas and along the boulevard than ever before. Music, laughter, and conversations filled the air, creating a loud cacophony of sound, but it wasn't an unpleasant sensation. The collective scents of eagerness and excitement filled the air, washing over me like the waves slapping up against the waterfront.

My friends and I climbed the steps and headed up toward the arena on the top of the island. And, as always, comments nipped at my heels as people caught sight of me.

"There she is!"

"That's the Bellonan queen!"

"Do you really think she can kill Maximus?"

"I guess we'll find out . . ."

All too soon, we left the steps behind, crossed the plaza, and reached the main archway that led into the arena. Thousands of people had already filed into the structure to watch the battle royale, and their cheers and conversations rang out like a low, rolling drumbeat that went on and on and on.

Even though I had been in this position before, nervous butterflies still danced in my stomach, but I swatted them away. I had beaten Emilie, another gladiator, in a black-ring match, and I had faced Vasilia and won. I could do the same to Maximus.

Paloma must have sensed my nerves, because she clapped her hand on my back, her great strength making me stagger forward.

"Don't worry, Evie," she said in her matter-of-fact voice. "If Maximus kills you, I will go into the arena and avenge you."

I groaned. She said that every single time I faced someone in battle, and I both loved and hated her for it.

"No." I stabbed my finger at her. "You are *not* going to avenge me. Remember the plan. If the worst happens and Maximus kills me, then Cho will kill him. Not you."

Paloma shrugged. "That depends on who gets to the bastard first."

I opened my mouth to argue, but she gave me a fierce look, as did the ogre on her neck. They wouldn't be dissuaded, so I sighed.

"Fine," I muttered. "You can avenge me to your heart's content. Just don't blame me if you wind up dead."

She grinned. I gave her a sour look, then glanced around. The others were a few steps away, scanning the crowd, so I reached into my pocket and pulled out a small gray envelope sealed with blue wax and my crown-of-shards crest.

"Here. This is for you." I gave the envelope to Paloma. "Just in case I don't make it out of the arena alive. Save it for when you're alone."

Late last night, I had written out everything I suspected about Paloma's mother and Xenia's daughter being one and the same. I just hoped it wouldn't be the final gift I ever gave my friend.

Paloma hefted the envelope. "What does it say? And why don't you just tell me now?"

"Because it's private, and I want to give you some time to think about what it says. Just promise me that you'll open it later, okay?"

She didn't like it, but she tucked the paper into her own pocket. "I promise."

By this point, most of the crowd, including the Bellonans, had streamed into the arena, although a few stragglers were still hurrying across the plaza. With every passing minute, the roars of the crowd already inside grew louder and louder.

It was time for me to leave my friends behind.

They knew it too, and they all gathered around me. Paloma. Captain Auster. Xenia. Cho. Serilda. Sullivan. They stared at me with a mixture of love, confidence, and determination glinting in their eyes, and they smelled of the same emotions too, although the strongest was their rosy love for me, and mine for them.

Seeing, sensing, feeling that love made the butterflies in my stomach finally, fully evaporate. I dipped into the traditional Bellonan curtsy, trying to show them all how deeply I respected them and how very much their friendship had meant to me over this past year.

Then I straightened, left my friends behind, and headed into the arena.

Cho was the only one who came with me. The others were going up to the royal terrace to keep an eye on Mercer, Nox, and Maeven. Maximus might have to finally face me himself, but I wouldn't put it past the king to order his other relatives to try to assassinate Heinrich, Zariza, or another royal during the bout. Today wasn't just about my winning—it was also about keeping our allies safe.

Cho and I stopped in the shadows that filled the archway, and I stared out at the spectacle.

I had always thought the Black Swan arena was massive, but the Pinnaculum easily dwarfed it. Thousands upon thousands of people were packed into the arena, and every available seat was taken. Those who hadn't been able to get a seat had lined up along the wall that circled the arena floor, as well as the one that cordoned off the very top of the structure.

Vendors carrying wooden trays filled with bags of cornucopia, cups of flavored ices, and other sweet and savory treats were hustling up and down the bleacher steps as fast as they could, desperately trying to make a few last sales before the battle royale began. Above the conversations, I could hear the distinctive *clink-clink-clink* of coins changing hands as people bet on the outcome. The sound was strangely comforting and reminded me of my first black-ring match against Emilie. I had given Serilda some gold crowns this morning and told her to make a bet for me. We'd see whether or not it would pay off.

"You're going to do fine, Evie," Cho said. "No, wait. Scratch that. You're going to go out there, and you're going to kick Maximus's ass. For everyone in Bellona and beyond that he's ever hurt. And then you're going to kill the bastard."

I smiled at him, and he winked back at me, as did the dragon on his neck.

"All right, then," Cho murmured, his black eyes gleaming with anticipation. "Let's start the show."

He straightened the sleeves on his red jacket, then squared his shoulders, lifted his chin, and stepped out into the arena.

The crowd erupted into cheers at the sight of him, and Cho raised his hand, smiling, waving, and playing the part of the ringmaster to perfection. I stayed in the shadows, shifting on my feet and trying not to notice how sweaty my palm was against the hilt of my sword.

Cho waved to the crowd again, then held up his hands, asking for silence.

"Welcome, lords and ladies, high and low!" His voice boomed out. "I know you thought yesterday's Tournament of Champions was the highlight of the Regalia, but we have an even better, bloodier treat today! A black-ring match between two royals!"

The crowd roared again, although they quickly quieted down. No one wanted to miss a word.

Cho looked across the arena at the archway opposite mine. "And now, introducing the king of Morta, His Royal Majesty Maximus Mercer Morland Morricone!"

For a moment, nothing happened, and I didn't see anyone lurking in the shadows. Then a figure strode forward.

Maximus was also dressed in fighting leathers—a sleeveless shirt, a knee-length kilt, and sandals—all done in a midnight-purple that was so dark it almost looked black. He was holding a sword that seemed to be made of pure gold, given how the weapon gleamed in the noon sun. He wasn't carrying a shield, and his face hadn't been painted like mine, but his glorious mane of golden hair was perfectly brushed and styled and gleamed almost as brightly as his sword did.

The crowd surged to its feet and roared, and Maximus held his arms out wide, just like Mercer had, further inviting the people to cheer, yell, scream, clap, and whistle. The applause went on and on and on, with Maximus smiling the whole time.

Finally, the Mortan king stepped into the ring in the center of the arena. The wood was painted a dull, flat black, signaling that this fight would be to the death.

The crowd slowly quieted, although tension and excitement filled the air.

"And now," Cho's voice boomed out again, "introducing the queen of Bellona, Her Royal Majesty Everleigh Saffira Winter Blair!"

I drew in a breath and let it out, knowing that this was perhaps the last—and most important—fight of my life. So I squared my shoulders, lifted my chin, and plastered a smile on my face. Then I stepped out of the tunnel and strode forward.

Showtime.

CHAPTER TWENTY-SIX

The second I appeared, the crowd erupted into cheers, yells, claps, screams, and whistles again. The atmosphere for a black-ring match at the Black Swan arena had been loud and raucous, but the noise here was *deafening*, and the overwhelming sound felt like a wave pushing against my body, trying to shove me back into the archway.

Unlike Maximus, I didn't preen, hold my arms out, and play to the crowd. I didn't need their applause. I only needed him bloody, broken, and dead at my feet. That would be satisfaction enough for me.

I crossed the arena floor and stepped into the black ring. The crowd continued to cheer, and Cho held up his hands, calling for quiet, although most people kept right on screaming. While he got the crowd under control, I looked up at the royal terrace.

Eon, Ruri, Cisco, Heinrich, Zariza. All the other kings and queens were gathered there, surrounded by their regular entourages, along with scores of guards. The other royals weren't taking any chances with their own safety. Good.

My friends were up there as well. Sullivan, Paloma, Serilda, Xenia, Auster. They cheered and clapped, letting me know once again how much they believed in me.

Leonidas was also on the terrace, still sandwiched in between some of the Bellonan guards. The boy looked even paler and more worried than before, and he kept glancing around the terrace, as though he was searching for someone.

Slowly, the cheers subsided, and everyone took their seats again, although not before another round of *clink-clink-clink*s rang out, as people placed one final round of wagers. No doubt most folks were betting on Maximus to kill me, but that didn't bother me. More than one person had underestimated me over the past year. Most of them were dead, but I was still here.

Cho held up his arms again, and the *clink-clink-clink*s of coins faded away. A tense, heavy silence fell over the arena, and the only sound was the royal flags snapping back and forth in the breeze at the very top of the structure.

"Lords and ladies, high and low," Cho repeated in a much more serious voice. "We are here to witness a royal challenge between the king of Morta and the queen of Bellona. This is a black-ring match—to the death. Are you both agreed?"

He looked at Maximus, who nodded, then at me. I nodded and tightened my grip on my sword.

Cho glanced back and forth between the two of us, his hands still raised high. This might be a fight to the death, but Cho was still a showman, and he was going to draw the moment out for as long as possible.

"Begin!" he yelled, dropping his hands and scrambling back.

Maximus didn't hesitate. With a loud roar, the Mortan king lifted his sword and charged forward.

I let out an equally loud scream, raised my own weapon, and rushed forward to meet my enemy.

Our swords clashed together in the middle of the arena, the concussive *boom* seeming even louder than the crowd's screams.

And I almost lost the match—and my life—right from the start.

Maximus was much, much stronger than I had expected, and he almost knocked my sword out of my hand with that first blow. His enormous strength made me drop to one knee. I gritted my teeth, my muscles burning and my arm already shaking from the effort of keeping him from cutting through my defenses and killing me.

Maximus leaned forward, his shadow falling over me. "What's the matter, Everleigh? Am I too powerful for you?"

I gritted my teeth again, still pushing back against his weapon. I didn't have the strength to answer him—not if I wanted to keep my head attached to my shoulders.

"You stupid bitch," he hissed. "Did you really think that releasing my strixes and my caladrius would cut off my supply of magic?"

For the first time, I noticed the hot, caustic stench of magic wafting off him—more magic than I had ever sensed from him before, even after he had drunk the strix blood during the kronekling tournament. Maximus was practically *dripping* with power, and the aroma was so strong that it scalded my nose, like I was breathing in fire instead of air.

"What . . . did you . . . do?" I rasped.

"I drank more strix blood." A cruel smile split his face. "But not just one little bird and one little cup. No, I drank the blood of the strixes that my guards and I flew here on."

Surprise spiked through me. I hadn't considered that he

might kill the larger strixes too, especially since they didn't have nearly as much magic as the smaller ones that I'd freed. I had assumed he would keep the older creatures alive in case he needed them to launch an attack, but I should have known better. Nothing mattered to Maximus more than amassing power.

"How . . . many of them . . . did you . . . kill?"

His smile widened, and a bright, fanatical light gleamed in his eyes. "All of them."

All of them?

Horror filled me, along with more than a little fear. The Mortans had had dozens of strixes. Maximus had slaughtered them all? Every last one? So that's why he was suddenly so strong. The older strixes might not have had very much individual magic, but their combined power would have been more than enough to augment his own, especially if he had added his tearstone powder to the mix.

Maximus smiled again and drew back his sword for another, harder blow. I wouldn't be able to absorb and stop this one, so I ducked down, threw myself forward, and rolled past him. Maximus's sword slammed into the dirt where my body had been, hard enough to open up a wide, jagged crack in the ground.

I got to my feet, whirled around, and snapped my sword up again. Maximus also whirled around. He let out a low, angry growl, lifted his sword, and charged forward. I stepped up to meet him.

And then we fought.

Back and forth we battled in the black ring. Well, it was more like Maximus battled. He was so strong that I didn't dare risk crossing my sword with his, lest he knock my weapon away. Instead, I lifted my shield and let it absorb his hard, brutal blows, although every single one of them still rattled my body and threatened to rip the disk off my forearm.

Maximus launched into a series of frenzied attacks, beating

his sword against my shield over and over again. Not because he thought he could cut through the tearstone shield, but just because he wanted everyone to see how strong he was.

I couldn't defeat him.

At least not like this. Serilda had spent much of the last year training me how to be a gladiator, but Maximus was by far the physically strongest opponent I had ever faced. I wasn't going to best him in raw strength, and he was hitting me so fast and furiously that I couldn't even swipe out at him with my own sword.

But I had to do *something*, or he was going to pound my shield into the ground and me right along with it. He might not be able to break through the shield, but he could certainly crush me to death with it. My mind raced, even as I huddled under the protective dome. I couldn't beat him with my fighting skills. Not when he had so much magic.

But I could fix that.

My nose twitched, and I drew in a breath and tasted the air. Maximus still reeked of magic, but the aroma wasn't quite as hot and caustic as before. He might have more power than me, but he was being reckless and burning through it quickly. I didn't know if my immunity was strong enough to counter all that stolen magic running through his veins, but I couldn't take much more of this beating.

So the next time he lifted his sword, I surged forward and shoved my shield straight into his chest. The move surprised Maximus, and he actually staggered back and lowered his blade.

Before he could recover, I whirled around the other way and lashed out with my own weapon. He jerked back, but he wasn't quite quick enough, and my sword sliced across his cheek, drawing a thin line of blood.

The crowd roared in response. They had grown tired of him hammering his sword against my shield. Yeah, me too.

Maximus clapped his hand to his cheek. Then he held his

palm out and stared down at it, as though surprised to see his own crimson blood glistening on his fingertips.

"You're going to pay for that!" he hissed.

I could barely hear him over the crowd's yells and screams, so I grinned and crooked my finger, daring the bastard to come at me again.

Maximus let out a loud roar and charged forward, but I spun away from him as coolly as I had before, doing a pretty twirl, as though I were on a dance floor. And I suddenly realized that I *was* on a dance floor. Somehow, despite all of Serilda's and Xenia's training, I had forgotten that. Whether it was in the arena or the throne room, dancing around my enemies was the thing that *I* did best, and it was going to help me win this battle, just like I'd won all the others so far.

I had been thinking about the fight all wrong. This was a long game, just like any other, and I didn't have to immediately kill Maximus with one blow. I just had to wear him down and make him bleed, one small slice at a time. The more he bled, the more magic he would lose. That would level the playing field. After that, all I had to do was wait for him to get angry and impatient enough to make a mistake. And *then* I could finally kill the bastard.

That phantom music started playing in my mind, even louder than the crowd's cheers, and I tuned out everything else. The people on the bleachers, my friends watching from the terrace, even Maximus spewing curses at me. Instead, I listened to that quick, steady beat, and I let it carry me away.

The king charged at me, and I spun to the side again. This time, I aimed lower and opened up a shallow slice above his right elbow. He howled and charged at me again, and I turned the other way, going lower still, and nicking the top of his left thigh.

Maximus growled and came at me yet again. This time, I threw my shield at him. He stopped, twisting to the side, although the shield bounced harmlessly off his chest and fluttered to the ground. But I was right behind it, slashing out with my sword and opening up a much deeper gash on his right thigh.

And then *I* went on the attack.

Spinning, turning, whirling, twirling. I danced quicker, better, and faster than I had ever danced in my entire life, even when I had performed the Tanzen Freund and the Tanzen Falter. And every time I moved, every time I whirled or twirled in close to Maximus, I cut the bastard, until thin lines of blood covered his skin like stripes of red paint.

Eventually, Maximus realized what I was doing, and he backed away and moved over to the edge of the black ring. "Do you really think all those little cuts are going to be enough to kill me?" he growled.

No, I didn't. I hadn't even come close to seriously wounding him. But I had made him bleed, which was far more important right now.

"I'm not trying to kill you," I snarled back. "Can't you feel what I'm doing? Can't you feel all that stolen magic leaking out of your body with every drop of blood? With every beat of your heart? Because I certainly can, you arrogant bastard."

Maximus frowned and stared down at the blood dripping off his fingertips. *Plop-plop-plop.* For a moment, I could have sworn I could hear all those precious drops hitting the dirt beneath our feet, each one taking a little bit more of his stolen magic along with it.

Now it was time to make him *really* bleed.

I lifted my sword and moved in for another strike, but Maximus was quicker, and he snapped up his hand. Only this time, he didn't attack me with his sword.

No, this time, he unleashed his lightning.

I should have been expecting the sneak attack, especially since Mercer had done the same thing to Paloma during the tournament. But the move took me by surprise, and the cold lightning slammed straight into my chest and knocked me away from him. In an instant I was flat on my back on the arena floor. My sword flew out of my hand, and I didn't see where it had landed.

All I could see was the lightning.

The bright, eerie purple lightning danced over my body much the same way that I had danced around Maximus. I screamed and pushed back with my own immunity, using my power to snuff out all that cold, crackling magic.

Slowly, much too slowly, the lightning dissolved in a shower of purple sparks. Just as slowly, I rolled over onto my knees and staggered back up and onto my feet. My skin was blue and numb, my hair was caked with frost, and my fighting leathers were stiff and frozen, but I faced Maximus again.

He grinned and unleashed another round of magic, this time shooting purple hailstones out of his fingertips. I snapped up my hands and held them out in front of me, using my immunity just like I had used my gladiator shield before. The hailstones slammed into the invisible barrier of my immunity and broke apart into brittle chunks. Maximus growled and went back to his cold lightning, but I stopped that as well.

The two of us stood there in the center of the ring, with him shooting hailstones and bolts of cold lightning at me over and over again, and me blocking them all with my immunity.

Finally, Maximus grew tired of throwing his power at me. He lowered his hand, and his lips curled back as though the mere sight of me made him sick to his stomach.

"The legends really are true," he said. "You're immune to magic. Just like Bryn Blair was. Just like so many Winter queens are."

I staggered back, trying to catch my breath. Legends? What legends? Mortan legends?

Maximus started circling me. "I thought they were just bed-time stories, tales to scare me away from my ambitions. Who would ever want to destroy magic? Much less actually be able to do it? But my grandfather always said that the Blairs and their accursed ability needed to be eliminated above all else. He was absolutely right. What a freak of nature you are, Everleigh." His voice dripped with disgust, and his lips curled back even more.

Me? A freak? He was the one who ingested crushed tearstone and amethyst-eye poison. *He* was the one who killed strixes, the symbol of his own kingdom. *He* was the one who drank blood like some undead monster. Maximus needed to look in a fuck-ing mirror.

"I'm so glad you're the last of your kind, Everleigh." He ac-tually shuddered a bit, as if I was some horror he just couldn't bear to contemplate. "Once I kill you, the Blairs and the Winter queen line will be forever dead. Then I can finally conquer your cursed kingdom, and Bellona and all its resources will be *mine*."

The thought of him invading my kingdom and killing my people filled me with disgust, along with almost paralyzing fear and horror, but I pushed my emotions aside. The only thing that mattered was ending him here and now.

I had put the first part of my plan into motion. I had made Maximus bleed and shed some of his stolen magic. I was just hoping that I had wounded him enough, and that I could use my immunity to destroy the rest of his power.

I expected Maximus to keep crowing about what a freak I was, but instead he charged at me. Before I could spin away, Maximus surged forward, locked his hand around my throat, and hoisted me up into the air.

Gasps rang out through the arena, but I didn't bother to kick or flail or fight back. Instead, I reached for my immunity. Nothing else mattered right now. Because if I didn't do this, then I was dead.

"I should have realized why Maeven was having such a hard time killing you," Maximus said. "Why you managed to slip out of every single trap she set. It's your immunity. It lets you sense magic, all kinds of magic, doesn't it?"

I ignored his question. Instead, I kept focusing on my immunity, pulling it up, up, up out of my body and then pouring the invisible strength of it out onto my hands, until it felt like gauntlets covering my fingers. I'd only get one shot at this, and I had to make it count.

Maximus must have realized that I wasn't paying attention to his words, because he gave me a vicious little shake. "Stay awake, Everleigh. I want you alive for as long as possible to witness my greatest triumph."

I still didn't respond, and a sly light flared in his eyes. Maximus hoisted me a little higher into the air, then lunged forward, dropped to one knee, and slammed me down onto the dirt.

He put a considerable amount of strength into the blow, and pain shot through my back, along with the rest of my body, but I forced it aside, just as I had done with my fear and horror.

"Did that get your attention? Are you finally ready to beg for your life, Everleigh?"

He loosened his grip on my throat, just a bit, and I sucked down a breath, readying myself. "Well?" he demanded. "Start begging. I might let you go on for a minute or two before I finally kill you."

"Never," I hissed. "But it's going to be so fucking sweet to hear you beg for yours."

He frowned, not understanding what I meant, but I didn't care. Instead, I shoved my hand forward, forcing my fingers through one of the openings I'd sliced in the front of his fancy leather tunic.

"What are you—"

Maximus never got to finish his thought. My fingers touched his bare skin, and I dug my nails into one of the shallow slices I'd opened up on his chest. His blood crackled against my fingertips, just like his lightning had earlier. Only this time, instead of blocking his magic, I went on the offensive and sent my immunity shooting out at him.

The cold, hard power of my immunity punched into his chest, tearing his hand from my throat and sending him staggering back. He also lost his grip on his sword, and the weapon flew out of his hand and landed on the ground.

I scrambled to my feet and surged forward, closing the distance between us. This time, I hit him in the stomach with my actual fist, but I also drove the force of my immunity into his body at the same time.

My fist didn't do all that much damage, but I felt something . . . *crack* deep inside him, like my immunity was a piece of gravel that had just flown up and chipped a windowpane.

So I hit him again.

And then again.

And then again.

Once again, I danced, spinning, turning, whirling, twirling. I landed punch after punch to Maximus's chest, and with each blow, I battered him with my immunity as well. Every time I hit him, I felt a little bit more of his stolen power crack away, and the sensation made me even more determined to finish him.

"You think I'm a freak of nature?" I yelled. "You want to kill the last of the Blairs? The final Winter queen? Well, let me show you just how strong I am!"

At first Maximus didn't seem to realize what I was doing, but he must have started feeling weaker, because he screamed and started punching me back. He hit me in the face, chest, and arms over and over again, putting his own stolen magic and strength into each and every one of the blows. But I'd been a Black Swan gladiator and I had taken more than one hard shot in the training ring, so I shrugged off the blows and concentrated on landing my own in return. Taking away his magic was more important than him giving me a black eye or bruised ribs.

Maximus drew back his fist for another blow, but I darted forward and kicked his leg out from under him. Maximus shrieked and crumpled to the ground. Then, before he could recover, I threw myself down on top of him and started pummeling him with my fists and my immunity.

And this time, I didn't stop.

Punch.

Punch-punch.

Punch.

I hit him over and over again, driving the brutal force of my immunity into his body with every blow. My knuckles busted open and started bleeding, but the small stings of pain made me even more determined to finish this. So I drew back both my fists and reached for even more of my immunity.

"No!" Maximus screamed. "Don't!"

He lifted one of his hands, and more purple lightning sparked on his fingertips, but I ignored the magic and focused on my own immunity. This was my chance to finally destroy his power once and for all.

We both struck at the same time.

Maximus blasted me in the face with his cold lightning, and I slammed my fists and my power down onto his heart as hard as I could.

CHAPTER TWENTY-SEVEN

For a moment, the entire arena turned that bright, eerie electric purple that I had come to despise so much. Then the lightning streaking toward me shattered like frozen glass, and another loud, concussive *boom* rang out. The force threw me away from Maximus and seemed to shake the arena from top to bottom, making the crowd scream in fear and surprise.

I landed hard on my ass on the opposite side of the ring, but I forced myself to stagger back up to my feet. Across from me, Maximus did the same. He snarled and lifted his hand to blast me with his cold lightning again.

But nothing happened.

No sparks flashed on his fingertips, no power flickered in his eyes, no gusts of magic swirled in the air around him. I drew in a breath, but he didn't even smell of magic anymore—just blood, sweat, and dust.

That's when I knew that I had finally *won*.

Maximus raised his hand and tried again, and again, but with the same nothing results as before. He glanced down at his fingers, then raised his harsh, accusing gaze to me.

"What have you done?" he said, his voice rising to a scream. "What have you done to me?"

"I took away your magic," I hissed back. "You killed all those strixes and drank their blood. Well, I *crushed* all that power. I crushed all the magic inside you. Just like that."

I snapped my fingers, and he flinched at the sound.

Maximus stared at me, horror filling his eyes, along with something that I had wanted to see for a long, long time.

Complete, utter, absolute *fear*.

Without that stolen magic running through his veins, Maximus was nothing but a bully with a crown, and he knew it as well as I did.

But he wasn't ready to admit defeat, and his hands slowly clenched into fists, even as fury shimmered in his eyes. "This isn't over," he snarled. "You haven't won anything, Everleigh. Not one fucking *thing*."

"Then let's finish it."

I leaned down and picked up my sword. Then I gestured at Maximus's weapon, which was lying a few feet away. But the idea that we settle this like real gladiators, with only our swords and our fighting skills, instead of tricks and stolen magic, further infuriated him, and he made no move to pick up his own weapon.

I tightened my grip on my sword. He didn't want to fight back with his sword? Fine by me. I would cut the bastard down where he stood with a smile on my face and a song in my heart.

More and more rage sparked in Maximus's eyes, and he finally gave in to it.

"This isn't over!" he screamed. "I'll get more magic! More power! No matter who I have to slaughter—"

"No, you won't." A low, silky voice cut him off.

We both whirled around.

Maeven was here.

She stepped out of the same archway I had come through and strode across the arena floor, heading toward us.

Cho was hovering just outside the black ring, and he waved his hand, catching my eye. He turned his arm to the side, giving me a look at the dagger clutched in his fingertips, but I shook my head the tiniest bit, telling him not to interfere. I wanted to see if this would play out the way I hoped it would.

Instead of fighting leathers, Maeven was dressed in a lovely lilac gown, and her blond hair was pulled back into its usual sleek bun. Amethysts glittered around her throat and on her wrists and fingers. Even across the arena, I could smell the power in the jewels, but it was nothing compared to the power that Maeven herself had—power that was all *hers,* and not what she had stolen from others.

Maeven picked up her skirt and stepped into the black ring. She glanced at me a moment, then moved over to stand in front of her brother. I kept my sword up, ready for her to whirl around, blast me with her lightning, and try to kill me the way she had so many times before.

But she didn't.

Instead, Maeven crossed her arms over her chest and studied her brother, her cold gaze flicking up and down his body and taking in his disheveled blond hair, his tattered fighting leathers, and the bloody cuts that crisscrossed his skin. Her lips puckered, but I couldn't tell if her sour expression was due to her brother's appearance or the fact that he hadn't killed me yet.

"Look at you," Maeven said, her voice dripping with disgust. "The mighty king of Morta crying like a petulant child at the loss of his precious magic."

Maximus's eyes narrowed. "How dare you speak to me like that. I'll—"

"You'll do *what*?" Maeven sneered, cutting him off again.

"Have me put in chains? Beaten? Tortured? You've already done all that and far worse."

"What does it matter?" he said. "Turn around and blast that Blair bitch with your magic. Kill her where she stands. That's your *duty*. So fucking do it."

Maeven tilted her head to the side, making the amethysts around her neck sparkle and flash in the sunlight. "I've been thinking a lot about *duty* lately, especially when it comes to my many years of service in the Bastard Brigade. Service that you've never rewarded me for."

"Why would I reward you for anything?" Maximus hissed. "You're just a bastard, just a tool for me to use however I like, just as all the other kings have done before me."

Maeven's lips curved up into a grim smile. "I know that I'm a bastard," she replied. "You never let me forget it. Not for one bloody *second*. Even though I was smarter than you as a child, and stronger, and had more natural magic, you always thought you were so much *better* than me. And now look at you. Without your precious tearstone drug and stolen magic, you're nothing but a whiny little brat." She shook her head. "You are so *weak*."

Maximus's hands clenched into fists, and he moved forward, that arrogant sneer still on his face as he peered down his nose at her. "Weak? I'm not weak. You're the one who's *weak*. Always trying to help the other members of your precious Bastard Brigade. Always coddling that younger son of yours. Always trying to protect and shield him from me. Well, this is the last time you insult me or disobey one of my orders, sister dear. I'm going to have that boy flayed alive right in front of you. Maybe then you'll finally remember your place."

Instead of being frightened by his threats, Maeven laughed in his face. Maximus blinked and reared back, as if he were utterly shocked that she would do such a thing, especially here, now, in front of thousands of people.

Finally, her chuckles faded away. "Face it, brother dear. You're not going to be doing very much of anything without your magic. Especially not torturing me and my son."

Maximus kept glaring down his nose at her. "I'll get more magic. You know I will. I always do."

Maeven shook her head, as if deeply disappointed that he hadn't listened to a single word she'd said, much less understood what they really meant. I did, though, and I knew exactly why she was here.

"I told you before," she said. "*No, you won't.*"

Maximus sucked in a breath, probably to insult her again, but he never got the chance.

Maeven plucked a dagger out of her long sleeve and buried it in her brother's heart.

Maximus screamed and tried to jerk away, but Maeven grabbed his shoulder and held him in place, slowly, brutally, methodically twisting the dagger in deeper and deeper. Maximus's eyes bulged in pain, and his panicked screams quickly died down to raspy, choking gurgles.

"Goodbye, brother," she said in a calm, cold voice. "My only regret is that I couldn't make your death last for days, weeks, months, years even. But we don't always get what we want, do we?"

Maeven stared her brother in the eyes a moment longer, then ripped the dagger out of his chest and sliced it across his throat. Blood sprayed all over the front of her dress, but Maeven didn't seem to mind, given her wide, satisfied smile.

Maximus let out a final, strangled gurgle. Then his eyes rolled up in the back of his head, and he crumpled to the arena floor.

The king of Morta was dead.

❦

A tense, heavy silence dropped over the arena. No one could believe what had just happened. That I had defeated Maximus, and that Maeven, his own sister, had so coldly executed him.

Maeven faced me, and I tightened my grip on my sword, expecting her to attack me next.

"You were wrong, Everleigh," she said, a satisfied sneer twisting her face. "I didn't have to run away from my brother, and I don't have to give up trying to kill you—"

"You bitch!" a voice roared out. "You traitorous bitch!"

Maeven and I both looked up. The screams were coming from the royal terrace. Mercer was on his feet, his face red with mottled rage, and purple lightning crackling around his clenched fists.

He stabbed a finger at Maeven. "You won't get away with this! I'll come down there and kill you myself, you murderous, treacherous bitch—"

Nox slipped up behind Mercer, dug his hand into his cousin's hair, yanked his head back, and cut his throat.

Mercer clapped his hands over his neck, as if he could somehow keep all that precious blood inside him where it belonged. Nox stepped to the side so that he could see his cousin's shocked face. He looked at Mercer a moment, then coolly lashed out with his boot and kicked his cousin off the terrace. The Mortan crown prince toppled over the wrought-iron railing, dropped down, and landed with a loud, sickening *crack* on the bleacher steps fifty feet below. People screamed and scrambled away from his broken, twisted body.

That tense, heavy silence dropped over the arena again. Nox looked at Maeven. He tipped his head to her, and she did the same to him. Then Nox held his bloody dagger high in the air before dropping to one knee.

"Long live the queen!" he yelled. "Long live Queen Maeven!"

For a few seconds, there was more tense, heavy silence.

Then several of the Mortan nobles and merchants on the terrace also dropped to their knees. It was easy to see which way the wind was blowing and what needed to be done in order to survive, and all the other Mortans, including the guards, quickly lowered themselves to the ground and took up Nox's chant.

"Maeven! Maeven! Maeven!"

Maeven lifted her chin, smiling at the sudden adoration, but not everyone was joining in with the cheers. Leonidas was staring at his mother with wide eyes, as if she were some strange, horrifying creature he had never seen before. Several of the Mortan nobles on the terrace looked stunned, while others were giving Maeven speculative looks, the wheels already turning in their minds as they thought about what her reign would mean for them.

Finally, the cheers died down. Maeven turned and gave me a traditional Bellonan curtsy. I couldn't tell if she was mocking me or not.

After a few seconds, Maeven climbed back to her feet. Then she moved forward and stopped right in front of me. "Like I said before, Maximus wasn't the only one who was wrong," she purred. "So were you, Everleigh."

"And what was I so wrong about?"

"I didn't have to leave Morta to escape my brother," she replied. "I just had to kill him and take the crown that should have been mine all along."

I didn't respond to her taunt, although I kept a tight grip on my sword, just in case she tried to kill me again. But Maeven had other ideas, at least for today, and she looked me up and down the same way she had Maximus earlier.

"Go get cleaned up, Everleigh," she purred. "You look a fright. After all, there is still a royal ball to attend tonight."

She sneered at me again, then picked up her skirt, stepped over her brother's body, and left the arena floor.

The second that Maeven vanished, everyone started talking and yelling, chattering on and on about this strange, shocking, brutal turn of events. I stayed where I was on the arena floor, watching, but Maeven didn't double back. Then again, why would she? She had just become the queen of Morta. She had far more important things to think about right now than killing me.

"Evie! Evie!"

I glanced over my shoulder. Paloma and Sullivan had made their way down the bleacher steps and were running across the arena floor, their weapons clutched in their hands.

"Highness!" Sullivan said, stopping in front of me. "Are you all right?"

"I'm fine. Just a little tired, bruised, and bloody."

Sullivan wrapped his arm around my waist and pulled me close. I leaned my head against his shoulder, soaking up his quiet strength and drawing his clean vanilla scent into my lungs.

Paloma looked down at Maximus's body, then over at the archway that Maeven had walked through. Finally, she turned to me.

Paloma frowned. "Why are you smiling? Maximus might be dead, but now Maeven is queen."

My smile widened. "I know."

Paloma frowned again. Sullivan frowned at me as well, as did Cho, but I didn't feel like explaining myself right now, so I grabbed my shield and jerked my head toward the same archway Maeven had used.

"Come on," I said. "Let's get out of here."

With my friends by my side, I stepped over Maximus's body and left the arena. The king was dead.

Long live the queens.

CHAPTER TWENTY-EIGHT

Many of the spectators were still gathered on the plaza outside the arena, and they started yelling, cheering, and clapping when I emerged out of the archway. I hadn't killed Maximus, but I had still given them a bloody good show, and they wanted to show their appreciation. I forced myself to smile, lift my hand, and wave to the people.

Captain Auster, Xenia, and Serilda were waiting for us there, along with Leonidas and the Bellonan guards, and we slowly threaded our way through the crowds. So many people were on the steps and packed into the plazas along the water-front that it took us twice as long as normal to get back to the bridge, especially since everyone started yelling and cheering when they caught sight of me. By the time we finally made it back to the Bellonan camp, my cheeks were burning and my arms were aching from smiling and waving for so long.

I gave a final round of smiles and waves to everyone in the Bellonan camp, then escaped into my tent. Calandre and her sisters helped me out of my bloody fighting leathers and into a hot bath, while Aisha healed my frozen skin and other injuries.

Once I got cleaned up, I crawled into bed, although I told Calandre to wake me in time to get ready for the ball.

I fell asleep almost immediately, and for once my rest was calm and devoid of any nightmarish dreams or memories. Perhaps that was because I knew I had finally beaten Maximus.

And Maeven too.

It seemed as though I had barely closed my eyes before Calandre and her sisters were back in my tent. Calandre dressed me in a gorgeous midnight-blue gown patterned with my crown-of-shards crest done in silver thread, while her sisters worked their usual magic on my hair and face. I thanked them for their services, then left my tent.

Sullivan, Paloma, Serilda, Cho, Auster, Xenia. My friends were waiting outside, and they updated me on everything that had happened while I'd been asleep.

Apparently, Maeven's plot was much larger and far more complex than I'd realized. Not only had she killed Maximus and Nox killed Mercer, but they'd also enlisted the guards who were loyal to them to swiftly slaughter all the ones who weren't. In the space of a few hours, Maeven had taken control of the Mortan camp, and everyone was bowing down to her as the new queen of Morta.

"Why are you smiling again?" Paloma asked after Auster had finished updating me. "Maeven is still alive, and now she's the fucking *queen*. That makes her even more dangerous."

"I know." Once again, my smile widened. "Since Maeven is queen now, I should bring her a present. After all, it's a Bellonan tradition to celebrate a new queen's reign with a gift." I looked at Auster. "Get Leonidas."

Auster returned with the boy a few minutes later. Leonidas was dressed in a dark gray tunic, along with black leggings and boots. He seemed to have recovered from his earlier shock in the arena, although his face was still tight and pale with worry.

"Auster told me that you asked to see the memory stone of the royal challenge," I said.

I had wanted a record of the day's events, so I had ordered the captain to discreetly place a memory stone on the royal terrace. I hadn't had a chance to view the images yet, but Auster had assured me that the memory stone had clearly captured everything that had happened, from my fight with Maximus to Maeven killing her brother to Nox assassinating Mercer.

Leonidas nodded. "Yes, I wanted to see . . . everything again. Thank you for letting me watch the stone."

He didn't say anything about what his mother had done to his uncle, but I could smell his relief. He was glad that Maximus was dead. Me too.

My friends and I crossed the bridge and made our way to the DiLucri castle. The mood in the grand ballroom was far more jovial than it had been last night, although an undercurrent of tension rippled through everyone's gossip, laughter, and chatter. The tides of fortune had shifted far more drastically than anyone had expected at this Regalia, and everyone was still scrambling to figure out what it meant for Morta, as well as for their own kingdoms.

Eon and Ruri greeted me warmly, but Cisco ignored me in favor of talking to Driscol and Seraphine. Driscol's shoulders were slumped, and he looked absolutely crestfallen. Whatever deal he'd made with Maximus had died the moment the king had. But Seraphine was smiling and nodding at Cisco as though nothing noteworthy had happened at all. Then again, Fortuna favored her ladies, and I had a sneaking suspicion that Seraphine was the one who truly ran things here.

I smiled at the other royals, then went over to Heinrich and Dominic, who both hugged me tight.

"Thank you for avenging my son," Heinrich murmured in

my ear. "And Lord Hans and everyone else who was lost at Seven Spire."

Tears filled my eyes, but I blinked them away and hugged him tighter.

Zariza came over to congratulate me as well. "I knew that aligning with you was the right thing to do." She toasted me with her brandy snifter.

Xenia lifted her cane and poked her cousin in the arm with it. "*You* knew it? *I* was the one who told you to align with Everleigh, even though it took you a while to listen to me."

Zariza sniffed and tossed her long red hair over her shoulder. "And once again, *I* did very well listening to *you*, even if it did take me a while."

I laughed at their bickering.

The ball continued, and everyone seemed happier and far more relaxed than they had been last night—until the Mortans arrived.

Everyone eyed the Mortan nobles, advisors, courtiers, servants, and guards as they streamed into the ballroom, but Driscol and Seraphine stepped forward and greeted them like usual, and the tension slowly eased.

A minute later, Nox escorted Maeven into the ballroom, and everyone turned to stare at her, including me.

The new Mortan queen looked truly stunning in a midnight-purple gown trimmed with cascades of silver thread, including the large, fancy cursive *M* of the Morricone royal crest that stretched across her chest. An amethyst-and-diamond crown was nestled in her long, loose golden hair, and more amethyst-and-diamond jewelry covered her neck, wrists, and fingers. Being queen seemed to agree with her.

Just like I'd hoped it would.

Maeven swanned around the ballroom for the better part of an hour, greeting the other royals, chatting with the nobles, and doing other necessary, queenly things, with Nox trailing along behind her. I wasn't the only one studying her. So was Leonidas, who was standing in the corner next to one of the coined-woman fountains, watching his mother move from one Mortan noble to the next, slowly but surely shoring up her power.

I walked over to the boy, and the two of us stood there, watching while Maeven chatted up yet another noble.

"Well, at least you won't have to worry about Maximus and Mercer anymore," I said. "Your mother made sure of that. If nothing else, I admire her for protecting you."

"Yes, she did. I still can't believe that she killed Uncle Maximus. And that Nox killed Mercer." Leonidas didn't seem as happy about the developments as his mother did, and I could smell his worry, fear, and dread.

"You don't have to go back to your mother or to Morta if you don't want to," I said. "You and Lyra could return with me to Seven Spire. I would find a place for you there and make sure that no one bothered you or your strix. The two of you would be free to come and go as you pleased. Perhaps you could even learn a trade. I'm in need of an apprentice for the new royal jeweler I wish to hire."

Leonidas jerked back, clearly stunned by the offer. "You would do that? You would help *me*, protect me? Even after everything that my family has done to yours?"

I shrugged. "Well, I would certainly enjoy rubbing your mother's face in the fact that you chose me over her. But you saved my life, and Lyra helped me free the strixes that Maximus wanted to use against me. Kindness is often in short supply in royal courts, and things like that matter a great deal to me."

Leonidas stared at me, and I could see the struggle in his eyes. It was no small thing to give up the life and the family you'd been born into, even if someone was offering you a chance to take an easier, safer path. To escape your birthright and all the horrors that came along with it. In the end, he shook his head, although I could smell his minty regret and dusty resignation.

"I can't abandon her," Leonidas said. "She might not realize it yet, but she's going to need me now more than ever. Mother protected me from Uncle Maximus, Mercer, and all the others as best she could. Now it's my turn to protect her."

Brave, stupid boy. My heart ached for Leonidas and everything he had suffered, and everything he would suffer in the future, but I admired his devotion to his mother, and I had to respect his decision. "Very well. If that's what you want."

He tried to smile, although the expression quickly melted into a grimace. "We very rarely get what we want. Mother said that when she killed Uncle Maximus in the arena. But I suppose you know that better than anyone, don't you?"

"I certainly do."

Maeven finally swanned over to the corner where I was standing with Leonidas. She held out her hand to her son, and he stepped forward and took it.

She squeezed his fingers, then tilted her head to the side. "Go say hello to Nox. Then later we'll see about getting you and Lyra back to our camp where you both belong."

He smiled at her, although the expression slipped off his face the moment Maeven glanced away. Leonidas shot me one more regretful look, then squared his shoulders and shuffled over to where Nox was standing with some of the Mortan nobles. They warmly greeted the boy, as though he had been one of them all along, and not just something they were suddenly interested in now that his mother was queen.

Even more sympathy filled me. I knew exactly what that was like, and I wondered what sort of life I'd doomed him to. But I'd given him a choice, and he had made it. Still, Leonidas was far stronger than he knew, and I thought that he would be all right. At least, I hoped he would.

Maeven pivoted back to me, a wide, triumphant smile on her face. Paloma and Sullivan were standing a few feet away. They both tensed, and Paloma dropped her hand to her mace and raised her eyebrows, silently asking if I wanted her to try to kill Maeven. I shook my head.

I had already beaten Maeven—the smug bitch just didn't realize it yet.

I studied Maeven the same way she was studying me. "Being queen agrees with you. Even I have to admit how stunning you look tonight."

She preened a little at my words. "Well, if the crown fits, I might as well wear it."

I couldn't help myself. I laughed.

Maeven frowned. "Why are you laughing? And why are you smiling at me like that?"

"Because I won—I finally, fucking *won*."

She stared at me like I was crazy. "You didn't win anything. You didn't kill Maximus. *I* did."

Her words made me laugh again, and it took me several seconds to get my merry chuckles under control.

"Well, one could argue that we killed him *together*. Clever of you to stand back and let me do the hard work of destroying his magic before you moved in to strike the fatal blow." I shrugged. "But let's not debate the semantics, not now, when I'm so happy."

She blinked. "What? Why are you happy?"

I shook my head. "You really don't see it, do you?"

She frowned again. "What do you mean?"

"You did *exactly* what I wanted you to. You're right. *You* killed Maximus in the arena, not me. Everyone saw *you* do it. And then, even better, Nox cut Mercer's throat. Everyone saw *him* do that too."

Maeven kept staring at me, still confused. So, for once, I decided to show her some mercy and explain what I'd done.

"I actually have to thank Felton," I said. "He's the one who first gave me the idea when I visited him in the Seven Spire dungeon a few months ago. He's still rotting down there, in case you were curious."

But Maeven didn't care about Felton, Queen Cordelia's traitorous secretary, only what he'd inspired me to do. "Idea for what?" she asked in a sharp voice.

I shrugged. "To make you queen of Morta."

Her eyebrows drew together in confusion. She still didn't understand what was going on and the cruel, cruel thing that I'd done to her.

"Felton told me how badly Maximus used you and your bastard relatives to carry out his dirty work. I knew how strong you are in your lightning magic, and I couldn't imagine why you would ever let anyone treat you like that. And I saw a way to potentially get rid of Maximus for good."

Maeven kept staring at me, although understanding was slowly beginning to creep into her eyes.

"So I decided to play a game with you," I said. "I didn't know if anything would ever come of it, but I decided to try. When I spoke to you through the Cardea mirror after all your schemes fell apart at Glitnir, I told you that you had two choices—die or leave Morta. What I didn't tell you was that you had a third choice—that you *always* had a third choice."

Her face paled, even as more understanding filled her eyes.

"Every time we've talked in the mirror since then, I've been playing my long game with you. Preying on your fears and your pride and especially your rage at Maximus for all the cruel things he did to you and your Bastard Brigade. And then you brought Leonidas to the Regalia. Maximus was even crueler to your son, which was something else I used to my advantage. And my plan worked, and you actually did the one thing I wanted you to do all along."

"Kill Maximus," she whispered. "You wanted *me* to be the one to kill him. But . . . why?"

"So you would be queen."

"But why would *you* ever want *me* to be *queen*?" Maeven threw her hands up. "Now I have more power, more money, more resources. Now I can fully devote myself to destroying you and Bellona."

I shook my head. She still didn't understand what I'd done to her. Not yet—but she would.

"Sullivan once told me that I didn't really know what it meant to be queen, and he was right. I didn't know just how demanding the nobles would be until I was actually queen. My nobles might not have expected me to be queen, but they've started to accept me. I doubt that your nobles will do the same."

I gestured at the people still gathered around Nox and Leonidas. "You might have killed the king and the crown prince, but there are still some legitimate royals left, including Nox, your partner in crime. How long do you think it's going to be before he or one of the legitimate royals challenges you for the throne? Or one of the wealthier nobles? You might have killed Maximus and Mercer, but in everyone's eyes, you're still just a bastard pretender. That's the Morricone tradition, the Mortan culture, and that pretty little crown on your head doesn't change any of that."

The last dregs of her smile slipped off her face, and she stared at the nobles as if she had never considered that they wouldn't be on her side—and that they might already be plotting against her.

Maeven shook her head. "It won't matter. I'll give them you and Bellona and Andvari, and they'll support me."

I laughed again, the sound much harsher and far more mocking than before. "*No, you won't.* Think about everything that's happened over the past few days. I freed Maximus's strixes, along with that caladrius. Even if you had Maximus's ability to absorb magic and could have actually stomached drinking their blood, those creatures are long gone, and their power along with them."

Maeven didn't respond, so I kept going.

"Maximus slaughtered the rest of the strixes your guards brought with them, and I killed your bastard relatives on that ship in the harbor. These might have all seemed like small defeats at the time, but they've added up to quite a bloody mess. In the space of three days, I've cut you to *pieces*," I snarled. "You're going to have to travel back to the Mortan capital by land, which will take *weeks*. And once you finally do arrive, I imagine that you'll have quite the struggle to secure your new throne. Why, I'd be surprised if you ever even get to sit on it."

"You lying, scheming, treacherous bitch!" Maeven hissed.

I arched an eyebrow. "Me? *I* didn't do anything. *You're* the one who killed the king, your own brother. Face it, Maeven. You won't be invading Bellona or Andvari or any other kingdom. You'll be too busy trying to hang on to your own. If you're lucky, you might avoid a civil war with the legitimate royals. But I wouldn't hold my breath about it."

Maeven kept staring at me, thinking about all the ramifications of what she'd done, of what I'd tricked her into doing.

"You told me yesterday that you made me queen. You were right about that, so I decided to do the same exact thing to you." I smirked at her. "I bet that amethyst crown doesn't feel so light on your head now."

Her hand drifted up, as if to touch the crown to make sure it was still on her head, but then she realized what she was doing, and she dropped her hand down to the side. "This doesn't change anything."

"Oh, it changes *everything*," I hissed. "Because while you're in Morta, fighting for your crown and most likely your life, I'll be in Bellona, building up my army and navy, securing my borders, and negotiating alliances with the other kingdoms. And by the time you finally kill all your rivals, or they kill you, I will be ready for anything that you or anyone else can throw at me. And then I will fucking *crush* you, just like I crushed Maximus and his magic."

Maeven didn't say anything, but concern darkened her eyes. Even better, I could sense her growing fear as she realized just how effectively I had trapped her. Sweetest bloody aroma I'd ever smelled.

Serilda had trained me to be a soldier, a fighter, a gladiator, and Xenia had schooled me in the subtle art of being a spy and twirling my enemies into corners. I had learned from two masters, and I would always be grateful for the hard lessons they had taught me.

But this scheme against Maeven was all *my* doing, from beginning to end. It had been *my* idea, playing to *my* strengths of waiting, watching, plotting, manipulating, and thinking ahead. It was my proudest accomplishment to date, and something that made me feel like I had finally *earned* my throne, just like a true Winter queen would.

"You know what people say about Bellonans, don't you?" I taunted her. "I'm sure you heard it often enough while you were at Seven Spire."

She wet her lips and whispered the words. "Bellonans are very good at playing the long game."

"Exactly! I'm so glad you remembered our little motto. I think that I did my kingdom, my people, and especially my family proud playing my long game with you."

Maeven pressed her hand to her stomach, as if she suddenly felt nauseous. The sight filled me with even more malicious glee.

"Although I have to pay my respects to you as well," I said. "You taught me an important lesson during the Seven Spire massacre, one that I've been thinking about a lot over the past year, one that I will never, ever forget. And now, thanks to me, you'll always remember it too."

Maeven couldn't stop herself from asking the inevitable question. "And what's that?"

I leaned forward and gave her a cold, vicious smile. "Someone *always* wants to kill the queen."

She kept staring at me, more and more horror filling her amethyst eyes, and more and more worry saturating her scent.

"Good luck with everything," I purred in a smug, satisfied voice. "I do hope that we can continue our chats through the Cardea mirror from time to time. I'm eager to hear about your progress in holding on to your throne. Goodbye, Queen Maeven. Long may you reign."

I dipped down into a traditional Bellonan curtsy, holding it far longer than necessary, just to mock her that much more. Then I straightened. Maeven was still standing in front of me, that same shocked, sick expression on her pale face.

I smiled at Maeven again, then turned and left her alone in the corner to think about the horrible thing that I'd done to her.

CHAPTER TWENTY-NINE

The next morning, I stood in the Bellonan camp and watched while the tents were dismantled and packed up for our trip back to Svalin. The work proceeded quickly and efficiently, and everyone was in a jovial, boisterous mood. There were plenty of reasons to celebrate. The Bellonan magiers, masters, and other competitors had done well in the contests, Paloma had won the Tournament of Champions, and the Mortan king was dead.

Without a doubt, it had been the most successful Regalia Games in Bellonan history.

I watched the workers a few more minutes, then walked to the edge of the rise. Down below on the plaza, merchants were trying to sell a few final things off their carts so they wouldn't have to carry their goods back home, but the constant, enthusiastic hawking had largely died down.

The massive crowds had already vanished from Fortuna, while workers were swabbing decks, hoisting sails, and getting ready to depart on the ships in the harbor. Everyone was packing up to return to their normal lives.

Including the Mortans.

Across the river, servants were breaking down the Mortans' tents, just like my own people were doing, but the Mortans all seemed quiet and tense, and I didn't hear any talking or laughter. Off to the left, several guards were digging what looked like a mass grave, probably to bury all the strixes Maximus had slaughtered before our arena fight.

Leonidas was standing near the guards, watching them dig and stroking Lyra's feathers. Sometime during the night, the strix had flown over to the Mortan camp, and she was stuck to Leonidas's side like glue. I was glad they had each other. Perhaps, together, they could survive all the dark days ahead.

Leonidas spotted me. He hesitated, then waved. Lyra also lifted her wing in greeting, and I waved back at both of them.

And then there was Maeven.

The new Mortan queen was also standing on the rise, overseeing the guards, and she noticed Leonidas's waving. She turned toward me, and the motion made her amethyst-and-diamond crown glint in the winter sunlight. I hoped it felt as heavy as an anchor weighing her down.

Still, I wasn't too eager for Maeven to lose her crown or her head. Not yet. At the very least, I knew how she thought and what she was capable of. As much as I despised her for what she'd done to my family, an enemy you knew and could prepare for was far better than one you didn't know.

Like Seraphine DiLucri.

She too was out and about today, walking along the waterfront over on Fortuna. Driscol was with her, and the two of them were strolling arm in arm. For once, Seraphine was gesturing and doing all the talking, and Driscol was nodding at her words.

Everyone might think that Driscol was the head of the Mint, but I knew it was really Seraphine. I should have known right from the start, by the way Driscol was always deferring to her. Plus, the geldjagers back in Svalin had said that they didn't take orders from *him*. I'd thought they meant Maximus, but now I realized they had been talking about Driscol. Seraphine was just using her brother as a prop, so that people wouldn't realize she was the true power and force behind the Fortuna Mint.

I still didn't know why Seraphine had ordered her geldjagers to bring me in alive, or what she truly wanted with me, but I would have to be careful of her.

Seraphine and Driscol headed for the Mint, so I put them out of my mind and looked at Maeven again. She was still staring at me, so I lifted my hand and snapped off a mocking salute to her. The queen's hands clenched into fists, and purple lightning crackled around her fingertips, but she couldn't hit me with her magic, not given the distance between us.

Maeven whirled around, stormed off, and vanished from sight. Leonidas followed her, with Lyra hopping along behind him.

I stayed on the rise, admiring the view, until the scent of cold, clean vanilla mixed with a hint of spice filled my nose. A strong arm slipped around my waist and pulled me close.

"What are you thinking about?" Sullivan asked. "Surely you aren't worrying about Maeven again."

I shook my head. "No. She'll be far too busy dodging assassins to send any of her own after me anytime soon. No, I was thinking about what I was doing this time last year."

"And what was that?"

"I was making gingerbread houses with the children of some senators who were visiting Seven Spire for the yuletide season. Doing my usual duties as the royal stand-in. Being invisible. Plotting my escape from the palace and my unhappy life."

"And look at you now," Sullivan murmured.

"And look at me now," I echoed.

His gaze searched mine. "Are you happier now than you were back then?"

I looped my arms around his waist. "Strangely enough, I

am. Oh, don't get me wrong. I would be ecstatic if I never had to face down another assassin or deal with a court full of scheming, demanding nobles, but we both know that's not going to happen."

Sullivan grinned. "No, probably not."

"But I *am* happy," I continued. "Not necessarily because I'm queen, but because I'm helping people and protecting Bellona. Or at least trying to."

"What? I don't even get a mention?" he teased, his blue eyes bright in his handsome face.

"Well, that depends. What have you done for me lately?" I teased him back.

Sullivan arched an eyebrow, but he leaned forward and whispered in my ear. "Well, there are certain activities we engaged in last night that can be repeated anytime you like, highness."

A delicious shiver ran through me as I thought back to all the things we had done together—and all the exquisite pleasure we had brought each other. "Oh, I think that can be arranged."

"Excellent," Sullivan murmured. "But why wait until tonight? Let's get started right now."

He lowered his head, and his lips found mine. I opened my mouth, stroking my tongue against his, even as I breathed in, letting his clean vanilla scent sink deep down in my lungs—

"Ugh! Are you two at it again?" a familiar voice sounded. "I thought you would at least wait until we got back to the palace before you started up with that again."

Sullivan and I broke apart to find Paloma standing a few feet away, rolling her eyes.

The rest of our friends were here as well. Serilda, Cho, Auster, Xenia. All happy and smiling, knowing that we had won this battle.

My friends stepped up beside Sullivan and me, so that we

formed a line on the rise. Once again, I looked toward Morta, but the guards had finished burying the strixes, and the servants had finished taking down the tents. The Mortans were gone, and they wouldn't bother us again for a good long while.

"Let's go home," I said.

Several days later, we arrived at Svalin and rode in open carriages through the city, slowly but surely heading back to Seven Spire. I was in a carriage with Sullivan next to me and Paloma and Xenia sitting across from us. Serilda, Cho, and Auster were in the carriage behind us.

People filled the streets and plazas, yelling, cheering, screaming, whistling, and waving flags and pennants bearing my crown-of-shards crest. Even though most of them hadn't been at the Regalia, they still had heard about everything that had happened, and they wanted to celebrate.

Paloma received the majority of the cheers, since she was the winner of the Tournament of Champions, and more than a few little girls and boys were waving flags with fierce ogre faces. Color tinted Paloma's cheeks, as though she were embarrassed by all the attention, but the ogre on her neck was grinning wide. I was so happy for my friend. My people had embraced both sides of her, just as Paloma herself had done by morphing in the arena in front of everyone.

Xenia leaned over and murmured something in Paloma's ear, and my friend nodded back. Xenia looked out over the cheering crowd again, but Paloma kept staring at the older woman, as did her inner ogre. On the way back to Svalin, Paloma had finally read the letter I'd given her. She hadn't talked to me about it yet, and she hadn't told Xenia my theory, but I could see the longing in her eyes whenever she looked at the other ogre morph.

I wasn't worried, though. The two of them would find each other when the time was right. But for now we all had this moment to enjoy, so I turned my attention back to the crowd, smiling, waving, and soaking up the adoration.

The cheers were louder and my sense of pride was greater than anything I had ever imagined in any childhood dreams.

Eventually, we crossed the Retribution Bridge and went over to Seven Spire, where the palace servants and guards cheered just as loudly as the people in the streets had. It was a raucous atmosphere, and I decided to throw my own ball to let everyone have one final, glorious celebration before we all got back down to the normal business of running the kingdom again.

That night, everyone gathered in the throne room to enjoy music, dancing, drinks, desserts, and more. It was a joyful occasion, and for once, everyone seemed to put their petty differences and scheming aside and just enjoy the evening. I even spotted Fullman and Diante having a somewhat amicable drink together.

Everyone was still talking, dancing, and drinking, but I wanted a moment to myself, so I grabbed a glass and a bottle of cranberry sangria from one of the servants, slipped out of the ball, and made my way outside to the royal lawn.

It was a chilly December night, and the wind brought the scent of impending snow along with it, but I welcomed the cold quiet after all the heat, noise, and commotion of the throne room. I wandered around for a bit, soaking up the silence, then headed over to the wall that cordoned off the lawn from the steep drop and jagged cliffs below. I opened the bottle, poured myself a glass of sangria, and sipped the sweet, fruity liquid.

I also pulled my sword from its scabbard and laid the blade out flat on the wall. The seven shards in the crown crest embedded in the hilt glimmered like midnight-blue stars. I traced my fingers over the symbol. With everything that had happened during the Regalia, I hadn't had time to think of a name for my sword, as Paloma had suggested. But now that I was back home at Seven Spire, a name had finally come to me.

Evermore—the same name as the main, center bridge that led from the palace over to the city. Evermore had been the first bridge built across the river, and it had weathered the test of time, just like I had weathered all the obstacles that had threatened to overwhelm me.

"Evermore," I whispered, testing out the name.

For a moment the crown-of-shards crest seemed to glimmer a little brighter, as though the tearstone pieces liked the name as much as I did. I took it as a good omen.

I lifted my gaze from the sword and stared out over Svalin. Across the river, lights burned throughout the city, making the gold, silver, and bronze spires on the rooftops gleam like bright metallic swords. I had always loved the view from the royal lawn at night, but never more so than this night when I knew I had finally avenged my queen, my family, and my kingdom against Maeven, Maximus, and the Mortans.

My thoughts turned to Maeven, as they so often did at quiet times like this. I wondered what she was doing. If she had returned to the Mortan capital yet. If she had secured her throne.

If anyone had tried to kill her yet.

But I had no way of knowing the answers. Besides, Maeven was a worry for tomorrow. Tonight was about me and everything that I had achieved over the past year.

I had killed a queen, protected a prince, and crushed a king.

But most of all, I had *survived*.

Oh, there were still plenty of threats and challenges to face. I might have blunted Maeven's power, but she would eventually hatch a new scheme against me. And I couldn't forget about the Fortuna Mint and why Seraphine had seemed so eager to get her hands on me.

And perhaps it was foolish, but I still hadn't given up hope that another Blair had survived the same way I had, and that I would one day find that person, and together we would rebuild the Blair family legacy—

Something cold stung my hand, interrupting my thoughts. I looked up and realized that it had started snowing. Big, fat, fluffy flakes poured down from the night sky, quickly covering the royal lawn, falling on the city, and making the view even lovelier than before.

By morning, the snow would cover Seven Spire with a solid sheet of white, making everything seem fresh and clean and new again. Maybe that's what being a Winter queen was really about—giving everyone a chance for a better tomorrow.

"Sleep well, Bellona," I murmured. "Sleep well."

I lifted my glass in a toast to my people, then stood there in the snow, sipping my sangria, and staring out over my kingdom, just as so many other Bellonan queens had before me.

Long live the Winter queen.

ABOUT THE AUTHOR

Andre Teague

Jennifer Estep is a *New York Times, USA Today,* and internationally bestselling author who prowls the streets of her imagination in search of her next fantasy idea.

In addition to her **Crown of Shards** series, Jennifer is also the author of the **Elemental Assassin, Mythos Academy, Black Blade,** and **Bigtime** series. She has written more than thirty-five books, along with numerous novellas and stories.

In her spare time, Jennifer enjoys hanging out with friends and family, doing yoga, and reading fantasy and romance books. She also watches way too much TV and loves all things related to superheroes.

For more information on Jennifer and her books, visit her website at www.jenniferestep.com or follow her online on Facebook, Goodreads, BookBub, and Twitter—@Jennifer_Estep. You can also sign up for her newsletter at www.jenniferestep.com/contact-jennifer/newsletter.